Not Until The End

A Hope Springs Novel

Valerie M. Bodden

Not Until The End © 2023 by Valerie M. Bodden.

Scriptures taken from the Holy Bible, New International Version®, NIV®. Copyright © 1973, 1978, 1984, 2011 by Biblica, Inc.™ Used by permission of Zondervan. All rights reserved worldwide. www.zondervan.com The "NIV" and "New International Version" are trademarks registered in the United States Patent and Trademark Office by Biblica, Inc.™

All rights reserved. No portion of this book may be reproduced in any form without permission from the publisher, except as permitted by U.S. copyright law.

This is a work of fiction. Names, characters, places, and incidents either are products of the author's imagination or used in a fictitious manner. Any resemblance to any person, living or dead, is coincidental.

Valerie M. Bodden

Visit me at www.valeriembodden.com

Hope Springs Series

Not Until Forever
Not Until This Moment
Not Until You
Not Until Us
Not Until Christmas Morning
Not Until This Day
Not Until Someday
Not Until Now
Not Until Then
Not Until The End

River Falls Series

Pieces of Forever
Songs of Home
Memories of the Heart
Whispers of Truth
Promises of Mercy

River Falls Christmas Romances

Christmas of Joy

A Hope Springs Gift for You

Members of my Reader's Club get a FREE book, available exclusively to my subscribers. When you sign up, you'll also be the first to know about new releases, book deals, and giveaways.
Visit www.valeriembodden.com/gift to join!

Need a refresher of who's who in the Hope Springs series?

If you love the whole gang in Hope Springs but need a refresher of who's who and how everyone is connected, check out the handy character map at https://www.valeriembodden.com/hscharacters

For this God is our God forever and ever; he will be our guide even to the end.

Psalm 48:14

Chapter 1

This was hard—harder than Owen had expected.

He pressed three fingers to his lips, then brushed them across the heart he'd carved into the closet door frame the day he and Katie had moved into this house. He'd done it secretly, before she could tell him not to, and when he'd shown her, she'd swatted at him, just as he'd known she would, and he'd pulled her into his arms, her pregnant belly a warm buffer between them.

He sighed and closed the closet door, wondering if the new owners would even notice the heart. Maybe they'd cover it with wood filler.

"I hope I'm doing the right thing here," he muttered to the empty room.

A horn sounded from the driveway below, and Owen jumped, then shook his head. Apparently, the kids were getting impatient. Whether this was the right thing or not, there was no turning back now.

He hurried down the stairs, resisting the urge to allow himself one last tour of the house and the countless memories it held.

They would make new memories in their new house. And the memories of Katie—those would be with them wherever they went. Always.

He stepped out the front door and pulled it closed behind him before he could change his mind. With a quick turn of the key, he locked it, then jogged down the front steps. His three youngest had already piled into the crowded minivan he would drive, while the older two girls sat in the car they shared. He'd prefer not to have them drive so far on their own—but with no other adults in the family, he really had no choice.

Besides, he reminded himself with a glance at Catelyn, who looked strikingly like her mother, with her dark hair and emerald eyes, his oldest *was* an adult. If you considered twenty an adult. Which he supposed he had to.

He made his way to the driver's side of their car, and Catelyn rolled down the window.

"You have your map open, in case we get separated?"

"Sure do." Catelyn gave him a patient smile—the one that said he was being overprotective but she wouldn't call him on it.

"We'll try to make it two hours and then stop for a break, but if you need to stop sooner, have Claire call me, and—"

"I've driven more than two hours at a time, Dad. We'll be fine."

"I know you will." Owen nodded, wishing he could feel the same easy assurance of his children's safety as they seemed to. "But Carter will need a bathroom break by then anyway. Drive carefully."

He looked past Catelyn to Claire. The sixteen-year-old was the polar opposite of Catelyn in appearance, the only one in the family with blonde hair and blue eyes. She sat with her arms crossed, staring out the window toward the house. Of all the kids, she'd been the only one strongly opposed to the idea of moving, and Owen still felt bad dragging her away from her friends for her junior year of high school. But an opportunity like this wasn't likely to come around again anytime soon.

"Make sure you get some rest," he said to Claire, "so you two can switch off when we stop."

Claire didn't indicate she'd heard him—not even a blink—but Catelyn patted his arm. "We'll be good, Dad," she reassured him again.

Owen nodded, grateful that Catelyn had been willing to change her original plan of staying on campus for the summer to instead come home and help them move. He patted the top of her car and forced himself to back away and turn toward the van.

Lexi, their golden retriever, had taken up residence in his seat and sat grinning at him, her tongue lolling to the side. He laughed, grateful for the slight easing of tension in his shoulders.

He pulled the van door open and poked his head in past the dog. "Should we let Lexi drive today?" he asked eleven-year-old Kenzie and nine-year-old Carter, who both sat in the back.

Kenzie gave him a weak smile and a shake of the head, pressing a hand to her stomach. Owen frowned. She hadn't said much about the move, but he could tell she was nervous. Carter didn't look his way at all but had his eyes fixed on something in the sky. His fingers flicked against his thighs, but Owen didn't try to stop him. It was one of his stimming behaviors, and the doctor had assured them after his diagnosis of level 1 autism that he wasn't hurting himself.

Owen swiveled his head to follow the boy's gaze. "Stratus today?" he asked.

Carter sighed and shook his head, not taking his eyes off the wispy clouds above. "Cirrus."

"Oh. Right." Owen nodded. He'd seen clouds from pretty much every angle conceivable, and yet he still couldn't get it through his head which were which.

He gave the dog a shove to dislodge her from his spot and got in, glancing at Cody in the passenger seat. The fourteen-year-old was usually loud and outgoing, but he was watching the house the same way Claire had been—as if working to soak in every last detail. A lump tried to form in Owen's throat, but he cleared it away.

"Hey," he said to Cody. "This is going to be good." He paused, half-expecting one of the kids to fill in Katie's customary response: "It's going to be *really* good." When no one did, he added, "I already talked to the baseball coach in Hope Springs, and he said you can join the team right away when we get there. They have a league that runs all summer."

Cody nodded, and Owen started the van. He supposed that was as much as he was going to get. *Please don't let me be making a big mistake,* he prayed as he backed the vehicle down the driveway, careful to avoid the moving pods they'd spent the past week filling with all of their memories.

When he and Katie had moved into this house, they'd had next to nothing. But twenty years and five kids later, it had taken three of those things to fit all of their furniture and boxes. He'd done the best he could to donate things ahead of the move—but, though he'd never really thought of himself as sentimental, all of this stuff held too many memories to part with.

He pulled onto the road, then waited, watching in his rearview mirror as Catelyn pulled out of the driveway too. Then, with one last glance over his shoulder at the house, he turned and pressed his foot to the gas. "Hope Springs, here we come."

Chapter 2

Glory in his holy name; let the hearts of those who seek the Lord rejoice. Emma reread the words from Psalm 105, then signed the card she'd written out for one of the shut-ins from church she was planning to visit tomorrow.

She knew from experience that it was harder to rejoice some days than others. But if God had taught her anything over the past year, it was that every day was a gift from him.

The sound of tires crunched on the gravel driveway outside, and Emma tucked the card into an envelope and tossed it on top of the plate of cookies she'd made, then rushed out the kitchen door onto the farmhouse's large porch. The gusty early June breeze caught at the short, spiky curls that had finally grown long enough to brush her forehead, and she zipped her sweatshirt, then waved to her brother James, his wife, and their daughter as they pulled up to the house.

The car engine was still running when eleven-year-old Ruby sprang out of the back seat. "Are they here yet?" She lunged toward Emma, tripping over her own feet. The girl must have grown a good six inches in the last few months, and sometimes she ran like a newborn foal still trying to figure out how to use its long limbs. She was nearly to the porch before she got her legs under control and came to a halt. "Did I miss them?"

Emma laughed, jogging down the steps to hug her niece. "You didn't miss anything." She greeted James and Bethany, who were both grinning oddly from one another to her.

"What's going on with you two?" She eyed them. "You're not going to try to talk me out of this again, are you? Because I told you, I've made up my mind." She crossed her arms defiantly.

But even James, who had been the most opposed to her latest plan, insisting that adding one more thing to her to-do list wouldn't be good for her recovery, shook his head. "Look at Ruby."

"Why? Does she have an extra head today?" She made a face at Ruby, who laughed but stood stark still—Emma was pretty sure it was the first time she had ever seen the girl not wiggling. "She's as beautiful as al—" Her eyes fell on Ruby's shirt, and she clapped a hand over her mouth.

James, Bethany, and Ruby all burst into laughter, but it took a moment before Emma could speak.

"Ruby," she finally gasped. "Why does your shirt say *big sister*?"

Ruby bounced up and down, the words bouncing with her. "Mom's pregnant."

Emma's eyes shot to James and Bethany, who were holding hands and grinning like newlyweds. Which, Emma supposed, they still were. "You're having a baby?" She ran and threw her arms around both of them.

"Wait. We are?" Bethany asked as Emma let go, but her laugh gave her away. Apparently this was one thing she remembered in spite of her short-term memory struggles.

Inadvertently, Emma's hand strayed to the spot where her own shirt covered the six-inch reminder on her abdomen that children were not in her future. Of course, her dreams of having a large family had already dissipated well before the radical hysterectomy. At forty-two and single, it hadn't been likely she would ever have children anyway. The hysterectomy just solidified it.

And it was fine. She may not ever have children. But she did have a family. And it was growing.

"I'm so happy for you." Emma gave her brother a quick glance, trying to tell if the news brought lingering sadness over the daughter he had lost years ago, before meeting Bethany and Ruby. But he looked absolutely radiant, and Emma's heart rejoiced for them. After all they'd both been through, she couldn't have imagined a happier ending for them.

"When are you due?" she asked, turning to lead them toward the chicken coop.

"In January," Bethany announced proudly. "On our one-year anniversary. Which means I won't have to remember another date."

"And also that we'll never be able to go out on our anniversary," James grumbled. But he wasn't fooling anyone with that gruff act. Emma had never seen him happier.

"I see a truck! I see a truck!" Ruby pointed to the end of the driveway. "Is that them?"

"I think so." Emma grinned at her niece.

"I've never seen anyone get so excited about chickens," James muttered.

"It's on Aunt Emma's life list," Ruby informed her father importantly. "Right, Aunt Emma?"

Emma nodded and wrapped an arm around her niece's shoulder. "That it is."

She'd made the list after she completed chemo last year, as a reminder to make the most of each day the Lord gave her. Actually, it was two lists: one that included "everyday" items—the things she strived to do every day, like spend time in the Word, serve others, pray for someone new. And the other list she liked to think of as her "possibilities" list—things she would love to do if God gave her the opportunity. Including today's item: raise chickens.

"I think Aunt Emma needs less lists, more rest," James retorted.

"That's why I'm here," Ruby explained patiently. "To help her with the chickens."

"Exactly." Emma smiled gratefully at her niece—one of the few people who didn't seem to think she was suddenly more fragile just because she'd survived cancer. "You two get going. You're going to miss the movie." She shooed James and Bethany away as the pickup truck from Ploughman Farms pulled to a stop.

She and Ruby jogged toward the truck, stopping at the open passenger window. "You can bring them right over there." Emma pointed across the yard toward the deluxe chicken coop she'd asked her friend Cam to build. Though it was a bit outside the scope of his usual landscaping work, he had outdone himself with a mini-replica of the stables that stood just beyond it.

By the time she and Ruby reached the coop, Mrs. Ploughman had already backed the pickup truck to it and was unloading large wire crates from the back.

"Oh, they're so pretty," Ruby gushed as Emma opened the mesh door on the large chicken run Cam had built surrounding the coop. She hefted one of the carriers and brought it inside, grateful she'd asked Cam to build the run and coop tall enough for her to stand up in.

She opened the carrier, and the big red and black chicken with a bright red comb stalked out as if she owned the place. She went straight for Ruby, who instantly dropped to the ground to pet her.

"She's soft," she called in delight.

"That's a Sussex," Mrs. Ploughman said. "And this beautiful gal is a blue Australorp." She opened a cage holding a striking bird with shimmery blue-green-black feathers.

They unloaded a large gray Orpington, a golden Friesian, and another Sussex. Emma chatted with Mrs. Ploughman a bit about their care, and then it was just her and Ruby and the birds.

"What do you think, ladies?" Emma asked. "Do you like your new home?"

Ruby giggled. "I think they *love* it. Can I help you name them?"

"You'd better." Emma adjusted the chickens' water dispenser. "I haven't been able to come up with a single good—"

She broke off as the chickens burst into a flurry of squawks and flapping. Reflexively, she raised an arm and ducked as one flew straight toward her face.

"Aunt Emma," Ruby cried, and Emma reached out a hand to pull her niece to her feet, hugging Ruby's face to her chest to protect her from the crazed chickens.

An involuntary shriek escaped as Emma felt a hen's weight settle onto her back, its thin toes stabbing into her skin as it fought for purchase.

"What is happening?" she cried, half hunched over, trying to shield Ruby and dislodge the bird at the same time. But the chicken's toes gripped harder as a large dog bounded right up to the chicken wire, its barks wild and frenzied.

"Shoo," Emma cried. "Go home."

The dog kept barking, and the chickens kept squawking and flapping, and Emma tried to figure out how to get the one off her back without injuring it—or herself.

"Let me see the dog." Ruby wiggled out of Emma's grip just as a voice shouted, "Lexi, come."

Emma scanned the yard for the source of the command, but the dog's only response was to perk its ears and keep barking.

"Lexi? Is that your name?" Emma spoke to the dog the same way she spoke to her horses, in a low, soothing voice, even though pain sliced through her back from the chicken's claws. "Your owner is looking for you. Go home now."

The dog tilted its head to the side, then crouched low and pounced at the chicken wire, sending the hens into a fresh frenzy. Fortunately, in the chaos, the one on Emma's back apparently decided there were safer places to be and dismounted. Emma straightened gratefully, waving her hands over Ruby's head so none would land on the girl.

"Lexi, come!" This time the voice was closer, and Emma followed the sound to a teenage boy, who was sprinting toward them. A girl who looked about Ruby's age chased behind him. Two more figures—one adult-size and one child-size—followed another hundred yards or so back.

"Hi, there!" Emma called to the boy in the lead. "This your dog?"

"Yeah. Sorry." The boy jogged closer and grabbed the dog's collar, then looked from her to Ruby to the chickens. "Are your chickens always this crazy?"

Emma laughed. "I don't know. I just got them today. But I sure hope not. They don't seem to be big fans of dogs though."

"Oh." The boy ducked his head. "Sorry about that."

"It's okay." Emma ushered Ruby toward the door, cracking it open just enough for the two of them to slip through, then latching it behind her. "But maybe we should bring Lexi away from the coop to let them calm down." The girl who had been running behind the boy reached them and drew to a stop.

"Hi," Emma greeted her. "Are you here for Lexi too?"

The girl nodded, her dark hair bobbing, but didn't say anything.

"What's your name?" Ruby asked. The girl didn't answer, but Ruby continued, undaunted. "I'm Ruby. How old are you?"

The girl stepped a little closer to the boy, who Emma guessed was her brother.

"I'm Cody, and this is Kenzie," he said, and Emma caught the protective note in his voice. "She's eleven."

"Me too," Ruby bounced on her toes. "Can she talk?"

At that, Kenzie smiled a little and nodded but still didn't say anything.

"She's shy," Cody explained.

"Where do you guys live?" Emma asked. She knew pretty much every neighbor who lived within five miles in every direction, not to mention most of the people who lived in town, but she didn't remember ever seeing these two.

Cody pointed across the field that bumped up against Emma's yard. "There, I guess. As of today."

"Oh, I saw that the house sold. I was hoping I'd be getting new neighbors soon." Emma waved to the adult and child who had almost reached them now, and Emma could see that one was a man—the kids' dad, she supposed—and the other was another, younger boy.

"I'm so sorry," the man called as he closed the last of the space between them. "Lexi doesn't usually run like that, but I guess she got excited to be out of the car and—"

"Please, don't worry about it." Emma waved off his apology, then held out a hand. "Welcome to Hope Springs. I was just telling the kids I'm glad to know I'll have new neighbors. I'm Emma, and this is Ruby."

"Owen." The man shook her outstretched hand. Up close, he looked to be about her age. A few grays shone from his dark hair and in the light layer of stubble on his cheeks.

"And this is Carter." Owen gestured to the young boy next to him, who was squinting up at the sky as he flicked two fingers against his leg.

"You have good clouds here," the boy announced.

Emma laughed, crouching down so she was at his level, though he didn't look at her. "Thank you. I think so too."

"Where are you guys from?" Ruby asked, bouncing as she always did when she was excited—and nothing excited her more than meeting new people.

"Tennessee." Owen gazed around him as if taking in the scenery for the first time.

Before Emma could ask what brought them to Hope Springs, Ruby jumped in. "Our friend Grace is from Tennessee. Hey, do you want to see our chickens?" The question was addressed to Kenzie, who sent a timid glance toward her dad.

He nodded and gave her what appeared to be a tired smile. "Go ahead. I'll keep Lexi over here."

Kenzie stuck a hand in his. "I want you to come with me."

"I'll take Lexi back to the house," Cody offered. "I already saw the chickens anyway."

"They weren't exactly at their best when you saw them." Emma raised a hand to her hair, suddenly realizing what a fright it must be after that whole debacle. She wondered vaguely if there were feathers in it.

"Come, Lexi." Cody pulled the dog across the yard toward the field.

Owen's face creased into lines of worry as he watched the boy go, but he didn't stop him.

"Don't worry," Emma reassured him. "You'll be able to see him all the way across the field." It wasn't until after the words were out that she realized they might make it sound like she regularly watched their house. She scrambled for a way to fix it, but Owen nodded, looking slightly relieved.

"Come on," Emma urged Kenzie. "Let's go meet the ladies."

Kenzie giggled. "The ladies?"

Owen glanced at his daughter, his mouth opening as if in surprise.

"Well, yes," Emma said, feigning seriousness. "These are no ordinary chickens. They're fancy chickens. So I call them my ladies."

"I know!" Ruby turned and walked backwards so she could talk to them all. "You guys should help us name them."

"That's a great idea." Emma smiled at her niece, always so eager to include everyone.

"It's perfect," Ruby crowed. "There are five of us and five chickens, so we can each name one."

Owen shook his head. "I'm sure you don't want complete strangers to name your chickens."

"You're not strangers, you're neighbors," Emma reassured him.

"You and I should name the matching ones," Ruby said to Kenzie. "Since we're friends."

Kenzie gripped her dad's hand but nodded, her eyes bright.

"I'm going to name mine Corazón," Ruby declared. "That's Spanish for heart, and her comb looks like a heart in the middle. What do you want to name yours?" She blinked eagerly at Kenzie.

"Um." Kenzie half hid behind Owen. "Maybe, um, Unicorn?"

"I love unicorns," Ruby cheered so loudly that Kenzie took another step closer to Owen, but she was grinning.

"That's perfect." Emma smiled at the girl, then turned to Carter. "Which one do you want to name?"

"The gray one," Carter announced, flicking his leg. "Its name is Stratus."

"Like the clouds?"

Carter turned and met her eyes, only for a fraction of a second but long enough for Emma's heart to melt. "Yes," he said. "Stratus clouds are low and gray, just like Stratus the chicken."

"Perfect." Emma smiled. "We'll call her Strat for short, if that's okay."

"Strat." Carter said the word a few times, as if testing it out, then nodded. "Strat for short is good."

"All right then." Emma looked to Owen, who had turned toward the field. She followed his gaze to where Cody was almost to their house, Lexi bounding ahead of him. "Which one do you want to name?" she asked him.

"Hmm." Owen turned to study the two chickens that were left. "I'll take the blue one."

"She's so shimmery." Kenzie stepped out from behind her father, apparently forgetting her shyness as she peered at the chicken. "What do you want to call her, Dad?"

"How about Sapphire?"

"Like Mom's ring," Kenzie said quietly. She slipped her hand back into her dad's, and Emma couldn't help but admire the picture they made together.

Owen nodded.

"Very elegant." Emma watched the blue chicken ruffle her wings proudly, as if she knew they were talking about her.

"What are you going to name yours?" Ruby asked, pointing to the golden chicken that had landed on Emma's back earlier. "Goldie?"

Emma shook her head. "That's a good name. But I think I'm going to call her Trixie. I have a feeling she's going to be a bit of a mischief-maker."

"Oh, I like that." Ruby clapped her hands. "Hey, do you ride?" She spun to Kenzie.

Kenzie blinked at her, moving closer to Owen again. "Ride?"

"Horses." Ruby gestured toward the pasture, where several of Emma's horses were currently grazing.

Kenzie shook her head, though her eyes lit up. "I don't know how."

"Oh, you should take lessons here," Ruby announced. "You'll love it."

Kenzie gave her dad a pleading look but didn't say anything.

Owen shook his head. "We should get going. The rest of our crew was picking up dinner, and they're probably getting impatient to eat. Or, knowing Cody, he's already polishing it all off without us." He smiled wryly and glanced over his shoulder. Emma followed his gaze. Sure enough, there was another car in the driveway now, and she imagined his wife—and possibly more children, the way it sounded—waiting at the house for them.

"Of course. It was nice meeting you." Emma tucked her hands into her pockets. "If you need anything, please don't hesitate to ask."

Owen gave a polite nod, then squatted to allow Carter to climb onto his back. He stood and took Kenzie's hand, and they started toward the field, the perfect picture of a family.

Emma brushed off a stab of longing. She had her own version of a family. It may not be what she'd once envisioned, but she was blessed, nonetheless.

"I like them," Ruby announced.

Emma nodded. "Me too." She watched them for another moment, then pulled her phone out of her pocket and checked *raise chickens* off her life list. Ruby grinned at her, then reached up and plucked something from her hair. She held it out.

It was a feather.

Emma took it from her with a laugh. "And I suppose this was in my hair the whole time?"

"Yep," Ruby answered cheerfully. "I didn't want to embarrass you by pulling it out in front of them."

"Gee, thanks." Emma fuzzed her hand over her niece's hair. "Oh well, now they know their new neighbor is a crazy chicken lady."

Ruby folded her arms into wings and let out a joyful bawk.

Chapter 3

"I don't see why we all have to go," Claire grumbled, climbing grudgingly into the back seat of the van Sunday morning.

"Don't you want to see the drop zone?" Catelyn asked. "It's always been Mom and Dad's dream."

"Yeah, well, mom can't see it either, can she?" Claire shot back.

"Claire," Owen started wearily. But he was at a loss as to how to finish the sentence, so he let it drop. He'd give anything for Katie to be here with them right now. But that wasn't how life—how cancer—worked.

He waited for Kenzie, Cody, and Carter to file into the vehicle, then closed the door and took the driver's seat, plugging the drop zone's address into his phone. He'd been to it a couple of times while he'd been finalizing details with his business partner Charles, but it was fifteen miles away from their new house, and he wasn't confident he could find it without a map yet.

"When is our stuff coming?" Cody asked as Owen turned right out of the driveway.

"Hopefully in the next day or two." Owen lowered his ear toward his shoulder to stretch his neck. He wasn't sure how many nights of sleeping on the floor his forty-five-year-old body could take.

"Oh, look at the horses." Catelyn pointed to the pasture behind their neighbor's house. Emma, Owen was pretty sure she'd said her name was, though Katie had always been the one to remember names and whisper them in his ear when he forgot.

"Can we take riding lessons, Dad?" Kenzie asked from the back seat.

Owen glanced at her in the mirror. "You want to?" He'd been trying for years to convince her to get involved in something where she could meet other people her age, but she had resisted anything that would take her away from him longer than necessary, aside from school—and he was sure she wouldn't go there either, if he didn't make her.

He'd never thought of riding lessons, though.

"It might be fun," she said in a small voice. "At least, Ruby seemed to like it."

Owen chuckled. That girl had certainly been outgoing—the complete opposite of Kenzie. But maybe that was what his daughter needed. "She was nice, huh?"

Kenzie seemed to consider this. Finally, she said, "She was nice. And kind of . . . bouncy. I liked her mom."

"What was her name again?" Owen was grateful that his kids seemed to have inherited Katie's knack for names.

"Emma," Kenzie replied. "She was nice. She reminded me of Mom."

"Don't say that," Claire hissed from the far back seat.

Owen's eyes flicked to the mirror in time to see the tears drop onto Kenzie's cheeks.

"Claire," he warned.

His daughter met his eyes in the mirror with a defiant glare. "I suppose you agree with her."

"What?" Where had that come from? "I hadn't—"

"Oh, a cherry orchard," Catelyn, ever the peace-maker, broke in.

Owen's eyes cut to the side of the road, where row upon row of pink-blossomed trees waved in the breeze. A sign at the end of a long driveway read, "Hidden Blossom Farms."

"They look like pink clouds," Cody said, and Owen grinned at his son's surprisingly poetic description.

"They do," he agreed, though his thoughts were still stuck on Kenzie's comment about Emma. He hadn't really thought about it when they were talking with her yesterday, but he could see why Kenzie had said Emma reminded her of Katie. It wasn't that Katie and Emma had the same personality. Like Ruby, Emma seemed to be outgoing and enthusiastic, while Katie had always been more like Kenzie—quiet and reserved. But both women gave off a feeling of warmth—like the person they were talking to was the most important person to them at that moment.

"Trees can't look like clouds." Carter's matter-of-fact statement cut into Owen's thoughts. "Clouds are made of—"

"I know, buddy," Owen interrupted before Carter could recite the same cloud facts he'd shared a thousand times already. "It's a figure of speech. Remember you talked about picture language at school?"

Carter shrugged and went back to looking out the window. A few minutes later, they came to a large complex of baseball fields that had Cody exclaiming in wonder. Owen pictured all of them going to watch Cody play—but he had to revise the image in his head when he remembered that Katie wouldn't be with them.

He swallowed down the sting of experiencing this new adventure without her and slowed the car as they came to the top of a hill.

Suddenly, Lake Michigan stretched out below them, its dark blue waves rising and falling in a rhythmic dance.

"Wow," Catelyn breathed.

"Yeah," Owen agreed, feeling like maybe this was God's way of telling him everything was going to be okay.

He glanced in the mirror to find that even Claire was watching the water with apparent interest—or at least not outright hostility.

"Look at those stratocumulus clouds!" Carter's voice burst excitedly through the vehicle.

Owen chuckled. "Yeah, bud. They're pretty, aren't they?"

The clouds seemed to brush against the water at the horizon, and closer to shore, dozens of colorful boats bobbed in a marina.

They continued through the town, past an antique store, a bakery, and a fudge shop. Farther down the road, past the downtown area, they passed a large church with a full parking lot.

"Hope Church," Kenzie read the sign out loud.

Owen nodded, a little nugget of guilt working at him. He'd made sure to take the kids to church nearly every week since Katie's death, and he knew he needed to prioritize finding a church here. But the truth was, church had become one more thing to check off his to-do list over the last few years, rather than the joyful worship he'd experienced when Katie was alive.

I'll find a church soon, he silently promised as they reached the far end of town. Another few miles, and he turned in at the small airstrip that would serve as his new drop zone.

"This is it?"

Owen knew Cody's question wasn't meant to sound skeptical. But the kids had been with him dozens of times to the much larger skydiving center he'd worked for in Nashville. The difference was, this one was his own. And he and Charles had plans to expand it.

"This is it," he said cheerfully, catching sight of Charles's truck parked in front of the large pole barn that would serve as both airplane hangar and headquarters for their skydiving business. He pulled the van up next to it, spotting Charles tinkering under the ten-passenger Caravan plane they'd purchased along with the facility.

Owen stepped into the cool morning, waiting for the kids to clamber out.

Carter's eyes immediately went to the large windsock near the runway. "This place is so cool."

Owen ruffled his son's hair. "Come on, let's go say hi to Uncle Charles."

He started toward the hangar, glancing over his shoulder to make sure that all of them—even Claire—were following. Kenzie slipped her hand into his, and Owen called, "Hey, Charles."

The other man didn't look in their direction, and Catelyn laughed. "He probably has his music cranked up too loud."

Owen chuckled. It was a standing family joke that Uncle Charles rocked out to classical music turned up louder than any rebellious teen had ever turned up their heavy metal.

Charles was no relation, since neither Katie nor Owen had any siblings, but he was the closest thing the kids had to an uncle. Owen had met him when he'd started working at the skydiving center in Nashville, and they'd become fast friends. They'd had plans to travel the world together, working at drop zones in all different countries—but then Katie had walked in for her first tandem skydive—and that had changed everything for Owen.

He'd settled down and started a family while Charles had moved on to drop zones in Germany, Ireland, Spain, Mexico, Argentina, and Australia. They'd stayed in touch, though, and whenever Charles returned to the states, he stopped by to visit.

When, on his visit last year, he'd mentioned wanting to purchase a drop zone in Wisconsin, Owen had nearly fallen out of his chair. And when he'd asked Owen to join him in the venture—well, it hadn't taken a ton of convincing. Though Katie had been an oncologist with a busy practice, they'd always planned to open their own drop zone one day. She'd gotten her skydiving B license and was working toward her C license and instructor rating. She'd only been fifty jumps away when she'd gotten her diagnosis. After that, the chemo left her too sick to jump. When they'd realized the treatments weren't going to be enough to save her, she'd made him promise to still carry out their dream.

And now here he was.

Emotion grabbed at his throat, and he had to clear it a few times.

"Are you okay, Daddy?" Kenzie looked up at him in concern.

Owen pushed his lips into a smile. "Yeah, baby. I'm good."

Catelyn met his gaze, tears shining in her eyes. "Mom would love this place."

Owen nodded, clearing his throat one more time.

The sound must have penetrated Charles's earbuds because his head suddenly jerked up, and his face broke into a giant grin.

"Well, if it isn't my favorite people in the world. And I see you brought your dad too." Charles pulled each of the kids into a hug. Even Claire halfheartedly wrapped her arms around him.

Then he stood in front of Owen, shaking his tousled blond hair that seemed to drive women all over the world wild. "Can you believe we're doing this?"

Owen shook his head. "Nope." The two men shook hands and pulled each other into a quick hug.

"So, how's our gal?" Owen gestured to the plane.

Charles patted its side. "She's a little tired, but I'll have her in top form soon enough."

Owen had always admired Charles's persistent optimism. He only hoped it was warranted this time. Purchasing a new plane wasn't really in their budget.

"You keep working on that," Owen said. "I'm going to take a look around and make a list of what we need to do before opening day." They'd already decided they wanted to open this summer rather than waiting until next season. It meant they would have to work fast.

"You and your lists," Charles ribbed him, stuffing his earbuds back into his ears.

"Lists keep people alive," he called back, as he always did. At least in skydiving. Owen had mental checklists for before, during, and after a jump—all of which enabled him to have an incident-free record. If only there could have been a list to save Katie.

But though they'd done everything the doctors recommended—everything she herself would have recommended to a patient—it hadn't been enough.

"Hey, cool pictures." Cody started toward a wall with a bunch of large pictures of the airfield over the years. Owen followed with the rest of the kids.

"You should put some pictures of skydivers up here too," Cody suggested.

"That's a great idea." Owen pulled out his phone and made a note to blow up some of his old pictures from Nashville—they could replace them with updated pictures from this drop zone once they had some.

"It's kind of crusty in here." Claire wrinkled her nose at a circle of scratched and dented folding chairs on a dingy rug.

"Nothing a little cleaning and remodeling won't fix," Catelyn said cheerfully. "I can help you pick out some furniture, Dad."

Owen nodded, making more notes. "We'll need a TV for training videos," he muttered, tapping that into the phone.

The kids wandered outside to explore, and Owen continued his tour, his to-do list growing long enough to make his head spin.

"So." Charles strode over after a while. "What do you think? Two months?"

Owen scanned his list and let out a breath. They'd already ordered all of the skydiving equipment, so as long as that came in on time, nothing else here should take too long to accomplish. "Two months," he agreed.

"Good." Charles plopped onto one of the dinged-up chairs and gestured for Owen to do the same.

He did, letting out a long sigh as every one of his vertebrae seemed to crack.

Charles chuckled. "Not getting any younger, eh?"

Owen shot his friend a mock glare. "And I suppose you are?"

Charles shrugged. "I'm not finding any gray hairs in the mirror." He reached as if he were going to pluck at one of the gray strands that dotted Owen's temple, but Owen swatted his arm away.

"You also don't have five kids," he growled.

"True." Charles nodded thoughtfully. "How are they doing with the move?"

Owen sighed. "Good. I guess? Kenzie met a new friend yesterday, and Carter likes the clouds."

Charles laughed softly.

"Cody starts baseball tomorrow, and Catelyn, well, you know Catelyn."

"Her mother's girl." Charles nodded. "Always there when you need her. And Claire?"

Owen groaned. "She hates me. I mean, she already did, but she hates me more now."

Charles tapped Owen's knee in sympathy. "It will get better. I think this will be a good place for the kids. And for you."

Owen nodded. He had no choice but to believe that too.

"You never know." Charles smacked his leg. "You might just meet someone here."

Owen shook his head. "*That's* not going to happen."

"Why not?" Charles's grin faded into a serious expression. "It's been five years."

Owen pushed to his feet and paced to the wall of pictures just for something to look at other than his friend. "It could be fifty years and it wouldn't matter. Unless Katie could come walking in here right now, there's no one I want to be with."

Behind him, he heard Charles's exhale, followed by the creak of his chair and then footsteps.

Owen glanced around, hoping one of his kids had moseyed back into the hangar so he wouldn't have to have this conversation. It was bad enough that his coworkers in Nashville had started to pester him about dating over the past couple of years, but Charles—Charles had known Katie as well as he'd known Owen. He'd been the best man in their wedding, for crying out loud. He knew there never was—never could be—anyone else for Owen.

"You're keeping your promise to her to open a drop zone," Charles said quietly. "Don't you think you should keep your other promise too?"

Owen exhaled loudly. "She told you about that?"

"Of course she told me about it. She knew you would never keep it on your own."

Owen scrubbed a hand down his cheek. "Why haven't you ever said anything about it before?"

"I knew you needed time."

"Yeah, well, there isn't enough time in the world." Anyway, he'd promised Katie that he'd move on—not that he'd fall in love again.

"That's kind of the point, isn't it?" Charles sounded oddly wistful.

Owen eyed his friend sharply. "There something you're not telling me?"

Charles shook his head. "Just starting to realize there's not a lot of time left for me to do the whole family thing."

Owen gawked at his friend. "I didn't know you *wanted* to do the whole family thing."

"Neither did I." Charles offered a rueful chuckle.

"Huh." Owen stared at his friend a moment longer.

"Yeah." Charles slugged his arm. "But we're not talking about me. We're talking about you. And the kids. It wouldn't be so bad for them to have a mother figure."

"Can we go now?" Claire's voice was hard, and both men jumped. Her glare moved from Owen to Charles and back again.

Owen checked his watch. "Oh, yeah, we should get going. I'll be back tomorrow, and we'll make a plan to tackle all of this." He waved a hand to encompass the entire hangar.

"Sounds good, man." Charles patted his shoulder, shooting Claire a quick wave she didn't return.

"About what Uncle Charles was saying," Owen murmured in a low voice as he walked with his daughter toward the open hangar door. "That wasn't— I'm not—"

"Good." But anger tightened Claire's voice, and she kept her arms crossed in front of her.

Owen rounded up the other kids and loaded them into the van. Carter spent the entire drive explaining wind speed and direction to them all, although Catelyn was the only one who nodded along.

Owen's thoughts had gotten caught on Charles's comment that the kids needed a mother figure.

They didn't, did they?

Since Katie's death, he had worked hard to be everything his kids needed. Sure, sometimes it would be nice to have another set of hands, another pair of eyes, to help with this whole parenting thing. But that didn't mean he wanted a replacement mother for them.

"I'm starved," Cody proclaimed as they passed the cherry orchard. "What's for lunch?"

Owen groaned. He'd meant to stop and pick something up on their way back through town, but he'd been so distracted that he'd forgotten. "I think there's still some peanut butter and jelly." He didn't add that he wasn't one hundred percent sure there was bread to put it on. They hadn't had room in the van to pack many groceries.

"It's okay, Dad. I can run to the store," Catelyn offered.

"That will take forever," Cody complained.

"Well, then come along and help and it will go faster," Catelyn shot back.

"Guys." Owen pulled into the driveway. "I'll—"

"Who's that?" Catelyn interrupted, pointing toward the front door, where a woman stood with a large box at her feet. Her back was to them, but her short curls blew in the breeze.

"It's Emma," Kenzie said joyfully.

"Who?" Catelyn gave her dad a quizzical look.

"The neighbor woman," Owen explained. "The one with the horses and chickens."

"She didn't bring us a chicken, did she?" Catelyn laughed, pointing to the box.

"Oh, I hope so," Kenzie breathed.

"Me too," Cody said. "I'm so hungry I could eat a whole chicken right now."

"Hey," Kenzie protested.

Owen pulled the van to a stop. He'd barely put it in park when Kenzie opened her door and hopped out, calling hello to Emma.

"Wow." Catelyn stared after her sister. "Is that really Kenzie?"

Owen shook his head. He wasn't quite sure what had come over his youngest daughter, but he would take it. The girl had always been shy, but ever since Katie's death, she rarely spoke to anyone outside of the immediate family. And there she was, chatting with Emma as if they were old friends.

He got out of the van as well, and Emma looked up with a smile and a wave. "Hi there. I was just about to leave you a note."

"A note about what?" Kenzie asked.

"About this box." Emma winked at the girl.

"I'm so hungry that I imagined I smelled food." Cody jogged over from the van, Catelyn, Carter, and Claire trailing behind him.

Emma laughed. "You didn't imagine it." She reached over to open the box at her feet. "I figured maybe you guys could use some food." She lifted out a plate wrapped with aluminum foil and held it out to Owen. He took it, the scent of fresh-baked cookies making his mouth water. "There's some fruits and veggies in here too. And a casserole. But I figured the cookies would be the biggest hit."

"You were right about that." Cody snatched the plate out of Owen's hands and peeled back the aluminum foil. He grabbed a cookie and passed it to Kenzie, then handed one to Carter and Catelyn as well. He held one out to Claire, but she shook her head and pushed past the rest of the group to get to the door. It didn't budge when she tried to open it, and Owen silently passed her the keys, still trying to wrap his head around the fact that his neighbor had made a meal for their entire family. Had he moved back in time as well as across the country?

"Wow." He really had no words. "You didn't have to— I mean, we—"

Claire pushed the door open, and Lexi came barreling out of the house, greeting the newcomer with paws to the chest and a tongue to the cheek.

"Lexi, stop." Owen tried to reach for the dog but missed and ended up grabbing Emma's hand instead. He let go quickly, reached again, this time locking his fingers around Lexi's collar and tugging her down.

The dog's tail continued to wag a hundred miles an hour as she strained to sniff Emma's jeans and cowboy boots.

"Hi there, girl." Emma squatted and held out her arms to the dog. Owen let go of Lexi's collar and took a step backwards.

"Do I smell like chickens?" Emma asked.

Owen almost said no, she didn't, she smelled like a mix of sunshine and wildflowers, but then he realized she had been talking to the dog.

After a moment, Lexi calmed enough to lie on the ground, letting Emma pet her side in long, smooth movements.

"Wow." Catelyn stepped forward. "I don't think anyone has ever gotten Lexi to calm down that quickly."

Emma grinned and stood, wiping a hand over the Lexi slobber on her cheek. She held out her other hand to Catelyn. "I'm Emma."

"Catelyn."

"My oldest," Owen added. "And the one who stomped past you is Claire, my second oldest. She's . . . struggling a little with the move. And the cookie monster here is Cody."

Cody shifted the cookie plate to his left hand and held out his right to Emma. "Nice to meet you."

Owen stifled a smile. As much as he wasn't ready for his kids to grow up, it was fun to see Cody growing into a polite young man.

"These are really good." Cody stuffed another giant bite into his mouth, saying around it, "Thank you."

Owen rolled his eyes. Okay, his son was becoming a *semi-polite* young man.

"Yes, thank you," Owen repeated, suddenly realizing that he hadn't said it yet.

"You're welcome," Emma said simply. "Oh, and I put some vouchers in there for a free trial of riding lessons. It's a great chance for kids to get to know a little bit about horses and how to be safe around them, if nothing else. We have classes for all ages, so any of the kids are welcome. And we have a great therapeutic program, if Carter wanted to try that. That's included too." She broke off suddenly, brushing her blonde hair off her face as if self-conscious. "I mean, if he—"

Owen nodded. "He's on the spectrum, yes. High functioning." He and Katie had agreed early on that there was no reason to hide their son's diagnosis. It wasn't as if it was anything to be ashamed of—and acknowledging it allowed them to get Carter the help he needed.

"Can we do the lessons, Dad?" Kenzie pleaded.

"I know Ruby would love to see you there," Emma added, as if she wanted to strengthen Kenzie's case. "She talked about you for an hour straight after you left yesterday."

"Where is she now?" Kenzie peered around as if expecting Ruby to jump out from behind a bush.

"She's at home," Emma said. "She lives in town."

Kenzie's forehead scrunched. "She doesn't live with you?"

Before Owen could figure out a subtle way to tell his daughter not to pry, Emma answered, "No, she lives with her mom and dad."

"But I thought *you* were her mom." Kenzie looked to Owen as if he could explain it, but he had thought the same thing.

Emma smiled. "I'm her aunt. My brother James married her mom earlier this year, but Ruby took lessons with me even before that. She's over at my house a lot."

"Oh good." Kenzie turned hopeful eyes on Owen. "So can we do the lessons?"

"Probably." Owen had meant to say *maybe*, which gave him a little more wiggle room than *probably*, but Kenzie hadn't been this excited about anything in a long time.

"Really?" Kenzie's eyes widened, and she threw her arms around him.

"Great." Emma smiled around at all of them. "Then I'll see whoever wants to ride on Wednesday. For now, I'll let you guys go eat before the food gets cold. If you need anything, you know where to find me." She started across the yard toward the field.

They all called thank you, and Owen bent to pick up the box, realizing suddenly that not only had she made them a meal, but she'd lugged it across the field to their house.

"See, isn't she nice?" Kenzie gushed to Catelyn.

"She is," Catelyn agreed.

"Like Mom," Kenzie added.

Catelyn opened the door for Owen, not replying to her sister's comment.

Owen decided it was best to let it go, since he had no idea how to respond either.

He set the box on the kitchen counter, then opened it. To one side, Emma had neatly stacked paper plates, plastic forks, cups, and even napkins. On the other side was a large casserole dish topped by a bag of rolls.

"Oh man, that smells so good." Cody nudged him out of the way and started emptying the box. "Here." He handed Owen an envelope.

"These must be for the riding lessons." Owen slit the envelope open, knowing Kenzie wouldn't give him a moment of peace until he did.

He pulled out a card and opened it to find a small stack of vouchers inside. But his eyes passed from the vouchers to the card. On it, in neat handwriting, it read: "Welcome, neighbors! I pray you'll love Hope Springs, and I trust that the Lord will bless your family here. If you need anything, please don't hesitate to call." She'd signed her name, followed by a phone number. And under that, in scrolling letters, the card said, "Trust in the Lord with all your heart and lean not on your own understanding; in all your ways submit to him, and he will make your paths straight." Owen blinked at the familiar words from Proverbs. This had been Katie's favorite passage. He'd been trying to hold onto it, trying to put his trust in the Lord after all they'd been through—but it wasn't easy.

He shook his head, marveling at God's ability to use a complete stranger to bring him the words he needed just when he needed them.

Not a complete stranger, he reminded himself. Their neighbor.

Charles's words from earlier flashed through his thoughts: *It wouldn't be so bad for the kids to have a mother figure.*

He shook his head. Emma may have been good with his kids, and she may have provided them with an excellent meal, but that didn't mean he had any interest in her as anything beyond a neighbor.

He grabbed up the plates and passed them to the kids. But he couldn't help thinking, as he filled his plate with a heaping helping of casserole, that she was a very good neighbor indeed.

Chapter 4

"You're sure you don't mind if we aren't there tonight?" Mom asked, looking up from the spot at the kitchen table where she was stitching a rip in one of Ruby's dresses.

Emma paused at the door. "Of course not. You already took me out for lunch." She rubbed her stomach, which was still stuffed from the giant meal she'd eaten at the Hidden Cafe. "Thank you again."

Mom still looked concerned. "But it's your birthday."

"And I'll have plenty more of them." Emma backtracked to drop a kiss on top of her mother's head. She knew what Mom was thinking—a year ago, she hadn't known if that was true. But God had brought her through that time.

"Besides," she added, "you haven't seen Nancy and Carl in years. They'd be disappointed if they came all this way and you ditched them. You can see me any old time."

Mom nodded, and Emma squeezed her shoulder. "I'll see you later. Have a good time." She smothered a yawn with her hand.

"Maybe someone else should take your lessons today," Mom said. "You look beat.

"Now you sound like James." Emma knew her family worried about her. But she was fine now. "I'm just sleepy from that big lunch. Nothing a few lessons won't wear off."

But as she headed out to the barn, she couldn't deny that her limbs were begging her to sit down for just a minute. Ever since the chemo, she got fatigued much more easily than she used to. Her doctor said she needed to allow herself time to get back up to full speed. She encouraged Emma to rest more. But Emma had had enough of resting. Life was short, and she wanted to *do* the things God had put her on this earth—kept her on this earth—to do.

Thankfully, in the barn she found that her team already had most of the horses saddled and ready to go. She headed straight for Big Blue and nuzzled the horse's velvety neck with her face. This old, dependable guy had been with Emma from the beginning, an always calm, always steady presence in her life.

She gave the horse one more pat, then went to greet the students who had begun to file in, forcing herself to put some "pep in her step" as her dad used to say. How could she expect the kids and horses to give one hundred percent if she didn't do the same?

"Happy birthday, Aunt Emma!" Ruby burst through the door, her gangly legs spinning as she raced to throw her arms around Emma.

"Thank you." Emma hugged her niece, marveling again at the unexpected gift of family God had given her through this girl.

"Happy birthday," James and Bethany chorused behind Ruby.

"We're still going to the Chocolate Chicken after lessons tonight, right?" Ruby asked.

Emma nodded. "Wouldn't miss it."

"I still think we should have thrown you another surprise party." Ruby scuffed her riding boots in the sand. "That was fun."

"It was," Emma agreed. "But now that you did it once, you wouldn't be able to fool me again. I'm on to you." She pointed two fingers at her own eyes, then at Ruby's.

Ruby laughed and mimicked the gesture. "Did you give Kenzie's dad the vouchers for lessons?"

Emma nodded. "He said they'd probably come."

"Goodie." Ruby jumped up and down with a clap. "Now you guys can meet her," she said to her parents.

"I feel like I already have with how much you talk about her." James rumpled Ruby's hair.

"Dad," Ruby moaned. "Don't mess up my hair."

"Why not? You're just going to put your helmet on anyway." James rolled his eyes, but Emma could see the way he glowed, just as he did every time he heard the word "dad."

It was funny how things had worked out. James, who had thought he'd never want to be called dad again after losing his biological daughter now relished the title. And Emma, who for years had dreamed of being called mom, never would be.

And God had given her contentment with that.

Besides, she had plenty of children in her life in the form of all of these students.

"All right." She led the dressage class to the horses. "Let's get to work."

For the next hour, they worked on perfecting their simple routine for the upcoming Hope Fest parade. Emma watched with a sharp eye, correcting form and posture, and by the end, she was confident they were ready for the parade. She walked with them all toward the gate that led to the seating area where parents usually waited, fighting past her fatigue to create a mental checklist of everything she needed to do before then.

"Kenzie!" Ruby's shriek sent Emma's thoughts scattering, and she laughed as her niece took off for the neighbor girl, who took a step closer to her dad as if afraid Ruby might bowl her right over.

Owen wrapped an arm around the girl but smiled at Ruby. "That was some fancy riding."

"Oh. Thanks." Ruby ducked her head, and Emma felt a surge of pride for the girl, who had medaled in every event she'd entered lately and yet remained humble and continued to encourage the other riders.

"I'm so glad you guys came," Emma said as she reached the group, spotting Carter still at the door, headphones on, eyes trained toward the sky.

"You must be the famous Kenzie." James and Bethany had made their way over, and James held out his hand to Kenzie, who took it timidly, then to Owen. "I'm Ruby's dad. James. And this is my wife Bethany." Emma loved the joy she heard in her brother's voice every time he introduced his family. It was like he was a different man from the one who had come here last spring, broken and surly. Love and family certainly agreed with him.

She suppressed a resurgence of longing in her own heart, reminding herself that God *had* given her a family, and she was content.

"Are you ready to get started?" she asked Kenzie and Carter, who had finally wandered toward them.

Carter nodded, but Kenzie bit her lip.

"Kenzie loves the idea, but she's a little nervous," Owen explained.

"I was scared at first too," Ruby said. "But the horses are so, so, so nice. You're going to love it."

"But it looked hard," Kenzie said quietly.

"Oh, don't worry," Emma soothed. "We won't start with the kinds of things Ruby was doing. She's been riding a long time, and the things she was doing are called dressage. Maybe you'll want to try that someday. But for tonight we'll just get to know the horses and equipment. Get on their back. That sort of thing. How does that sound?"

"Good, I guess." Kenzie looked at her dad uncertainly, and he patted her back.

"You'll do great."

"You will," Emma agreed, holding out a hand to Kenzie.

Shyly, the girl let go of Owen's hand and took Emma's instead. Emma gave her fingers a gentle squeeze.

"Kenzie, you'll be with me. And Carter, you get to work with my awesome friend Kayla." She pointed across the arena to where Kayla was greeting the other riders in the therapeutic program, who came up to her wheelchair to give her fist bumps and high fives. Carter flicked his leg and nodded.

"She's my other aunt," Ruby announced proudly. "She's married to my Uncle Cam."

"Did she get hurt riding a horse?" Kenzie asked, looking even more nervous.

"Kenz," Owen scolded.

But Emma smiled. "No. She was in a car accident. She was actually afraid of horses until a few years ago, and now . . . well, you can see how much she loves them."

Kenzie nodded, laughing as Ace nuzzled Kayla's hair with his lips. "They do look nice."

"You should put her on Big Blue, Aunt Emma," Ruby said. She turned to Kenzie. "He's the sweetest one of all. And the handsomest."

Kenzie looked slightly reassured, and Emma nodded. "That's a good idea, Rubes."

"We're waiting for Aunt Emma to finish lessons so we can go to the Chocolate Chicken," Ruby told Kenzie. "So I'll sit over there and watch you."

Kenzie nodded as if she wasn't quite sure what to say about that, but Carter said, "What's a Chocolate Chicken? That sounds gross."

The group from Hope Springs all laughed. "It's an ice cream shop," Ruby explained. "The best ice cream shop in the whole world. Hey, you guys should come with us!"

"Can we dad?" The prospect of ice cream seemed to pull Kenzie out of her shell.

Owen looked conflicted. "Maybe," he said finally.

"Yay!" Ruby and Kenzie both cheered, and Emma laughed at the expression on Owen's face. Clearly, he knew he wouldn't be able to say no now.

"All right." Emma started toward the arena with Kenzie and Carter. "Let's ride some horses so we can get some ice cream afterward."

"I said maybe," Owen called behind them.

Emma only laughed as Kenzie gave a little skip at her side.

Chapter 5

"Kenzie is doing really good. I think she's a natural. I bet she'll be doing dressage in no time. And then we can hang out together even more. Hey, do you think she could sleep over at my house sometime?"

Owen laughed at Ruby's constant barrage of questions. She'd kept up a steady stream of chatter through the entire lesson, but Owen didn't mind. Anyone who wanted to befriend his shy daughter was a good person in his book.

"I'm sure she could," Owen answered.

"Yay. How about this Friday? Is that okay, Mom?" Ruby glanced over her shoulder to James and Bethany, who were sitting behind them.

Bethany nodded. "I think so."

"You have children's choir this Friday," James said, his arm resting lightly on his wife's shoulder. "But we can definitely find sometime soon to do it."

Bethany shook her head with a laugh. "That's why I shouldn't agree to things before checking my calendar." She pulled out her phone, and James wrapped an arm around her shoulder. From what Owen had gathered, Bethany suffered from short-term memory loss after an aneurysm had almost taken her life.

"That's what I'm here for," James said to his wife, dusting a kiss over her forehead.

Owen had to look away for a moment. How many times had he taken that simple gesture for granted over the years with Katie?

His eyes fell on Emma, who was leading Kenzie and Carter toward them, all three of them smiling and waving.

"Did you see me, Dad?" Kenzie called, her voice more animated than it had been in months.

Owen stood and made his way down the bleachers with Ruby and her family. "I saw you. You did great. You both did. What did you think of the horses, buddy?" He looked to Carter.

"They smell funny."

Owen chuckled. Leave it to Carter to say exactly what he was thinking.

"You get used to it after a while," Emma assured him. "I hope you guys will come again next week."

"Oh yes. You *have* to come," Ruby said dramatically. "You're so good. You did better than I did the first time I was on a horse." She moved to Kenzie's side. "Your dad said you can have a sleepover at my house sometime. I wanted to do it this week, but then my dad said I have choir, which I totally forgot about. But the week after that, maybe. If you want to, I mean."

Kenzie sent Owen a panicked look, but he gave her a reassuring nod. She'd only been to one sleepover—and Owen had gotten a teary call in the middle of the night asking him to come pick her up. But he had a feeling Ruby would keep her so busy she'd forget to be homesick.

"Um, maybe." Kenzie moved closer to Owen. "Thanks."

"I'm starving," Ruby announced. "Are we ready to go to the Chocolate Chicken now?"

Emma glanced over her shoulder, to where her team members—six full-time employees, Ruby had informed him—were leading the horses out a large door at the back that Owen assumed led to the stables.

"I should really help with—"

"Not today," James said firmly. "Your team has it under control."

Emma looked ready to protest but said on a sigh, "Fine."

Ruby led the way to the door and held it open for all of them to pass through.

It wasn't until they were outside that Owen realized the flaw in their plans. "I forgot that Catelyn took the van," he murmured to Kenzie. They'd dropped her car off at the shop this morning to have the air conditioning looked at. "I'm sorry, but we're going to have to go another time."

Kenzie's face fell, but she didn't say anything—which only made Owen feel that much worse.

"That's okay." Emma pointed to a large pickup truck. "You guys can ride with me."

"Oh, you don't have to do that." Owen brushed off the offer. "We can just go another time."

Emma tilted her head toward the road. "Come on. It's not like it's out of my way to take you. I'm going anyway."

Kenzie and Ruby both turned pleading eyes to him, and even Carter said, "I like orange ice cream."

Owen shook his head. He knew when he was beaten. "All right."

The kids cheered and Emma grinned at him as if to say he'd made the right decision.

"See you there," Ruby called as she ran to her car with her parents.

Owen and his kids walked with Emma to her truck.

He helped Kenzie and Carter into the back seat, then climbed into the passenger seat. Emma had already started the vehicle, but she sat for a moment, staring out the windshield.

Just when Owen was about to ask if everything was all right, she put the truck into gear and started down the driveway. Owen pulled out his phone to send a quick text to the family chat. Catelyn and Claire had gone to the beach and were supposed to pick Cody up on their way home in a little bit. *Meet us at the Chocolate Chicken after you get Cody,* he texted. *It's an ice cream shop.*

They could look up the address on their phones.

When there was no immediate reply, Owen set his phone in his lap. This whole having-the-family-go-in-different-directions thing was still hard for him to adjust to, even though Catelyn had been in college for two years now. He much preferred when his whole crew was together. Not that that could ever truly happen again, without Katie.

"So what brings you guys to Hope Springs?" Emma's question cut into his thoughts

"Do you know Above the Blue?"

Emma's gaze jumped to him, her eyes wide. "The skydiving place off Old River Road?"

"Yeah. Have you been there?" He had no trouble imagining her skydiving. After all, people of all ages and walks of life did it.

She shook her head, directing her gaze back at the road. "It closed."

"It will be opening again soon."

"How do you—" Emma's eyes came to his again. "Did you buy it?"

Owen couldn't suppress a grin at what felt like the sheer audacity of his and Charles's venture. "My business partner and I did, yes."

"Wow." Emma sounded impressed. "Do you skydive?"

Owen chuckled. "You could say that, yeah. I'm working toward my eight-thousandth jump."

"Eight-thousandth?" Emma repeated, sounding disbelieving.

"Well, I've been doing it for twenty-seven years." He puffed out a breath, still blown away by how much time had passed. "Wow, that makes me feel old."

Emma laughed easily, her short hair bouncing against her temples. "I know the feeling."

He eyed her. He wasn't terribly good at estimating people's ages, but if he had to guess, she was probably a few years younger than him.

"What made you choose Hope Springs?" Emma asked.

"Lack of options." Owen gave an apologetic chuckle, realizing how that probably sounded. "Not that Hope Springs isn't a great place. It's just, my wife and I had always dreamed of opening a drop zone, but we hadn't really gotten to thinking through the logistics, like the fact that they don't come on the market every day. But then one did, and my friend Charles called, and, well, here we are." He clamped his mouth shut. That was probably way more information than she wanted.

"That's really great." Enthusiasm rang from her words. "So your wife skydives too?"

"I, uh. No. I mean, she—" Owen fumbled. It had been five years. Why was it still so hard to say this? He took a breath. "She did. But she passed away. Cancer."

"Oh, I'm so sorry." Emma's voice registered her shock, and she lifted a hand, as if she was going to touch his arm, but then put it back on the steering wheel.

Owen was grateful. He'd received many a sympathetic squeeze on the arm over the years, and though he knew people meant well, all it did was remind him that he'd never feel Katie's touch again.

"Thank you," he said quietly. "It's been hard, but we're doing okay."

Emma gave him an understanding smile, and he wondered if she'd known someone who had died of cancer too. Maybe even her husband. His eyes went to her bare ring finger.

"I don't know if you guys have a church home or not." Emma lifted her hand off the steering wheel to point out her window. "But this is where I go. We'd love to have you join us."

Owen gave a small laugh, and Emma shot him a questioning look.

"Sorry." He shook his head. "Finding a church was on my to-do list, but it looks like I can check that off now."

"You keep a to-do list?" Emma raised an eyebrow.

"Yeah. Why?" Owen leaned his head back on the seat, realizing suddenly that this was the first time since Katie's death that he'd been in a vehicle and not been the one driving. It was rather relaxing.

"No reason." Emma shook her head. "I just figured someone with a job as exciting as skydiving would be less of a list maker and more . . . spontaneous."

Owen chuckled. "Sorry to disappoint you, but I don't have a spontaneous bone in my body. In my work, lists keep people alive."

Emma nodded thoughtfully. "I guess that makes sense. Although I'd argue that you can be at least a little spontaneous. You're here, aren't you?" She pulled over to the curb and gestured out his window, where a giant metal chicken statue held a sign that said Chocolate Chicken.

Owen shook his head but grinned. He supposed he was.

Chapter 6

Owen's wife had died of cancer.

Emma eased herself out of the truck, trying to figure out why the thought shook her so much. She knew people died of cancer every day. She had even wondered for a while if she might be one of them.

But that was the point.

She hadn't died.

And Owen's wife had.

Even though she'd had a husband and five children who needed her.

Whereas Emma had no one who really needed her. Sure, her friends and family would have missed her, but she also knew they would have been okay without her.

She walked around the truck, standing a few feet off as Owen helped Carter down.

Bethany, James, and Ruby had parked in front of them, and Ruby barreled toward Kenzie as if they had been separated for days. Kenzie shot her dad one panicked look, but when he offered an encouraging smile, she held her ground.

Ruby stopped inches from her and whispered something in her ear that made Kenzie giggle.

They all moved toward the Chocolate Chicken, James and Bethany hand in hand, Kenzie and Ruby side by side, and Owen with Carter, his hand resting on the boy's shoulder.

Emma brought up the rear, reminding herself that just because she didn't have anyone to walk next to didn't mean she was alone.

Owen and Carter stopped to hold the door open for her.

"Thanks." She addressed her comment to Carter, feeling self-conscious about talking to Owen now that she knew about his wife.

"Surprise!" The enormous shout made Emma leap backwards like a spooked horse.

She smacked into something solid that she thought was the door until it let out a soft "oof!"

"I'm so sorry," Emma gasped, thrusting herself away from Owen. Her hands clutched at her chest, and she couldn't catch her breath. "You're all evil," she called to the large group crowding the tables and open spaces of the restaurant.

"You said we couldn't surprise you again," Ruby danced from foot to foot. "But we did."

Emma let out her breath on a laugh. "I guess you did. That was some pretty good acting."

"Happy birthday," someone called, and dozens of voices echoed the words.

Realizing suddenly that Owen and his kids must be as stunned as she was, she turned to apologize.

But Owen was already backing his kids toward the door. "We didn't mean to crash your birthday party. We'll get ice cream some other time."

"Don't be silly." Emma gestured them into the restaurant. "The more the merrier. Besides, you can't promise kids ice cream and then take it back. Right, guys?" She looked to Kenzie and Carter. "Sorry if the shouting scared you though. My friends are loud."

"Ruby told me outside, so I wasn't scared," Kenzie beamed.

"Ah, that's what you two were giggling about." Emma smiled at the girls as Ruby grabbed Kenzie's hand and pulled her off to introduce her to the other kids.

Owen watched her go, looking torn.

"Don't worry," Emma tried to reassure him. "They may be noisy and giggly, but they're a good group."

Owen pulled his eyes off his daughter. "Kenzie's always been shy, but after her mother . . ." He shook his head. "I have a feeling Ruby is going to be good for her."

Emma laughed. "Ruby is good for a lot of people."

"Happy birthday, sweetheart." Emma spun toward the voice. In all the chaos, she hadn't even noticed Mom and William.

"I thought you were going out with Nancy and Carl."

"As you were supposed to think." Mom grinned and gave her a big hug. William did too.

"I can believe you would do this, Mom. But you, William," Emma joked. "I thought I could trust you not to let them do this to me again."

William's smile was affectionate. "After the year you've been through, we all thought—"

"Mom. William." Emma cut him off, unwilling to let her cancer come up in front of Owen, not after what he'd revealed about his wife's death from the disease.

"This is Owen and his son Carter. And his daughter Kenzie is over there with Ruby. They're our new neighbors. Owen, this is my mom Anne and her husband William."

"Ah, the chicken namers." William held out his hand. "Ruby told us all about you."

"Can't say I've ever been called that before, but yeah." Owen returned the handshake with a chuckle, then shook Mom's hand. "It's nice to meet y'all."

"Did I just hear someone say y'all?" Grace was suddenly at their side.

Owen looked sheepish. "Yeah, sorry. I'm—"

"Oh, don't be sorry." Grace waggled her head back and forth. "It's a little taste of home."

"This is Grace," Emma filled in. "Grace, this is Owen. My new neighbor," she added before her friend could get any ideas. "They just moved here from Tennessee."

"You're kidding. I'm from Tennessee. A little town in the Smokies called River Falls. No one's ever heard of it."

"I've heard of it," Carter said, and the adults all looked at him in surprise. "Lydia St. Peter lives there."

"That's right, she does." Grace grinned at the boy. "Do you like her music?"

"She has a song about clouds."

Grace looked confused.

Owen chuckled. "He's fascinated by weather. I think he means *Lift Me Up in the Storm*."

"Ah." Grace nodded seriously to Carter. "That's a good one. What would you say if I told you that Lydia St. Peter is my sister?"

Carter's eyes widened. "Really?"

Grace nodded. "Next time she visits, I'll make sure she sings it for you."

"Are you guys Titans fans?" Emma turned to Owen and Carter.

"Of course. Why?"

Emma considered telling them but decided it would be more fun to let them be surprised when they met Grace's husband Levi in person. He must be manning their bed-and-breakfast tonight. "No reason. Why don't you guys go get some ice cream, and then I'll introduce you to everyone else."

Owen led Carter to Kenzie and then the three of them got in line.

"He seems nice," Grace said in a low voice.

"His wife died five years ago. Of cancer." Emma rubbed her hands, which had started tingling and burning the way they did sometimes ever since the chemo. Her doctor said it was neuropathy and that it would probably get worse before it got better.

"Oh, that's too bad." Grace frowned in sympathy.

Emma could only nod. Apparently the news didn't raise the same questions for Grace as it did for her. Like, why would God take a woman who had a family who needed her, and leave Emma here?

God kept you here for a purpose. As if to prove it to herself, she decided right then and there that she would do everything she could to be a good neighbor to Owen and his kids.

Chapter 7

Owen licked his chocolate-vanilla swirl ice cream cone—a flavor Katie had always teased was his way of avoiding making a decision—and handed Carter a bowl of orange sherbet. Kenzie had already taken her mint chip back to Ruby and the other girls and was smiling quietly as their talk whirled around her.

His eyes skimmed the crowded ice cream shop. If sheer numbers were any indication, Emma was one popular lady. But then, he supposed that made sense, given how friendly and outgoing she seemed to be.

Katie had always been quieter, more contemplative. Not that she wasn't friendly—she would do anything for anyone—but it took her awhile to get comfortable with new people. Owen had been the more social of the two of them, and she'd usually been happy to let him carry the conversation when they talked with others. It was only with him that she'd been completely open—completely unguarded.

Emma, on the other hand, seemed to be perfectly at ease with this large group of people.

As if she heard his thoughts, Emma caught his eye, waved, and made her way over to them.

"Good pick." She nodded to his cone. "Then you don't have to make a choice."

Owen took another lick of his ice cream so he wouldn't have to answer. If she were Katie, he would have said, "I chose you, didn't I?"

"And is that orange sherbet?" Emma turned to Carter, who nodded, an orange mustache rimming his top lip. "I used to love that kind. It made me feel like I was eating the sun."

"You can't eat the sun," Carter said seriously.

Emma nodded just as seriously. "Nope. But it's fun to pretend, isn't it?"

Carter half-smiled and took another bite, and Owen had to smile too. Emma may not be a mother, but she sure was good with kids anyway.

A group of people approached them, and Emma gave hugs all around before introducing Owen and Carter as her new neighbors.

Turning to Owen, she said, "This is Sophie and Spencer. They own the cherry orchard just down the road from your place. Hidden Blossom Farms."

"Welcome to the neighborhood." Spencer held out a hand. "Be sure to let us know if you need anything."

Owen nodded, though he knew he wouldn't. He could still hear his father's motto: "The Lord helps those who help themselves." It had taken Katie years to convince Owen that those words weren't actually biblical, but he'd still never been able to shake the feeling that asking for help was wrong. Or at the very least, weak. Katie had called it his one flaw—though he was perfectly aware that he had plenty more.

"Mom, when are we going to get ice cream?" A girl who looked a little younger than Kenzie ran over to Sophie.

"Right now." Sophie laughed and steered the girl toward the counter. "It was nice meeting you."

Owen nodded.

"That's Aubrey," Emma said. "And her twin brother Rylan is over there next to Kenzie and Ruby. And that's Gabby on Kenzie's other side. Her mom, Isabel, is over there—" She pointed to a woman who was laughing with another couple. "And her dad is Tyler. He's Spencer's brother, and they're partners in the cherry orchard. Oh, and he's the baseball coach, so maybe you've met him?"

Owen nodded, trying to keep up. "Yeah, I think so." He was already lost with all the names.

"His boys play too. They'll probably be here soon. I think baseball practice should be done by now."

Owen nodded. It should be. So where were Catelyn and Claire and Cody? He pulled out his phone, but there were no texts or missed calls. Maybe they'd decided to go home instead of coming for ice cream—but would it kill them to let him know where they were?

"Happy birthday, Emma." A woman holding a toddler on her hip wrapped Emma in a one-armed hug.

"Thank you." Emma gestured to Owen. "This is Owen, my new neighbor. And this is Violet. And her little Liliana." Her voice went up as she reached to tickle the girl, who let out a giggle straight from the belly. Owen smiled, missing the days when his own children had laughed like that.

"It's so nice to meet you." Violet held out a hand. "My husband is here somewhere." She scanned the room. "Oh. He's talking to Jade."

"That's perfect." Emma smiled warmly. "Owen's daughter Kenzie is Ruby's age, so they should both be in Jade's class this year."

"Oh, wonderful." Violet smiled. "Come on, she'll be thrilled to meet you."

Owen dutifully followed, tugging Carter along with him, trying to run through the names of the people he'd already met. Katie had always said it worked best to repeat the person's name silently to yourself while picturing their face—but there were too many faces in here.

"Nate, this is Owen." Violet passed her wriggling toddler to a man Owen assumed was her husband. He nodded and smiled at Owen, though his hands were too busy juggling the little girl to shake Owen's.

"He just moved in next door to me," Emma added. "And his daughter will be in your class." Emma turned to the woman Nate had been talking to. "This is Jade. Mrs. Zellner, to her students. And her husband . . ." She scanned the room, then pointed to a man juggling four cones. "Is Dan. He's the pastor at our church."

Dan stopped to hand one of the cones to a girl at Kenzie and Ruby's table. "That's our daughter Hope," Jade said.

Owen's heart lifted as the girl said something that made Kenzie laugh.

"And the little guy next to Dan is Matthias," Emma added.

After Owen said hello to Dan, Emma brought him to a section of tables that had been pushed together. Every last seat was occupied, and Owen braced himself for the barrage of names.

"You already met James and Bethany. And this is Jared and Peyton and their sweet little Ella Lynn." A small girl with dark hair smiled shyly at him. "And Ethan and Ariana. Their daughter Joy is part of the giggly gaggle over there." She gestured to Kenzie's table, and all the girls—including Kenzie—waved and then broke into a fresh fit of giggles.

"And Carter already got to know Miss Kayla." The blonde woman in a wheelchair who had taught Carter's lesson smiled as the baby on her lap tried to grab for her ice cream cone.

"And this is Evelyn." Kayla moved her cone to her other hand. "And my husband Cam." She gestured to the man who stood with a hand on her shoulder.

"He built my chicken coop," Emma added.

"Don't forget about us." A woman waved from the far end of the table, and Emma led Owen and Carter closer.

"This is Leah. She's Dan's sister."

"It's so nice to meet you. This is my husband Austin and our son Jackson." Leah gestured to a dark-haired young man who looked to be in his early twenties, and Owen was suddenly relieved that his oldest daughter wasn't there.

"Hey, Dad. Sorry it took us so long to get here." Catelyn appeared suddenly at his side. Behind her, Cody stood in the middle of a group of baseball players who had flooded into the place as well.

"Oh, Catelyn." Emma gestured her forward. "I'm so glad you made it. Have you met Jackson?"

Owen nearly growled as Jackson got up from his seat to shake Catelyn's hand, especially when Catelyn tucked her hair behind her ear the same way Katie had the day they'd met. Oh brother, he was not ready for this step.

"Where's Claire?" Owen asked.

Catelyn rolled her eyes. "That's why we're late. I couldn't convince her to leave the beach. She made some friends there. She said she'd get her own ride home."

"She what?" Owen stared at his daughter. "Why would you let her do that?"

"Right. Like anyone *lets* Claire do anything." Catelyn laughed, but Owen could see the worry in her eyes.

More than once, Owen had heard Claire remind her sister that just because their mother had died, it didn't make Catelyn the new mom.

Owen would have to take care of this himself.

He held out his hand. "Give me the keys."

Catelyn blinked at him for a moment, as if debating whether or not to argue. She glanced at Jackson, who looked concerned and also a bit lovestruck—Owen would deal with that later—then set the keys in Owen's hand.

"Keep an eye on your brothers and sister. I'll be back in twenty minutes."

It wasn't until he was out the door that he realized he probably should have apologized to Emma for running out on her birthday party.

Chapter 8

Emma tried not to stare after Owen as the door to the Chocolate Chicken closed behind him. She didn't blame him for being worried about his daughter, but Hope Springs wasn't exactly a hotbed of gang activity. She was sure Claire was fine. Then again, she'd never been a parent, so she had no right to judge someone else's parenting.

"Sorry about that." Catelyn turned to the group with a rueful smile. "He's been a little overprotective, ever since Mom died."

"I'm so sorry to hear that." Jackson took a step closer to Catelyn, and Emma exchanged a small smile with Leah. She knew her friend worried that her son spent so much time on his premed studies that he would never marry, but maybe meeting Catelyn would change that.

"Catelyn." Carter pulled his sister's arm, interrupting her conversation with Jackson. "It's loud in here."

"I know, buddy. Put on your headphones."

"I left them in Miss Emma's truck."

"Oh." Catelyn gave Emma a startled look, as if wondering why her brother's headphones would be in Emma's vehicle.

"They rode with me since you had the van." Emma didn't know why she felt compelled to give an explanation. "I'll take Carter out to get his headphones."

Catelyn only hesitated a second. "Okay. Thank you." She turned back to Jackson, and Emma shot another look at Leah, who had definitely noticed too.

Outside, Emma took in a breath of the fresh, lake-scented air. She dearly loved being with all of her friends, but right now, she, like Carter, was feeling a bit overwhelmed.

She retrieved Carter's headphones from the truck, and he pulled them on.

"Are you ready to go back inside, or do you want to stay out here for a bit?" she asked.

"Out here." His answer was decisive.

"Do you want to see the boats?"

Carter nodded, and Emma led him down the steep hill to the marina.

The boy tipped his head skyward as they walked, and Emma kept an eye out in front of him so that he wouldn't trip over anything. But he seemed to have a remarkable sense of what was in front of him, even without looking.

Emma glanced at the sky too, wondering what had him so fascinated. "That cloud looks like an elephant."

"It's a cumulus mediocris," Carter informed her. "If it keeps growing vertically, it might become a cumulus congestus. Or it could become cumulonimbus. Those are my favorite."

"Aren't cumulonimbus thunderstorm clouds?" Emma was pretty sure she'd learned that somewhere.

Carter looked at her as if impressed. "Yep. I love thunder."

"Where did you learn so much about clouds?" Emma asked.

Carter shrugged. "My mom gave me a book. She used to read it to me because it was too hard. But she said someday I'd grow up and be able to read it myself, and now I can."

Emma wasn't sure what to reply. Her heart hurt just thinking about Carter and the other kids being raised without their mom—not to mention the grief she could still hear in Owen's voice when he mentioned his wife's death.

They walked in silence for a bit, until Carter said abruptly, "My mom is dead now."

Emma nodded. "I know. I'm so sorry. You must miss her."

They reached the edge of the lake, and Emma stopped walking. Carter's gaze was still turned skyward.

"Daddy says she's in heaven, and I should think of her whenever I look at the clouds, but I don't think heaven is in the clouds because they're just water and ice and cold, and Mom didn't like the cold."

Emma nodded, fighting back a sudden sting of tears before Carter could see them. "I think you're right about that. I'm sure in heaven it's just the right temperature all the time."

Carter nodded, as if satisfied, and finally seemed to notice they'd reached the marina. Within its shelter, water rolled quietly against the docks, but beyond it, waves crashed up against the boulders of the breakwater.

"Do you want to take your headphones off so you can hear the lake?" Emma asked.

Carter nodded and pulled them off, grinning broadly. "It sounds like it's laughing."

Emma grinned back. "It sure does. If you promise not to let go of my hand, I'll take you out on the docks."

Carter nodded and stuck his hand in hers. It was more than a little sticky from his sherbet, but warm and sweet.

Their footsteps sounded in unison on the wooden pier, and Emma let herself enjoy the play of the breeze over her face as the sun lowered itself toward the water, lighting the clouds in brilliant shades of pink and orange.

"Wow. Look at that." She knelt at Carter's side and pointed into the distance, where a large cargo ship was backlit by the sun.

"It's huge!" Carter flapped his free arm in excitement.

Emma smiled, letting herself soak in his sheer wonder for a moment before pushing to her feet. "We should probably head back to the Chocolate Chicken. Your dad will be back soon, and he might wonder where you are."

Carter nodded, and they made their way off the pier. His hand remained tucked into hers as they started up the hill toward Hope Street. By the time they were only a quarter of the way up, Emma was nearly dragging him, and before they reached the halfway point, Carter slowed to a stop. "I'm tired."

Emma eyed him. He wasn't a big kid, and she'd seen Owen give him a piggyback ride, but was she strong enough to do the same?

She nodded to herself. Of course she was.

She lowered herself into a squat, ignoring the protest of her knees, and Carter hopped on.

She grunted as she stood. Either Carter was heavier than he looked, or she wasn't as strong as she used to be.

Probably both.

But after a couple of staggering steps, she found her footing and started to make her way up the hill.

Her progress was slow and somewhat painful, but Carter didn't seem to mind as he kept up a running commentary on the clouds, which apparently had begun to flatten, meaning it shouldn't storm.

"That's good," Emma panted.

They were nearly to the top of the hill when her hands began to tingle again, making it impossible to keep her grip on Carter's legs.

"I think this is where the horsey stops." She squatted until she felt his feet hit the ground.

To her relief, Carter giggled and got off easily. She leaned forward to push herself up off the ground, but a sharp pain shot through her back, freezing her in place. She tried to reach behind her to massage it, but the tingling in her hands had given way to numbness.

"Oh, for goodness' sake," she breathed to herself. Her back loosened for a moment but spasmed again before she could straighten. "Let's rest here for just a second."

"Okay." Carter plopped to the ground and tilted his head skyward, as if this were the most natural resting place in the world.

At the top of the hill, a car door slammed. Carter swiveled and peered up the hill.

Emma considered calling out to whoever was up there for help. But what would she even say?

No, the spasm would pass, and then she and Carter could finish their walk.

But the boy was already jumping to his feet.

"Carter, wait." Emma tried to straighten, but a burst of pain ripped through her back.

"We're taking a break on the sidewalk," Carter called to someone.

"Who's taking a break?" The voice that responded sounded confused—and familiar. Emma let out a breath. She didn't exactly want her new neighbor to see her like this, but at least he could take care of his son while she figured out how to make herself move.

"Emma? Is that you?" Footsteps hurried down the pavement, and Emma gave one more desperate attempt to stand upright. This time she managed to straighten a few degrees, but it drew a grunt of pain from her.

"What happened?"

She couldn't see Owen's face, but she could hear the concern in his voice.

"I'm fine." She concentrated on keeping her voice breezy. "Carter and I were just coming up from a little trip down to the marina, and I threw out my back."

"Her piggybacks aren't as good as yours," Carter informed his father, and Emma laughed through her pain.

"You gave Carter a piggyback ride?" Owen must have bent over because his face suddenly came into her field of view. "Up this hill?"

Emma shook her head. "It's fine. I'm fine."

"Yeah, you look fine." From this angle it was hard to tell if Owen was frowning or smiling. "Can I help you somehow?"

Emma shook her head, trying to look like she wasn't in agony. "I just need a second. It'll pass."

Owen wrapped his fingers around her elbow, making her very aware that she still had sensation in her arm, even if not in her fingers.

His grip was warm and solid and . . . nice.

Nice enough that she should move away.

She shifted her arm a little, but his hand remained locked in place.

"Do you think you can walk?" His other arm came around her back, and a pleasant shiver went up her spine. It was enough to get her feet moving.

Her pace was agonizingly slow, and Owen's hands remained firm on her arm and her back. Carter walked ahead of them, turning around every few seconds to check their progress.

"There we go," Owen murmured. "Nice and easy."

Emma breathed out a soft, slightly painful, laugh. "That's what I say to the horses."

Owen laughed too. "What were you doing giving Carter a piggyback ride during your birthday party, anyway?"

"We came outside to get his headphones from my truck." Emma panted out the words between breaths, and Owen pulled her to a stop.

"Let's rest a second. Hey, Carter, hold up, buddy." Owen readjusted his grip on her arm. "Your truck is at the top of the hill," he pointed out.

Emma nodded. "It was just so nice and . . . peaceful out here. And so loud inside. So I asked Carter if he wanted to see the boats for a minute." She suddenly realized how inappropriate that might have been. She'd only known these people for a few days. "I'm sorry. I hope you don't mind."

"Mind?" Owen sounded perplexed. "No. I appreciate it. I shouldn't have run off so quickly without taking him. Or at least making sure Catelyn or Cody would keep a better eye on him."

"Did you find Claire?" Emma managed to straighten a few more degrees. So now she only had to angle her head a little to see his face.

"Yeah." Frustration rippled off the word. "I found her right away, but it took me ten minutes to convince her I wasn't leaving until she came with me. I finally had to threaten to pick her up and carry her away if she didn't come voluntarily. She says she'll never forgive me for humiliating her in front of her new friends."

Emma hadn't realized the feeling had come back to her fingers until she brushed them across his hand, which was still wrapped around her arm. Fresh tingles started through her, but she was pretty sure they weren't caused by the neuropathy.

She dropped her hand to her side.

"If it makes you feel better, there are plenty of things I told my mom I would never forgive her for when I was a teenager," she said. "And now she lives with me, so I guess I got over it."

Owen gave her a wan smile. "That does make me feel better, thanks. It was just easier when there were two of us, you know? Like I didn't have to figure out all the answers myself."

Emma nodded. If she weren't in so much pain right now, she would be giving herself a swift kick. She'd been standing here, so busy enjoying how nice his arm felt around her, that she'd let herself forget that the man was still mourning for his wife. His wife who had died of cancer, no less.

"I think I'm ready to keep going now." She pushed herself to straighten a little more. A few more degrees, and she'd be fully upright.

Owen studied her as if assessing her condition. "You're sure?"

She nodded, and they started up the hill again. It only took a minute to get to the top, and then they turned toward the Chocolate Chicken.

Owen slowed as they approached her vehicle. "I can send the kids home with Catelyn and drive you home in your truck if you want."

"That's okay." Emma gestured to the restaurant. "I should go in and say goodbye to everyone. Thank them for the party. I'm sure Mom and William can drive me home."

Owen didn't say anything but steered her toward the Chocolate Chicken.

"I think I can make it on my own now," she said quietly when they reached the door. The last thing she needed was to walk in there with Owen's arm around her. She knew her friends well enough to know they'd jump to all sorts of conclusions.

Owen nodded and pulled his arm off her back as Carter opened the door for both of them.

"Thanks, buddy." Emma tried to straighten more as she stepped inside, but she couldn't quite manage to get fully upright. Still, she did her best to walk normally. She could feel Owen only half a pace behind her, and she wondered if he was staying close just in case she needed help or because it had grown even more crowded in here while they were gone.

Probably the latter.

"There you are." Bethany was seated at the table closest to the door and was the first one to spot her. "We thought maybe you tried to— What's wrong?" Her sister-in-law slid her chair out and headed straight to Emma.

"Nothing." Emma tried to smile but felt her face freeze into a grimace as her back tightened again. "Just a back spasm."

"Oh no, you poor thing. Come sit down." She gestured to the table, where James was scrambling to his feet. Mom and William pushed their chairs back too.

"I'm fine." Emma tried to reassure them all, but a wave of pain shot up her spine, making her hunch forward again.

"Here, let me help you." Owen's hand landed on her back, and he guided her the few steps to the table.

Bethany's eyes widened, but she pulled out a chair and helped Owen lower her into it.

"What happened?" James demanded. Emma didn't miss the suspicious look he cast at Owen.

"Just a back spasm. No big deal."

"What were you doing outside anyway?" Apparently James wasn't going to give up his interrogation.

"It was my fault." Carter stared at his feet, the fingers of each hand flicking at his legs.

"It wasn't your fault," Emma reassured him. "I had a lot of fun with you. And I learned about cumulus mediocris and cumulus congestus."

James looked at her as if she had started speaking a foreign language, but Owen laughed. "I bet you did."

"I wish you'd be more careful," James's frown deepened. "You know you're still—"

"I'm fine, James." Emma gritted her teeth and forced herself to sit completely upright. "See? I'm feeling much better already." She ignored the waves of pain sliding up and down her spine.

"That's not the point." James glared at her. "You can't just—"

"James." Bethany's voice was low, and she set a calming hand on her husband's arm. He shook his head but let it drop, and Emma sent her sister-in-law a grateful look.

"We should really go," Owen said quietly. "Claire is still out in the car. Are you sure I can't give you a ride home?"

Emma shook her head. "I'm fine. Thanks for coming. And for, you know, picking me up off the sidewalk."

"It was the least I could do after we crashed your birthday party." Owen's smile sent a little ripple through Emma that made her forget for a moment the pain in her back.

He collected his kids, and they all said goodbye—and then they were gone.

Emma braced herself, waiting for Bethany or Mom or one of her friends to say something about how attractive Owen was or how he was nice or how he would be perfect for her—any of their usual reactions when a single man her age came into their midst.

But no one said anything.

And Emma was left wondering why her relief felt more like disappointment.

Chapter 9

"Carter, could you please stop opening and closing the door?" Owen looked up from the laptop balanced precariously on his lap as he sat on the stairs—only slightly more comfortable than the living room floor he'd been sitting on most of the week.

The next time they moved, he'd stuff some bean bag chairs in the van—and retain a healthy skepticism when the moving company said their stuff would arrive within a few days.

Then again, if all went well with the drop zone, Owen wouldn't have to worry about moving ever again. He could easily envision remaining in Hope Springs for the rest of his life. The weather was pleasant, the scenery beautiful, and the people friendly. So friendly that they'd let Owen and his kids crash a birthday party.

Owen had considered texting or calling Emma to see how her back was doing. But every time he picked up his phone, he changed his mind. After all, he barely knew the woman, and she had plenty of friends and family to check up on her. Still, he'd found his mind drifting to her more often than not, and he was looking forward to the kids' next riding lesson so he could find out how she was doing—and then stop thinking about her.

The door creaked open again, and Owen pressed his lips together. If their moving pods didn't arrive soon, he was going to have to go out and buy some new tools to fix that.

"Daddy, look." Carter's shout pulled Owen's eyes off his laptop. His son rarely raised his voice. "It's our stuff!"

Owen snapped the computer shut and jumped to his feet. On the other side of the room, Lexi woke and scrambled to her feet as well, her claws scrabbling against the hardwood floor.

The dog and Owen reached the door at the same time.

Sure enough, a semi-truck loaded with three moving pods was slowing to make the turn into their driveway.

"Oh, thank you, Lord," Owen patted Carter's shoulder, scratched the dog's ears, and strode back to the steps.

Before he could even finish calling, "The moving pods are here," Kenzie and Cody were barreling down the steps, both cheering. Catelyn emerged a few seconds later, grinning at him. "It's about time."

"I know." Owen let out a breath. Hopefully this was just what his family needed to get back to normal. Or if not normal—they'd never be that without Katie—at least the new normal they'd established over the past few years.

"Claire," he called up the steps, when his second oldest hadn't come out of her room. She was most likely still sulking that he'd grounded her for her incident at the beach the other night. "Come on. If you want to sleep in your own bed tonight, we need to get these things unloaded."

It took another solid minute, but she finally emerged. Though she didn't say a word to him as she jogged down the steps, she also didn't glare at him. Owen grinned a little to himself. *Progress.*

They all gathered on the front porch to watch the driver unload the pods, Cody grasping Lexi's collar so she wouldn't run down to welcome the man with her kisses.

Carter danced in place and flapped his arms as the driver operated the large wheeled frames that lifted the pods off the truck and lowered them onto the long driveway. But the rest of the kids chattered about the things they were most eager to have back in their possession. Somehow, the week they'd waited for their stuff to arrive seemed like nothing compared to the half hour it took the guy to unload all three pods.

When he was finally done, Owen thanked him, then turned to the kids. "We'd better get to it." He tried not to think about the days and days it had taken them to load the pods—and that had been with the help of friends. He supposed he could call Charles to see if he was available—but knowing his friend, he was probably either tinkering with the plane or off in pursuit of his sudden goal to find a woman to settle down with. Either way, Owen didn't need to disturb him. He and the kids could manage this themselves. However long it took, it would be worth it.

But an hour later, he mopped his brow and studied the first pod. They'd barely made a dent in it, and Carter had already wandered off to examine the rocks in the flowerbed. Kenzie had gone inside to get some water. Claire had carried a few boxes up to her room and not returned. Even the dog had lost interest and plopped herself under the tree for a nap. Only Catelyn and Cody continued to haul boxes back and forth with him—but even they weren't going to be able to help him carry some of the heaviest furniture.

"Think we'll be done by the time I have to move back to school?" Catelyn stopped next to him, twisting her dark hair into a ponytail.

"If we're not, will you stay here?"

Catelyn gave him a patronizing smile that said she knew his question was only half in jest, then picked up another box and headed inside. Owen sighed and did the same, grimacing as his eyes fell on the label: toys for grandchildren.

Not that he was anywhere *near* ready to think about being a grandparent. But he also hadn't been able to part with some of the kids' favorite toys—especially the ones Katie had loved to play with them—so he'd used saving them for future grandchildren as an excuse to hold onto them. He lugged the box through the propped-open door and stacked it along the dining room wall, where all the boxes he didn't quite know what to do with yet had ended up. He shook his head at the size of the pile already. He probably should have donated more stuff before the move. But how did you decide what to keep from a lifetime of memories?

His eyes fell on a box that said *Katie's stuff*. One of the kids must have put it there by mistake. He scooped it up and carried it to the master bedroom. Katie would have been the first to tell him that her stuff was just stuff and he could get rid of it—in fact, she *had* told him that before her death. But in a lot of ways, it felt like all he had left of her, and he wasn't ready to let go of that yet.

He deposited the box in the closet—its door frame smooth and unmarred by the heart he'd carved into their old one—then headed back through the house.

"Claire," he called on his way. "Come outside and help us, please."

His daughter didn't answer, and Owen kept moving. They needed to pick up the pace if they were going to—

He lurched to a stop in the doorway.

A small cluster of people stood talking near the closest pod, while a group of children chased each other—and Lexi—around the yard.

"Dad." Catelyn stepped out from the group, beaming. "We have help."

"Help?" Owen scanned the group next to his daughter. He counted nine people, most of whom he'd met at the Chocolate Chicken the other night, though he couldn't recall everyone's names. Except for Jackson—the guy who was standing a little too close to his daughter. That name he hadn't forgotten.

"What are— How did—" Owen jogged down the porch steps, his eyes catching on an even larger group of people stepping out of the field next door into his yard.

He immediately picked out Emma's short curls and brilliant smile.

Although he still had no idea what was going on, Owen felt his lips lift in return. At least now he knew her back must be doing better.

"I hope you don't mind," she called.

"Mind what?"

Before Emma could answer, Ruby burst out from behind her and sprinted the rest of the way into the yard. "We came to help you move in. Where's Kenzie?"

"She's, uh—"

"Never mind, I see her." Ruby darted past him, pulling up just shy of Kenzie, who was gathered with some of the girls she'd met the other night. Her smile nearly rivaled the sun.

Emma's laugh was closer than Owen expected, and he turned to find that both groups had converged near him.

"I saw your moving pods arrive this morning," Emma said, as if that explained everything.

But Owen must have still looked confused because she added. "We thought maybe you could use a little help."

"A little help?" Owen repeated, scanning the dozens of faces gathered around them.

"Tyler's just waiting at my house for the baseball team." Emma brushed her hair back from her face and turned to squint at the field. "I figured everyone should park at my place since you have those big pods in your driveway. Speaking of which, put us to work. Where do you want everything?"

Owen stared at her, still dumbfounded. He barely knew these people. He couldn't expect them to move his stuff.

"Listen, this is really nice of you all, but I can't accept—"

"You don't have a choice," a man called from the middle of the group. Owen didn't remember seeing the guy at the Chocolate Chicken the other night, but he still looked strangely familiar.

"Holy cow, you're Levi Donovan." Cody's voice cracked with excitement as he barreled toward the group.

Owen did a double-take. Sure enough, the man did resemble the former Titans quarterback.

So that was why Emma had asked if they were Titans fans.

"Guilty as charged." Levi stepped forward to shake first Cody's hand, then Owen's.

"Oh man, my dad and I were so bummed when you blew out your ACL." Cody examined Levi's leg, as if he might be able to see the injury. "You were the best quarterback ever."

"Well, thanks." Levi laughed. "But it worked out pretty well for me. Brought me here to these folks. And my wife." He glanced over his shoulder and the woman who had said she was from Tennessee grinned. "I didn't even pay him to say that."

A jolt went through Owen. He missed bantering like that with his wife.

"All right." Emma clapped her hands twice. "Put us to work."

Owen shook his head. He really couldn't accept all this help.

"Before you try to argue, you should know that it doesn't pay." Emma crossed her arms in front of her. "I always win."

"That's the truth," James called from the back of the group. "Trust me. She's stubborn."

Emma raised her eyebrows at Owen in a challenge.

He let out a slow breath. "In that case . . ." His lips lifted a little. "I guess I really don't have a choice. The master bedroom is on the first floor. The kids' bedrooms are upstairs. The den is the room at the back of the house. Everything should be pretty well labeled."

Emma grinned in triumph as the group dispersed toward the pods.

He watched in awe as they methodically began to empty boxes out of the first pod. But when Emma reached for a box, he grabbed her arm. "I don't want you to hurt your back again."

"I'm fine." She was still smiling, but her eyes went to his fingers, wrapped around her elbow, and he quickly let go. He didn't know what he'd been thinking.

He let her pick up a box, then grabbed one himself, glancing around the pod. In one trip, Emma's friends had managed to unload more than he and the kids had in an entire hour. And some were already on their way back out for more.

He dropped his box off in Kenzie's room, meeting up with Emma again outside.

"Carter informs me that it's going to be a beautiful day." She glanced up at the sky, where a few fluffy clouds dotted the blue.

Owen nodded, a lightness he hadn't felt in years buoying him. He had a feeling that his son might just be right about that.

Chapter 10

"Lunch is here!" Emma closed the door to her truck with her hip, balancing the large stack of pizzas Owen had insisted on ordering for everyone. She had a feeling the reason he'd asked her to be the one to pick them up was that he was afraid she'd throw out her back again—she hadn't missed the way he sized up every box she lifted, as if trying to decide whether it was going to be the one to do her in. Though she didn't need one more person worrying that she was too fragile, it didn't rub her quite as raw when it was Owen worrying about her as when it was her brother. But she wasn't going to examine the reason for that right now.

Or ever.

"Let me grab those." Owen swooped down on her, a light sheen of sweat dotting his forehead. He tucked his arms under the boxes and tugged.

Their arms brushed, but Emma didn't loosen her grip. "I've got them." Okay, maybe it did rub her just as raw to have Owen see her as weak as when James did. But they were just pizza boxes, for heaven's sake. Not boxes of bricks.

Owen gave her an odd look but relinquished his hold. "Thanks for picking them up."

He looked so genuinely grateful that Emma regretted not turning them over. Owen wasn't trying to be overprotective. He didn't even know about her cancer. He was just concerned about her back—and no wonder, when he'd found her barely able to move the other day.

"It looks like we've made good progress." She nodded to the pods, two of which were now empty.

"Yeah." Owen shook his head as if he couldn't believe it. "I thought this was going to take days."

"It's amazing what a little help can do." She'd had to learn that lesson the hard way when she spent weeks recovering from her hysterectomy, then going through chemo. If it hadn't been for her friends and family, everything would have fallen apart.

And now she had a chance to repay their kindness by helping others.

"Pizza!" The kids spotted the delivery first, and Emma and Owen were immediately surrounded.

"The dining room table is set up now," Owen called over the din as the kids drove them apart. "You can put them in there. I'll let everyone else know it's time to eat."

Emma lost track of him as she helped the kids get food, chatted with her friends, and finally grabbed a plate for herself.

She brought it outside, where everyone had sprawled on the grass.

"Aunt Emma, come sit over here." Ruby waved from where she sat in a circle with Kenzie, Carter, Owen, Bethany and James, and Sophie and Spencer.

Bethany slid over so that there was a spot right between her and Owen.

Emma glanced at her sister-in-law but didn't detect any sign of an ulterior motive in placing her there. She sat, chiding herself again for thinking her friends and family would assume she would be attracted to Owen. Obviously she wasn't.

And the friendly—but nothing more—nod he gave as she sat reassured her that she didn't have to worry about him being attracted to her either.

"So Owen, what do you do?" Bethany asked.

"I, uh—" Owen looked confused.

"He bought the skydiving center," James said patiently to his wife, and Emma marveled yet again at how good Bethany was for her once-grumpy brother.

"I've already asked that, haven't I?" Bethany said easily, the self-consciousness that used to accompany the question nowhere to be found. James had been good for Bethany too, helping her see that her memory issues were nothing to be embarrassed about.

James nodded. "At riding lessons the other day."

"Sorry." Bethany turned to Owen. "I do that sometimes."

"No problem." Owen laughed. "If we're being completely honest, I'm terrible with remembering names. My wife always had to whisper them in my ear. But now . . . I've been wracking my brain all day to come up with your names." He gestured across the circle, and Emma answered automatically, "Sophie and Spencer."

She bit her tongue the moment the names were out. "Sorry, I—" Now she was the one who was confused. She hadn't meant to take on the role he said his wife had always taken.

Fortunately, Ruby sprang up from the ground as if a catapult had shot her to her feet, grabbing everyone's attention. "I know! Owen can take you skydiving, Aunt Emma! Then you can cross that off your life list!"

Emma choked on a piece of her pizza. "Ruby, I don't think—" she barely managed to gasp out before she was attacked by a fit of coughing.

"What's a life list?" Kenzie asked.

"It's a list of all the things you want to do in your life," Ruby explained, as if she were an expert. "I have one too."

"You do?" Kenzie's eyes widened. "What's on it?"

"A whole bunch of stuff," Ruby answered. "Like get an A in spelling. And ride dressage in the Olympics. And skydiving too. But I can't do that until I'm eighteen, right?" She looked to Owen.

He nodded. "That's right. But when you're old enough, I'll be happy to take you."

James directed a glare usually reserved for suspects at Owen, and Emma cringed. She'd have to warn him later that James wasn't a fan of anything that would put someone he loved at risk—no matter how small that risk was. She'd researched it, and there was like a 0.000 28 percent chance of dying from skydiving. But she knew even that wouldn't convince James.

"But you could take Aunt Emma, right?" Ruby seemed oblivious to her father's expression.

Emma just barely managed to swallow her food without choking this time. "Oh, Ruby, I don't think—"

"I sure could," Owen cut her off. "We're still waiting for our tandem rigs to come in, but that should only be another week or two. You could be our first customer. Before we even open."

James's eyes bulged. "Emma's not going to risk her life on something so dangerous after—"

"It's actually quite safe," Owen said calmly. "We have checks and double-checks and triple checks for everything: chutes, backup chutes, ripcords, backup ripcords, automatic activation devices . . ."

"Doesn't matter." James crossed his arms. "There's no sense in taking needless risks."

"My mom used to skydive," Kenzie said quietly. "That's how she met my dad."

Everyone turned to the girl, and she ducked her head.

Owen patted her leg. "That's true."

Emma directed a glare at James, and he shrugged helplessly.

But at least Kenzie's comment had ended the argument between the two men.

"We should get back to work." Emma carefully pushed to her feet, ignoring the tightness in her back muscles.

"Come on, Kenzie." Ruby pulled her friend up, and the two went to join a game of tag already in progress.

James stood and then helped Bethany up, dropping a kiss on her forehead and leading her toward the house.

Emma glanced at Owen as he got to his feet as well. "Sorry about James." She felt a sudden need to defend her brother. "He's always been the protective type. Comes with the territory for police officers, I guess."

"That's okay." Instead of annoyed, Owen looked wistful as he tracked James and Bethany, who had their arms looped around each other's backs, and Emma wondered if he was missing his wife. "I tend to be fairly protective too, in case you didn't notice the other night." He made a self-deprecating sound. "I just like people to realize that skydiving isn't as risky as they think. If I thought I wasn't going to come home to my kids one day . . ."

"I know," she said quietly. "I've done some research, and I was surprised by how safe it is."

"So you want to go?" Owen sent her a mischievous smile. "I won't tell your brother."

Emma laughed. "I'm just not sure I can actually convince myself to step out of the plane."

"That's the hardest part. But it only lasts a second. And once you do . . ." He whistled. "Trust me, you'll want to do it again."

"It's that fun, huh?"

"It's . . ." Owen tilted his head toward the sky just like Carter so often did. "Incredible. Like you're just floating above everything, and you couldn't even think about your problems if you tried—" He cut off, shooting her a sheepish grin. "Sorry. I tend to get carried away when it comes to jumping."

"Don't apologize. You almost make me want to try it." She started toward the last moving pod, Owen striding eagerly at her side.

"Yeah?" He grinned. "Well, anytime you want to go, I'm your guy."

Emma's heart jumped a little.

Oh, for mercy's sake. He hadn't meant he was *her guy*. He had meant that he was the guy to take her skydiving. Since that was his *job*.

They reached the pod, and James intercepted Owen to ask where to put a dresser. Emma picked up a box and started toward the house, grateful to put a little distance between herself and Owen.

She couldn't explain the silly way her heart seemed to be acting toward him. Maybe it was just because she knew he could help her cross off a big item on her life list. One that she'd put on as more of an impossible challenge than a realistic goal.

She dropped the box off and went out to get another. Everyone seemed to have caught a second wind after lunch, and within an hour, the pod was empty.

Emma stood on Owen's porch, grinning at her friends, who still stood talking and laughing in the yard. Her back throbbed, and she didn't even want to think about all the chores waiting for her at home. But she couldn't help feeling satisfied. They had done it.

"I don't know what to say." Owen came up next to her, looking slightly stunned. "I'm going to go thank people before they leave." He jogged down the steps, and Emma went inside to grab a garbage bag and gather up the empty pizza boxes and paper plates scattered around the dining room. No reason to leave that mess for Owen and his family. They had plenty of unpacking to do the way it was.

Boxes stacked three or four high lined every wall of the dining room and living room. Her eyes caught on one labeled *Katie's stuff*, and she set down the garbage bag, drawn toward the box. There was nothing else written on it, and she found herself wanting to know what was in it. What Owen's wife had been like. What he had saved from their life together.

She pressed her hand to the box as a wave of guilt washed over her. Everything she had gained through her treatment—a second chance at life, more time with her family—this family had lost.

"What are you doing?" The sudden, sharp voice made Emma jump, and she spun to find Claire glaring at her.

"Oh, you startled me." Emma smiled at the girl, who only narrowed her eyes.

Emma scurried for her garbage bag. "I was just cleaning up the pizza boxes and stuff. I figured you guys would want it out of the way so you could unpack. Are you excited to get your room set up?"

"No." Claire's voice was flat and hard, and she turned and stalked back up the stairs.

"Okay." Emma let out a slow breath. There was no need to take Claire's attitude personally. Owen had said she was struggling with the move.

Quickly, Emma finished her cleanup and brought the trash bag outside. The only people left in the yard were James and Bethany, who stood talking to Owen. They were all smiling, which meant James must not be holding a grudge from their earlier argument about skydiving.

Emma reached them just in time to hear Owen say, "All five of ours were born so fast that I was afraid Katie was going to have them in the car."

Bethany's eyes widened, and her hand went to her stomach, which showed no sign of a baby bump yet. "I hope this one comes that fast. I was in labor with Ruby for eighteen hours."

As if on cue, Ruby popped into the group, dragging Kenzie behind her. "But I was worth it," she finished Bethany's story, and they all laughed.

Emma joined in, pushing aside the feeling that she didn't really belong in this conversation, since she would never have her own parenting story to tell. It didn't matter.

"Hey, Mom." Ruby turned pleading eyes to Bethany, and Emma thought suddenly that maybe it was a good thing she wasn't a mother. She never would have been able to say no to any kid who looked at her with that expression. "Can Kenzie sleep over next weekend?"

Emma didn't miss the pleading look Kenzie sent Owen as well.

"You have dressage practice Friday night," James reminded Ruby. "And then the parade on Saturday."

"After the parade, then." Ruby was well-known for her persistence.

"After the parade you're staying at Aunt Emma's, remember? So your mom and I can have a date night."

"Oh yeah." Ruby frowned for a microsecond before turning to Emma with bright, pleading eyes. "Hey, Aunt Emma, do you think Kenzie could come too?"

"Ruby," James sounded exasperated, but Emma grinned.

"I think that's a fantastic idea. If it's okay with Kenzie and her dad."

Kenzie clasped her hands under her chin. "That sounds fun. Please, Daddy?"

Owen glanced at Emma. "You're sure you want to do that?"

Emma shrugged. "Of course. That way Ruby will have someone to keep her entertained when I get boring."

"I'm going to guess that doesn't happen too often." Owen's eyes crinkled, and Emma couldn't tell if he meant it as a compliment or a joke, but either way, she felt her face warm. She prayed no one else noticed.

"As long as Miss Emma is sure it's okay, it's fine with me," he said to Kenzie.

Wild shrieking met this answer, and the two girls threw their arms around each other.

"Well, on that note." James gestured toward the field that led back to Emma's house. "We should get going."

Emma joined James, Bethany, and Ruby for the walk back, Ruby buzzing the whole way about all the things they should do at the sleepover.

It wasn't until James and his family had left and Emma had finished taking care of the horses and chickens and made monkey bread for fellowship time at church tomorrow that she allowed herself to drop into her favorite rocking chair on her porch and pull out her phone.

She opened her notes app and scanned her "everyday" life list, her eyes falling on the words *pray for someone new*.

That one would be easy today. *Please, Lord, bless Owen and his family in their new home. Help them adjust to life in Hope Springs and let this be a place where they experience the full richness of your blessings. Give them peace and comfort in the loss of their wife and mother, and show them, Lord, that you know the plans you have for them—and those plans are for their eternal good. In Jesus' name. Amen.*

She opened her eyes, letting the peace of the prayer wash over her as she gazed at Owen's house. She couldn't see anyone out there, but she imagined them inside, busily unpacking their boxes. All except, maybe, the ones labeled as *Katie's stuff*.

She turned her eyes back to her phone, scrolling to the "possibilities" list. In addition to raising chickens, she'd already crossed off *read all of Jane Austen's books, explore a cave,* and *learn the violin*. That one was a work in less-than-beautiful progress.

If God gave her the opportunity, she still wanted to check off throw pottery, go kayaking, climb a tree, laugh so hard I cry, watch the sunrise and sunset every day for a month. And, maybe . . . skydive.

Owen had said anytime she wanted to . . .

And the way he talked about it made it sound so . . .

But that didn't mean she was actually ready to go through with it.

She clicked off the phone and set it in her lap, gazing toward the lowering sun and trying not to think about the things she hadn't added to her list. Things like *kiss in the rain* and *stay up all night talking* and *walk down the aisle* and *raise a family*.

She hadn't added them because they weren't possibilities anymore. And she didn't need them. They may have been things she longed for once. But not any longer.

She glanced toward Owen's house again.

She'd be content if he helped her check off skydiving. Someday.

Chapter 11

"Hurry up, Daddy. We're going to miss it." Kenzie tugged Owen's hand harder, but it was nearly impossible to maneuver through the packed street. Everyone in Hope Springs and all the surrounding towns for miles around must have come out for the Hope Fest parade.

"Hold up, Kenz." He tightened his grip on Carter's hand and scanned the sidewalk for a place to sit. He only needed room for the three of them since Cody was walking in the parade with the baseball team, Claire had refused to come, and Catelyn had said she was going to the parade with a friend—whom Owen strongly suspected might be named Jackson.

"Owen," someone called.

He glanced around before he realized that they were probably talking to another Owen. He didn't know anyone here well enough that they'd be calling out to him through a crowd.

"Owen," the voice shouted again. "Kenzie. Carter."

Okay, well the chances that there was another Owen here with a Kenzie and a Carter were pretty slim.

"Over there." Kenzie pointed to the other side of the street, where he recognized a bunch of the people who had helped them move in last weekend. Several of them were waving, and they had spread blankets along the curb in front of the antique store.

"Should we sit with them?" Kenzie adjusted her backpack, which she'd filled to the point of busting for her sleepover with Ruby.

"Sure." Owen scanned the group as they approached, working hard to recall names. He was pretty confident he actually remembered most of them. It helped that he'd seen them in church yesterday, and Emma had reintroduced them all.

"Have a seat," a dark-haired woman he was pretty sure was named Violet offered, bouncing a toddler on her knee. "Kenzie and Carter, if you want to sit on the blankets, that's the best place to get candy. And Owen, feel free to grab a camp chair. Or actually, it looks like Nate has one for you."

Owen took the camp chair Violet's husband held out to him. "Thanks."

"No problem." Nate gestured to the antique store behind him. "We always keep some inside for just this occasion."

"This is your store?" Owen gave the building a closer look. The brick exterior and deep blue door gave it a timeless feeling, and one window displayed a collection of glass jars of all shapes and sizes, while the other sported a washboard and spinning wheel.

"Technically, it's Vi's." Nate rested his hand on his wife's shoulder. "I'm just along for the ride."

Violet shook her head with a laugh. "Don't listen to him. I would have lost the store after my first husband died if it weren't for Nate."

Owen's eyes jumped between the two. He never would have guessed Violet had been a widow. She was so young.

Then again, he wasn't so old himself, and he'd been a widower for five years now.

Nate settled into a chair on the other side of Violet, and Owen tried to catch any indication that this was a second marriage as opposed to a first. But as far as he could tell, there was no difference.

"You can put your chair here." Violet gestured to the open spot next to her. "That way you'll be close to Kenzie and Carter." The two had settled onto the curb next to some of the other kids.

"Look, Mommy, fire truck." The little girl on Violet's lap pointed down the street, her pudgy cheeks lifting into a wide grin as she clapped her hands.

"Yes, Liliana," Violet kissed her daughter's head. "Fire truck. The parade is starting."

Owen made sure Carter put his headphones on—just in time, as the fire truck honked.

Fortunately, Carter waved his arms in excitement.

Candy rained down on the street, and Owen kept an eye on Carter and Kenzie as they joined the rush to grab it. A few pieces landed on Violet's lap, and she laughed as Liliana squealed. "Say thank you to Jared and Ethan."

The girl called out an adorable thank you, and Owen shaded his eyes against the sun to peer at the truck. Two of the guys who had helped them move were waving from inside and tossing more candy. Owen hadn't realized they were firefighters.

The fire truck was followed by a string of classic cars, a marching band, and a float promoting Hope Church's jungle-themed vacation Bible school. A young boy stopped to hand Kenzie a flyer.

She turned and waved it at him. "Everyone was talking about this last weekend. They said it's so fun. Can we go?"

It took Owen a moment to get over his shock before he nodded. Last year he'd tried to talk her into going to VBS, but she'd been so nervous about it that he'd ended up letting her stay home.

"Here come Miss Emma and the horses," Violet told Liliana, and both Owen and Kenzie turned back to the parade.

Owen's gaze went straight to Emma, who rode the horse at the front of the group. Though she wore formal-looking riding gear—white pants, a fitted blue coat, black boots, and a helmet that her light hair just barely poked out under—she looked at ease in the saddle. Behind her, six girls in matching uniforms rode in two lines. When Emma reached the spot just in front of the antique store, she turned her horse 180 degrees to face the riders as they moved their horses in fancy-looking sideways steps.

Owen had no reason to be, but he was proud of them anyway.

"I'm so glad Emma could ride this year. After last year . . ." Violet was turned toward Nate, but her words caught Owen. "Praise the Lord that—"

"Candy!"

It took Owen a moment to register that Carter was lunging away from the curb and into the street.

"Carter, no."

But the boy kept going, headed for an orange-wrapped piece in the middle of the street—only a few feet from Emma's horse.

"Carter." Owen leaped to his feet and charged after his son. Fortunately, Carter wasn't very fast, and it only took Owen a few strides to catch up with him. He scooped the boy up just as he was about to grab the candy.

Carter screeched his resistance.

At the sound, Emma's horse crouched low, wheeling its hindquarters and raising its front legs a few inches off the ground. The movement brought the horse within a foot of Owen, and he pulled Carter in tighter to his shoulder.

"Whoa, girl. Easy now," he heard Emma say as she tugged the reins. The horse sidestepped in the other direction, hindquarters still low, then wheeled one more time before coming to a standstill. Emma patted its neck, but her gaze came to Owen.

He saw the question in her eyes, and he nodded. They were all right. He wanted to ask the same of her, but she returned her focus to her riders as if nothing had happened.

Owen took a few slow steps backwards, careful not to spook the horse again. When he reached the sidewalk, he heard Emma call out, "Walk on," and the crowd applauded.

He dropped into his seat, Carter still in his arms.

"Are you guys okay?" a whole chorus of voices asked.

Owen let out a shaky breath. "Yeah. I think so." He sat back to watch the rest of the parade, finally letting Carter wriggle down after he promised he wouldn't run into the road even for orange candy.

The moment the parade was done, Kenzie sprang to her feet. "Can we go find Ruby and Miss Emma now?"

Owen nodded and jumped to his feet too—he needed to apologize to Emma and make sure she was okay.

He folded up his chair, thanking Violet and Nate, then scooped Carter onto his back so they could make better time and weaved through the crowd with Kenzie.

"There they are." Kenzie pointed, picking up speed. Owen tightened his grip on Carter and worked to keep up with her, his eyes on Emma.

She had taken off her helmet, and her hair bounced around her face as she nodded at something one of her riders was saying.

Owen's heart jumped, and he let out a breath. She was all right.

She looked up at that moment and unleashed a big smile in their direction. Owen's heart jumped higher.

"You guys are all right?" she called before he could say anything.

He nodded. "Are you?"

"I'm good. I'm sorry about that, though. Scarlet is usually bomb proof, but she got a little skittish before the parade today, so she was already on edge. I should have ridden someone else."

Owen shook his head. "I'm the one who's sorry. I should have kept a better eye on Carter." He suddenly recalled Nate and Violet's conversation that had distracted him. It had been something about Emma and having a tough year. A divorce maybe? The death of a spouse? Did they have that in common?

"Well, anyway, everyone is fine, so that's the main thing." Emma sounded cheerful. "Are you ready for our sleepover, Kenzie?"

Kenzie nodded, her cheeks flushed.

"Good. Ruby is just getting changed, and I need to get the horses untacked and trailered. But you guys can head out if you want. Kenzie can hang out with us."

"Oh." Heaven knew Owen had plenty to do at home. He really should go. And yet—he didn't want to. "Is there anything we can help with? I mean, as a thank you for all your help moving us in."

Emma looked surprised—but pleasantly so, he thought. "That's not necessary. But if you want to, I could use someone strong to load the saddles onto the saddle racks in the trailer. Do you think you could do that, Carter?"

"I'm strong." Carter kicked his feet against Owen's legs.

Owen winced. "I can confirm that." He lowered Carter to the ground, and Emma led them all to the trailers, where Ruby greeted Kenzie with a shriek and a hug that Kenzie returned.

Owen accidentally met Emma's eyes, and they both smiled. His heart did that same little jump from before, and Owen told himself it was only because he was grateful to her for facilitating this friendship between Kenzie and Ruby.

He and Carter busied themselves hauling the saddles to the racks in the trailer. It was a laughably easy job—one he was certain Emma hadn't really needed them to do, but he was glad she had asked anyway. Even if Carter quickly lost interest and wandered to the end of the trailer to watch the sky.

"This is the last one," Emma announced much too soon, holding out a black and brown saddle with elegant scrolls worked into the leather.

Owen whistled as he took it from her. "That's a pretty one."

"Thanks." Emma unbuttoned the fitted blue jacket she still wore and peeled it off, then tugged at the high collar of the white shirt she wore underneath it. "I much prefer the saddle to the clothes."

Owen laughed. "I believe it." Afraid that might have come across as insulting, he added. "You look nice though."

Emma's eyes widened, and Owen realized too late that that might make it sound like . . . Like he was hitting on her. He turned to place the saddle on the rack, taking much longer than necessary to situate it. Maybe by the time he finished, Emma would be gone, and he could escape without saying something else ridiculous.

When he finally turned around, Emma wasn't gone. But she was busy sorting through a large drawer of what looked like bandages and such.

"Well, uh, I guess we should go." Owen stuffed his hands awkwardly in his pockets. "Unless there's anything else we can help with."

Emma shook her head. "I don't think so." She looked up but kept her hands in the drawer. "Thanks for your help. I guess I'll see you tomorrow? I can bring Kenzie to church with us, unless you're going again?"

He nodded. "We'll go. But if Kenzie wants to ride with you, that's fine. We can meet you there."

Emma closed the drawer, her smile wide. "Sounds great. See you then."

He nodded, telling himself that the only reason her words lifted his heart was that he'd have Kenzie back with him tomorrow. It had nothing to do with the thought of seeing Emma again.

Chapter 12

You look nice.

Emma shook her head and focused on the road in front of her. Why could she not get those words—or Owen's rich, deep tone—out of her head? He hadn't meant *she* looked nice. Only that the formal dressage uniform fulfilled its purpose, even if it wasn't comfortable.

"Aunt Emma, can we have a bonfire tonight?" Ruby asked from the back seat.

Emma glanced in the rearview mirror, grateful for the distraction. "I think we'd better. How else are we going to have s'mores?"

Ruby cheered, and Emma's gaze flicked to Kenzie. The girl had been quiet on the drive, but she didn't look upset or anxious. Maybe she was just tired.

Goodness knew, Emma was. The parade had been more taxing on her body than she'd anticipated, partly because of the way Scarlet had spooked.

She could still see Owen's expression as she'd fought to regain control of the horse—not upset or angry but . . . concerned.

For her?

Emma pushed the thought away. Obviously he had been concerned for everyone involved. As had she.

She was only grateful he hadn't been upset about the incident and that he'd still let Kenzie sleep over. Otherwise, Ruby would have been devastated.

Emma pulled the truck and trailer into her driveway. A long line of trailers already stood in front of the barn, and Emma's limbs felt heavy just thinking of all the work there was to do yet.

Thank goodness she had a staff and parent volunteers who would help put away the horses and tack. Even so, it was a big task, and Emma tried not to slump at the wheel at the thought of how much energy it would take.

She needed to push on.

She was recovered now. She could do this.

"Do you girls want to take care of the chickens for me?" she asked Ruby and Kenzie as they climbed out of the truck. "Change their water, give them some food. There are some grapes in the refrigerator. They'll be your best friends if you give them those."

"They can't," Ruby said. "Kenzie is my best friend. But they can be second best."

Emma laughed and shook her head at her goofy niece, who was leading Kenzie toward the chicken coop.

Emma headed to the barn to get to work. Fortunately, with so many people to help, it went quickly, and by the time everything was done, Emma thought she might have time to close her eyes for a few minutes—though she knew her body wouldn't actually let her nap, no matter how exhausted she was.

She was halfway to the house when she nearly tripped over a chicken. "Strat!" She squatted to pick up the bird, tucking it under her arm. "How did you escape?"

She stroked the bird's soft feathers as she carried it toward the chicken coop. Her heart sank when she spotted the open door.

The run was empty.

"Oh, I hope you're all in the chicken house," she murmured.

She stepped through the door and hurried to the barn-shaped chicken house at the other end. But there was only one chicken in there.

"Trixie." She set Strat down and moved to the golden chicken, rubbing her head. "I guess you're not such a troublemaker after all. Where's everyone else?"

The chicken blinked at her.

"Well, I suppose you're not going to answer me, are you?" Emma sighed and headed out through the run, careful to close and latch the door behind her.

She lifted a hand to shade her eyes and scanned the yard. The chickens couldn't have gotten far.

There. Sapphire was pecking her way through the garden near the house, oblivious to the vegetables and flowers she was crushing. Emma sped toward her, slowing when she got closer so as not to scare the bird.

But Sapphire seemed unperturbed as Emma stepped next to her. She simply dropped her beak to the ground and pecked again.

"All right, young lady. Back to the coop with you." Emma bent and hefted the chicken—who was much larger than Strat—in her arms, her muscles quaking with fatigue.

She tried to blow at a hair that was tickling her forehead, but sweat from the long day had slicked it in place.

With a groan, she deposited Sapphire in the run, then searched for Unicorn and Corazón. Unicorn she found around the back side of the barn, but Corazón was nowhere in sight. After spending another half hour looking, Emma had to admit that she might have to search farther afield. But for that she was going to need help.

She headed for the house and grabbed a long drink of water.

"Emma, is that you?" Mom strolled into the kitchen. "I told the girls— You look exhausted."

Emma shook her head and set the water glass down. "I'm fine. The chickens got out. I found them all except Corazón. I was just coming in to ask Ruby and Kenzie to help."

"I'll go out with them. You sit down for a minute." Mom's voice was gentle, and Emma couldn't deny that sitting sounded lovely, but still, she hated the implication that she needed a break.

"I'll sit down later."

Before Mom could say anything else, Emma strode past her and jogged up the stairs to show just how much energy she had left. She hurried past Mom and William's room—they'd refused to accept her offer of the downstairs master bedroom when they'd moved in last year to help take care of her through her chemo—a bathroom, and two additional rooms. She slowed as she reached the room she'd decorated for Ruby to use whenever she slept over.

The door was open and the girls' voices drifted out.

"Five years ago," Kenzie was saying.

"Is it okay if I ask what she died of?" Compassion covered Ruby's words, and Emma was proud of the empathy in her niece's voice.

"Cancer," Kenzie said quietly. "She had ovarian cancer."

Emma inhaled sharply enough that the air sliced against her throat. It had been bad enough knowing that Owen's wife had died of cancer. But she hadn't realized it was the exact same cancer she had survived.

"My aunt—"

"Ruby," Emma nearly shouted, lunging toward the room before her niece could say anything that would accidentally hurt Kenzie.

"Oh, hey, Aunt Emma." Ruby looked up with a smile. "We gave the chickens food and water, and they really liked the grapes." She looked so proud that Emma almost didn't want to bring up the open door. But she needed help finding Corazón.

"Did you possibly forget to latch the door?" she asked.

"No," Ruby said. "I told Kenzie to—"

But Kenzie had clapped a hand over her mouth, and tears filled her eyes. "I'm so sorry. I thought I—"

"Oh sweetie, it's okay." Emma stepped into the room and squatted in front of the girl. "It was an honest mistake. You couldn't know." She patted Kenzie's leg, and the girl nodded, though Emma wasn't one hundred percent sure the tears wouldn't still fall. "I found all of the chickens except Corazón. I thought maybe you two could help me look for her?"

Ruby nodded and jumped to her feet. "Of course."

Kenzie was slower to get to her feet, but she nodded too. "I'm sorry," she said again.

Instinctively, Emma wrapped an arm around the girl's shoulder. "I forgive you," she reassured her.

"And so does Jesus," Ruby said cheerfully.

"True." Emma squeezed Kenzie's shoulder, then ushered her out of the room and trailed the girls down the stairs. Mom gave Emma a look as she followed the girls to the door but didn't say anything.

"Come on." Ruby grabbed Kenzie's hand and pulled her down the porch steps. "I think I know where to look."

Kenzie swiped a hand over her cheek, and Emma regretted saying anything. The last thing she wanted to do was hurt the girl. The poor thing had been through enough already.

Emma's hand strayed to the incision on her stomach. Had Owen's wife had a radical hysterectomy too? Had it been too late?

The questions weighted Emma's feet, but she forced herself to keep walking. God had spared her life, and she was going to use every moment of it wisely—even if that meant searching for a wayward chicken.

Chapter 13

"Daddy," Carter called from the front door, which he was once again opening and closing.

"Yeah, bud?" Owen sat at the dining room table, staring at the numbers on the screen in front of him. Had they really already spent that much on renovations of the drop zone?

"There's a chicken here."

"Okay, bud." Owen rubbed at his eyes. He and Charles were going to have to talk about what they could cut if they didn't want to go broke before they even opened.

"I think it's one of Miss Emma's chickens. But it's not Strat."

Owen looked up from his laptop just in time to see Carter stepping out the door.

"Carter, wait." Owen pushed his chair back and hurried to the door. Their driveway was long enough that he wasn't terribly worried about Carter wandering into the road, but he still didn't like the boy to go outside alone.

"Hi, chicken." Carter headed toward the driveway where a chicken with white and black feathers and a red comb seemed to be on a mission to march right to the road.

"Hey, chicken." Owen repeated his son's greeting, glancing over his shoulder to make sure he'd closed the door to the house. The last thing they needed was for Lexi to come tearing out here.

He crept closer to the chicken, trying to remember its name so he could call for it. Not that he knew whether chickens would come when called anyway.

"Here, chicky, chick, chick," he tried anyway, throwing in a couple of clicks of his tongue for good measure.

Carter did the same, flapping his arms.

Owen watched out of the corner of his eye, wondering if he should mimic the movement, but decided he had to draw the line somewhere.

"Here, chicky," he clucked again. "Does Miss Emma know you went for a stroll? I bet she's worried about you." He was within a couple of feet of the bird now. The chicken barely spared him a glance before continuing toward the road.

"Come on, little lady," Owen cooed. "You don't want to become the punchline to a bad joke. Let me take you back to Emma." He took a giant step and swooped down, gathering the bird in his arms. The chicken squawked and flapped her wings wildly, but Owen held on tight, trying to make soothing sounds, though for all he knew he might be riling the hen up more.

In the background, Carter was cheering and laughing and clapping his hands—which probably didn't help calm the bird either, but Owen was too busy concentrating on not losing his grip to tell his son to settle down.

Finally, the chicken stopped flapping, and Owen got a better grip on her. She was lighter than he'd expected, and she settled into his arms much like a cat, though she swiveled her head so that her beak was pointed right at his face. He lowered her enough that she wouldn't be able to peck his eyes out if she got angry again.

"There we are." Owen breathed heavily. "See that wasn't worth all the fuss, was it?" He turned to Carter, who was still cheering and clapping. "What do you say we take her back to Miss Emma?"

"Can we bring Lexi?" Carter asked.

Owen laughed and tightened his grip on the bird. "No. We absolutely cannot bring Lexi."

As they started across the field that separated their property from Emma's, the bird seemed to relax in his arms, and Owen could almost see the appeal of keeping one. Almost, but not quite.

"There's Kenzie," Carter cried.

Sure enough, the girl was halfway across the field, walking toward them, her head down. Several yards to her left, Ruby was doing the same. And a little farther away, Emma was too.

"Looking for this?" he called.

Kenzie's head jerked up, and a smile tore across her face before she set off toward him at a run.

"Corazón! You found Corazón!"

"Is that your name?" he muttered to the bird. He felt tension ripple through the chicken's wings as Kenzie got closer.

"Slow down, Kenz," he called. "She's a little jumpy."

Kenzie slowed to a walk, but the moment she got to him, she burst into tears.

"Oh baby, what's wrong?" Owen dropped to one knee in alarm, careful to keep his grip on the bird.

"It's all my fault." Her lip trembled, but at least she wasn't full-out sobbing. "I didn't latch the chicken coop right, and—"

Owen frowned. Kenzie didn't know the first thing about chicken coops. Why had Emma expected her to—

"Corazón!" Ruby's cry tugged Owen's head up. "Where did you find her?"

Emma jogged over too, and Owen stood and passed the chicken to her, their arms getting momentarily tangled in the handoff.

"Oop. Uh. Sorry. Oh." Emma made funny sounds as she tried to extract her arms and the bird.

Owen would have laughed if he weren't so upset that she'd made Kenzie cry.

"There we go." Emma cradled the bird as if it were the most natural thing in the world.

"She wandered into our yard," Owen explained, wrapping a protective arm around the still-crying Kenzie.

"Oh, sweetie." Emma gave his daughter a look filled with compassion. "I tried to reassure her that it wasn't her fault, but she's been so worried."

The sincerity of Emma's words reached right into Owen's heart. He rubbed his daughter's back. "She does that."

"Should we go put Corazón away and get this sleepover going?" Emma asked Kenzie. "I was just about to make the pizzas and start the bonfire."

"I don't know." Kenzie sniffed.

"It's okay, Kenz," Owen said in a low voice. "You can go."

Kenzie shook her head, and Ruby's face fell, right along with Owen's heart. His daughter had been making so much progress in opening up to others. He'd hate for this to stop it.

"How about just coming over for some pizza and s'mores for now?" Emma asked. "You can decide about the sleepover later."

When Kenzie still didn't answer, Emma added, "Your dad and Carter are welcome to come too, if you want."

Kenzie nodded, and Emma lifted her gaze to Owen, raising an eyebrow.

"Kenzie knows I'd never pass up s'mores." He looked to Carter. "What do you think, buddy?"

"Fire is orange," Carter said, and Owen and Emma both laughed.

"That it is," Owen answered. "But please don't try to eat it."

"Come on," Ruby called. "Let's go see if Grandma and William want to join us." She gestured for Kenzie to follow her, and Owen gave his daughter a gentle nudge. Kenzie sniffed but ran ahead with Ruby.

Carter half-ran, half-marched behind the girls, and Emma fell into step next to Owen.

"Thank you for catching Corazón." Emma still had the chicken tucked into her arms. Its feathers ruffled in the breeze, as did Emma's hair. "I hope she didn't give you too much trouble."

"None at all." Owen was thankful that she hadn't seen him stalking the chicken—or heard him clucking.

"Oh good." She held the chicken up so that she was eye to eye with it. "Well, Corazón," she scolded. "Looks like we're going to have to lock you up tight to keep you safe."

Owen glanced at her out of the corner of his eye as his own heart gave the tiniest protest that it might be safest locked up tight too.

Chapter 14

"Sit down, Emma," Mom ordered, pointing to the hay bales where Owen, Carter, Kenzie, and Ruby sat around the bonfire Owen had helped her build. "William and I will clean up the pizza stuff and bring the marshmallows out."

Emma prepared to object, but Mom shook her head. "No arguments, young lady."

Emma snorted. "It's been a long time since I was a young lady." But she passed the tray holding the few remaining slices of pizza to Mom and returned to the fire.

She'd been sharing a bale with Kenzie and Ruby, but they had turned and put their feet up between them to play some sort of clapping game, so there was no longer room for Emma.

There was an empty hay bale where Mom and William had been sitting, but Emma didn't want to steal their seat. Which left the bale Owen and Carter had been sharing—although Carter was now examining something in the grass on the other side of the fire.

"Mind if I sit?" Emma gestured to the empty space next to Owen.

"Of course not." Owen's voice was warm, his smile soft, and—she couldn't help but notice as she took a seat—his scent kind of cottony and warm.

NOT UNTIL THE END

"It's beautiful out here." Owen sounded content as he leaned back and tilted his head to the sky, which had slowly begun to deepen into the hues of night.

"Mmm hmm." Emma leaned back too, but before she could say anything else, she felt herself tipping backwards in slow motion. She stretched her arm out, grasping for something solid, and it landed on Owen's arm. But even that didn't slow her fall, and the next thing she knew, she was lying flat on her back in the grass, the hay bale pressing against the back of her legs, which were now resting on top of it.

Shrieks of laughter came from the other side of the fire, and a low chuckle sounded from next to her.

Emma turned her head to find Owen lying in the same position she was. Her hand was still on his arm, and she quickly retracted it.

He grinned at her, then swiveled his legs to the opposite side and sat up. He jumped to his feet and held out a hand to her.

Emma blinked at it, still trying to catch up with exactly what had happened.

"Is it your back?" The mirth on Owen's face transformed to concern, and she took his outstretched hand, pretending not to notice that her heart skipped the same way it did when she cleared a low jump with Scarlet. "I'm fine. Just trying to figure out what happened."

"We toppled over is what happened." He pulled her to her feet. Emma wasn't sure if it was the setting sun or the firelight that made his eyes glow a deep honey color. "You're sure you're okay?"

Emma nodded, retracting her hand from his warm and strong and slightly calloused one and ignoring the tingles that zipped up and down her fingertips. It was just the neuropathy, she told herself.

"Who wants marshmallows?" Mom's voice sang out across the yard, and Emma spun toward her in relief, running her fingers through her hair to make sure there was no grass in it. Owen righted the hay bale and sat down, but Emma hurried to grab the marshmallow sticks, which—fortunately—meant she had to move to the opposite side of the fire.

"Grandma," Ruby called. "Aunt Emma and Mr. Mitchell just tipped over. It was hilarious."

"It wasn't that funny," Owen retorted, but Emma could hear the laughter in his voice.

"I don't know. I think it might have been." She felt her own lips tug upwards as she imagined what they must have looked like, suddenly flipping upside down like that.

She handed out the sticks, relieved to see that Carter had taken her spot next to Owen. Until Owen said, "Hey, buddy, why don't you scoot closer so Miss Emma can sit too?"

Emma shook her head. "That's okay. I'm not sure I trust sitting by you anymore."

"You tip a person over once," Owen muttered with a laugh.

Emma laughed too. There was no need for him—or anyone else—to know that wasn't the part that she didn't trust.

She poked a marshmallow onto her stick and held it over the fire, her eyes inadvertently tracking to Owen as she tried not to think about the way her fingers still tingled pleasantly from his touch.

She caught Mom watching her and quickly dropped her gaze.

She didn't need her mother thinking she liked her new neighbor.

Because she didn't.

Or, well, she liked him just fine as a neighbor. It would never—could never—go beyond that.

"I'm going to get you!" Owen called as he chased Emma toward the hay bale that Ruby had declared the base for their game of ghost in the graveyard.

"Not a chance." Emma threw a playful glance at him over her shoulder, and he stumbled over a rut in the ground.

"Are you all right?" Emma paused, and Owen used the opportunity to lunge for her, his hand landing on her arm. It was smooth and slightly cool in the night air.

Her eyes widened. "Did you just use my kindness against me?"

Owen laughed as he gulped to catch his breath. He hadn't thought he was out of shape, but they'd been playing this game for an hour, and mostly he and Emma had traded off being the ghost, as Anne and William had gone inside and the kids seemed to have come up with a trick for not getting caught—either that or they were just faster.

Owen didn't mind though. He'd heard Kenzie and Carter laugh more tonight than they had in the last five years. And he'd done his fair share of laughing too, he had to admit. It had been a long time since he'd had this much fun.

"Oh my goodness." Emma bent over and rested her hands on her knees. "I'm not sure how much more of this I can take."

"I know what you mean. I don't think I've been this exhausted since the time Katie and I entered a triathlon. She was great at it. Me, not so much."

Emma stood, studying him as she swiped a short curl off her forehead, and Owen suddenly wished he hadn't mentioned his wife. Not because he didn't want to talk about Katie but because every time he mentioned her, it tended to change the whole atmosphere of the conversation. Like people felt they had to say something sympathetic or stop smiling and enjoying their own lives.

But Emma was still smiling. "She must have been an amazing woman."

Owen nodded, swallowing. "She was. Come on." He inclined his head toward the kids. "Let's see if they'll let us quit."

Emma chuckled, the sound as warm and bright as he was feeling right now. "I thought we were supposed to be in charge here."

Owen shook his head. "That's what they want you to think."

They started toward the bonfire, which they'd let die down to embers. The kids were already there, jumping from one hay bale to the next, their laughter ringing across the yard.

"Thank you for doing this." Owen suddenly needed her to know how much this meant to him. "It's been really good for Kenzie. Ever since her mom died . . ."

Emma drew to a stop and so did he. "I lost my dad when I was a little older than Kenzie is now. I know how hard it is."

"Oh." Owen studied her. He never would have guessed she'd lost a parent at a young age. Though he was sorry she'd had to go through that, he was relieved too; she had clearly turned out just fine. It gave him hope that his kids would as well.

"One of the things that helped me the most was that my mom was always there for me." Emma met his eyes. "And I can tell you're there for your kids in the same way."

The words made Owen's chest oddly tight. Katie had always been an encourager, and he missed hearing her words of support. "Thanks." He cleared his throat to loosen his chest. "I think some of my kids would agree with you more than others."

"I'm sure they all know it, at some level."

Owen made a sound halfway between agreement and disagreement. "Ninety percent of the time, I have no idea what I'm doing."

Emma's laugh was understanding. "Don't worry, based on what my friends all say, that's totally normal." She gazed at the sky in the distance, looking wistful. "And I feel that way about my chickens," she added brightly.

"Look." She lifted her arm to point, and he followed her gesture toward the east. "The Hope Fest fireworks."

Sparks of gold and red popped against the night sky, and Emma clapped her hands. "Come on, we don't want the kids to miss this." She started toward them, calling, "Look up at the sky, guys."

Owen stood frozen for a moment, watching her, a strange sort of fireworky feeling spreading through his chest.

He let out a breath. He was not interested in his neighbor. It was just the dark and the fireworks and her kindness that had him mixed up.

But he had his kids and his memories of Katie. And that was all he wanted.

Emma glanced over her shoulder, as if she'd just realized he was no longer next to her.

He took a step, and she smiled, then kept walking.

He kept his pace slow enough that he wouldn't catch up with her and settled onto a hay bale with Carter while she sat next to the girls, who immediately drew her into a conversation about horses.

Owen wrapped an arm around his son and watched the fireworks. And whenever Emma's low voice or warm laughter pulled his eyes in her direction, he pulled them right back again, ignoring the little whisper at the back of his mind that said he had promised Katie he would move on. He'd known from the moment he made that promise that he wouldn't keep it. And sitting here at a bonfire, watching fireworks with his kids and his neighbor didn't change anything.

Chapter 15

Emma tugged her fingers through her curls in one last, desperate attempt to tame them. She'd tried a headband, barrettes, and bobby pins, but there was no helping it. She longed for the day when it would be long enough to pull back into her once-standard ponytail again—and maybe lose the curl. She'd had straight hair her entire life—though in middle school she'd made one misguided attempt to go curly with a perm. She'd learned from that experience that curls were not the look for her—and these chemo curls only confirmed it.

There was a knock on her door. "The girls are ready to go," Mom called.

"Coming." Emma sighed, giving up the fight with her hair. It wasn't like it mattered any more today than any other day what her hair looked like. She slipped on a pair of strappy sandals that left her feet feeling oddly exposed.

She kicked them off and tugged on a pair of brown boots. They may not exactly go with the blue sundress, but at least they made her feel a little more like herself.

Without another glance in the mirror, she opened her bedroom door and rushed out. She'd taken longer than usual to get ready, and Mom and William had already cleared away the dishes from the oatmeal waffles she'd made the girls for breakfast. "Thanks, you guys. I would have done that later."

Mom eyed her with a small smile. "You look nice."

"Oh." Emma smoothed a hand self-consciously down the simple fabric. "Thanks."

Ruby thundered down the stairs but came to such a short stop at the bottom that Kenzie crashed into her.

"Careful, Ruby," Emma chided with a laugh. "We need to get you some brake lights. Come on. It's time for church."

But Ruby didn't move. "Aunt Emma, you're wearing a dress."

"Yes, Ruby." Unbidden warmth rose to Emma's cheeks. She only hoped it wasn't as noticeable on the outside as it was on the inside. But judging from Mom's quiet smile, it was.

"You never wear dresses." Ruby didn't let it go.

"Well, today I am."

"You look pretty," Kenzie said softly.

"Thank you, Kenzie. You do too." The girl wore a pink skirt with a white top, and Emma wondered who helped her pick out her clothes. Her sisters? Or maybe Owen. She supposed she could imagine it—he certainly had shown a soft side when it came to his kids. But still, her heart hurt for the little girl who wouldn't have a mother to help her pick out a prom dress or a wedding dress one day.

"All right, folks, let's load 'em up and move 'em out." William jingled the car keys in his hand. Usually Emma drove Mom and William to church in her truck, but with the two girls, it would get pretty crowded in there, so William had offered to take them all.

Emma followed everyone outside, relishing the feel of the morning sun on her bare shoulders. Wearing the sundress had been a good idea. A hint of the smoke from their bonfire last night hung in the air, and Emma glanced at the firepit. She could almost still see them all—her and Ruby and Kenzie and Carter and Owen—sitting around the fire, watching the fireworks, and a sharp desire for more nights like that swept over her.

She tried to push it away as she climbed into the back seat with Ruby and Kenzie. But their conversation rehashing the evening didn't help.

They pulled into the church parking lot, and William directed the car into an open spot. Emma reached to open her door but paused as another vehicle pulled in next to them. Her heart jittered as her eyes met Owen's smiling wave.

"Daddy!" Kenzie called joyfully, scrabbling to get her seatbelt off.

Emma opened the door and jumped out before Kenzie could try to climb over her. She nearly collided with Claire, who was stepping out of the van.

"Oops. Sorry." She laid a hand on the girl's arm, but Claire scowled and jerked away.

Cody climbed out of the van behind Emma, stuffing a muffin into his mouth. "Morning," he mumbled cheerfully around it.

Emma laughed. "Good morning."

Carter followed Cody out of the vehicle, a book clutched in his hands. "No clouds today," he said, wrinkling his nose.

Owen got out of the driver's seat, and Kenzie flew to give him a hug that made Emma's heart squeeze. She'd always imagined a little girl running to her like that after a sleepover.

Catelyn came around from the other side of the van, and they all started toward the church with Mom and William.

"I hope they let you get some sleep." Owen fell in next to Emma, with Kenzie between them.

"They were asleep by midnight," Emma assured him. She, on the other hand, had been awake well past that time courtesy of the insomnia that had been her companion since the chemo. So she'd worked on her jigsaw puzzle until two a.m. and then had finally been able to fall asleep.

"Midnight?" Cody scoffed. "The last time I had a sleepover, we stayed up until four in the morning and got up at seven."

"Oh really?" Owen frowned at his son. "Maybe you don't need to go to any more sleepovers then."

"Oh wait, did I say four *a.m.*? I meant four *p.m.*," Cody joked, and Emma laughed, enjoying the easy family banter.

When they reached the church, Owen held the door open for everyone, and Emma was the last one through.

"Thank you," she murmured, feeling unaccountably shy.

She felt the warmth of his presence as he came in behind her, and she scooted a few steps away, to the far side of Ruby.

Owen was listening to something Carter was saying and didn't even seem to notice.

And why should he?

Someone else had though.

Violet hurried toward them, her eyes wide, pupils darting from Emma to Owen and back again, a half-smile on her lips.

Emma shook her head discreetly at her friend. Violet raised an eyebrow at her but simply said good morning to everyone.

Within moments, a group had gathered around them in the lobby, talking with Owen and his kids as if they had always been part of this church family. Spencer and Sophie chatted with Owen. Isabel and Tyler's twins, Jonah and Jeremiah, swooped on Cody to talk baseball, while Gabby and Joy and Hope circled Ruby and Kenzie. Catelyn made a beeline for Jackson, and Dan and Jade's five-year-old Matthias struck up a conversation with Carter. Only Claire stood apart, her arms crossed.

Emma stepped tentatively toward her. "Do you have any plans for the summer? I know they're always looking for lifeguards at the beach."

"No." Claire's answer was short and clipped, but Emma had never been easily deterred.

"Or there's always the Chocolate Chicken. I know for a fact that you get free ice cream on your breaks." She ignored Claire's scowl and continued cheerfully. "Or the new bookstore. Or I know Cam is always looking for people to help mow lawns and stuff."

"Hey, that's a great idea." Owen's voice startled Emma. She hadn't seen him approaching, and when she met his eyes, his smile did that jittery thing to her heart again.

"It's a terrible idea." Claire's glower lost none of its potency as it traveled from Emma to Owen and back again.

"Claire," Owen started, but the church bells rang, indicating that the service was about to start. The whole group moved toward the sanctuary. Emma gestured for Claire to enter ahead of her. The girl tucked her chin to her chest and stepped inside.

"I'm sorry about her," Owen said in a low voice, leaning over Emma's shoulder so that she smelled his warm, clean scent. "She's mad at me for making her come to church this morning, and she's taking it out on everyone."

"Nothing to apologize for," Emma said quietly. "I was a teenage girl once too." It may as well have been yesterday for how ridiculously fast her heart was running around her chest with him standing so close behind her.

Owen's chuckle rippled up her back. "Nothing quite as mysterious as that species."

The church was already fairly full, and each family found seats where there was room.

Emma spotted James and Bethany just as they looked over with a wave, and Ruby made a beeline for their row, pulling Kenzie with her. Cody and

Catelyn filed in after the girls, followed by Claire and then Carter. Emma stepped aside so Owen could sit next to his family.

But Carter looked over just as Dan stepped to the front of the church. "I want to sit next to Miss Emma," the boy declared loudly.

"Shh." Owen hushed his son but angled his head to indicate that Emma should enter the row ahead of him.

She did, sliding close to Carter so Owen would have room too. Even so, when Owen sat, the sleeve of his dress shirt brushed against her shoulder.

She scooted closer still to Carter, searching for a way to still her heart, which had taken off at a full gallop.

"What are you reading?" she whispered to the boy.

Carter held up the book so she could read the title: *The Complete Guide to Clouds and Weather*.

"That sounds like a good one."

Carter nodded. "It's my favorite book." His voice was a few notches too loud to be a whisper, and Owen leaned across Emma to tap him on the knee.

"Hey, buddy, we need to be quiet in church, remember?"

Carter nodded and Owen sat back. Emma dared to breathe again.

She folded her hands as Dan led the congregation in prayer, silently adding one of her own: *Take away these ridiculous feelings I've been having around Owen, Lord. I want to be a good neighbor to him and his family. Nothing more.*

She lifted her head and reached for a hymnal, her hand landing on it at the same time as Owen's.

The tingle that skipped across her fingers only meant that God hadn't answered her prayer yet. But she was confident he would. And hopefully soon.

Chapter 16

Owen could not stop marveling as he listened to the sermon. He barely knew Dan, and yet it felt like the pastor had written the message just for him.

For the past five years, he'd felt like he was only going through the motions of faith, maybe even retreating from it. Not because he was angry with God. More like he was . . . confused. Uncertain. Not sure what the point of it all was.

But this morning, God's Word seeped into his soul and penetrated the thick calluses on his heart. He only hoped it was doing the same for his kids. He'd fallen down on his job of encouraging them in their faith the last few years—it had been hard when he was struggling with his own. But he was going to get back to it. Starting with a return to their family devotions tonight.

"And this is a cumulonimbus capillatus." Carter's pseudo-whisper carried across Emma.

Owen was about to shush him yet again, but Emma's quiet, patient "Mm hmm" stopped him.

He allowed himself a peek at the two of them. Emma's arm was draped easily across the back of Carter's seat, and her head was bent close to his, her light hair a contrast to Carter's dark locks.

She lifted her head as if she felt his eyes on her, and Owen snapped his gaze to the front of the church.

"And now, may the God of grace restore to us all the joy of his salvation, today and every day, until we meet him in life everlasting. Amen." Dan concluded his sermon, and Owen stood along with the rest of the congregation. That's what he felt like this service had done—restored to him the joy of his salvation. It was a joy he didn't intend to let go of again anytime soon.

Next to him, Emma stood, half bent over, listening to something Carter was saying. When she straightened, her arm bumped against Owen's, and her light floral scent drifted over him. He'd never thought he'd enjoy another scent as much as Katie's fruity one, but this was . . . nice too.

Owen stepped to the side to give Emma a little more room, but Pastor Dan invited the congregation to be seated, and Owen had to move closer again to avoid sitting on the armrest at the end of the row.

The music for the next hymn began, but a few rows in front of them, there was a slight stir as two men Owen recognized from the fire truck at the parade climbed over the people in their row to get to the aisle.

Emma cast a worried look in their direction as they hurried out the doors, and Owen saw one of them pulling a pager off his belt. From what he'd gathered, the town's fire department was entirely volunteers, and he wondered how often they got calls during church.

He turned his attention back to the song, listening to Emma's quiet voice next to him to figure out which verse they were on.

Ten minutes later, the service concluded, and Dan made several announcements about upcoming events like vacation Bible school and an anniversary celebration and all kinds of things Owen could suddenly see getting his family involved in—the same kinds of things they'd been involved in when Katie was alive.

The moment the announcements were done, Owen turned to Emma. "I'm so sorry. You probably didn't hear a word of that service."

Emma's laugh sparkled over the chatter that had started up all around them. "It's fine. I learned a lot." She patted Carter's knee. "Thank you for telling me about all the kinds of clouds."

Owen groaned. "He doesn't need any more encouragement in that department." But he couldn't help smiling at the pride on Carter's face. A lot of people dismissed the boy without listening to a word he said because he was different. But Emma seemed to appreciate him for exactly who he was.

Owen stood and stepped into the aisle, waiting for Emma and his kids to join him.

"I'm so glad you guys could make it today." Dan approached from the front of the church, holding out his hand with a warm smile. He had already loosened his tie, and he carried his sport coat over his arm.

Owen returned the handshake. "I'm not sure how you knew exactly what I needed to hear, but I really appreciated the message."

Dan's smile grew. "That's all God's doing. But I'm grateful to be a part of it."

Jade came up next to Dan and kissed his cheek. Owen noticed the way their hands instantly interlaced—the same way his and Katie's always had. He rubbed the spot on his finger where his wedding ring used to rest. It was one of the few things he'd already unpacked and was tucked safely into a drawer of his dresser.

"Your children claim they are going to starve to death if they don't get some food soon," Jade told her husband with a laugh. "Anyone else want to come to the Hidden Cafe for lunch? I think Nate and Vi and Sophie and Spencer and Tyler and Isabel and maybe Leah and Austin are coming too."

Bethany groaned and pressed a hand to her stomach, her face going green. James wrapped an arm around her. "Not us. Bethany's morning sickness seems to be getting worse."

"Poor thing." Emma reached over to pat her sister-in-law's arm, and Owen wondered if she ever had anything other than a compassionate word for anyone.

"I don't think I can go either," Emma added. "I rode with Mom and William, and I know they are planning to golf in Silver Bay this afternoon, so they need to drop me off and then head over there."

"We could give you a ride." Kenzie's comment drew everyone's eyes to her, and her cheeks colored, but she added meekly, "Right, Daddy?"

Owen considered insisting that they didn't need to go out to lunch. But going home meant an afternoon staring at spreadsheets and trying to figure out how to get the drop zone ready to open without going broke, whereas going to lunch meant a chance to spend more time with Emma.

With Emma's friends, he corrected himself.

Right. More time to spend with Emma's friends. Who were starting to feel like his friends too for how often he saw them and how much they had already done for his family.

"Sure," he answered Kenzie's question, then turned to Emma. "We can give you a ride. If you want to go."

"Oh yes, say you will," Kenzie pleaded, and Owen kind of wanted to echo the plea, but he resisted.

Emma's smile lit up her eyes. "You've convinced me. Let me just tell my mom and William."

They all followed her to the lobby.

"Do we have to go?" Claire muttered as they waited for her. "I just want to go home."

"Maybe you should think of someone other than yourself for once," Catelyn retorted.

"And maybe you should think of someone other than your new boyfriend," Claire shot back. "He's the only reason you want to go."

"Girls." Owen ran a hand down his cheek. His two oldest had been the best of friends when they were little, but over the last few years, their relationship seemed to deteriorate little by little. Owen wasn't sure if that was a result of Katie's death or simply their differing personalities, but he sure wished he knew how to fix it.

"That's not true." Though Catelyn was usually his dependable rule-follower, she ignored Owen's reprimand. "I want to go because I can see that Kenzie and Cody and Carter and even Dad want to go. And unlike you, I think Dad should—"

She cut off as Emma approached.

"Ready when you are," she said cheerfully. If she noticed the tension between his kids, she didn't let on.

"We're ready." Owen led his crew to the door and held it open for everyone.

When they reached the van, Emma and Catelyn had a friendly debate over who should sit in the front seat. He knew his daughter could hold her own, so he was surprised a moment later when Catelyn climbed into the seat next to him.

"What can I say, she's good." Catelyn lifted her shoulders with a laugh. "She got Kenzie on her side."

Owen glanced in the rearview mirror to see Emma climbing to the far back of the van with Kenzie and Cody. Claire and Carter sat on the bucket seats in the middle of the vehicle.

"You really could have sat up here," Owen called.

But Emma turned and settled into her seat, pulling her seatbelt over her shoulder. "I told you, sometimes my stubbornness can be a good thing."

Owen shook his head and started the vehicle. Emma chatted with Cody and Kenzie as they drove, although she also called out directions to the restaurant.

When they arrived, Owen opened the sliding door and waited for his kids to clamber out. Emma came behind them, bending her head low so she wouldn't hit it on the ceiling.

Owen held out a hand to help her down. It was one thing for the kids to come springing out of there, but the back of the vehicle definitely wasn't adult-friendly.

Emma's eyes came to his for a second, then jumped away. But she set her hand in his. It was colder than he'd expected, and instinct told him to wrap his other hand around it to warm it up. That was what he would have done if she were Katie.

But she wasn't Katie.

Confusion poked at his heart, and he let go of her hand as soon as her feet were on the ground.

They started across the packed parking lot, and Owen let Kenzie, Carter, and Cody come between them, while Catelyn hurried ahead and Claire dragged behind.

They were almost to the door when someone burst out and headed straight for them.

"Soph." Alarm rang from Emma's voice. "What's wrong?"

"You didn't see the text?" Sophie squinted against the sun, and even though Owen didn't know her well, he could pick out the concern in her expression.

His heart jumped as her eyes shifted to Emma. Had something happened to her mom or William or maybe Ruby's family?

Emma was digging in her purse, probably for her phone. "What did it say?" She sounded much calmer than Owen expected. Maybe she hadn't jumped to the same conclusions he had. After losing Katie, it seemed like he'd become pretty good at inventing worst-case scenarios.

"I'm so sorry." Sophie stopped in front of him, her eyes glassy with unshed tears.

Owen's heart clattered, and he braced a hand on Cody's shoulder.

"They didn't have your number, so they texted us all."

Owen blinked at her. He had no idea what any of that meant.

"Oh no." Emma's low groan pulled his eyes in her direction. She had her phone in one hand, her other hand pressed to her lips. Owen wanted to move closer, to ask her what was wrong, but his feet were locked to the ground.

"It's your house," she whispered.

"What's my house?" Owen's chest constricted so tight he could barely get enough air to ask. His voice was hoarse and raspy, and he was afraid he already knew the answer.

Emma's tortured eyes met his, and it felt like it took forever for her to get the words out.

"The fire."

Chapter 17

Helplessness washed over Emma as she watched Owen's face register her words. His eyes showed his emotion first, and then his mouth fell. Around them, the kids' cries and voices broke out, and Emma felt Kenzie's hand slide into hers.

She clutched it tight. "It's going to be okay," she said, grateful the wobble in her heart didn't register in her voice.

The words seemed to snap Owen into action. "We need to go."

She nodded. "Go. I can get a ride with someone else."

Kenzie's grip on her hand tightened, and Emma looked down into pleading brown eyes.

"Unless you want me to come." She lifted her head to meet Owen's eyes. "Please."

It was only one word, but it went straight to Emma's heart.

She nodded and wrapped an arm around Kenzie.

"They won't want us all to get in the way," Sophie said. "But we'll be praying. Please let us know what you need."

Owen gave a terse nod and led his family and Emma back to the van. Emma kept her arm firmly around Kenzie, who was crying quietly.

Catelyn climbed into the back with the other kids, leaving Emma the passenger seat. Owen already had the vehicle running, and he pulled out the moment the last door clicked shut.

Aside from Kenzie's sniffles, the car was eerily silent.

Emma wracked her brain, searching for something to say, the right Scripture verse to share, but her mind seemed to have become one giant, blank canvas. Owen's fingers choked the steering wheel, and his jaw was clenched so tight Emma was afraid his teeth would break.

Please, Lord. This family has already lost so much. Emma clasped her hands together in her lap and did the only thing she could—prayed. *Give them your peace and your hope, whatever happens. Show me how to help them, Lord.*

They crested a hill, and a sharp gasp went through the vehicle.

Though they were still a couple of miles away, the higher vantage point gave a clear view of the fire trucks crowded into the driveway of the Mitchells' house, where the moving pods had been just a week ago. Dark smoke billowed from the house in ominous clouds.

The van dipped down the hill, taking the house out of sight, but there was no way to forget what they'd seen.

She glanced at Owen, whose throat rippled with a rough swallow.

"God's got this." The words felt small, but Emma prayed they'd bring comfort. Small words did not change the size of their big God.

Owen's lips flattened into a grim line, but he nodded.

"Lexi!" Kenzie cried suddenly. "Lexi was in the house."

A sharp inhale was the only sign Owen had heard his daughter.

Emma reached back to grab Kenzie's hand. She desperately wanted to tell the girl the dog would be fine—but the words stuck in her throat. The way that smoke had looked . . .

Please, Lord, she started up her prayer again, but it evaporated as they came around a bend that gave them a full view of her house, and, beyond it, theirs. Flames clawed out of two upstairs windows, licking against the siding and crawling up the roof. Below them, charred siding smoldered and broken windows gaped. Firefighters in full uniform aimed hoses at the flames, sending waves of smoke billowing. Its smell pierced the van's closed windows.

Owen pulled into the driveway, then steered into the grass to avoid the fire trucks. He slammed the vehicle into park and turned off the engine.

"You all stay in here," he ordered as he opened his door. The scent of smoke was overpowering now, and Emma couldn't hold back a cough.

"Dad, no, we have to—"

"Stay," he barked.

"I'll stay with them," Emma offered.

He nodded roughly, then slammed his door and sprinted toward the nearest fire truck.

"It's going to be okay," Emma tried to reassure the kids, gripping Kenzie's hand. The girl sniffed and nodded but didn't wipe the tears from her cheeks.

Next to her, Carter was staring out his window at the flames still working their way up the side of the house. In the back seat, Cody had his head bowed, and Emma wondered if he was praying. Catelyn was watching the fire almost as intently as Carter. And Claire was scowling fiercely at Emma.

Emma brought her eyes back to Kenzie, who was looking at her as if she'd know how to make everything better.

"Why don't we pray," Emma suggested.

A derisive huff came from Claire. "We're not going to pray." She unfastened her seat belt and leaned over Carter's back to open the sliding door.

"Claire, stay in here," Emma reached for the girl's arm, but Claire wrenched away and was out the door.

"I'll go get her." Catelyn opened the other sliding door, and before Emma could say anything, she was gone too.

Well, great. Owen had asked her to do one thing, and she couldn't even manage that. She debated going after the girls but decided it was more important to stay with the younger children. Besides, she could see that Claire was headed for the picnic table under the big tree in the backyard, Catelyn only a few yards behind. She supposed they'd be safe and out of the way there.

"Close the door," she instructed the other kids, and they immediately obeyed.

As soon as Claire settled on top of the picnic table and Catelyn sat next to her, Emma let her eyes seek Owen.

He stood next to one of the fire trucks, talking to a firefighter who held his helmet in his hands. When the man turned, Emma could tell it was Ethan, and she let out a breath. He would break any news to Owen gently.

Owen said something, and Ethan shook his head, laying a hand on Owen's shoulder.

Emma's chest tightened. She wanted to be out there, offering Owen her support. But she also wanted to be in here for his kids.

"Look, there's Lexi," Cody cried suddenly.

Sure enough, the dog had come barreling around the garage, and she ran straight to Owen, who squatted to receive her in his arms.

Emma shook her head, a shaky laugh making its way out. At least that was one less loss this family would have to face.

Owen petted the dog for a minute, then stood and shook Ethan's hand before striding toward the van, Lexi at his heels.

He opened his door and let the dog jump in. Lexi swiped Emma's cheek with a kiss on her way past, and if the giggles from the back seat were any indication, she was greeting the kids in the same way.

"What did they say?" Emma asked quietly.

Owen sighed, leaning into the vehicle to look into the back seat. "Where are Claire and Catelyn?"

"I'm sorry. I tried to tell them to stay here, but Claire got out and Catelyn went after her. They're on the picnic table." Emma pointed to the spot where both girls sat staring at the house.

Owen glanced over his shoulder, then turned back to her. "The fire is about sixty percent contained. They hope to have it out in the next hour or two. The back of the house isn't as bad, so if they can keep it from spreading, it might not be a total loss." Though his voice was staunch, his expression broke her.

"Oh, Owen." She reached a hand toward him, but he was too far away. "I'm so sorry."

He nodded, his lips pressed tight together, a muscle in his cheek working as he looked over his shoulder again at the house.

He turned back to the kids. "I need to make some calls to insurance. You three stay in here. You do not get out for anything. Got it?"

Cody, Kenzie, and Carter nodded meekly, but Emma hated the thought of them sitting in the vehicle watching their house burn. "I could take them over to my house for now."

"I couldn't ask you to—"

"Of course you could." Emma tried to smile, though her heart was cracking right along with theirs. "Anyway, don't worry, I'll put them to work. There are chickens to feed and horses to muck and—"

That muscle in Owen's cheek was working again, but he nodded. "Thank you," he said hoarsely.

"You're welcome." She turned to the back seat. "Come on, kiddos." She opened her door. "We'll walk."

She rounded the van to meet Kenzie and Cody and Carter on the other side. "Come on, Lexi," she called. "You too." The dog bounded to them, and Owen gave her a tight smile as she led the group toward the field.

She had never wanted to be in two places at once so badly. But right now, the best thing she could do for Owen was make sure his kids were safe and cared for. That, and pray for him, which she did all the way across the field.

Chapter 18

Owen could barely lift his feet as he trudged across the field toward Emma's house. The smell of smoke still filled his nostrils and clung to his clothing. The fire was finally out, but the firefighters had said they couldn't enter the house until an inspector gave the all clear, which wouldn't happen until tomorrow at the earliest. Either way, they wouldn't be sleeping there for a good long time, not with the extent of the damage, which Ethan had said included all of the bedrooms, as well as the living room.

Owen glanced over his shoulder to make sure Claire and Catelyn were still trailing behind him. They both looked as haggard as he felt.

He had thought he'd already been through the worst day of his life the day Katie died. But today was definitely a contender. At least with Katie, they'd known it was coming. They'd had a chance to hug her and say their goodbyes.

But this—on top of everything else. Owen wasn't sure how they were going to get through it.

He knew it was just stuff. But it was *their* stuff. *Their* memories.

He'd moved boxes and boxes of things with them because he couldn't bear to part with them. Because they seemed to keep a part of Katie close.

And now they might all be gone.

It could have been worse, he reminded himself. If a driver who happened to be passing by hadn't called the fire department when they did . . . If he'd let Claire stay home as she'd wanted . . .

He shuddered, rubbing the sting of smoke and loss from his eyes. He had to be strong for his kids. It shouldn't be hard. He'd been doing it for five years now.

"Daddy!" Kenzie's broken voice pulled his head up, and he found her running across Emma's yard toward him. Cody followed behind her more slowly, holding Carter's hand. And behind them, Emma hovered, her forehead creased into lines of worry.

Owen squatted to catch Kenzie in his arms. "It's okay, sweetie." He smoothed a hand over her hair as she cried into his shirt. "It's going to be okay." He had no idea how he could expect his daughter to believe that, but she nodded into his shoulder.

"I know, Daddy. Miss Emma prayed with us. She said God is still with us."

"Yeah, baby, he is." Owen swallowed, trying to believe that was true. Was it only this morning in church that he had thought God had restored to him the joy of his salvation? It felt like three lifetimes ago, that joy three light years away.

He lifted his head, his eyes landing on Emma's, and she offered him a compassionate smile. "We tried to stay busy, but they've been watching for you."

Owen nodded, pushing to his feet, though he kept an arm around Kenzie. "I don't know how to thank you."

Emma shook her head. "There's no need." She bit her lip. "I hope you don't mind, but I called my friends Grace and Levi, the ones who have the bed-and-breakfast, to see if they had anything available."

Mind? Owen gaped at her. Finding somewhere to stay was next on his list of things to do. But if she'd already done that for them . . . A tiny bit of the weight pressing on his shoulders lifted. "Thank—"

Emma shook her head. "Both their bed-and-breakfast and their new cabins are fully booked. For the whole summer."

"Oh." Owen felt the weight slam back onto him. "That's okay. I'll call some—"

"I called everywhere," Emma said quietly. "There's nothing."

"Nothing?" Owen stared down the road as if he could make a hotel materialize. He'd take a rundown shack at this point. He just needed to put a roof over his children's heads.

Emma shook her head. "It's the height of tourist season. Things book up a year or more in advance."

"We never should have moved here," Claire muttered.

Owen ignored her. "It's okay. We'll just—"

"Stay here," Emma finished his sentence.

"Yeah. What?" Owen stared at her hand, which was gesturing toward her house.

"Mom and William and I talked it over," she said. "We have more than enough space. I mean, the kids will have to share rooms, but—"

"We can't stay here." Claire crossed her arms, and Owen threw her a look. As much as he agreed with her, he didn't appreciate her attitude.

"That's a very kind offer." Owen turned back to Emma. "But we couldn't possibly—"

But Emma was already shaking her head. "Of course you could. Bethany and James and Ruby stayed here a few months ago while their house was being renovated, so—"

"But they're family," Owen protested.

Emma shrugged. "We're all brothers and sisters in Christ, right?"

Owen half-laughed, half-sighed. "I'm not sure that's the same thing."

"It is." Emma insisted.

"It's way too much of an imposition," Owen argued. In the back of his mind, he could hear his dad's voice, telling him that you made a way for yourself. You figured things out on your own. You didn't ask for help.

But over his dad's voice, he could hear Katie telling him not to let his stupid pride get in the way.

"Dad," Catelyn said. "Where else are we going to go?"

Owen sighed. There was Katie's voice in the form of her daughter. And as much as he hated to admit it, she was right. They had no other options.

"Only until we can find somewhere else to stay," he said with resignation.

Emma nodded, her smile filled with understanding and compassion and . . . something that made Owen wish she could help him walk through this whole thing. But giving them a place to stay was more than enough. The rest of it, he'd handle on his own.

Chapter 19

"Thanks, you guys." Emma hugged Leah and Austin as she stepped out onto the porch with them. Somehow, they'd managed to throw together an amazing meal to feed her new guests. Jackson had come with them—and Emma was guessing it wasn't just to help carry the food. At the moment, he stood with Catelyn on the other side of the porch, his hands wrapped around hers.

Leah caught the direction of Emma's gaze and smiled. "I'm glad he can be here for her."

Emma nodded, although, based on the dark looks Owen had been shooting his daughter's suitor all evening, he would disagree.

"We should go." Leah patted her arm. "I'm sure Owen's going to want to get the younger kids to bed. If you need anything else, let us know."

Emma nodded. She knew her friend's offer was sincere. When she'd sent out a text to let her friends know what the Mitchells needed, they'd responded in a big way. Anyone with kids around the same age as Owen's kids had stopped by to drop off piles of clothing. Ruby had brought a whole bag full of stuffed animals—even though most of Owen's kids were older than her. "Everyone needs to hug a stuffed animal sometimes," she'd said. And Cam, who was about the same size as Owen, had even dropped off some clothes for him.

Leah called to Jackson that it was time to leave, and he leaned to give Catelyn a quick hug before joining his parents. Catelyn waved as they got into their car, then turned to Emma. "Maybe my dad doesn't need to know about the hug."

Emma laughed. "I'm sure he would understand. All of you could probably use a hug right about now."

Catelyn gave her a strange look. "Yeah, probably."

They stepped back into the house to find Owen washing the dishes.

"Just leave those," Emma protested. "I'll take care of them later."

"I tried to tell him." Mom bustled around, putting away leftovers. "He listens about as well as you do."

That made Owen laugh a little, and Emma was so grateful to hear it that she laughed too.

Owen shook his head. "We're staying in your house. The least I can do is wash the dishes."

"Seriously, Owen, you don't—"

He turned to her. "I'm washing them." His voice was practically a growl, and Emma nodded silently. She busied herself helping Mom. "Where are the kids?"

"William talked the younger kids into a game of checkers," Mom answered easily, as if they had a houseful of kids every day. "Catelyn and Claire and Cody are setting up the air mattresses."

"Oh good. I think we have enough for everyone to use two." Emma laughed. In addition to bringing over clothes and stuffed animals, her friends had brought air mattresses, sleeping bags, and toiletries.

"There." Mom put the lid on a dish of cheesy potatoes—the ultimate comfort food, according to Leah. "I think I'm going to go get in a game of checkers."

She left the room, and Emma felt suddenly awkward, alone with Owen. She concentrated on scooping brownies into a container. Aside from the splashes of water from the sink and the low mumble of voices from the living room, there was no sound.

"Your friends didn't have to do all of that." Owen broke the silence after a while. "The clothes and food and stuff."

"They know that," Emma said patiently. "They wanted to."

Owen nodded, his lips pressed into a tight line. He'd resisted the first few offerings from her friends but after a while had simply thanked them.

"Insurance will cover replacement costs for clothes and stuff. And a place to stay, for that matter. We'll pay you all back."

Emma stopped with a brownie halfway to the container. "I can guarantee not a single person will accept payment."

She watched his shoulders drop and had a sudden vision of the way her dad used to come up behind her mom and wrap his arms around her when she was having a bad day. If only she could . . .

She pushed the thought away.

There were other ways to offer comfort. Ways that were much more appropriate for one neighbor who barely knew the other.

She cleared her throat and turned her focus back to the brownies. "It's nothing to be ashamed of, accepting help. God tells us to bear each other's burdens."

Owen exhaled, the sound close to a laugh. "That's what Katie always said."

"Smart woman." Emma peeked at him again.

"Yeah." He glanced over his shoulder, his eyes coming straight to hers. Emma's heart jumped a little at the sudden eye contact—which translated into a jump of her arm holding the spatula. The brownie that had been resting on it plopped to the floor.

She yanked her eyes off of his, but before she could bend to pick it up, Lexi had swooped in and swallowed it whole.

"Oh no." Emma dropped the spatula. "I'm so sorry. I didn't mean for her to get—"

A chuckle from the sink made her look up. Owen's lips had tipped upwards, and the heaviness that had visibly weighed on him seemed to lift slightly. "There's nothing you could have done. The kids call her a food vacuum."

"But it was chocolate," Emma moaned. "Should we call the vet?"

Owen shook his head. "Trust me, she's gotten into a lot more chocolate than that before. She's indestructible."

"Phew." Emma couldn't imagine this family losing one more thing today.

"I don't know what I would have done if she hadn't made it out of the fire." Owen's voice was low, and Emma wanted to go to him. Instead, she squatted by the dog and rubbed her silky ears. Lexi licked her chops, her mouth stretching into what looked like a smile.

"You're sure you don't mind having her in the house?"

"Of course not. I've considered getting a dog more than once myself. This will be a good trial run."

"Hear that, Lex?" Owen turned back to the dishes. "You're Miss Emma's test dog. Don't screw this up."

Emma laughed and stood, returning her attention to the brownies. She finished and pressed the lid onto the container, then picked up a towel to at least dry a few of the dishes.

Owen shot her a look but didn't say anything, and they worked in silence for a while. Emma tried not to think about the fact that this—doing dishes side by side with someone, the sound of children's voices in the other room—was more like how she'd always pictured her life when she was younger and dreaming of the future.

She'd long since put that dream aside.

So while Lexi may be a practice dog, Owen and his kids most definitely weren't a practice family.

"Thank you," Owen cut into her thoughts suddenly. "For everything."

Emma added the plate she'd been drying to a stack on the counter, then carried the pile to the cupboard. "There's no need to keep thanking me."

Owen made a disbelieving sound. "I'm pretty sure there is."

She waved off the comment. "I don't know if any of the kids want to shower, but there's a whole bag of little shampoos and soaps and conditioners from Grace. There's a bathroom upstairs and one down here, but sometimes when someone uses the hot water in one, the water in the other becomes cold. I didn't discover that until Mom and William moved in last year." She was babbling, and she needed to stop.

Owen's lips had lifted into not quite a smile—but something close.

He wrung out the dishrag and draped it over the side of the sink, the same way Emma always did.

"I'll go have Carter get started." He moved past her to grab the bag of stuff from Grace. Smoke from the fire clung to him, and Emma was suddenly reminded of why his family was here.

They had lost everything.

She rubbed at her heart as Owen disappeared, then returned a moment later to usher Carter upstairs.

Once everything was in order in the kitchen, Emma moved to the living room to check on Kenzie. The girl sat with Mom on the couch, strategizing how to beat William at checkers. Kenzie looked tired, but she rested her head near Mom's shoulder, and Emma backed out of the room. Mom and William had everything under control in there.

She headed upstairs to see if the older kids needed any help setting up their rooms.

She'd put the girls in the room Kenzie and Ruby had shared for their sleepover—had that only been last night? It seemed impossible that so much could have changed since then. But then again, she knew from firsthand experience how quickly a life could be upended. The day before her cancer diagnosis, she'd gone about life as if nothing would ever change. And then . . . It had all changed.

But God had brought her through that, and he would bring Owen and his family through this. And she would do whatever she could to help.

The door to the girls' room was open, but Emma knocked anyway. Catelyn looked up from the one actual bed in the room, which she'd claimed as the oldest. "Come on in." Her smile was tired and a little sad, but still inviting.

Emma stepped into the room. A small air mattress was pushed up against the bed—that one must be for Kenzie, as it held Ruby's favorite stuffed unicorn, which she'd given her friend earlier. Claire lay on a larger air mattress near the closet. She faced the wall, her arms wrapped around herself, and Emma couldn't tell if she was awake or asleep.

She whispered just in case. "I just wanted to see if you guys need anything else."

Catelyn shook her head. "I don't think so." She didn't whisper, so maybe Claire wasn't asleep after all.

"Okay, well, your Dad brought up the shampoos and stuff from Grace, but if there's anything you need that isn't in there, let me know."

"Thank you." Catelyn's green eyes shone with gratitude. "I don't know what we would have done if it weren't for . . ." She gestured around the room. "All of this."

Claire flipped onto her back suddenly, eyes open, staring at the ceiling.

"What about you, Claire?" Emma asked. "Do you need anything?"

Claire snorted. "Let's see, my house just burned down, I lost everything I've ever owned, and, oh yeah, my mom is dead. No, I don't think I need anything."

"Claire." Catelyn's voice was sharp.

"It's okay," Emma said quietly. She knew the girl's vitriol wasn't directed at her. She was hurting, and she didn't know how else to deal with it. Emma had felt the same way after her dad died.

She longed to sweep over to the air mattress and pull Claire into a hug, but she had a feeling that might result in a black eye. So she backed toward the door. "Please let me know if you need anything."

Catelyn nodded. "We will."

Emma reached the hallway just as Carter stepped out of the bathroom. His wet hair stuck up all over his head like a hedgehog, and he wore a pair of pajamas that was two sizes too big, but he smiled at Emma. "The shampoo was orange."

Emma laughed. "I bet you liked that."

The boy nodded solemnly. "But I didn't eat it."

"That's good," Emma responded, working to keep her lips straight.

Owen stepped out of a room across the hallway. James and Bethany had used that room while their house was being remodeled, so it was already set up with a bed and desk and dresser. Emma sometimes used it as an extra office space when she didn't want to go over to her main office in the barn, but she could do without it for now.

"Hey, bud, all done with your shower?" he asked, and Carter nodded.

"He did not eat the orange shampoo," Emma added.

"It's the small victories," Owen said with a tired laugh. He held out a hand to Carter. "Come on, bud, let's get you tucked in."

"Goodnight, Carter. Sleep tight." She smoothed his wet hair as he walked past her but then realized that really wasn't her place and quickly pulled her hand back. "Let me know if you need anything," she mumbled as she turned toward the stairs.

"Wait," Carter cried, and Emma turned back.

Instead of speaking to her, Carter tugged on Owen's arm and whispered something in his ear. Owen groaned, eyeing his son. "Do you really need it?"

Carter nodded solemnly, and Owen turned to Emma. "Do you by chance have any old spoons, maybe some wind chimes, and some bubble wrap?"

"Probably." Emma laughed at the strange list of items. "Why?"

Owen looked to the ceiling. "Carter likes to set up a monster trap in his room. Just in case."

"A monster trap?" Emma smacked her forehead. "I knew I was forgetting something." She waved for Carter to follow her. "Come on, you can help me find stuff."

She caught Owen's grateful smile before she turned and led Carter down the stairs.

She'd do a lot more than set up a monster trap for this kid if it helped bring that look back to Owen's face after the day he'd just had.

Downstairs, she and Carter collected a handful of spoons, the wind chimes from Emma's front porch, and—since they couldn't find any bubble wrap—a package of balloons she used for birthday parties at the stables. "Oh, and how about some of these." Emma grabbed a handful of wrapped hard candies. "Monsters don't like mint."

Carter grinned and nodded. "Good idea."

They carried their haul upstairs, where Owen had collapsed onto the smaller of the air mattresses in the room, while Cody sprawled on the other. Owen sat up as Carter explained Emma's plan with the mint to his dad. Owen's gaze came to her, and her heart caught.

"I want to blow up the orange balloons." Carter tugged the package out of Emma's hands, pulling her attention back where it belonged.

While Cody helped Carter blow up the balloons, Emma surrounded the air mattress with spoons and mints, and Owen hung the wind chimes over the top of it. Balloons scattered around the bed made a final barrier.

"All right, buddy, now do you think you can sleep?" Owen's voice hung with weariness.

Carter shook his head solemnly.

"What do you need now?" Only the tiniest edge of impatience bled through Owen's words, and Emma admired his ability to keep everything under control even after all they'd been through today.

"You," Carter said simply, and Emma was pretty sure her heart was going to melt.

"Tell you what." Owen groaned as he lowered himself to the air mattress. "How about I lie down with you for a little while? Just until you fall asleep."

"Will you tell me stories?" Carter asked.

Owen laid back. "One story," he mumbled, and Emma wondered if he would even make it through one before he fell asleep.

Carter hopped onto the mattress too, and Owen wrapped an arm around his son. A sudden, sharp ache tore through Emma's middle. How many times had she dreamed of seeing an image like this in her own house?

"Are you going to bed too, Cody?" Owen's words were slow and drowsy.

"Not yet." Cody scrambled off of his mattress. "Can I watch a movie on my phone?"

"For a little while." Owen's speech grew slower still.

"Thanks." Cody zipped into the hallway, and Emma turned off the light and closed the door, whispering "goodnight" after it had already latched.

Chapter 20

Owen woke with a start, his eyes raking the darkness. What time was it? Where was he? And why did his back feel like it was about to break?

He tried to check his watch, but something heavy weighed his arm down, and he glanced to his side. Carter.

An onslaught of images hit him suddenly—church, the fire, putting Carter to bed. Right. They were at Emma's. And he had told Carter he'd lie with him for a little while. He was pretty sure he'd started to tell a story about a boy who wanted to catch a cloud, but he couldn't remember finishing it.

Carefully, he eased his arm out from under his son and rolled toward the wall, groaning as quietly as possible as he pushed to his feet. He glanced across the room, where Cody lay asleep on the other air mattress, then took a step toward the door, his foot coming down on something crinkly. He pulled his foot back as he recalled the monster trap. Quietly, he turned on his phone screen, which gave him just enough light to tiptoe through the trap without waking the boys. He blew each of them a kiss before closing the door behind him.

He checked the time on his phone. 1 a.m. He glanced at the door to the room the girls were staying in, but it was closed, and no light seeped under it. Catelyn must have gotten her sisters to bed.

Rubbing at his bleary eyes, he caught a whiff of the smoky smell that still clung to him. He really needed a shower. But he didn't have any clean clothes to wear—unless he went downstairs and grabbed the ones Emma's friends had brought.

Carefully, he tiptoed down the steps. But he didn't know them well enough to be familiar with where they squeaked, and he felt like his progress was painfully loud. Not that he was worried about his kids—they could sleep through a tornado. But he didn't want to wake Emma or Anne or William. It was bad enough that Owen's family had taken over pretty much their entire house. He didn't need to go ruining their sleep too.

He let out a breath as he reached the bottom of the steps without waking anyone. A muted light glowed above the kitchen sink, and Owen wondered if Emma always left that on or if she'd done that for his family.

He crossed the kitchen and rummaged through the bags of stuff Emma's friends had brought. Uneasiness still clung to him at the thought of accepting so much help, but he wasn't sure what else he could do. Other than keep saying thank you—which Emma didn't seem to think was necessary either. He shook his head. That woman was—

"Is Carter asleep?"

He wheeled around, almost calling his wife's name, even though he knew the whispered voice wasn't hers. But it was a question they'd asked each other plenty of times.

"Yes," he whispered. "Sorry if I woke you."

She shook her head, and he realized she was still wearing the shorts and t-shirt she'd had on earlier. "I was just working on my puzzle."

"At 1 a.m.?"

She lifted a shoulder. "It's when I usually do it. I have a hard time falling asleep, and it relaxes me."

"Ah, I see. I'll have to try that sometime. Although I apparently didn't have any trouble falling asleep tonight. Sorry about that."

"It was a long day." Emma rested her hand on the back of a dining chair, and Owen suddenly realized how exhausted she must be. It had been a long day for her too.

"I didn't mean to stick you with taking care of the other kids. It won't happen again. I hope they didn't give you any trouble."

Emma shook her head with a soft laugh. "They were so little trouble, I wasn't sure what to do with myself. Cody watched a movie. Claire didn't come down at all. Catelyn had Kenzie go to bed around nine. Then Catelyn chatted with my mom and William and me for a while. She's a very impressive young woman. I had no idea she wanted to be a pediatric neurologist."

Owen nodded. "She decided that the day she learned Carter's diagnosis. She was fourteen at the time."

Emma dropped her gaze. "She said she considered switching to oncology when her mom . . ."

Owen swallowed. He had always been proud of his daughter's desire to help others—just like her mother. "She did, but we talked about it, and she wasn't sure she could handle seeing so many families go through that." He pushed a hand through his hair. "I thought maybe that would protect her from experiencing any more loss, but . . . Here we are again."

"I know." Emma's voice was sort of choked, and she seemed to lean more heavily on the chair.

"I'm sorry." Owen blew out a breath. "I didn't mean to— I should let you go to bed."

Emma shook her head. "I'm not tired."

Owen grunted his disbelief. Her eyes had grown heavier by the moment.

He, on the other hand, was sure he'd never be able to get back to sleep after his long nap in Carter's bed.

"After Catelyn and my mom and William went up to bed, Cody turned off his movie." Emma's words were measured, and Owen felt the shift in her tone.

His shoulders tensed.

"He asked why I thought God was letting all of these bad things happen to your family."

Owen let out a sharp breath and pulled out the nearest chair, sitting with a heavy thud. He wanted to know the same thing. "What did you say?"

The chair next to him scraped quietly across the floor, and Emma sat too. "I said—" Her voice was gentle. "That I didn't know."

Owen swiveled his head to find her tracing the grain in the table's wood with her finger. He wasn't sure that answer would help Cody, but he couldn't have given his son a better one, so he didn't say anything.

"But," Emma continued, her eyes lifting to meet his. They were gray-blue in the dim light but filled with a soft peace that Owen longed for. "I told him that God promises that he works all things for our good and his glory. And then Cody said something really insightful." Her hand stilled, and her smile reached for him. "He said, 'So I guess we can be optimistic as we wait to see how God is going to work through this.'"

Owen considered his son's words, then rubbed his face. "I think he has more faith than I do," he confessed. "Because I'm having a hard time feeling optimistic right now."

Emma gave him an empathetic look. "It's not about how much faith you have. It's about how faithful God is."

Owen startled at the words. They felt familiar. Had Katie said that to him? After her diagnosis, maybe?

"I know it's hard to see right now," Emma said quietly. "But he really is faithful. Always."

Owen swallowed, but before he could say anything else, a little voice called out, "Daddy."

He pushed his chair back with a sigh. "Looks like I'm going back to bed. Thanks for . . ." He had no idea how to fill in that blank. There was too much to thank her for.

Her understanding smile made him want to stay and talk longer, but Carter called again.

"Goodnight," he said quietly. "I guess I'll see you in the morning?"

A quiet laugh puffed from Emma. "I'll be here."

Chapter 21

Emma closed her Bible and lifted her face toward the sky, drawing a large breath of the soft early morning air. The sun had risen less than an hour ago in a blaze of yellow and pink that had now settled into a delicate blue with a few fuzzy clouds she'd have to ask Carter about.

She spent a few more minutes in the willow rocking chair, absently petting Lexi, who had followed her outside as if they did this every day, and turning over the verses she'd just read from Job 36: "He is wooing you from the jaws of distress." The words had caught and captivated her. She'd never really been wooed by a man before. But God—God had wooed her in so many ways, including in her distress, though she hadn't always seen it at the time. But God had used all of those hard moments—including her cancer—to draw her closer to him and remind her of his tender, all-encompassing love.

Do the same for Owen and his children, Lord, she prayed as she pushed up from her seat and returned to the kitchen.

Lexi's paws clicked on the tile next to her. Footsteps creaked across the floor upstairs, and Emma paused to listen. She couldn't even count the number of times she'd been startled by that sound when Mom and William had first moved in. After living alone in the old farmhouse for sixteen years, it had taken awhile to get used to hearing other people moving around. Now the sound was familiar, but she was pretty sure it wasn't them—or at least not just them. There were too many different cadences.

Quickly, she pulled out the breakfast foods her friends had dropped off yesterday—orange juice and muffins and fruit and yogurt and granola and even breakfast burritos—then started mixing pancake batter. Lexi stuck close by her side, directing wide puppy eyes at the food.

By the time footsteps thundered down the stairs, she was flipping the first batch onto a plate.

"I smell something—" Cody bounced down the steps, his eyes going as wide as the pancakes Emma held. "Whoa!" He stopped a foot in front of the stairs, and Owen nearly ran him over.

"Hey, dude. What's the— Whoa." Owen stopped too. He was clean-shaven and wearing a t-shirt she recognized as belonging to Cam. His jaw went slack, and his eyes moved from the table to Emma. A slight spark of pleasure went up her spine at the surprise in his eyes. Only because it was good to see him looking less weighed down than he had last night.

"I hope you're hungry." Emma busied herself plopping the next load of batter onto the griddle. Lexi looked torn between the sizzling food sounds and her owners but finally ran to Cody. "Everyone brought a lot of food."

"And you're making more." Owen's light laugh held a note of bemusement.

Emma shrugged. "I figured you'd all be hungry, since no one ate much last night." And she had no frame of reference for how much a family of six ate for breakfast, so she'd figured it was better to have too much than too little.

She beckoned Cody to the spread. "Grab a plate and help yourself."

The boy didn't have to be told twice, and Emma watched in awe as he heaped his plate with some of everything.

She turned back to the griddle.

"Did you get any sleep?" Owen must have followed Cody across the room because his voice was much closer than Emma expected.

"Yep." Cody's answer sounded like it came through a mouthful of food.

"I know *you* did," Owen retorted. I heard you snoring all night. I was asking Miss Emma."

"Oh." Emma flipped a pancake. She hadn't realized he was asking her either. "I did. Thanks." Actually, she'd slept better last night than she had in probably months. It must have been because of the exhausting day. "Did you?"

Before Owen could answer, a voice called, "Good morning, Daddy," and Kenzie appeared at the bottom of the steps, followed by Catelyn.

"Ew, gross, Cody. Chew," Catelyn called to her brother.

Emma glanced at Cody, who sheepishly nodded, his cheeks bulging, and muffin crumbs on his lips. "Sorry," he mumbled, expelling more crumbs in the process. Lexi gobbled them up.

Emma laughed at the repulsed look on his sisters' faces.

"Boys are so gross," Kenzie proclaimed.

"Tell that to your sister," Owen grunted, throwing a look at his oldest.

Catelyn laughed off the remark. "I believed that for twenty years, Dad. I think that's long enough. Besides, you're one to talk, since you got married when you were only a few years older than I am."

Emma's gaze swung to Owen, trying to picture him as a twenty-something. She imagined he'd look much like he did now—firm jaw, broad shoulders, trim build—but without the light touches of silver in his hair and maybe a little less sorrow behind his dark eyes.

"That's really not the point," Owen spluttered. He turned to Emma. "When you get married young, you're not thinking about the fact that one day your kids could use that against you when they want to get married young too."

Catelyn rolled her eyes. "No one's talking about getting married, Dad. Don't be so dramatic."

"That's good," Owen retorted. "Since you're not allowed to get married until you're forty-five."

"Dad," Kenzie protested on her sister's behalf. "That's as old as you. Even Miss Emma couldn't get married if that was the rule. She's only forty-two. Ruby told me."

"Miss Emma can get married if she wants," Owen replied. "*She's* not my daughter."

"Do you want to get married?" Kenzie's bright eyes turned to Emma.

"I— Uh," she stammered. "No, not really. I mean, unless—" *Stop.* She had to stop right now. "I don't think marriage is in God's plans for me."

Kenzie's brow wrinkled. "How do you know?"

Emma shrugged, her mouth going suddenly dry as she felt Owen's eyes come to her again. "I mean, I guess if I haven't met the right man by now, it's probably not— I'm probably not—"

She accidentally looked up and made eye contact with Owen.

"Kenz, why don't you get some breakfast?"

His gaze lingered on Emma's a moment longer, and then he pulled it away to pass his daughter a plate.

Emma poured her concentration into watching the pancakes bubble. Fortunately, the food seemed to have taken Kenzie's attention off of Emma's marital status.

She scooped the pancakes onto the plate, then moved to set it on the table. "Oh, I forgot to grab glasses for the orange juice."

She swept past Owen to grab them out of the cupboard. When she turned around again, he was right there. He reached past her to grab a few more, his clean, soapy scent tickling her nose.

"Thanks," she murmured.

He laughed. "I'm pretty sure *we* should be thanking *you*."

"Yeah, these pancakes are amazing," Cody said through another full mouth. Lexi rested her head on the boy's lap, her eager eyes watching his every bite.

"Seriously, bud, chew." Owen set the glasses on the table next to the ones Emma had carried over, then started filling them with orange juice. He passed one to each of his kids, then one to Emma.

"Oh." She took it in surprise. "Thank you."

Owen nodded and passed her a plate too, then took one for himself and started filling it.

"Dad, we have to go." Cody shoveled the last bite of his pancake into his mouth. "Practice starts at eight."

Owen gave a sad look at his half-filled plate.

"I can take him," Catelyn offered. "Jackson and I are supposed to have breakfast together before work anyway."

"There's breakfast right here." Owen pointed to the spread, and Emma noticed that Catelyn hadn't taken a plate.

"Dad," Catelyn said in a warning voice.

"Miss Emma and her friends went to a lot of work to—"

"It's okay," Emma interrupted. "Really. I won't be offended."

Owen threw her a dark look, but Emma couldn't feel bad when Catelyn looked so happy.

"Come on, Cody." She gestured for her brother, and the two of them were out the door.

"Thanks for that," Owen muttered.

"Jackson is a good kid," she said. "He just finished his junior year in college. Premed. Volunteers at church. Never gets in trouble anymore."

"Anymore?" Owen growled, his eyes coming to her.

Oops.

"He had some issues when he first came to Hope Springs," Emma tried to explain. "Got into some fights and— Well, his mom had died of a drug overdose so—"

Owen's eyes went to the door and he took a step, like he was ready to chase Catelyn down and tackle her to keep her from going out with Jackson. Emma skipped to the punchline. "But Leah fostered him and then she and Austin adopted him, and he's really flourished with them. You would never know he was the same kid. Truly, Owen, he's a good one, I promise."

Though Owen still looked like he wanted to go after his daughter, he nodded, then finished filling his plate.

"What are we going to do today?" Kenzie asked.

Owen turned to his daughter. "I need to go over to the house to take some pictures and see—" He stopped, clearing his throat and running a hand through his hair. "See what's left."

"Can I come?" Kenzie asked quietly.

Owen shook his head. "I don't think that would be a good idea, baby. Not yet. I'll wake Claire up before I go so she can watch you and Carter."

"I can watch them," Emma offered.

"Really, Emma, you can't keep doing more and more for us." Owen sounded half incredulous, half amused.

"And why not?" Emma set her plate down next to Kenzie and pulled out a chair. "This is what neighbors do."

"Trust me, you've gone far above and beyond the call of a neighbor. This is just . . ." He shrugged helplessly, as if the word he was looking for didn't exist.

"It's just me trying to get some free labor," Emma filled in. "I fully intend to put Kenzie and Carter to work, helping with the chickens and horses again."

Owen stabbed a bite of pancake and eyed her. "Don't you have lessons to teach?"

"Not until later. And Kenzie and Carter can watch those. It will be good for them to see."

"Please, Dad," Kenzie added. "Claire will just make us watch TV all day."

Emma could see Owen's resolve weakening as he cut another bite but didn't pick it up.

"You'd really be doing me a favor," she put in for good measure. "Honestly, I don't know how I'll get everything done if they don't help me." She winked at Kenzie.

"Well, in that case." The tension in Owen's posture relaxed a little. "I guess I can't say no."

"Thank you." Emma held her hand out to Kenzie for a high five.

Owen shook his head. "You got the thank you backwards again. Do you want me to wake Carter and Claire up before I go?" He scooped a big bite of pancake, and Emma noted with satisfaction that it seemed to release his tension a little more.

"Let them sleep. They have to be exhausted. I'll be here when they get up."

Owen swallowed, his face going serious. "Thank you. Really. That means a lot to me."

The breath got caught in Emma's throat, and she had to look away from his grateful gaze.

They finished eating in silence, and Emma could tell his thoughts were already on what he'd find at his house.

When he stood and said, "I guess I should go," Emma wished suddenly that she had offered to go with him. She hated the thought of him going through his burned out house alone.

He kissed Kenzie on the head, patted the dog, then aimed heavy steps at the door.

"Owen," Emma called.

He turned, but she had no idea what she was supposed to say next.

"I'll be praying for you," she said finally.

He nodded. "Thank you." He stepped out the door, and her gaze moved to the window as he crossed the yard.

Please be with him, Lord, she prayed. *Give him strength. Show him that you can make beauty even from literal ashes.*

Chapter 22

Owen dragged his feet, barely able to lift them high enough to push through the field's thick grasses that brushed against his knees. With each step, it felt like he was being driven further and further into the ground. He had spent most of the day pacing outside the house as the fire inspector combed through it. When the inspector finally stepped out to tell him the fire had been caused by faulty wiring, Owen had barely listened. He'd been too anxious to get inside. He'd stepped through the door, expecting to find the worst. But although streaks from smoke and water covered everything, the kitchen was largely intact, and he'd let out a breath. Maybe Cody had been right about being optimistic.

Then he'd moved into the bedrooms, and the sight there had bent him double. Blackened beds. Scorched stuffed animals. And all the boxes and boxes they hadn't yet unpacked—the cardboard burned away, their contents charred and unrecognizable on the floor. The inspector had suggested he box up everything he wanted to salvage before having a restoration company come in. Owen had thanked him and started digging through the rubble of his room. But when he'd come across the remains of what appeared to be the box of all the letters he and Katie had ever written to each other, he'd fled.

He stepped into Emma's yard and made it as far as the bonfire pit before collapsing onto one of the hay bales. He had to compose himself before seeing his kids. The most important thing was to be strong for them. He'd brought them here, and he needed them to believe he had everything under control—even if that wasn't at all close to the truth.

A light breeze stirred the ashes in the fire pit, and Owen buried his face in his hands. Katie would tell him to turn to the Lord. She would take his hands and pray with him and things wouldn't seem to be so bad after that.

But Katie wasn't here.

"Owen?"

The gentle voice made him jump. He lifted his head to find Emma standing just a few feet in front of him.

"Sorry." He cleared his throat. "I didn't hear you coming." His eyes darted behind her.

"The kids are inside," she reassured him. "Helping with a project for the church anniversary. I was just coming out to see if I left my phone in the stables." Her forehead was creased in worry lines, though she wore the same calm smile as usual.

"Okay, thanks. I should get back to the kids." He started to stand, but Emma's hand landed on his shoulder and pushed him down.

"My mom and William are with them. Take as long as you need out here. I just wanted to see if you were all right."

He laughed sardonically. "I have no idea what I am right now."

She nodded. "Trust me, I've been there."

He highly doubted that, but he didn't say anything.

Emma settled onto the hay bale next to him. "I read a verse this morning that made me think of you. Well, not—" She shook her head, looking slightly embarrassed. "I mean, it made me think of your situation."

"Yeah?" For some reason, knowing she'd thought of him as she'd read her Bible was comforting.

"It was from Job," Emma continued, and Owen grunted a humorless laugh. He was starting to feel like Job.

"It said God woos us from the jaws of distress."

Owen grimaced. "If God wanted to woo me, he could have spared all of our stuff. Or, you know, kept the fire from happening in the first place." He cut off and shook his head. "Sorry, I don't mean that."

"It's okay." Emma touched his knee for a second. "It's natural to feel that way. I've had the same thought about plenty of things in my life."

"I highly doubt that." This time Owen couldn't hold back his skepticism.

"Doubt it if you want. It doesn't make it any less true." She smiled graciously.

"I'm sorry." Owen didn't know why he was feeling so contrary all of a sudden, but it was unfair to treat her like this when she'd bent over backwards to help his family. "I didn't mean— I guess I'm just . . ." What was he, even? Words rolled around in his head. He wasn't angry or even depressed. "Confused, I guess." He lifted his eyes to hers. "And . . ."

"Hurting," Emma filled in.

He nodded, feeling his throat go all thick and scratchy.

"Have you prayed about it?" Emma asked.

His breath leaked out. "I was trying to just now, but . . ." He stared into the fire pit.

"Would you like me to pray for you?" Her voice was soft and yet solid, certain.

"Yes." The word barely made it past his lips.

He felt her shift on the hay bale and looked over to find that she'd bowed her head and folded her hands in her lap. Her eyes were closed, and her short hair brushed against her cheeks.

Owen closed his own eyes, gulping in a breath and holding it as if he were about to dive under water.

"Holy God." Emma's voice slipped over Owen, and he released his breath. "You have promised that you are with us in all things, including our troubles. You invite us to cast all of our cares on you, Lord, and to leave our burdens at your feet. Please take this burden that Owen feels crushed under right now."

Owen swallowed against the burn in the back of his throat. That was exactly what he felt. Crushed.

"Ease his fears and worries, Lord. Give him renewed hope in you. Even though we don't know why you allowed this fire to happen, we know that even in this you are working for Owen's good and his children's good."

Owen sniffed and cleared his throat, and he felt Emma's hands land on his. Instinctively, he wrapped his fingers around hers.

"Help us even when we are confused, even when we don't see the fullness of your plans for us, to trust in you and in your goodness. Clear away our confusion and replace it with your peace, Lord. The peace that comes only from knowing that Jesus died for us and that whatever else we may gain or lose in this world, nothing can separate us from that promise. In Jesus' name we ask this, Lord. Amen."

Owen heard the end of the prayer, but he couldn't bring himself to move.

Not yet.

He needed to remain in this moment of peace a little longer.

You're holding her hand. The thought finally penetrated his skull, and he released his grip.

"Thank you." He cleared his throat again and pinched the moisture from the corners of his eyes. He could still hear his father telling him that real men didn't cry, and to this day, Katie was the only person who had seen him cry as an adult—and that was only once, when they'd gotten her diagnosis. He had come close to falling apart at her funeral, but he wouldn't let himself—not when his kids needed him.

"Of course." Emma's voice was soothing, and he could still hear it lilting over her prayers. He had no idea how she had known exactly what to pray for, but every word she'd said could have come from Owen's own heart, if he could have gotten them out.

She jumped to her feet suddenly and brushed a blonde strand off her face. "I'll let you have some time to yourself. I thought I'd make chicken for dinner, if that's okay?"

Owen stood too. "I'll take the kids out for dinner. You don't need to feed us."

Emma waved off the comment. "Mom and William and I have to eat anyway. What's a few more people?"

"In case you hadn't noticed, there are six of us." Owen walked next to her, his feet easier to lift now, the load on him just a little lighter.

"So what do you think, grilled or baked?"

Owen shook his head. "You weren't kidding when you said you were stubborn."

"Nope." Emma's gentle smile morphed into an all-out grin. "Better get used to it."

Chapter 23

Emma examined the puzzle piece in her hand, letting it hover over the card table she kept set up in the corner of the living room. She had just started this puzzle earlier in the week, and though Owen's kids occasionally stopped on their way through the room to find a piece or two, only the edges and a small corner were complete. Other pieces were attached in twos or threes off to the side, waiting for Emma to figure out how they fit with the bigger picture.

A yawn shook her frame, and she considered going to bed like everyone else already had. She probably wouldn't have to worry about insomnia tonight. She'd been sleeping better this week than she had in a long time, and she was pretty sure it was thanks to hanging out with Kenzie and Carter so much—they were delightful but tiring.

Owen had taken them with him to the drop zone whenever he'd managed to find time to go there, but mostly he'd spent the week dealing with insurance and trying to salvage what remained of his family's belongings. She'd gladly watched Kenzie and Carter during those times, though she knew Owen felt bad about it. The poor man was shouldering a load heavier than anyone should have to bear, but Emma was pretty sure the big group dinner at Sophie and Spencer's house earlier had lifted his spirits—at least until he'd spotted Jackson and Catelyn holding hands.

Good thing he hadn't noticed the sweet peck on the cheek Jackson gave Catelyn on the way out the door.

Absently, she ran a finger over her own cheek. No one had ever . . .

She chased away the thought. It wasn't like she wanted anyone to kiss her cheek.

"Hard at it again, huh?" Though the voice was barely above a whisper, Emma jumped. Her face warmed as she dropped her hand from her cheek to her lap.

"Sorry. Didn't mean to scare you." Owen stepped into the living room. He wore shorts and a t-shirt that was slightly too tight across the shoulders.

Emma directed her gaze back to the puzzle. "Couldn't sleep?"

He exhaled heavily. "Not really. I keep dozing off, then waking up with some new worry pecking at me."

Emma's eyes fell on the exact place where her puzzle piece belonged, and she snapped it into place with a satisfied, "There."

Owen chuckled. "One down. Eight hundred-some more to go?"

"Something like that." She dared to look up. "You're welcome to join me. It might help you relax."

"That's okay." But Owen took a step closer. "I'm sure you appreciate your alone time."

"Trust me, one thing I have plenty of is alone time." As soon as the words were out, Emma realized they probably made her sound like a bitter old spinster. "I don't mean— It's not that—"

Owen laughed mildly. "Don't worry, I know what you meant. One of the hardest adjustments after Katie died was figuring out what to do with myself once the kids were in bed. All that alone time can get kind of . . . lonely."

Emma's throat went dry, and she couldn't seem to swallow.

"You're sure you don't mind the intrusion?" Owen took another step closer, and Emma managed to shake her head.

He grabbed the gray ottoman from in front of the couch and slid it over to use as a chair.

Emma passed him the top of the puzzle box, which was full of green pieces she'd sorted from the rest.

"Thanks." But he set the box down and stared at the part of the puzzle that was already done.

"Do you think," he said slowly, and Emma looked up from digging through the puzzle pieces that remained in the other half of the box. "That all of this—the fire, the problems at the drop zone—is God's way of saying I made a mistake moving the kids to Hope Springs?"

Emma studied him as she considered the question. Was he thinking about moving away from Hope Springs already? She tried not to let her personal feelings about that possibility color her answer. "I think—" She spoke as slowly as he had, trying to formulate her thoughts. "That life is kind of like a puzzle. If you just look at an individual piece—" She picked one up and showed it to him. "It's pretty unclear what it is or where it goes or how it fits into the big picture. But once it's all together, it seems obvious. The problem is, we can only see all these little pieces, all these things that happen to us and to others, good and bad, but we can't see how they fit together to make the big picture. But God is the master puzzle, uh . . ." She searched for the word. "Puzzle maker, I guess. He knows exactly where each piece goes, and he forms them all into this beautiful picture. It's scary for us when we can't see exactly where each piece we're experiencing fits into that picture, but we can trust that he isn't going to let even one piece end up out of place. He has a purpose for them all."

Owen was staring at her, and she ducked her head. "And now you think I'm the world's biggest nerd, using puzzle analogies."

He laughed, but it wasn't a laugh of derision. It was more like . . . hope. "No. I actually like that analogy. It helps."

"Oh. Well, good." She gave silent thanks to the Lord for that. She'd had no idea if her words were making sense.

Owen picked up a puzzle piece and studied the parts that were already assembled. "I guess the advantage of a puzzle over real life is that you can see the whole picture before you start." He lifted the box above his head so that he was looking up at the image on it.

"What are you doing?" Emma cried, turning her head away so she wouldn't see.

"Looking at the picture." Amusement and confusion mingled in Owen's voice.

"You can't do that." Emma kept her eyes averted but grabbed for the box.

Owen held it out of her reach. "Then how am I supposed to know what we're making?"

"You see it when it's done," Emma explained as if it were the most obvious thing in the world. "And not a moment sooner."

"But that's not fair. *You* saw the picture when you opened the puzzle. I should get at least one peek."

But she shook her head. "I keep the puzzles upside down in my cupboard."

"You do not." Owen laughed, as if the very idea was preposterous.

But Emma nodded vigorously, a short curl bouncing against her forehead. "Go look." She pointed to a set of built-ins on the far wall.

Still looking dubious, Owen set the box down and crossed the room, stopping in front of the built-ins.

"On the left side," she called.

But he didn't move, and Emma realized his eyes were on the pictures on the shelf. "You used to have long hair," he said in surprise.

"Oh. Uh—" Before she could figure out how to answer without getting into her health history, he bent and opened the left cupboard door.

A stifled laugh rang out. "Sure enough. They're all upside down."

"Told you," Emma gloated.

Owen squatted and began to rummage through the piles. "There must be thirty of them here," he said in awe.

Emma put another puzzle piece in place. "Those are just the ones I haven't done yet. The rest are in my closet."

Owen burst into laughter, and she had to join in. "It's possible I have a puzzle problem."

"Don't worry." Owen was still laughing as he moved back to the footstool. "I'm sure we can get you some help for that."

Chapter 24

A low murmur of voices and clanking dishes carried up the stairs as Owen got ready Saturday morning. Emma certainly had been right about the power of puzzling. He'd fallen asleep the moment his head hit the pillow and slept the whole night through without waking to new worries. Even this morning, a feeling of peace remained with him. His eyes fell on the small pin on his dresser, and he picked it up, wiping away a layer of soot. When he'd discovered it in a pile of rubble at the house the other day, it had almost brought him to his knees. Katie had loved these things and had a whole denim jacket covered with them. The jacket was destroyed, most of the pins that were on it melted and blackened beyond recognition. Except this one. He'd given it to her for their first anniversary, and it was a simple silver pin engraved with a tiny heart and the words "Trust in the Lord."

"I'm trying," Owen whispered, setting the pin down. He stepped out of the bedroom, the smell of coffee and something freshly baked beckoning him down the stairs.

"Good morning." Anne and William looked up from the kitchen table, where they were eating breakfast and sharing the newspaper, Lexi looking eagerly between them. William passed the dog the last bite of his muffin, and Lexi gobbled it up, then looked at Owen with gleeful eyes as if to say, *We can never leave this place.*

"There are muffins on the counter." Anne pointed to where they still sat in the muffin pan. "Help yourself."

Owen shook his head but grabbed a still-warm pastry off the plate. "Y'all really have to stop spoiling us."

"Nonsense." Anne pushed to her feet and filled a coffee cup for him. "I hope you don't mind that I told Carter and Kenzie they could watch a little TV."

"Of course not." Owen moved to the living room to check on his kids.

They were watching The Weather Channel, which meant Kenzie must have let her brother choose.

"Good morning, Daddy." His daughter beamed at him. "Look how far Miss Emma got on her puzzle."

"Oh wow." Owen glanced over, as if he didn't already know a third of it was finished, not quite sure why he didn't tell Kenzie he had helped with it.

"What are we doing today?" Kenzie asked.

"I have some things I need to do at the drop zone."

"Do we have to come along?" Kenzie made a face.

"I thought you liked the drop zone."

She hadn't complained the few times he'd brought her and Carter there during the week.

"There's nothing to do there. Why can't we stay here?"

"There's no one to watch you. Catelyn has to work, Cody has baseball practice, and Claire is supposed to start her new job at the Chocolate Chicken." He thanked the Lord for that. Hopefully working would give Claire something to do other than resenting him.

"Miss Emma can watch us," Kenzie said as if it were that simple.

But Owen shook his head. Emma had been kind enough to watch them several times during the week, but he had to stop taking advantage of her hospitality. "We can give Miss Emma a little break today."

"Miss Emma doesn't like breaks," Carter said, eyes still on the thunderstorm on TV. "She told us."

Owen laughed. He believed that. Other than when she was reading her Bible or working on her puzzle, he rarely saw her sit down. "Even so, I think she probably needs one. You two are a handful."

"Dad," Kenzie protested. Then she lifted a finger excitedly. "I know, we should bring Miss Emma to the drop zone."

"That wouldn't exactly give her a break from you two," Owen pointed out.

"She doesn't want a break from us," Kenzie insisted. "And anyway, maybe if she sees the drop zone, she'll see that skydiving isn't scary. And then she'll be able to cross it off her life list."

Owen considered his daughter's reasoning. It was actually pretty sound. "I guess it wouldn't hurt to ask her," he said at last, ignoring the little spark that went through him at the thought of spending the day with Emma.

"Yippee!" Kenzie jumped off the couch. "I'll go ask her. She's out by the chickens."

"Hold up there." Owen caught his daughter. "You're still in your pajamas. You two go get ready, and I'll go ask Emma."

"You promise you'll try to convince her to come?" Kenzie narrowed her eyes, as if she wasn't sure he was up to the task.

"Kenz." Owen gave his daughter a nudge toward the stairs. "She doesn't have to come if she doesn't want to. Now go."

But as he marched out the door and toward the chicken coop, he found himself making a list of ways to overcome any of Emma's potential objections. The most powerful was, "Kenzie wants you to come," and he decided he'd lead with that one, both because it was true and because it didn't risk giving Emma the impression that he was the one who wanted her to come.

As he neared the chicken coop, he thought he heard voices, so he slowed. One thing he'd learned over the past week was that Hope Stables was a busy place, with employees, riders, and friends often milling about—and somehow Emma managed to make time for all of them.

Emma emerged from the chicken house into the run, the sun catching on her hair, a chicken following at her heels. She looked back at the bird and let out a laugh that seemed to shimmer in the morning air. "I think Ruby should have named you Goofy instead of Corazón," she said to the chicken. "Then again, I suppose the heart can be pretty goofy sometimes."

Owen couldn't hold back a snort-laugh, and Emma's head jerked up, her eyes widening, a soft pink blush stealing up her cheeks. "I didn't know anyone was out here."

Owen let his chuckle carry him the rest of the way to the coop. "Do you always talk to your chickens?"

"Of course." Emma seemed to regain her composure. "You should try it sometime. It's very therapeutic."

"I'll keep that in mind." He managed to keep a straight face.

"Good." Emma pulled a small bag of what looked like grapes out of her pocket. "Do you want to feed them?"

Owen shrugged. "Sure." If he were to make a life list, feeding chickens wouldn't be on it, but maybe it would distract him from what he'd come out here to do, which suddenly had him feeling oddly nervous.

Emma gestured for him to enter the run, and he did, careful to latch the door behind him.

She passed him the bag of grapes. "They'll eat them right out of your hand."

Owen squatted and plucked a grape out of the bag. Before he could even hold it out, one of the chickens snatched it from his hand.

"Unicorn," Emma scolded. "Be polite."

"Yes, be polite," Owen echoed. "Hey, you're right. It is therapeutic." His lips twitched, and Emma swatted his shoulder.

"Laugh if you will. Just remember, I've seen you talking to your dog."

"That's different." Owen dug out another grape, and Unicorn stole that one too. He shifted his position to give the other chickens a chance. But the chicken who had been following Emma refused to come to him.

"I don't think she likes me," he said finally.

"Corazón?" Emma looked at the chicken who still hung close to her heels. "She's just shy. Come on, Corazón." Emma moved closer to Owen, then squatted down next to him. Owen passed her the grapes, and the chicken took them willingly from her hand.

"I guess she likes you better," he murmured.

"We can get her to like you too. Here." Emma held out a grape to him, not letting go even when he grabbed it. "Here, Corazón."

She stretched their hands together toward the chicken. Owen's arm accidentally brushed against hers, but he didn't want to scare the bird, so he didn't pull it away. Corazón crept closer and stuck out her neck. Then, faster than he could blink, the chicken grabbed the grape in her beak and scurried to the other side of the run.

"There! We did it!" Emma pulled her arm back.

"I'm not sure that was a resounding success, but I guess it's a good start." Owen pushed to his feet, then held out a hand to help her up.

She hesitated, and Owen realized that although helping Katie up had become as natural as getting up himself, helping his neighbor up really shouldn't be. He let his arm fall to his side, and Emma scrambled gracefully to her feet without it.

"All right, ladies. See you later." Emma scooped up a basket of eggs near the door, then stepped outside.

"See y'all later," Owen said, Emma's wide grin totally making up for any awkwardness he felt in talking to the birds.

"So do you have any plans for today?" Owen asked as they walked toward the house.

"I have a bunch of stuff to get ready for the church anniversary. Plus, I should start writing the new dressage routines for my more advanced riders. And then if I have time, I need to catch up on some paperwork."

Owen's heart dipped. "So you're busy?" Kenzie would be so disappointed.

She nodded. "I guess so. Why?"

He shrugged. He didn't want to pressure her. "I thought I'd take the kids to the drop zone today. Kenzie wanted to know if you'd like to come along. I told her you probably needed a break from them after spending so much time with them this week—"

Emma made a sound of disagreement. "Of course I don't need a break from them. They're great kids."

"I know, but you have other things—"

"That can wait," Emma insisted.

"Really, Emma, you don't have to—" Why was he trying to talk her out of this all of a sudden?

"Really, Owen, I want to. Besides, if I'm ever going to skydive, I should probably have an idea of what I'm getting into."

"That's what Kenzie said." Owen let himself relax a little.

"Smart girl you have." Emma gave him a teasing grin. "Must take after her mother."

Owen chuckled. "I have no trouble admitting that." They climbed the porch, and Owen opened the door for her.

"Is she coming?" Kenzie sprang at them the moment they entered the kitchen.

"She is," Owen announced, reminding himself that the joy he felt was only on Kenzie's behalf.

He was indifferent to whether or not Emma came.

But then Emma's eyes met his, and he had to admit that a tiny little piece of the joy might be for himself.

Chapter 25

"This place is great." Emma looked out over the airstrip and the green space Owen had said he and his partner planned to turn into a picnic area for spectators and jumpers.

"Thank you." Owen looked pleased. "I hope other people think so too."

"Show her the chutes, Dad," Kenzie urged. "They're green and gold. Because this is Packers country."

"Smart move." Emma followed Owen and the kids back into the large pole building that served as both headquarters and hangar. He stopped at an area that was separated from the rest of the space by a wall that was just higher than Emma's head.

Carter went straight to the window to watch the sky. Not that Emma blamed him. The clouds were low and heaped up today, making fascinating shapes and shadows.

"It's going to rain," he announced.

"There's no rain in the forecast," Owen answered, then turned to Emma. "This is where we pack the chutes." He pointed to a neat line of backpacks along the wall. "Charles and I are both certified riggers, so we'll pack them ourselves until we get busy enough to hire a couple more."

"I'm sure that will be in no time." Emma could already picture the place bustling with people. The only question that remained was whether she'd be one of them. At this point, she couldn't imagine actually strapping a parachute to her back, but the more she saw of this place, the more she thought she might be brave enough someday—especially if Owen was the one jumping with her.

Owen moved to pick up one of the backpacks. "This is the container." He stepped into two loops that hung down from it, then pulled the backpack up and slipped his arms into the straps and cinched a belt around his waist. "It holds the main chute and the reserve chute. We don't have our tandem rigs in yet, but those also have a drogue chute to slow the free fall."

He said all of this as if it were a matter of business as usual. Which, for him, Emma supposed it was.

She was about to ask if he'd ever had to use his reserve chute when a man's voice called, "Hello?" The sound echoed through the building, and Owen grinned. "Back here." He started to peel the straps off.

"Come on." Kenzie grabbed Emma's hand. "It's Uncle Charles."

Emma let the girl pull her, glancing over her shoulder at Owen. He nodded her forward. "I'll be right there."

"Uncle Charles!" Kenzie pulled Emma faster. "This is Emma."

She stopped in front of a man with windblown blond curls and a sparkling smile.

"Ah, so *you're* the famous Emma." Charles held out a hand. "I'm honored to finally meet you."

"The famous? No, I'm uh, not—" Emma stuttered as she shook his outstretched hand. His grip was warm and confident.

"Oh, trust me, you're famous." Charles winked at Kenzie. "According to my sources, you have a cool niece, awesome horses, and amazing chickens. Or was it amazing horses and awesome chickens?"

Kenzie giggled. "Both."

"And that makes you famous," Charles concluded.

"Hey, partner," Owen called before Emma could figure out how to respond.

Owen's eyes flicked to Emma's hand, still locked in Charles's handshake, and the skin around his lips tightened. Emma slid her hand out of Charles's grip and brushed it through her hair.

"I half-expected you to come complete with a halo, the way Owen talks about you." This time Charles directed his wink at Owen, who shifted uncomfortably, looking suddenly flustered.

Emma felt her own cheeks warm, but she managed to keep her tone light. "Nope. No halo. Just the love of Jesus."

Charles grinned. "Well, could you slow down a little bit with that? You're making me look bad, giving them a house and food and clothes. I mean, how's a guy supposed to keep up?"

"You live in a loft," Owen pointed out. "There's no room for us. And you can't cook to save your life, so we don't really want your food. And your clothes are . . ." Owen eyed Charles's button-up white shirt with the silhouette of a palm tree on one side. "Not my style."

Charles mock staggered and grabbed his chest. "That cuts deep, man."

Owen rolled his eyes. "How's Carrie doing?"

"Give me half an hour, and I can show you." Charles sent a wink Emma's way, then jogged past them to the other side of the hangar.

"So that's Charles." Emma watched as the other man disappeared into the room Owen had pointed out as the office earlier. Somehow she'd assumed he'd be more like Owen.

"That's Charles." Owen let out a bemused laugh. "Never a dull moment with him around."

"I bet."

Owen gave her an odd look, his mouth tightening and relaxing again so quickly that Emma was sure she'd imagined it.

"Who's Carrie?" she asked, glancing again toward the office. As far as she knew, no one else was here, but maybe Charles had gone to call someone.

"You'll see," Owen said mysteriously.

"Well, that's cryptic." Emma studied him, but he didn't reveal anything.

"I need to move some things so the contractors who are refinishing the concrete floor can get to it. It shouldn't take too long, if you want to hang out in the rigging room. Or outside."

"Or I could help," Emma pointed out.

Owen shook his head. "I didn't bring you here to put you to work. You do enough of that the way it is. Just relax."

Emma lifted a shoulder. "I've had more than enough relaxing to last a lifetime." She bit her tongue as soon as the words were out, praying Owen wouldn't ask *when* she'd done all of that relaxing.

But he just snorted. "You must have a different definition of relaxing than I do."

Still, he didn't object when she followed him to the training area—a section of the hangar surrounded by a half-wall, with a rug, folding chairs, and several boxes inside. Huge pictures of skydivers floating in the air hung on the wall. Emma hadn't really looked at them closely before, but now she smiled at the face grinning back from one of them.

"Hey, that's you."

Owen looked up and followed her gaze. "Oh. Yeah."

Emma moved closer to examine it. It was a tandem dive, and there was a woman strapped to his harness. A woman who looked a lot like Owen's daughters.

"And this is Katie," Emma said quietly.

"Yes." Owen had come closer too, and the love and sorrow reflected in his eyes as he looked at it was too much for her. "It was our first jump together. The first day we met."

"Oh." Emma felt like she had intruded on something personal. "Not many people get that moment captured on camera."

Owen looked at her in surprise. "I never thought of it that way, but you're right."

"You both look very happy."

"We were." He looked at the picture another moment, then walked away and picked up a box, heading for a small back room. Emma grabbed her own box and followed. Wordlessly, they cleared the area. By their last load, the storage room was fairly full, and Owen apparently didn't anticipate how close Emma was behind him because when he turned around, he nearly bowled her over.

His hands came to her shoulders to steady her, and Emma's breath hitched.

They stood like that for a moment, and all Emma could hear was Charles's comment: *the way Owen talks about you*. But all she could see was the way Owen had looked at that picture of his wife. There was no comparison.

"Where did everyone go? We're ready." Charles's voice echoed through the hangar, and Owen yanked his hands off Emma's arms.

"Sorry." His voice sounded scratchy. "You okay?"

She nodded and spun to exit the room. Charles was on his way toward them, Kenzie and Carter on his heels. Charles's eyes went from Emma to Owen, a small smile pricking his lips. "And where were you two?"

"Clearing the training room," Owen said brusquely.

"Mmm." Charles nodded conspiratorially, and Emma felt her face grow hot again. "Are you ready?"

"For what?" Emma wished she could fan at the stupid heat radiating from her cheeks.

"To meet Carrie, of course." Charles gestured toward the open hangar door, where the plane now rested on the tarmac.

"Where is she?" Emma stared at the plane, trying to pick out a figure.

Charles's laugh played against the walls. "You're looking right at her. Carrie the Caravan."

"Carrie the— Oh, it's the plane." She laughed. "I was looking for a woman."

"Me too," Charles quipped, and Owen rolled his eyes.

"I told you it didn't work as a nickname."

Charles waved off the comment. "Well, whatever we call her, she's ready to take us up."

"Up?" Emma's mouth went dry. "In the sky?"

Owen chuckled. "That's where we usually fly."

"But who's going to fly it?"

Charles pointed his thumbs at himself. "Guess I should have worn my pilot's uniform."

"*You're* the pilot?" Emma's eyes cut to Owen for confirmation. For some reason, this made Charles laugh.

Owen threw an arm over Charles's shoulder. "Don't worry. He may be a big goofball, but he's the best pilot I've ever worked with."

"Aw, I'm touched." Charles shoved Owen's shoulder, then turned to Emma. "And he's right. I'm the best."

"Sorry." Emma laughed through the nerves coiling in her stomach. "I've just never been on a plane before."

"You haven't?" everyone seemed to say at once, even the kids.

She shook her head. "I'm sort of afraid of heights." It was one of the reasons she'd added skydiving to her list in the first place. She figured if she could jump out of a plane, it would cure her fear once and for all.

"That settles it." Owen tilted his head toward the plane. "If we're ever going to get you to jump out of one of these, first we'll have to get you in one."

Emma bit her lip, but Kenzie's hand slipped into hers. "Don't worry. I'll hold your hand the whole time."

Owen grinned and raised an eyebrow as if daring her to say no to that.

Emma let out a breath. "All right." The words came out before she consciously registered making the decision. "Let's go."

They all cheered, and Charles raised an arm as if in victory.

But the moment they stepped outside, he stopped. "Where did these clouds come from?" he muttered, pulling out his phone. "I thought we had a couple of hours yet."

"I told you it was going to storm," Carter crowed, grinning at the clouds as if they were a great prize. "That's why there were stratocumulus clouds before."

"You did tell me that." Owen patted the boy's head. "I should really know to listen to you by now." He turned to Charles. "Let's get Carrie back inside."

Charles nodded, looking like a little boy who'd lost his favorite toy. He jogged inside the hangar and came back out pulling what looked like a large, low wagon without sides. He lined it up with the plane's front wheel, and Owen moved to help him fix a strap around the metal leg that attached the wheel to the plane. Once they had it in place, Charles pressed a button, and the lift pulled the planes' wheel onto a low platform. The platform hoisted the wheel off the ground, and Charles grabbed the lift's handle, pulling the plane toward the hangar.

"All right." Owen turned to Emma and the kids. "Let's get home before the storm hits."

Emma's head snapped to him, the word "home" rumbling against her heart harder than a roll of thunder.

Of course he hadn't meant that her house was *home* to him; just that it was where he and his family were staying right now.

But after spending the last week with them, she was starting to wish—

No. She gripped Kenzie's hand and followed Carter and Owen toward the parking lot. Being there for them right now was fine.

Wishing for more was out of the question.

Chapter 26

Thunder rattled the windows of Emma's sturdy house, and sheets of rain obscured the view outside so thoroughly that Owen couldn't even see the barn.

Emma had gone out to check on the horses the moment they got home—and now she was stuck out there.

He didn't know why that bothered him.

Emma was a grown woman—she could certainly take care of herself in a little thunderstorm.

Still, unease hung over him as he chopped onions for the tacos he'd promised to make for dinner, the same way it always did when he was separated from one of his family members during a storm. Fortunately, Claire was safe at work, and Catelyn had texted to let him know that the lifeguards had been sent home due to the weather—and by home, she meant she was going to Jackson's house. But at least she was safe.

Emma wasn't part of his family, he reminded himself.

Even if it was starting to seem like she was at times. But that was only because he saw her so often. And because she did such a good job with the kids. Not because of his own feelings.

"Daddy?" Kenzie sat at the kitchen table with a book open in front of her, but Owen could tell she hadn't read a word.

"It's okay, baby," he reassured her automatically. The poor girl had always been terrified of storms. She used to crawl in bed with him and Katie every time there was even a hint of rain, and she still often called for him in the middle of the night when it stormed.

Carter, on the other hand, couldn't get enough of storms. Thunder was the one loud sound that he not only tolerated, but sought out. Owen chalked that up to Katie's brilliance in getting him interested in weather at such a young age.

At the moment, the boy was in the living room, watching the storm out the big picture windows, and Cody was upstairs, probably oblivious to the storm.

Poor Lexi, who felt the same way as Kenzie about storms, shivered under the kitchen table.

"Maybe you should check on Miss Emma." Kenzie's brow furrowed, and her voice shook a little.

"I'm sure she's fine." Owen kept his response carefully worry-free.

He slid the onions aside and turned to stir the meat browning on the stove.

He glanced out the window just in time for a blinding flash of lightning to split the sky. At the same time, a deafening crack of thunder exploded, and the room went black.

"Daddy," Kenzie's plaintive voice cried.

"I'm still here," Owen called back. "Just stay put, and I'll come to you." He had left his phone in the other room, so he didn't have a flashlight, but the frequent flashes of lightning were enough to allow him to stumble toward the table.

"Carter, you okay?" he called in the direction of the living room.

"This is so cool," Carter called back. "The trees are bending."

Kenzie whimpered, and Owen rested a hand on her shoulder.

"Hey, Dad, I think the power is out," Cody called from upstairs.

"You think so?" Owen called back with a laugh. "Do you have your phone on you?"

"Yeah. Why?"

"Mine's in the other room, and we could use some light down here."

"Oh, sure." Footsteps ran down the steps, and Cody appeared in a pool of light. "Something smells good."

"Don't get too excited." Owen grabbed his son's phone and angled it at the stove. "This is only half cooked."

Cody groaned. "I'm starved. Coach worked us hard today."

"We'll figure something out," Owen reassured his son. "I haven't let you starve yet."

He glanced toward the window, squinting through the slashes of rain. A flash of lightning illuminated the barn, and Owen thought he caught movement near the door. He waited a beat for another flash, and this time he was sure—a figure was darting toward the house.

"What is she doing?" Owen let go of Kenzie and rushed to the door, yanking it open and stepping out onto the porch.

"Daddy!" Kenzie called.

"My phone," Cody cried.

"Cody, stay with your sister," Owen ordered as chill air swallowed him. It must have dropped twenty degrees since they got back. He peered into the dark, waiting for another flash of lightning. Emma's form glowed from the middle of it. She was halfway to the house, and he debated running down to meet her.

But what was he going to do? Scoop her up and carry her to the house?

He strode to the edge of the porch. The wind drove pellets of cold rain into him.

"What are you doing?" he called, but a fresh roar of thunder covered his words.

It seemed to take forever before Emma reached the porch and raced up the steps, nearly mowing him down.

He caught her arms, and her head snapped up. Her mouth had formed into an O, as if she were about to scream, but instead she let out a breath with a short laugh.

"What are you doing?" Her words came in rough heaves, and water streamed from her plastered hair onto her face.

"Me?" Owen gestured to the yard. "What are *you* doing?" He still had her other arm in his hand, and he led her toward the house, shining the light from Cody's phone ahead of them.

"Miss Emma!" Kenzie jumped out of her chair and threw herself at Emma. "We were so worried about you."

"You were?" Emma sounded surprised, and her head turned toward Owen.

He realized he was still holding her arm and let go. "Well, we weren't sure—"

"I was worried about you guys too," Emma interrupted. "I realized you probably don't know where the flashlights and candles are."

"We were fine," Owen said gruffly, waving Cody's phone. "You should have waited until the storm passed."

Emma ignored him, moving to a drawer near the refrigerator. "For future reference, there are flashlights in here." She pulled two out and switched them on, passing one to each of them.

Then she moved to the laundry room off the back of the kitchen. "Can you shine your light in here, Kenzie?" she called. Kenzie obeyed, and Owen heard rummaging for a few minutes. When she returned, she triumphantly held up two jars and a lighter.

"They're different scents, but at least they'll give us some light."

She set them on the dining room table and tried to light one, but her hands were shaking.

Concern tightened Owen's chest, and he moved closer. "You're soaked through. Go change, and I'll do this." He held the flashlight out to her and opened his palm for the lighter.

Emma tried one more time, then silently set the lighter in his hand and reached for the flashlight. But it hit the floor with a loud clatter.

"Ach, sorry." Emma bent to pick it up, but Owen was quicker. "I've got it." He held it out to her again.

This time, she reached for it slowly, as if she were concentrating all her energy on grabbing it. Her fingers brushed his as they closed around it. They were icy, and his first instinct was to warm them. "Are you all right?" His eyes met hers, but she looked away, sliding the flashlight out of his hand.

"I'm good." She sounded cheerful as usual, and her cheeks were red in the glow of the flashlight. "I'll be right back."

Owen's eyes followed the light until it disappeared. Then he turned and lit the candles.

"Come on hands, cooperate." Emma had already tried twice to unbutton her jeans, but it just wasn't happening.

Her hands were numb and tingly, rejecting every movement.

The cold had likely triggered the neuropathy. Once she warmed up a little, she'd get the feeling back in her fingers. Of course, the best way to warm up would be to get out of these wet clothes. But it wasn't like there was anyone she could ask for help. Mom wasn't home—she and William had gone to a friend's for dinner.

She supposed she could possibly ask Kenzie.

But how would she explain that she'd walked away from cancer with only some lingering neuropathy and fatigue, while the girl's mom had died from it.

No, she would deal with it.

She went into the bathroom and ran her hands under warm water. The tingling morphed into an intense burning sensation, and she pressed her lips together to keep from crying out.

When she couldn't stand it any longer, she pulled her hands out of the water and dried them. Pain still shot up and down her fingers, but at least she could feel them now.

She reached for her button again and this time managed to work it free.

She breathed out, giving her hands a moment to rest before she peeled off the wet denim. She dried her legs, then moved into her bedroom to find a new pair of pants. She scanned her jeans but decided she couldn't put herself through working a button again and chose a pair of sweatpants instead. She pulled on a hoodie and a pair of fuzzy socks, then gave her hair one more towel dry, avoiding the mirror so she wouldn't see just how atrocious her curls must look.

It didn't matter.

It wasn't like she was trying to win a beauty contest.

Or impress Owen.

Right. Exactly. She wasn't trying to impress Owen. She hurried out of her room.

"Hey, Carter," she said as she passed through the living room. "How's the storm?"

"Almost done," he answered mournfully.

"Cheer up." Emma glanced out the window, where the pitch black sky had given way to gray clouds laced with streaks of deep blue. "It looks like we're going to get some great clouds."

Carter brightened, and Emma continued to the kitchen.

"Hey." Owen looked up as she entered the room, his expression somewhere between warm and worried. "I thought maybe you fell asleep in there."

Emma shook her head. "Just trying to warm up a little."

Owen's eyes scanned her, and Emma suddenly wished she'd chosen something other than sweats.

"You look cozy," he said, and for some reason, it sounded like a compliment.

"Thanks." She touched a hand to her hair but then dropped it, reminding herself that it didn't matter. "Carter says the storm is almost over."

"But the power is still out," Kenzie said. "So we're having tacos *sans* meat for supper. Sans means without."

"That sounds tasty. And you know what, I think I have some black beans we can put on them." She moved toward the cupboard, but Owen stepped in the same direction at the same time. He caught her shoulders as they crashed into each other.

"Oh, sorry." Emma tried to dodge out of the way, but Owen still had her shoulders in his hands.

"My fault." Owen moved her gently to the side, then let go.

Emma stared at the cupboard, but she couldn't for the life of her remember what she'd been about to do.

"Beans on tacos?" Kenzie asked. "That sounds gross."

"Kenzie." Owen's voice took on a warning tone, but Emma could have hugged the girl. That was what she was doing—getting out the beans. Not standing here thinking about how she'd wanted Owen's arms to wrap her tighter.

"Oh, trust me, you'll like it," she said to Kenzie, pulling open the cupboard. The motion sent a fresh tingling through her fingertips, but she ignored it.

She wasn't short, but the cupboards in this kitchen were high, and she had to stand on her tiptoes to reach for the beans. Her fingers brushed against the can, and the tingling sensation intensified, but she closed her hand around it anyway. She slid the can to the edge of the shelf, but it slipped out of her grip and plummeted toward the ground. Without thinking, she stuck out her foot to break its fall.

Too late, she realized her mistake and yanked her foot back—just in time for the can to smash her big toe. It ricocheted from her foot to the floor with a solid clunk that was accompanied by her cry of pain.

She grabbed the counter with one hand and grasped her toes with her other hand.

"What is it?" Owen was right there, eyes filled with concern.

"Nothing," she gasped. "I'm fine." She turned away so he wouldn't see the tears that had gathered at the corners of her eyes. She swallowed them down. She'd survived much worse than this.

"You're not fine." Owen wrapped his hand around her elbow. "Cody bring that chair over here."

"No, really, I'm—"

"Sit."

Somehow the chair was there, and she couldn't resist as Owen shifted to ease her into it. "Let me see it."

Emma shook her head. If she let go of her toe, the pain would be so much worse.

"Come on." He squatted in front of her and carefully peeled her fingers back. "I'm going to take your sock off, okay?"

She nodded, biting her lip so she wouldn't hiss out loud as he slid the fluffy sock over her toe.

"Ooo." He hissed for her. "I think you definitely broke a toe or two."

Her big toe and the one next to it were already a dark black-blue. The big one was nearly twice its normal size.

"You need ice," Owen declared. He stood and moved to a drawer to pull out a sandwich bag. Emma tried not to think about how natural it felt that he knew where she kept those. He pulled open the freezer and quickly filled the bag with ice. "As long as the power comes on in the next couple of hours, we should have enough ice to get you through the night." He stepped in front of Emma but instead of handing her the ice, bent over and slid his hand behind her back. "Let's get you to the couch so you can elevate it."

"That's really not—" But he was already pulling her upwards, and Emma had no choice but to wrap her arm around his neck so she wouldn't tip over.

"Can you walk?" Owen kept his arm around her back, supporting her as she took a tentative step.

Her whole foot throbbed with the movement, and she leaned into him more than she meant to. His fresh, warm scent wrapped around her, and she tried to lean the other direction, but his arm cinched tighter around her waist.

"I'll carry you."

Kenzie giggled. "Like you did when Mommy broke her foot."

Owen's shoulders stiffened under Emma's arm, but he didn't loosen his grip on her.

"You're not going to carry me," she protested. "I'm really fine." She took a tentative step, biting down hard on her lip to keep from crying out.

"You're not fine," Owen growled. "At least lean on me and hop."

Emma wanted to protest that too, but she had to admit that it was probably the only way she was going to get to the living room.

She took a careful hop, and Owen's arm tightened around her even more, practically doing all the work for her.

"Good job," Kenzie encouraged.

By the time they reached the other side of the kitchen, Emma's foot was throbbing and her breaths came in short gasps.

"Let's take a break." Owen drew to a stop, and Emma tried to slide away to give him a break too, but he tugged her in close, so that her weight was resting against his arm.

"Did you see the— What are you doing?"

Owen swiveled at the sound of Catelyn's voice behind them, nearly knocking Emma over. She grabbed his arm with her other hand to keep from toppling.

Catelyn's eyes went between the two of them, a slight smile forming on her lips, but behind her, Claire scowled at both of them.

"Emma broke her toe," Owen answered, though Emma couldn't decide if his tone was defensive or just explanatory. "I'm helping her to the couch."

"Oh, no." Catelyn rushed across the room. "Let me help too. Put your other arm around me."

Emma obeyed, and they started toward the living room again.

When they reached the couch, Catelyn ducked out from under her arm and grabbed a couple of throw pillows while Owen took Emma's arm and lowered her to the couch. Catelyn tucked the pillows under Emma's foot, and Owen gingerly settled the ice onto her toes.

"How's that?"

"Good." She leaned back on the armrest of the couch and closed her eyes against the pulsing pain that traveled up her toes and into her foot.

"I'll get you some ibuprofen," Owen offered.

Before she could argue that she didn't need any, he was gone.

"And I'll get you some food," Catelyn added.

"No, you don't have to—"

But Catelyn was already gone too.

Emma closed her eyes, listening to the low rumble of voices in the kitchen. A knot of emotion rose in her throat. This was the sound she'd always longed to have fill her house—the sound of a family.

Chapter 27

Owen opened his eyes to a dark room, trying to figure out what had woken him.

He reached for his phone to check the time. But it had died hours ago—and the power must not have come on yet, since it was plugged in but not charging.

Footsteps creaked in the hallway, and a faint light moved under his door.

He swung his feet out of bed, grabbing his shirt and pulling it on, then strode to the door.

Someone screamed and aimed a flashlight right at his eyes, and he jumped backwards.

"Shh. It's just Dad," he whispered. "Lower your light."

It took a moment after the light was lowered for his eyes to adjust. When they did, it took another moment to process what he was seeing. Emma stood there, one hand pressed to her heart, the other gripping Kenzie's. His daughter wielded the flashlight.

"What's going on?" His gaze swiveled between them.

"Kenzie had a bad dream," Emma whispered, "and she came down to ask for a glass of water. I was just tucking her back in."

Owen looked to his daughter. "You should have come to me, Kenz."

Kenzie shook her head. "I knocked on your door, but you didn't answer."

"Oh." He couldn't deny that was likely. It had driven Katie crazy, the way he could sleep through the kids' cries when they were babies. "Well then you should have woken Catelyn or Claire up."

Kenzie shook her head. "When I was little and I had nightmares, I always went to Mom."

Owen sucked in a breath. "Sweetheart, Miss Emma isn't—"

"I know," Kenzie interrupted. "But she says the same kinds of things Mom always said. About how God protects us. She even said the same prayer with me as Mom always did. I taught it to her."

"Kenz . . ." Owen had no idea what to say to that. He agreed that Emma was like Katie in some ways. But that didn't mean . . .

"It's okay," Emma said, lifting her eyes to his. "I was still awake anyway."

Owen glanced over his shoulder to the inky window. "What time is it?"

"Two a.m." Emma moved her hand from her heart to the wall, bracing herself against it, and Owen suddenly remembered her broken toe.

"You shouldn't be walking around on that foot," he scolded. "Let me tuck Kenzie back in, and then I'll help you down the stairs."

Emma shook her head. "That's okay. I'm—"

"Can Miss Emma tuck me in?" Kenzie asked quietly.

Emma's eyes came to his, the question in them clear even in the dark.

He blew out a breath. He supposed he could understand why Kenzie would want that—and yet, he couldn't really let her start thinking their living situation with Emma was a permanent thing.

"I guess that's fine," he finally answered. "If Miss Emma feels up to it."

Emma studied him a moment longer, as if trying to read his expression, then nodded slowly. "Sure, Kenzie. I can tuck you in."

"I'll wait here," Owen said. "So I can help you down the stairs when you're done."

"You don't have to—"

But Owen crossed his arms, and she cut off.

Using the wall for support, she limped alongside Kenzie to the bedroom, setting a hand lightly on the girl's shoulder as they disappeared through the door.

A strange feeling jabbed at Owen's middle, and he ran his hands over his face. Did Kenzie see Emma as a stand-in for her mom?

Worse . . . Did he?

Owen shook his head against the thought. It wasn't that he saw Emma as a new mom for the kids—it was that he'd relied too much on her help lately. He had to stop doing that. And get serious about finding somewhere else to live. Before Kenzie—or anyone else, including himself—got too attached.

"You're still out here." Emma hobbled into the hallway, her whisper not sounding surprised in the least.

"I told you I would be."

She took another limping step, trying to hide a grimace.

"Come on." He moved to her side, but after the turn his thoughts had been taking, he suddenly found it awkward to put his arm around her. Still, he couldn't make her navigate the steps on her own.

Carefully, he slid his arm around her back, trying not to notice the subtle summery scent of her shampoo. She braced a stiff arm over his shoulders, and they made their way silently down the steps.

At the bottom, she started to pull away, but he held her close and kept walking. If he was going to help her, he might as well help her all the way.

When they reached the door to her bedroom, Owen unwrapped her arm from around his neck and leaned her against the door frame.

"Thanks." Her voice was barely a whisper.

"Thank you," Owen whispered back. "For taking care of Kenzie."

"Of course." Emma turned toward her room.

"About what she said." Owen forced the words out. "About her mom and . . . you. She didn't mean— She wasn't trying to—" He floundered.

"I know," Emma said quietly. "She said her dream was about her mom, so I'm sure that's why . . ."

"Yeah . . ." Owen blinked at her. Moonlight from the windows on the other side of the room lit her curls, making them shine like a halo.

He couldn't help a soft laugh. Emma gave him a quizzical look.

"Sorry. Apparently Charles was right. You *do* have a halo."

He pointed to her head, and she laughed but smoothed her hair.

Owen suddenly wondered if it felt as silky as it looked.

He jammed his hands in his pockets. "Well, goodnight."

"Goodnight," Emma whispered. "See you in the morning."

Owen nodded, wishing he didn't like the sound of that quite so much.

Chapter 28

Emma searched her closet, looking for a pair of shoes that would fit her still-swollen toe.

From the kitchen, she could hear Owen and the kids and Mom and William all finishing breakfast.

Fortunately, the power had come back on shortly after she'd returned to bed from tucking Kenzie in.

She'd still been awake, Kenzie's remark about going to her mom when she had a nightmare playing over and over in her head.

She knew Owen was right that Kenzie hadn't meant anything by it, but...

A knock on her bedroom door made her jump.

"Are you ready?" Mom's voice was filled with a smile, and Emma could tell she enjoyed having Owen and his family here as much as she did. Maybe more.

After all, Mom had always wanted a whole troop of grandchildren to spoil.

They're not her grandchildren, she reminded herself. Or your children.

Although if she'd ever had children, she'd want them to be an awful lot like Owen's.

She shook off the ridiculous line of her thoughts and grabbed a pair of sandals. But the moment she attempted to slide one onto her left foot, she recoiled with a whimper. If those didn't work, she didn't know what would.

Her eyes fell on her slippers. She would look ridiculous, but at this point, it was either that or go barefoot. She eased one onto her injured foot, then slipped a black flat onto the other and turned to the full-length mirror.

Well, her feet looked comical. But her flowy sleeveless blue shirt and white linen pants looked decent. And her hair had even almost cooperated for once.

She limped toward the door. The pain wasn't quite as overwhelming this morning, but the dull throb intensified every time she took a step.

When she finally reached the kitchen, she found a riot of glorious chaos as kids and adults scurried around the room, putting on shoes, filling water bottles, crashing into each other.

Kenzie was the first to notice her feet. "You're wearing a slipper." The girl giggled.

"It's wet outside." Owen frowned. "Your slipper will get soaked."

Emma shrugged. "I couldn't find any shoes that fit over my toe."

"Hold on a sec." Owen disappeared up the steps.

"William is pulling the car up," Mom said. "So you don't have to walk as far."

"That's sweet of him."

"Well, he's a sweet guy," Mom replied with the same glow she seemed to have worn since her wedding day. It was a look Emma would never tire of seeing, especially after Mom had spent so many years on her own after Dad's death. She'd never expected to get remarried. And then she'd met William and "God changed my mind," as she liked to say.

Emma wondered, if Owen ever remarried, would the sorrow etched on his face be replaced by a glow too?

"Here. Try this." Owen reappeared in front of her, holding out a man's shoe that looked about five sizes too big for her.

"That will look even sillier than the slipper."

"It will keep your foot dry, won't it?"

Emma couldn't deny that, but that didn't mean she could show up at church this morning wearing his shoe.

"But it's brand-new," she protested. The new shoes he'd ordered for the whole family had arrived just yesterday.

"Either try the shoe or I'll carry you to the car," Owen half-growled.

Emma didn't doubt that, but she looked to Mom for backup.

Mom only smiled and said, "It will make a fashion statement."

Emma rolled her eyes and looked at the kids. Kenzie grinned widely, and Catelyn watched her dad with a slight smile. Cody nodded—shoveling a handful of granola into his mouth, and Carter said, "It's going to rain some more."

The only kid who probably would have taken Emma's side was Claire, who glowered at her from the other side of the room. Emma didn't quite have the courage to ask her for help.

"Fine," she sighed. "I'll try it." She reached for the shoe. and set it on the floor, carefully sliding her foot out of the slipper. Gingerly, she eased it into the shoe. It definitely didn't press on her toes—there was probably enough room to fit her whole other foot in here too. She tied it tightly so it wouldn't fall off, then stood and took a tentative step.

"Will that work?" Owen asked.

"I look like a clown, but yeah, I think it will work."

"I bet no one will even notice." Owen rolled up the slightly too-short sleeves of his dress shirt.

"Ha." Clearly he didn't know her friends—or Ruby—very well. "You willing to put money on that?"

"Better." The edge of Owen's lip crept upward. "I bet the dishes."

Emma laughed. "You're on." She almost hoped she lost, since he hadn't actually let her or Mom or William do the dishes once in the past week.

Owen held out a hand, and Emma set hers into it, expecting a quick handshake to seal the deal. Instead, his warm fingers wrapped fully around hers, and he tugged her to her feet.

"Oh." The unexpected movement pulled her off balance, and his other hand cupped her elbow to steady her.

"Thanks." Her gasp was much too breathless, and she was acutely aware of all the eyes on them.

"We should get going," she said briskly, sliding her hand out of his and starting for the door, nearly tripping over her own foot in the process.

This time it was Mom who caught her. "Owen, maybe you'd better help her."

Emma stabbed a look at her mother, but Mom blinked innocently.

Owen reappeared next to her, and she tried to prepare herself for the feel of his arm around her waist. But this time he simply took her arm and bent his under it to support her. His fresh, cottony scent toyed with her senses, and she had to concentrate hard on not leaning closer to pull in a deep breath.

Fortunately, once they stepped outside, the earthy scent left behind by last night's rain overpowered everything else.

Owen led her to the edge of the porch, murmuring, "Careful," as she took the first step.

For some reason, the word brought an ache to her chest. Mom had probably told her a thousand times to be careful on these steps after her hysterectomy, and mostly that had only annoyed her. But the way Owen said it—somehow, it felt different. Or it made *her* feel different.

She ignored the feeling and sped her walk to the car William had pulled up as close to the bottom step as possible without driving in the water-logged grass. Owen easily kept pace with her.

He opened the back passenger door and probably would have helped her in too, but she said, "I'm good. Thanks."

He silently nodded but didn't move away. She ducked into the car.

"See you at church." With a quick smile, Owen closed her door, then led his kids to their van.

Emma swallowed back a sigh.

"I'm getting very fond of that family," Mom said brightly as William turned the car toward the road. From the van, Kenzie waved wildly at them, and Mom, Emma, and William all waved back.

"Me too," William replied. "Owen was saying that the contractors think repairs on their house will take six to eight weeks. I hope you don't mind, but I told him they're more than welcome to stay until it's all done." He turned his head a little to look over his shoulder at Emma.

"Of course not." Emma tried to sound businesslike and indifferent, but she was afraid Mom and William could hear the smile in her voice just as well as she could.

Chapter 29

Owen parked the van and hurried the kids out of it. William had dropped off Emma and her mom at the church doors, and Owen wanted to get over there to help Emma inside. She should stay off that foot as much as possible.

But before they were halfway to the doors, James and Ruby appeared next to Emma. They talked for a moment, and Owen could tell exactly when Ruby noticed Emma's mismatched shoes. James looked down and frowned. Emma said something that made his frown deepen, and then he took her arm to help her inside. Owen told himself that the feeling in his chest was relief.

"Hurry up." Kenzie pulled his hand. "I want to sit by Miss Emma."

"I don't," Claire muttered.

Owen shot her a look, but they had reached the church doors, so he didn't say anything. She'd been less than gracious to their hostess all week, though, and Owen would have to have a talk with her about that later.

Cody pulled the door open and held it for his siblings and Owen.

"Thanks, Cody." Owen reached to ruffle his son's hair, but Cody ducked out of the way with a muttered, "Dad."

Inside, Kenzie made a beeline across the lobby, straight for Ruby and Emma and James, who were disappearing into the sanctuary.

"Kenz," Owen whispered, tugging her hand to slow her down. "Maybe we should let them sit by themselves, as a family. Anne and William will probably want to sit with them too."

Just then, Emma glanced over her shoulder, her smile hitting Owen right in the chest, even though she was looking at Kenzie. "Are you guys going to sit with us?"

Kenzie tossed an I-told-you-so look at Owen, and he sighed. James entered an empty row, Ruby right behind him, then Kenzie, and then Emma. Owen didn't want to subject her to Carter's nonstop talking again, so he filed in after her.

The moment he sat down, the heaviness of everything that had happened in the past week seemed to bear down on him. He dropped forward to rest his elbows on his knees, bracing his forehead with his fists.

Had it only been last week that he'd sat here and felt like he was finally rediscovering the joy of his salvation? While his house had probably been burning that very moment.

"Good morning." Pastor Dan's warm greeting rang across the church, and Owen forced himself to sit upright.

"Are you okay?" Emma's whisper was barely audible over the music Nate's worship band had begun to play, but Owen nodded and reached for a hymnal.

He tried to focus on the service, but whenever Carter wasn't whispering to him, his mind wandered from his giant to-do list for the drop zone to the things he needed to remember to tell the contractors working on the house to the woman sitting next to him, who had opened her house to them. He let himself dwell on that one least of all.

"Have you ever gotten a bruise?" Pastor Dan's question grabbed Owen's attention, and he was startled to realize it was already time for the sermon.

Emma's soft laugh pulled Owen's gaze in her direction. Kenzie was whispering something, and Emma's head was lowered toward her. She grinned at Kenzie and wiggled her foot, clad in his shoe.

He lasered his attention back to Dan.

"And you know, when you have a bruise and you hit that spot again." Dan hissed and made a face. "It hurts that much worse, right?" The pastor paced in front of a small podium. "Sometimes life can leave us bruised, can't it?"

A puff of assent escaped Owen's lungs. Life had left him more than bruised lately. It had left him trampled.

"And somehow, those bruised spots get hit over and over again," Dan continued. "Until we don't think we can take anymore."

Owen swallowed around the rough lump in his throat. That was exactly how he felt.

"So what do we do with a verse like Isaiah 42:3? 'A bruised reed he will not break, and a smoldering wick he will not snuff out'?" Dan asked. "When we feel like we're about to break? When we feel like our faith is on the brink of being snuffed out?"

Owen clasped his hands in his lap. Because he really had no idea what the answer was anymore. Once upon a time, he would have said, just trust in the Lord. But after all he'd been through, that felt almost impossible these days.

"It would be easy for me to stand up here and tell you that when that happens, all you have to do is trust in the Lord." Dan echoed Owen's thoughts, and Owen couldn't help but feel let down. How was he supposed to do that?

"And that's true," Dan continued. "And biblical." He flipped open the Bible in his hand and looked down at its pages. "Psalm 20:7: 'Some trust in chariots and some in horses, but we trust in the name of the Lord our

God.'" He turned a few pages. "Psalm 28:7: 'The Lord is my strength and my shield; my heart trusts in him, and he helps me.' Psalm 37:5: 'Commit your way to the Lord; trust in him.'"

Dan looked up as his fingers flipped the pages ahead. He didn't even look down as he recited, "Proverbs 3:5: 'Trust in the Lord with all your heart and lean not on your own understanding.'"

Owen sucked in a breath. That verse—Katie's verse—seemed to follow him wherever he went lately. Katie would tell him that was because God knew he needed to hear it.

Dan closed the Bible and looked up. "Those are great verses. Comforting. All we have to do is trust. Piece of cake." His voice was thick with sarcasm, and he shook his head. "I don't know about you, but many a time I've wondered *how*. How can we put our trust in the Lord when everything around us seems to be falling apart? When it seems like we've lost control—or worse, like *he's* lost control?" Dan paused and scanned the congregation, and Owen leaned forward. *That* was the question he needed the answer to.

"Actually, let's take it back a step further," Dan said. "What does it even mean to trust in the Lord?"

Dan gave the question a moment to sink in, and Owen pondered it. Once upon a time, he'd thought he knew the answer, but after everything his family had been through, he wasn't so sure anymore.

"Let me put it another way," Dan said. "Is our faith in God a blind faith? A sort of wishful thinking or a hoping for the best? Or is it a faith based on something solid and secure? Something unshakable?"

Those were more questions Owen wasn't sure he knew the answer to anymore.

"Maybe the easiest way to come at those questions is to look at someone in Scripture who often showed extraordinary trust in the Lord," Dan said.

"And other times, he—well, let's just say he failed pretty hard. You know who I mean, right? Your favorite disciple and mine: Peter. I mean, this guy—" Dan shook his head in wonder. "When Jesus came to him and said, 'Hey, Peter, come, follow me, Peter didn't even think twice. He dropped his fishing net and became a fisher of men."

"And then later," Dan continued, "when Jesus asked the disciples if they understood who exactly Jesus was, Peter's answer was immediate and certain: 'You are the Messiah.'"

Dan scanned the room. "That's some pretty strong trust, isn't it? So maybe it's not all that surprising when Peter and the disciples are out on the Sea of Galilee in the middle of the night and they see Jesus walking toward them on the water and Peter cries out, 'Hey, Lord, should I join you out there?'"

Dan gave an incredulous laugh. "I mean, come on. That takes some *trust*. I'm pretty sure it wouldn't have been my first response. I'd have been like, 'Jesus, what are you doing? Get in the boat. People can't walk on water.'" The congregation laughed, and Owen gave in to a smile. He may be willing to jump from a plane, but even *he* wouldn't try to walk on water.

"So anyway," Dan continued. "Jesus invites Peter to come out to him, and Peter doesn't even hesitate. He throws his feet over the side of the boat, and *he does it*. He stands on water. I feel like sometimes we skip too quickly over this part. Because we all know what comes next. But let's just hang out with Peter on top of the water for a second. Imagine what that was like. Doing something he knew was impossible for him to do on his own. Something he knew had to be the work of God. I mean, he must have just been in awe of Jesus' power. He must have wanted to stay there forever. He must have thought he would never doubt the Lord again." Dan paused, and Owen felt the sting of his words. He'd thought the same thing just last week.

"But then we move on to the next sentence." Dan's voice was low as he read, "But when he saw the wind, he was afraid and, beginning to sink, cried out, 'Lord, save me!'"

Dan shook his head. "Oh Peter, Peter, Peter." He chuckled. "Not that I have a right to judge, since I've already admitted that I wouldn't have gotten out of the boat in the first place. But Peter *did* get out of the boat. He *did* walk on water. He *did* see Jesus' power firsthand. So what happened? Why did he sink?"

Next to him, Owen felt Emma shift, and his eyes went to her. She was leaning forward, listening intently, as if she needed the answer to the question as badly as Owen did.

"The answer is easy," Dan was saying. "Peter sank because he looked down and he saw the wind, he saw the waves, he remembered that people aren't really built to stand on top of the water. In other words, he took his trust off the Lord and leaned on his own understanding."

Dan's eyes scanned the congregation. "And who of us wouldn't do the same, when what we *see* contradicts what we *believe*? When the problems of this world seem so much larger, so much stronger, than even the God who made someone walk on water." Dan moved toward their side of the church. "What do you see in front of you right now? Bills? Grief? Loss?"

Owen swallowed. Yes. Yes. And yes. He saw all of those all around him.

"Do those things seem bigger than the One who stands in front of you, promising to hold you up under them?"

Owen had to admit that sometimes they did.

"You're not alone," Dan said gently. "Look what happened to Peter. He thought the wind and the waves were bigger than Jesus, and he started to sink. But even here, we can see his trust. Because he didn't start flailing his arms and trying to figure out how to keep himself afloat. Instead, he cried, 'Lord, save me!'"

Dan paused, apparently contemplating the words. "Now, there are a lot of things Peter could have said here. Like, 'Lord, how could you let me fall?' Or, 'What are you doing, Lord?' Or even, 'Why did you tell me to get out of the boat?' But instead, Peter, in trust, cried out, 'Lord, save me!'"

Dan's eyes traveled over their row. "Was Peter right to put his trust in God?"

"Yes," Carter said out loud, though his eyes were still on his book.

"That's right." Dan smiled at the boy, and laughter rippled through the congregation. Owen's lips lifted too. It always amazed him how much Carter picked up.

Dan looked down at his Bible and read, "Immediately Jesus reached out his hand and caught him." The pastor looked up and shook his head. "That word gets me every time. *Immediately*. Jesus didn't make Peter wait. He didn't say, 'I'm going to teach you a lesson and let you sink a little.' No. He reached out his hand and *immediately* rescued Peter. He didn't let his disciple drown. And he won't let us drown either."

Dan paced to the far side of the sanctuary. "So *how* do we trust in the Lord? We cry out to him. It may not feel like it, but that's an act of trust. That's saying, 'God, I can't handle this on my own. But I know you can.' And we *do* know he can. Because he has shown us. He has shown us in his Word, like in this account with Peter. And he has shown us in our lives. I know I could ask each one of you, and you could tell me about a time in your life when you didn't think you could handle all that you faced, but God saw you through it."

Out of the corner of his eye, Owen caught Emma nodding, and he nodded internally too. He wouldn't have gotten through those weeks after Katie's death without the Lord.

"Paul tells us in 2 Corinthians 5:7 that 'we live by faith, not by sight.' That doesn't mean our faith is blind. It means that we know the One our faith is founded on and that no matter what things look like around us, we know that he is in control. We seek him in his Word, we turn to him in prayer. We remember all the ways he has been faithful in the past. And we trust that he will be faithful forever. The writer to the Hebrews reminds us that 'faith is confidence in what we hope for and assurance about what we do not see.' The hope he's talking about here isn't a wishful kind of hope, like 'I hope the Packers go to the Super Bowl this year.' As much as we might love our team, there's no guarantee that particular hope will be realized. But the hope we have in Jesus, that's a certainty. There are no questions. He hasn't failed to keep a single one of his promises. He proved that on the cross, where he died for every one of our sins—including the many times we, like Peter, have failed to trust in him."

He moved to the podium and braced his arms against it. "So what do we do when we're feeling bruised and battered and broken and like we can't take one more thing? The answer is simple. 'Trust in the Lord with all your heart and lean not on your own understanding.' Amen."

Owen let out a breath as he stood with the rest of the congregation and bowed his head for prayer. Dan's words washed over him, but Owen found himself forming his own prayer. *Lead me to trust in you and lean not on my own understanding, Lord. Give me confidence in what I hope for and certainty in what I do not see.*

Something brushed his arm, and he glanced to his side.

"Sorry," Emma whispered, her head still bowed, one of her hands wrapped around Kenzie's.

Owen dropped his chin and added: *A little certainty about what I do see would be helpful too.*

Chapter 30

Emma slipped silently out the door, her Bible and journal tucked in her arm, anticipation tickling her insides. This was her favorite time of day—just her, God, and the sunrise. She wondered what colors the Master Painter would use today.

The porch floor was warm and damp under Emma's bare feet, and she limped to the set of rocking chairs at the far end of it. She'd felt foolish, when she'd commissioned them from Spencer, asking for two. At the time, she'd hoped that maybe she'd sit out here with her husband one day. Although that had never happened, the second chair had been occupied by nearly every one of her friends over the years, and Emma was glad she'd invested in it.

She eased herself into the chair closest to the door, sighing as the throbbing in her toe eased. It was definitely better than it had been yesterday, but it would probably be a few days before she could walk normally—or wear her boots. She'd have to ask Owen if she could borrow his shoe again today.

She flipped her prayer journal open and watched the sky as she brought her requests to the Lord. She prayed for a woman from church who was having surgery, for Jared and Peyton, who were starting the process for a second international adoption, for Bethany, who hadn't been in church yesterday because her morning sickness had gotten so severe, for her new little niece or nephew.

As she prayed, the tufted clouds transformed from gray to pink to gold. Birds sang their wake-up songs, and a cherry blossom breeze stirred against her bare arms. She sighed with contentment and added a prayer for Catelyn and Jackson's budding relationship.

A low creak cut through her thoughts, and she looked over to the door in surprise—usually she had an hour or so before anyone else got up.

"Hello?" she called softly.

"Hi." Owen's head poked around the door, his lips lifted in a sheepish smile that made her heart roll. "I hope I'm not— I don't want to— Wow." Owen's eyes went past her to the sky. The clouds had broken up into long streaks so that now they looked like rivers of molten gold flowing toward the horizon.

The view seemed to compel Owen out the door.

"I told you it was worth getting up for." She'd mentioned it last night when they were working on the puzzle, and he'd asked how she got up so early after staying up so late.

His eyes came to hers. "Totally worth it."

She swallowed, noticing the book under his arm. "Your Bible?"

He nodded. "Dan and Jade gave it to me after the fire. Said they had plenty of extras."

Emma laughed. "That's for sure. They have a whole bookshelf of them in their house." She gestured to the rocking chair next to her.

Owen eyed it, as if not sure he should sit.

"You can have this one instead if you want." She made as if to get up.

"Stay there," he ordered, his voice firm but amused as he moved past her to the other chair. "How's the toe?"

Emma lifted her foot to examine it. "A little better, but I think I may need to borrow your shoe for another day or two if you don't mind." It suddenly felt like a strangely intimate request, and she wanted to take it back.

But Owen chuckled. "Considering that I'm borrowing your house, I think that would probably be okay. I still have the ones Cam gave me."

They sat silently for a bit, and Emma finished her prayers, then opened her Bible. After a moment, Owen opened his too.

Emma tried to tune out the fact that it was her and God and Owen out here and focus on the words of Ephesians 5. She pulled out a highlighter when she came to verse 20: "Always giving thanks to God the Father for everything, in the name of our Lord Jesus Christ."

Owen glanced over. "Can I borrow that?"

She passed it to him. "It's purple."

He shrugged and slid it over the page, a look of concentration on his face.

Emma found herself wanting to know what verse he was highlighting, but it felt too personal to ask.

"Thanks." Owen passed the highlighter back without looking up, his fingers skimming hers as she grabbed it.

She ignored the tingle in her fingertips and forced her attention back to the page. But she'd reached the section of Ephesians 5 dedicated to husbands and wives. Verse 25 had already been highlighted—and underlined. "Husbands, love your wives, just as Christ loved the church and gave himself up for her." Years ago, she'd written in the margin, "The kind of husband I want!"

Her eyes strayed to Owen as he turned the page of his Bible. Of all the people who had ever sat in that chair, he was the only one who even offered a possibility of fulfilling the purpose for which she'd bought it.

As if he felt her eyes on him, Owen lifted his head, and Emma jumped out of her seat.

"All done?" Owen sounded surprised—rightly so, since she usually read a few chapters, and today she hadn't even finished one.

"Uh, yeah, I just remembered I have to . . ." She gestured toward the stables, hoping his mind would fill in something plausible since hers didn't seem able to. She limp-scurried toward the door.

When she reached it, she dared a glance over her shoulder. Owen was still reading his Bible, still sitting in the second rocking chair, still looking like that spot was made just for him.

And her heart was still galloping in a wild longing for something that could never be.

Chapter 31

"It's good to see you smiling, partner." Charles strode into the rigging room, where Owen was inspecting the canopies, then folding and packing them into the containers. From the other side of the building, he could hear the contractors refinishing the floors.

"Am I?" Owen kept his focus on the long white strands of the brake lines, separating them with his fingers to ensure they weren't tangled, then draping them over his shoulder so that the canopy hung at his side.

"Come on, don't play coy with me."

Owen snorted and lifted his head. "I'm not playing coy. Who even uses that word?"

Charles picked up a container Owen had already packed and examined it. "Nice. And I do, when my friend acts like everything is business as usual, even though he's grinning like a fool."

Owen rolled his eyes. "I'm not grinning like a fool." He stretched his lips into a flat line just to make sure. "I'm just feeling the tiniest bit better about everything, that's all."

"Mmm hmm." Charles looked exuberant. "And why is that, I wonder?"

Owen shrugged, shaking out the fabric of the canopy. "We have the rigs. The floors are getting done. It feels like things are starting to come together."

"Anything else?" Charles crossed his arms, but his eyes glinted with mirth.

"I don't know. I guess we went to church yesterday, and that was good. The sermon was exactly what I needed to hear."

"That's good." Charles's eyes still glinted, but his nod was serious. Owen knew his friend had found a church on the other side of the peninsula, closer to where he lived.

"And I read my Bible this morning," he continued, grabbing the front end of the canopy and pinching it between his knees. "First time in a while."

"Also good." Charles scrutinized him. "But can you honestly tell me that not even the tiniest slice of your smile has to do with a certain someone whose name begins with Em- and ends with -ma?"

Owen rejected the idea with a sharp headshake and focused on flaking the canopy—separating the fabric of each cell so that the chute would open properly when deployed. "Of course not." Good thing he hadn't mentioned that his Bible reading had been with Emma at his side—he still wasn't sure what had possessed him to join her on the porch this morning, but he was glad he'd done it. The company had been nice.

"Really?" Charles moved closer, but Owen's attention remained deliberately on his task.

"Really." He kept his voice even.

"So you wouldn't mind if I asked her out?" Charles's question yanked Owen's chin up.

His friend stared him down as if daring Owen to call his bluff.

"Be my guest," Owen said defiantly, ignoring the hardening in his gut. "I'm not sure she's exactly your type, but . . ."

"Oh?" Charles cocked an eyebrow. "And what type is she?"

Owen shook his head. He wasn't going to fall for that one. He'd start listing Emma's good qualities, and Charles would use that as proof that Owen liked her.

He grabbed the slider and tucked it into the canopy. This small, rectangular piece of fabric would control air flow through the chute at opening. Owen had always marveled at how such a small component could be so critical.

"Just, you know, don't . . ." he mumbled.

"Yes?" Charles leaned closer. "Don't what?"

"Don't screw it up." Owen met his friend's eyes.

Charles let out a stream of air. "So you're really going to let me go through with it?" He suddenly sounded uncertain. "Do you think *I'm* her type?"

Owen peered at his friend. Charles was never uncertain when it came to women. Unless . . . Maybe he wasn't bluffing. Maybe he really did want to go out with Emma, and he was just prodding Owen to test whether it would affect their friendship.

"I really couldn't tell you what her type is." He pulled his gaze off Charles and bent to grab the canopy's tail. He pulled it up, wrapping it around the bundle of fabric in his hand.

"But you could find out." Charles sounded eager.

Owen snickered. "What are we, in grade school?"

"No." Charles didn't sound embarrassed in the least. "We're two friends who want the best for each other. Who would do anything for each other." He put a heavy emphasis on the word *anything*.

Owen let out a breath and carefully laid the folded canopy on the ground, then dropped to his knees next to it. It was true that he'd do anything for Charles—so why not this?

He leaned his forearm onto the canopy to push out the air, telling himself the reason for his resistance was that he'd look like a fool asking.

But he'd willingly been a fool for Charles more than once in the past.

"Listen, man, all you have to do is say the word, and I'll back off." Charles's teasing tone from earlier was gone. "I honestly think the two of you—"

"I told you, I'm not interested," Owen said flatly. "In anyone."

"Owen." Charles squatted next to him as Owen worked the canopy into a tight bundle. "I saw the light in your eyes for the first time in a long time the other day when she was here with you. And that's okay. It's good."

"It's your imagination. I'll ask her for you."

Charles waved off the idea. "Forget about it. That was just me trying to get to you. Clearly psychology is not my calling." He patted Owen's shoulder and used it to push himself to his feet. "Flying, however, is. I hope the reason you're preparing that rig is for a jump. I want to work out some trajectories."

"Yeah." Owen grabbed the parachute bag from the floor next to him and pushed the folded canopy into it. "I'll be there in a couple of minutes." He kept his head down, concentrating on stowing the lines as his friend's footsteps retreated.

When he was done, he sat staring at the rig. Why did it bother him so much, the thought of Emma and Charles together?

Because he knew Charles's reputation with women, that was all. He didn't want to see Emma get hurt.

That didn't mean he wanted to date her himself.

Satisfied, he jumped to his feet, snatching up the packed bags. He grabbed a rig, already packed with a reserve chute, and shoved the parachute bag into it, methodically going through each step to secure it.

But even the work couldn't set him free from thoughts of Emma.

He pulled on his harness and strapped it up. He'd just have to hope that a jump from 15,000 feet above the ground would help him forget everything else.

Chapter 32

"Great job tonight." Emma held open the arena gate to dismiss her students, holding out a hand for fist bumps. Kenzie and Carter were the last ones out, and they stuck next to her as Owen made his way from the bleachers, where he'd grabbed a seat halfway through the lesson.

"Sorry I was late." His apologetic smile traveled from his children to Emma. Her heart sped up just a little, so that it was halfway between a walk and a canter. She knelt and busied herself unfastening Carter's helmet.

"It's okay, Daddy," Kenzie replied for her. "Miss Emma got us ready."

"I know." Emma felt his eyes on her. "Thank you."

She shrugged and stood, handing him the helmet. "It's not like it was out of my way."

Owen's chuckle seemed to warm the barn. "No, I suppose not. But I'm still going to make it up to you with some teriyaki chicken. You have soy sauce, right?"

"Um yeah, we—uh, I—should have some." She cleared her throat. "But I'm sorry I can't stay. I have to clean up and then head straight to a meeting at church for the anniversary committee."

"You mean you won't be home for family devotion?" Kenzie cried.

"Kenz." Owen's voice held a low warning. "Miss Emma has a lot going on. She's nice enough to let us stay in her house, but that doesn't mean—"

"You promised," Kenzie interrupted, stabbing Emma with a hurt look. "The other day you couldn't because you had shut-in visits, and yesterday you couldn't because you had Bible study, and you promised you would soon."

"I know," Emma answered gently before Owen could reprimand his daughter again. "And I will. But I have to go to this meeting tonight. A lot of people are depending on me, okay?"

Kenzie nodded sullenly. "Will you be home before I go to bed?"

"Kenz." Owen sounded completely exasperated. "Miss Emma doesn't have to—"

"I might be," Emma interrupted. "I'll try."

"Can I hug you now, just in case?"

"Of course." Emma held out her arms to the girl, swallowing down the hard ache of emotion that grew at the back of her throat.

When Kenzie pulled away, Carter waved, and Owen gave her a look she didn't know how to interpret but that sent her heart back into canter-mode. He shepherded his children to the door, and Emma watched out the window as they ambled across her yard toward the house. Her heart still throbbed from the force of Kenzie's hug, and somewhere deep down inside, she wished this could be her view forever.

"So . . ." Kayla's drawn-out syllable pulled Emma's attention off the window. Her friend sat in her wheelchair, which was tipped back with its front wheels in the air so she could better maneuver the sandy floor of the arena. "How are things going with Owen and the kids?"

"Fine," Emma answered brusquely. "The kids seem to be settling in well. Except for Claire, but Owen says that's pretty normal for her." Even after a week and a half of living in the same house, the girl had barely spoken a dozen words to Emma. But Emma tried not to take it personally, since Claire hadn't spoken a total of a hundred words to everyone combined.

"Oh, and—" She felt herself warming to the topic. "I was talking to Leah the other day, and she said Jackson is head over heels for Catelyn. As far as

I can tell, she feels the same way." Emma walk-hobbled across the arena. She'd finally been able to get her foot into her boot today, but after a full day on her feet, her toe was starting to throb again.

Kayla wheeled alongside her. "And what about Owen?"

That stupid thought she'd had the other day on the rocking chair came back to her, but she shoved it out. "He's fine too. A little stressed maybe, but I've been trying to— What?"

Kayla had stopped and lowered her front wheels to the ground. She wore an expression Emma could only describe as Cheshire Cat. "You are so cute. And either dense or oblivious."

Emma rolled her eyes and resumed her limping walk. "Don't start."

"Start what?" Kayla feigned innocence as she kicked her wheels back and rolled toward Emma again.

Emma didn't slow down. Her friend won wheelchair marathons, so if Emma wanted to escape this conversation, she was going to need a head start.

"Why won't you even talk about it?" Kayla had already caught up.

"Because it's ridiculous," Emma huffed.

"That a single man and a single woman might be interested in each other," Kayla teased. "Yes, absolutely preposterous."

"Widower," Emma corrected quietly.

"What?"

Emma stopped walking and turned to her friend, who stopped her wheelchair as well.

"He's not single, he's a widower," Emma repeated.

Kayla's brow wrinkled. "Yes, true, but—"

"His wife died of cancer, Kayla." Emma swallowed roughly. "Ovarian cancer."

"Oh." Kayla's lips remained parted as she took in this news. "But that doesn't mean—"

"Yes." Emma hit her friend with a hard look. "It does."

"Have you told him about . . ."

Emma shook her head. "There's no reason to. He's my neighbor who happens to be using my house temporarily. There's no reason to get into our health histories."

"Emma." Kayla's voice was gentle, but there was an edge of reproof under it.

"You know I don't date anyway." She must have been in her early twenties the last time she'd had a date.

"But you could," Kayla insisted. "If you wanted to. If the right guy came along." She raised her eyebrows as if to suggest perhaps he already had.

But Emma shook her head. "I *don't* want to. Besides, every group needs its spinster."

Kayla snorted. "Being single does *not* make you a spinster. And I know you have a very fulfilling life as a single woman. But so did I . . . And now I have a fulfilling life as a married woman." She shook her head. "I still don't know how that happened."

Emma laughed, eager to encourage the change of subject. Kayla had resisted the idea of falling in love with Cam so hard that Emma was pretty sure no one had been as shocked as Kayla herself when she'd announced they were getting married. And now they had a baby girl that they both doted on.

But that was Kayla's life. Not Emma's.

"All I'm asking," Kayla said as they resumed their progress toward the stables behind the arena, "is that you don't rule out the possibility. God can work some pretty big changes of heart. I'm living proof."

Emma stepped into the stables without agreeing to her friend's request.

Chapter 33

"Amen." Owen looked up as Carter finished his prayer. "All right. Time for bed." He set the devotion book he'd started reading with the kids a few nights ago on the coffee table and pushed to his feet.

"But Miss Emma isn't home yet," Kenzie protested. "I want her to tuck me in."

"Sorry, kiddo, looks like you're stuck with me." Owen made a funny face at his daughter, and it was enough to make her laugh.

"I'm going to get a snack." Cody headed for the kitchen, though they had just finished supper an hour ago.

"Eat some of the stuff I bought," Owen called after him. "Not all of Miss Emma's food." He'd tried to restock her pantry to replace everything his family had already devoured, but he was sure there were plenty of things he'd missed.

He shepherded Carter and Kenzie toward the stairs. He wished they could have waited for Claire and Catelyn to do the devotion, but Claire was still at work, and Catelyn was at Jackson's—again. Owen ignored the knot of anxiety that caused. He trusted Emma's assurance that Jackson was a good kid—he just didn't like the idea of his daughter going off and having a family of her own someday. And it felt like that was where this was headed.

"Going to bed?" Anne looked up from the kitchen table, where she'd struck up a conversation with Cody.

"Yes." Kenzie studied Emma's mother. "Do you know you look a lot like Miss Emma?"

Anne laughed. "I've been told that, although I always figured she looked like me, since I'm the mom."

Kenzie nodded thoughtfully. "I guess that makes sense. I look like my mom too."

"Well, then, your mom must have been a very beautiful lady," Anne said gently.

"She was." Owen squeezed Kenzie's shoulder. "Come on, kiddo, no more stalling."

"I'm not stalling. I'm conversing."

Anne chortled. "That sounds exactly like something Emma would have said at your age."

"Really?" Kenzie sounded pleased. "Can you tell her I said goodnight?"

"I will consider it my mission." Anne saluted Kenzie, and Kenzie returned the gesture, then started up the stairs after Carter, who was already at the top.

"Oh." Kenzie stopped halfway up the steps, and Owen had to grab the railing to keep from plowing her over. "Goodnight, Miss Anne."

"Goodnight to you too, dear. Sleep tight."

Kenzie giggled. "That's what Miss Emma always says too. I bet she got it from her mom. What did my mom always say?" Kenzie's smile dimmed. "I can't remember."

"She said, 'Sweet dreams for dreamy sweethearts.'" Owen's chest ached at the words, but they also brought a smile to his lips.

"I like that." Kenzie sighed. "But I like Miss Emma's too. And yours," she added quickly.

Owen snorted. He usually stuck with the tried and true "goodnight" or "see you in the morning."

"Get in your bed. I'll be there to tuck you in after I say goodnight to Carter."

Kenzie scampered into the girls' bedroom, and from the hallway, Owen heard her inventing a song about dreamy sweethearts sleeping tight.

He tucked Carter and Kenzie both in, promising Kenzie that he would make sure Anne kept her promise to say goodnight to Emma. As he headed down the stairs, he tried to push aside his growing concern that Kenzie was getting too attached to Emma. He'd made a couple of attempts to find somewhere else to stay, but it seemed that every hotel, cabin, or short-term rental within a hundred miles was booked. The one place he had found—a miniscule one-bedroom condo—insurance had denied.

He tried to tell himself it would be fine if they stayed here until their house was ready. After all, once they moved out, they'd be just down the road. They could still see Emma often—just maybe not every day.

His heart stumbled a little at the thought.

"Hey, Dad." Cody looked up as Owen reentered the kitchen. The boy held a peanut butter and jelly sandwich and Lexi sat drooling at his feet. "As soon as I'm done with this, Miss Anne and I are going to play Scrabble."

"William went to bed so he wouldn't have to watch." Anne's eyes gleamed. "He and Emma both refuse to play with me. They always accuse me of cheating."

"Do you?" Cody asked pointedly.

Anne arched an eyebrow at him. "Of course not. They're just not as good at the game as I am. No one is."

"We'll see about that." Cody tossed a chunk of sandwich to the dog, then popped the last quarter of it into his mouth in one bite and sprang up from his seat. He went to the cupboard and grabbed a glass, filling it to the brim with milk, which he downed in a single gulp.

"Sorry about him," Owen apologized to Anne. "Apparently I failed in my duty to teach him manners."

Anne dismissed his comment. "A growing boy has to eat."

"Yeah, Dad, a growing boy has to eat." Cody carried his dishes to the sink. "All right, Miss Anne. I hope you're ready to meet your match."

"I'm always ready." Anne winked at Owen and followed Cody to the living room.

Owen couldn't help grinning at their interaction. His kids hadn't really had much experience with grandparents. He'd never been close to his own parents, who had died shortly after Catelyn was born. And Katie's parents lived in Arizona. They'd come to visit occasionally over the years, but after Katie's death, her mom had gotten sick and they had withdrawn. Owen and the kids had gone to see them once, but his in-laws had resisted any further visits, and now Owen and the kids usually only heard from them at Christmas, when they sent a card.

Anne and William, though, they were the kind of grandparents he'd always wanted for his kids. The kind of grandparent he wanted to be someday. Owen sighed and grabbed his laptop bag off the hook by the door. It was hard to imagine becoming a grandfather without Katie at his side as a grandmother.

He shook off the thought. That was waaaay in the future.

Right now, he had other things to worry about. Like designing a new sign for the drop zone. He pulled out a chair and opened his computer. But before he could put his fingers to the keyboard, Emma blew through the door as if the wind were pushing her.

"Am I too late?" Her voice hitched as if she were trying to catch her breath. "Are the kids already in bed?"

"I just tucked them in."

"Miss Emma, is that you?" Kenzie's voice carried down the stairs.

Owen rolled his eyes. "Apparently I didn't do a good enough job."

"Do you mind if I . . ." Emma gestured toward the stairs.

"I'm afraid she won't close her eyes until you do."

Emma set her notebook on the table and limped gingerly toward the stairs.

"Toe still sore?" Owen resisted the urge to get up and help her across the room. She'd been getting around on her own for three days now.

"It's just the boots." Emma stopped to pull them off. She sighed. "That's better." Her limp was less pronounced as she started up the stairs.

"Did you eat yet?"

"I'll find something when I come down," she called back. "I'm sorry I didn't make it home in time for your devotion." Her voice was softer, and Owen realized she was talking to Kenzie.

He moved to the fridge and pulled out the leftovers from dinner, filling a plate with rice and teriyaki chicken and broccoli. He popped it in the microwave and got out a glass and a jug of milk. When the food was ready, he brought it to the table, sliding Emma's notebook aside.

His eyes fell on her neat handwriting. It appeared to be a to-do list—with her name written behind half the tasks.

Organize and collect items for silent auction - Emma

Create photo collages - Emma

Sort memorabilia and write up histories - Emma

Design and hang posters around town - Emma

Indignation rose in Owen's chest. How was she supposed to do all of that on top of everything else she did? The people on the committee—he recognized many of the names as her friends—were taking advantage of her kindness.

Like you are? The thought hit him hard.

"Something smells . . ." Emma stopped at the bottom of the stairs, her eyes locked on the meal Owen had set out.

"It's the teriyaki chicken I promised."

Her eyes came to his, wide and wondering. "It's for me?"

He laughed. "As long as Cody doesn't smell it and get to it first."

"I heard that," Cody called from the living room.

"Ask him who's winning." Anne sounded gleeful.

Emma's eyes came to Owen's with a question.

"They're playing Scrabble," Owen explained.

"Brave kid," Emma murmured.

"The game is definitely bringing out a side of your mom I haven't seen before." Owen pulled out the chair where he'd set the food, and Emma moved toward it, a grin growing on her lips.

"This looks delicious."

"Tell that to Carter." Owen still wasn't past the battle he'd had with his son over the meal. "He said the sauce was too red, not orange. I ended up melting cheese on top of some rice for him."

Emma laughed. "You're a good dad." She folded her hands, and Owen slid back into his own seat as she prayed silently.

When she lifted her head, he asked, "How was the meeting?"

"It was good." Exhaustion hung from her words as she scooped rice and chicken onto her fork. "We have a lot to get done in the next five weeks, but we'll get there." She popped the food into her mouth and closed her eyes, the exhaustion replaced momentarily by bliss. "This is so good. You're going to have to give me the recipe."

"It's in here." Owen tapped his head. "But I can write it down for you. Why do you have so much more to do than everyone else?" He hadn't meant to ask, but it still bothered him that people—her friends—would take advantage of her like that.

She glanced up, looking surprised. "What do you mean?"

"For the anniversary." He pointed to her notebook. "I saw your to-do list. Your name is behind half the items."

Emma shrugged. "That's no big deal."

"Yes it is." Owen pushed his computer aside. "You're too nice for your own good. People take advantage of you."

Emma laughed and took another bite. "No one is taking advantage of me. I volunteered. Everyone else has family commitments. I don't." She said it breezily enough, but Owen wondered if that ever bothered her. If she'd ever wanted a family.

"Family or not, you're one of the busiest people I've ever met." Owen eyed her. "Between the stables and your chickens and church and . . ." He almost said *us* but bit it back at the last second, finally filling in, "Your friends."

Emma lifted a shoulder. "I like to be busy."

"Well, we're going to help you." Owen didn't know where the offer had come from, but once he made it, he felt better. "The kids and I. To thank you for everything you've done for us."

"That's not necessary," Emma started to protest.

But Owen cut her off. "It is, and we are, so there's no point in arguing. I can be pretty stubborn too when I want to."

"Trust me, I know," Emma muttered, and Owen stared at her a moment, then chuckled. It sounded like something Katie would have said. He'd missed her teasing banter.

"Okay, then. I saw you need to design some posters," he said. "I can help with that, and then the kids and I can go around town and hang them up."

Emma raised a brow. "Do you know *how* to design a poster?"

Owen grabbed his computer and spun it toward her. "I'm designing signs for the drop zone as we speak."

"Wow, Owen," Emma gasped. "Those are great."

"Thanks." Owen's chest filled. "I feel like there's still something missing, but . . ."

Emma tapped a finger to her lip, her eyes on the screen. Owen tore his gaze away from her and back to the computer.

"What if . . ." she said slowly. "You added a wavy blue line under the words *Above the Blue*, to kind of give the idea that you'll see views of Lake Michigan."

"Hold on." Owen pulled the computer back to him and selected a tool. He leaned forward, concentrating. After a few minutes, he turned the computer to her. "Something like this?"

"Yes!" Her eyes sparkled, almost the same color as the line he'd drawn. "I mean, if you like it."

"I do." Owen saved the file, then opened a new one. "Now, those posters. What size do you need?"

Two hours later, Owen clicked save on the fourth sample poster, grinning at Emma.

She grinned right back at him. "I thought this was going to take me two weeks. Thank you."

Owen closed his computer. "Of course."

The rest of the house was quiet. Cody and Anne had finished their game of Scrabble over an hour ago, Cody running into the kitchen in triumph to announce his win. Anne too, had seemed happy with the results, and Owen suspected she may not have played her hardest. But when he'd suggested this to Emma after Cody and Anne had gone up to their rooms,

Emma had looked at him in all seriousness and insisted her mother would never do that.

"Right, just like you'd never take on more work than you should just to be nice," had been his reply.

To which she'd aimed a playful swat at his arm—just as Claire and Catelyn walked in. Claire had glared, Catelyn grinned, and they'd both quickly made their escape upstairs.

Which was exactly what he should do right now. But working on the poster with Emma had energized him, their ideas flowing back and forth and building into concepts neither of them would have come up with on their own. That energy still pulsed through him, and he wasn't ready to call it a night.

"Are you planning to work on the puzzle?" he asked, seeking a casual tone. "Or are you too tired?"

Emma's eyes crinkled at the corners. "I'm game if you are."

"I could be convinced." He pushed his chair out and stood, stretching his back.

Emma grabbed two oatmeal cookies off a platter on the counter and passed him one. "A reward for our hard work."

They headed into the living room, Lexi close on their heels, and took what had become their "usual" spots around the card table, Emma in the blue armchair and him on the gray ottoman across from her. It meant that he ended up working on the puzzle upside down, but he didn't mind. She usually put together twice as many pieces as he did anyway. Lexi settled at Emma's feet, looking up hopefully. Emma laughed and passed the dog her last bite of cookie.

"Who's a good dog?" Emma spoke in baby talk, reaching down to pat Lexi's head. "You're a good dog, aren't you?"

Owen chuckled. "So I take it she's won you over to getting your own dog. Once we . . ." He couldn't bring himself to add "move out."

"If I could guarantee the dog would be as sweet as Lexi, I would get one in a heartbeat. Where'd you get her?"

"You wouldn't believe me if I told you."

Emma tucked a strand of hair behind her ear, smiling from him to Lexi and back again. "Well now I have to hear it."

Owen grabbed a puzzle piece and started the story. "Katie convinced me we needed a dog, probably eighteen years ago now."

Emma gave Lexi a dubious look. "You've aged well, girl."

Owen laughed. "It wasn't Lexi. It was Molly. She was a good dog. A lot smarter than Lexi."

"Hey." Emma patted the dog defensively.

"Trust me, it's true. Anyway, she died a few months after Katie." Owen shook his head. Man, that had been hard on the kids. "I swore then that we'd never get another dog."

"What changed your mind?" Emma's voice held compassion and curiosity.

"*She* did." Owen nodded to the dog. "Just wandered into our yard one day and plunked down as if she'd always belonged there. Kind of like we've done here." He gave an ironic laugh. "Anyway. We tried to find the owner—put up signs, posted online, even took her to the shelter. But when no one claimed her, she became ours for good."

"Sounds like it was meant to be." Emma stroked the dog's nose.

"I guess so. But don't worry. We don't expect you to keep us for good."

Emma laughed softly, and they turned their attention to the puzzle—or at least Emma did. Owen's eyes refused to stay focused on the picture. Instead, they drifted to Emma's face—the tiny smile of concentration that tickled her lips. To her hair—the way it rippled in uncontrolled waves toward her chin. To her hands—roughened by hard work and yet elegant as she snapped another piece into place.

"Oh, it's a picnic," she cried in sudden delight.

Owen squinted at the pieces under her hand, but upside down it looked like a flat-topped tree. He stood and moved to her side of the table, stopping next to her chair and leaning in a little to get a better look.

Her sunshiny floral scent drifted up to him, and he stood near enough that he could have brushed the curl off her cheek.

"Sure enough. It is." His voice went ragged, and he found himself wanting to lean closer still. Wanting to jump into that puzzle and enjoy a picnic with her and the kids.

He jolted upright and scampered back to his side of the table.

What was wrong with him?

If he was going to jump into that puzzle with anyone, it would be Katie.

Katie is gone. The voice in his head sounded like Charles, who had brought up Emma again today. His partner seemed to think that the fact that Owen hadn't yet asked Emma if she was interested in dating Charles was proof that Owen wanted to date her himself.

"Charles has been asking about you." The words leaped out of Owen's mouth before he could think them through.

"Oh?" Emma looked up in surprise.

This is a good idea, Owen told himself. He wasn't going to ask her out, so Charles *should*. He sincerely believed his friend wanted to settle down and raise a family. Why shouldn't it be with Emma? She was kind and funny and compassionate, giving to a fault, beautiful.

So why don't you ask her out? he could hear Charles asking.

"Does he want to take riding lessons or something?" Emma scooped up another puzzle piece and snapped it into place, her eyes meeting his with a tiny look of triumph.

Owen swallowed. He could say yes, that was all Charles wanted, to take riding lessons. "No, uh—" He hesitated. Once he told her, he couldn't take it back. For all he knew, he could be planting the seed that would lead to Emma and Charles's marriage.

His gut twisted, and as if to prove to himself that he had no problem with that, he expelled the words in a single breath: "He actually wants to date you."

Chapter 34

Emma blinked at Owen. Then blinked again. Had he just said that Charles wanted to date her?

So all those feelings she'd been getting all night . . . Like Owen was watching her, like he was maybe interested in her . . .

They'd all been so far off as to be laughable.

Well, she blamed Kayla. If her friend hadn't put such a ludicrous idea in her head, then she wouldn't have misinterpreted the situation so badly.

She tried to figure out why disappointment curled through her heart. She knew nothing could ever develop between her and Owen anyway, just as she'd told Kayla. It had just been nice to feel like someone was interested in her.

Someone is, she reminded herself. *Charles.*

"So?" Owen had been studying his pile of puzzle pieces carefully, but now he looked up. His eyes were earnest and hopeful . . . But for what? Did he really want her to date his friend that badly?

"Um." Emma licked her lips, trying to figure out how to say this without sounding rude. She supposed she'd just have to be honest, even if it was embarrassing. "I'm flattered. And I'm sure Charles is a great guy."

Owen nodded stiffly.

Emma forced herself to go on. "But I don't really date."

"Oh." Owen sounded surprised—and relieved. Had he been afraid Emma was going to say *he* was the one she couldn't take her mind off of?

"Why not? You're so good with kids, I figured you must want a family of your—" He cut off. "I'm sorry. That's none of my business." He dropped his gaze to the puzzle and picked up a piece, turning it over in his fingers.

"That's okay." Emma focused on her own pieces. "I used to want my own family. A big one. Five kids at least."

A soft puff of laughter came from Owen. "You do like a lot of work."

"Yeah." Emma fingered the figures on the puzzle. "For a while there, I wanted a family so badly that I coveted it. The thought of finding the right person and starting a family became my idol."

Owen's hand stilled, and he looked up.

Emma swallowed. She had never told anyone this before, and she wasn't really sure why she was telling him now. But she knew she wanted to. "So I finally surrendered that desire to God and asked him to help me be content with what I have."

"And are you?" Owen asked quietly.

She nodded. "I am. And I do have a family. My mom and William, James and Bethany and Ruby, my friends." She hesitated, then added, "My neighbors."

"That's a good way of looking at it." Owen's gaze was so intense that Emma had to lower her eyes.

"So what about you?" She picked up a puzzle piece that looked like part of a building and searched for its location.

"Do I date?"

Somehow, Owen had followed the line of her thoughts, though she hadn't been brave enough to express it out loud. She nodded silently, still not looking at him.

"No." His sigh was weighted, and Emma lifted her head to find him staring out the dark window. "People tell me I should, but the truth is . . ."

"You're not ready," Emma said softly.

Owen started to nod, then switched to a head shake. "Even if I was . . ." He seemed to be thinking out loud. "I just can't see doing that to the kids. You've seen how easily they get attached. What if I was dating someone and it didn't work out . . ." He directed an anguished gaze at her. "What if they lost another mother?" He shook his head. "I just can't put them through that."

Emma's eyes stung, and she looked away, clearing her throat to banish the tears before they could fall.

"Oh, hey. I didn't mean to upset you." Owen reached across the table, his hand coming to rest on hers.

At that, a tear did fall. She sniffed and shook her head. "I'm sorry. I just hate to think of you guys going through that."

"It's okay. We're okay." Owen's thumb stroked the back of her hand.

Emma nodded, trying to convince herself that was the only reason for her tears—not the fact that he had just confirmed what she'd already known. They could never be together.

Chapter 35

In a way, it was a relief to know that Emma didn't date. Now Owen didn't have to worry that someday he'd get an invitation to her and Charles's wedding. His friend had taken the news quite well—so well, in fact, that he continued to press Owen to ask her out.

But that was the other good thing about knowing she didn't date. Now he didn't have to worry about whether he was ready to date again or not. Any tension he'd experienced over his confused feelings for her had disappeared, and over the past week, they'd become even better friends. The only problem was—

"Good morning." Emma breezed inside, her smile bringing with it the sunshine. Owen's heart leaped higher than the first time he'd jumped out of an airplane.

And that was the problem. He couldn't seem to get his heart to understand that Emma had no interest in dating—and neither did he.

"Good morning." He was proud of himself for keeping his voice in the friend zone.

"Is the birthday girl up yet?"

Owen shook his head just as there was a pounding of feet on the stairs. "I stand corrected."

"Happy birthday," he and Emma cried at the same time, and Owen's heart did another little leap.

"Thank you." Kenzie's grin covered her entire face as she gave first him and then Emma a hug.

"What do you want to do today?" Owen moved to the cupboard to pull out flour and baking powder. He and Katie had always made pancakes for the kids' birthday breakfast, and he'd continued the tradition over the years.

"I want to play mini-golf," Kenzie announced exuberantly.

Emma laughed. "You didn't even have to think about that."

Kenzie shook her head. "Nope. Ruby told me you took her once and it was so fun. Will you come with us?'

"Oh. Uh." Emma's eyes darted to Owen's, and he nodded eagerly. If he was honest with himself, he had hoped Kenzie would invite her.

"Absolutely." Emma's smile was almost as big as Kenzie's.

"Go get ready and make sure your siblings are up." Owen grabbed some vanilla and some sugar. "After breakfast, we can do presents and then we'll go."

"Yippee, presents!" Kenzie skipped back up the steps.

"Remember when birthdays used to be that exciting?" Emma chuckled, going to the fridge and pulling out milk, butter, and eggs.

"As I recall, yours was still pretty exciting." It seemed impossible that that had been only a month ago, just after they'd met—and yet, in some ways it felt like he'd known her forever.

Emma groaned. "That was a little more excitement than I needed." But she was smiling as she started cracking eggs into a bowl. She cut up a stick of butter and stuck it in the microwave, and Owen realized she was helping with the pancakes, as if they'd planned to make them together all along.

He added the dry ingredients to a bowl, warmth tightening his chest at the familiarity but also the newness of the routine. He glanced at Emma, who was measuring out the milk. If she were Katie, he would sneak up behind her, wrap his arms around her waist, and drop a kiss onto her neck.

She turned, and he yanked his attention back to the bowl of flour. She wasn't Katie. She was Emma. His friend who didn't date. And neither did he.

"Daddy," Kenzie called down the stairs. "Claire says she won't get up and she's not coming."

Owen sighed, kneading a sudden knot at the back of his neck.

"Go ahead." Emma tilted her head toward the stairs. "I've got this."

"Thanks." Owen slid his bowl toward her with more force than he intended, and it nearly careened off the counter. They both lunged for it, and his hands landed on top of hers.

"That was close." Emma's voice was breathless, and her eyes came to his.

"It was." He should let go. She clearly had the bowl. But he couldn't quite figure out how to make his hands move.

"Daddy," Kenzie called again.

"Coming." Owen kept his eyes on Emma's. "Got it?"

She nodded, and he slowly let go and stepped around her, his arm accidentally brushing her shoulder on the way past. Sparks ignited the spot, but he ignored them.

Catelyn was coming down the stairs as he went up. "Good luck," she breathed.

Owen steeled himself and marched through the girls' open door. Kenzie was still in her pajamas, though she had laid out her clothes on the bed. She sat next to them with her arms folded, glaring at her sister, who lay on her air mattress with her face to the wall.

"Claire," he said sternly.

She didn't answer.

"Get up. You are not going to ruin your sister's birthday."

"I'm not." Claire rolled over, shooting defiance at him. "She can still celebrate. She doesn't need me. Mini-golf is so embarrassing."

Owen rolled his eyes. That was what this was about? "We're all going. You know birthdays are family days."

Claire sneered. "Then why is Emma going? She's not family."

Kenzie made a sound of protest. "She is too."

Owen looked between his daughters. "Emma is our friend," he said slowly, hoping each girl would get what she needed from that sentence. "And she's done a lot for our family. It's Kenzie's birthday, and she invited her. It's as simple as that. Now get up and get dressed. The pancakes will be ready in ten minutes."

He strode out of the room, praying that had been the right way to handle the situation. He didn't want Claire treating Emma badly, but he also didn't want Kenzie to think that Emma was always going to do everything with them.

He reached the kitchen and found Catelyn had taken over his role helping Emma. Anne, William, Cody, and Carter had all come down too.

Within a few minutes, Kenzie appeared as well, smiling around the gathered group. Claire trailed a few steps behind, still looking sullen but at least dressed and ready to go.

Emma handed out pancakes to everyone, and Owen led them in prayer. "Heavenly Father, thank you for this day that you have blessed us with to celebrate Kenzie's birthday. Thank you for the gift she is to everyone here. Bless her, Lord, as she continues to grow in faith and knowledge of you. And let everyone in this . . . room be an encouragement to her. Amen."

"Amens" chorused around the room, followed by the sound of eager forks on plates.

Owen glanced around, his heart full. He'd almost said "everyone in this family" in his prayer. But Claire was right—Emma and Anne and William weren't part of their family.

But Kenzie was right too: It sure felt like they were.

***

"Hole-in-one!" Emma raised her arms above her head in exultation.

"Hey, careful where you're swinging that." Owen laughed, reaching over her shoulder to catch her club in midair.

"Oops, sorry." Emma laughed and turned to face him, but he was much closer than she'd expected, and she took a quick step backwards, tugging the club with her. "How many shots did you take on that one?" She turned to Kenzie with a smile, and the girl giggled.

Owen rolled his eyes. "You know how many. You're the scorekeeper."

"I forgot." Emma tried to look innocent but couldn't keep a straight face.

"It was eight," Owen play-growled. "You know how I said Scrabble brought out a whole different side of your mom?" He lifted his eyebrows.

Emma laughed. "Sounds like someone doesn't like to lose." She pushed his arm without thinking, then yanked her hand back. She couldn't seem to stop doing that today. Not that she was too worried about it. She already knew that he didn't date—and neither did she. So a couple of playful shoves didn't mean anything.

"Yeah, even I beat you," Kenzie gloated to her dad. She took the scorecard from Emma. "And so did Cody and Catelyn."

"Yeah, yeah," Owen grumbled, but his eyes twinkled, and Emma wished he could always look this carefree.

They moved toward the small building that housed the mini-golf course's pro shop. Claire already sat on a bench outside the door. She'd retreated there the moment she'd halfheartedly completed the last hole.

"That was so fun," Kenzie chanted. "Thank you for coming, Miss Emma." It was the sixth time Kenzie had thanked her, and Emma got the feeling she was trying to make up for Claire, who had spent most of the day directing evil looks at Emma.

Emma understood if Claire would have preferred she not come along. She hadn't wanted to intrude on their family day. But she also hadn't wanted to disappoint Kenzie on her birthday.

Inside the pro shop, they all returned their clubs, then headed for the parking lot, Claire bringing up the rear.

"Here," Emma heard the young woman at the desk say. "Why don't you give this to your mom? For next time you guys come."

"She's not my mom." Claire's voice was sharp enough to slice right through the paper the woman held out.

"Oh. I'm sorry— I thought . . ." The woman looked mortified. "You were all together, and you two look so much alike . . ."

"It's okay." Emma offered the woman a reassuring smile and took the piece of paper.

"It's a coupon for twenty percent off your next visit." The woman still looked apologetic. "I hope you'll come back soon."

Emma nodded and gestured for Claire to file out ahead of her. The girl gave Emma a hard look but obeyed.

Once they were in the van, Owen announced that they were headed for the Chocolate Chicken. A cheer went up from the kids—but Emma watched silently out the window, Claire's words battering her temples. "She's not my mom."

The words shouldn't hurt. Of course she wasn't Claire's mom. Or Kenzie's. Or anyone else's.

And she was content with that. She really was.

It was just . . .

Nothing.

It was just nothing. She was content. Period.

The only thing she needed now was some ice cream.

Chapter 36

Emma dug her hands into the pizza dough she was kneading, her heart light as she watched Kenzie dance around the kitchen singing, "This has been the best day ever," into the karaoke microphone Owen had given her as a gift this morning.

"I knew I was going to regret getting her that," Owen muttered, leaning into the rolling pin he was using to shape the dough Emma handed him.

"Oh, you know you love it." Emma grinned at Kenzie. "And anyway, she's right. It has been a great day."

Owen nodded, his lips hiking into a smile. "It has."

After the Chocolate Chicken, they'd come back here, and everyone except Claire had joined in a game of boys vs. girls Pictionary, which, despite Emma's rudimentary drawing skills, the girls had won. Then they'd played Clue, followed by Uno, which the birthday girl had won. Emma had ducked out to do chores and lead a couple of private lessons after that.

She'd come back to find Mom and Cody locked in a Scrabble rematch, William reading with Carter, Kenzie singing, and Owen making pizza dough. The scene had struck her immobile for a moment, her earlier discontentment that this couldn't last morphing into joy that God had given her an opportunity to get to know and serve this wonderful family.

"There." Owen lifted the rolling pin off the dough. "How does that look?"

"Like a football," Cody said, barely looking up from the Scrabble board.

Owen chucked a piece of dough at his son. It hit Cody on the cheek and stuck. "Real mature, Dad."

"Don't worry, Cody. I'll get him back for you." Emma pulled a wad of dough off her ball. In a flash, she rested her empty palm on one of Owen's cheeks, pressing the dough into the other.

"I— What—" Owen spluttered, and Emma pulled her hands away, suddenly realizing the rough feeling under her fingers was the light layer of stubble that grazed his cheeks.

The kids hooted with laughter, and Owen gave her a mock betrayed look. "I thought we were on the same team here."

Not bothering to remove the blob of dough, he pressed his palms against the flour-covered table, then patted them to Emma's cheeks.

The kids laughed harder. Emma reached up to pull his hands away. But her eyes snagged on his, and her heart locked, and she forgot everything else.

The way he was looking at her was so . . .

"You look like a ghost," Kenzie cried gleefully, and Emma zapped back to life.

She let go of Owen's hands, and he dropped them quickly to his side, wiping the excess flour onto his jeans.

"You still have—" Emma pointed to his cheek, where the dough still clung.

"Oh. Thanks." Owen pulled it off, leaving behind a powdery circle.

Emma almost reached up to brush it away but caught herself just in time.

"What on earth is— Oh." Catelyn appeared at the bottom of the stairs, her eyes going from Owen's cheeks to Emma's. Too late, Emma realized she must still be covered in flour too.

"Miss Emma and Dad are having a food fight," Cody said, as if this happened every day.

"Oh." Catelyn smirked, but she too acted as if it were completely normal. "Is the pizza almost done?"

"If your father stops throwing the dough, it will go faster," Emma said lightly.

"Me?" Owen spluttered. "You're the one who—" He touched his cheek where she had stuck the dough, and she could almost feel his whiskers under her fingers again.

"Hey, we should have a movie night," Kenzie said into the microphone.

Owen and the other kids froze, exchanging shocked looks.

Emma glanced at Mom, who looked just as confused as Emma felt. When no one said anything, Emma asked, "What's a movie night?"

Kenzie lowered the microphone and spoke quietly. "It's where you eat pizza in the living room and watch a movie."

"Oh." That sounded innocent enough. She glanced at Owen, but his face had gone as pale as the flour on his cheek. "I mean, that would be fine with me if it's okay with your dad."

"Is it, Daddy?" Kenzie asked.

Owen looked at Cody and then Catelyn. They both nodded slowly. "Sure," he finally said, his voice strained. "We can do that."

Emma wanted to ask what the big deal was about a movie night, but she had a feeling, based on the way Owen and the older kids were acting, that it had something to do with Katie, and she didn't want to upset Kenzie more.

Owen picked up the rolling pin and attacked the remaining dough.

"Hey, Kenzie." Emma desperately wanted to restore the lighter mood. "Can you sing us a song?"

But Kenzie shook her head and turned off the microphone. "We don't have to have a movie night," she whispered.

"Oh, but I've never had one." Emma glanced at Owen to make sure he was okay with her intervention.

He stopped slathering sauce on the dough to offer his daughter a tight smile. "We should have a movie night, Kenz. It's a good idea."

"Okay." Kenzie's voice wavered a little.

"What movie do you watch on a movie night?" Emma asked.

"Whatever movie you want." Kenzie perked up a little.

"And what movie *do* you want?"

"*Beauty and the Beast.*" The girl didn't even hesitate.

"Oh, that's my favorite."

"Mine too. And Mommy's." Kenzie glowed, but Emma's eyes went to Owen. He met her gaze with a silent nod.

"Should we go see if we can find it?" She led Kenzie to the living room, where William had fallen asleep on the couch. Carter sat next to him, still reading.

"We're having a movie night," Kenzie informed her brother.

"Cool." Carter didn't look up from his book.

Emma turned on the TV and did a search for *Beauty and the Beast*. "Live action or cartoon?" she asked Kenzie.

Before the girl could answer, shouting came from the kitchen.

"What in the world?" Emma hurried toward the commotion.

"It *is* a big deal," Claire was yelling. "That was Mom's thing." She grabbed a set of keys off the little table by the door.

"Claire." Owen's voice was edged with steel. "Don't you dare—"

But Claire shoved the kitchen door open and ran down the porch steps, sprinting for Catelyn's car on the other side of the driveway.

"Claire." Owen followed her out the door.

But the car's engine roared to life, and gravel sprayed behind the tires as Claire raced down the driveway.

Owen banged back inside and grabbed another set of keys off the table.

"Dad," Catelyn said quietly. "Let her go."

Owen blinked at his daughter, then looked to Emma as if she might have the answer. She looked back helplessly. She had never wished more that she knew how to be a mother.

"Catelyn's right." Anne said gently, and Emma sent her mom a grateful look. Somehow, she always knew what to do or say. "If you follow right now, she'll only run harder and faster."

Owen nodded tightly.

"I'm sorry, Daddy." Kenzie was near tears, and Emma wrapped an arm around her shoulder.

"This isn't your fault," Owen said firmly. He crossed the room and bent to kiss his daughter's head, close enough that Emma could feel the warmth of his breath on her arm. "Come on. Let's get things set up."

They stuck the pizzas in the oven, spread a big blanket on the living room floor, and made a pitcher of lemonade.

But every few minutes, Emma saw Owen's eyes stray to the window. Once everyone had their pizza and headed to the living room, she caught his arm.

"I can call James if you want," she murmured. "Ask him to keep an eye out for her."

Relief crossed Owen's face. "Do you think he would do that?"

"I know he would." She let herself hold his arm just a moment longer in support, then pulled out her phone. "You go start the movie. I'll be right there."

Chapter 37

Owen paced Emma's living room, staring into the deep darkness that had fallen. It was 11 p.m., the movie night long over, Carter and Kenzie in bed, and still Claire hadn't returned. Nor responded to a single one of his or Catelyn's texts or phone calls.

Tension pressed against the walls of the room.

Cody and Anne hovered over the Scrabble board, neither of them speaking as they built words. William sat in a chair with a book open in front of him. Catelyn tapped into her phone, her forehead creased, and Owen wondered if she was texting Jackson. Emma sat at her puzzle table, but Owen hadn't seen her put a single piece in place. She picked up her phone, and Owen knew she was checking for an update from James. So far he hadn't spotted any sign of Claire. If she didn't come back soon, he'd offered to start an informal search. But it wouldn't come to that.

It *couldn't* come to that.

Please, Lord.

Maybe he should have gone after her. Maybe he should go now.

Emma stood, and Owen's heart jumped, but she shook her head. "No news." She moved to his side and looked out the window as well.

"She'll be okay." It was the kind of thing people said in situations like this, a platitude. But it didn't sound like a platitude coming from her. It sounded like conviction.

"I know," Owen lied.

Emma's phone rang, and the whole room jumped. Emma snatched it out of her pocket.

"It's James." Her wide, reassuring eyes came to his, and she hit the answer button, then put the phone on speaker.

"James." Emma closed her eyes, and Owen wondered if she was praying even right that moment. "Did you find her?"

"I did." Something in James's voice made Owen's heart stop.

Apparently Emma heard it too because she opened her eyes and grabbed Owen's arm. "What is it?"

"She was at the gas station with some friends."

Owen let out a breath. She was alive. Anything else he could handle.

Emma let go of him. "What a relief. Thank—"

"That's not all, Emma," James interrupted, and Owen froze. "The reason I found her was that we got a call from the station saying some kids were making a mess of the place. Some of them were shoplifting."

No.

Not Claire.

Sure, she was angry with him, but she would never do anything like that.

"There has to be some kind of mistake," he managed to choke out.

"She had a handful of candy bars in her bag." James's voice was low, and Owen could hear the shocked gasps from Cody and Catelyn on the other side of the room. "She hadn't left the premises yet, and she's returned them now, so I'm going to make her help clean this place up, then take her to the station and write up a warning. Hopefully that will scare her enough not to do it again."

Owen could only stare at the phone, still stupefied.

"It's up to you," James continued. "You can pick her up at the station, and I'll release her into your custody, or I can escort her home."

"I'll pick her up." Owen was already on his way to the kitchen.

He heard Emma say something else to her brother, but her voice faded as he grabbed his shoes and blindly shoved his foot into one. It wouldn't go on. He stared at it for a moment before realizing it was Cody's. He chucked it aside and grabbed his own shoes.

"I'm coming with you." Catelyn marched into the kitchen, shoes already on her feet.

Emma stood behind her. "We'll take care of things here."

He nodded tightly. "Thank you."

He and Catelyn got silently into the van. The drive to the police station seemed to take six years.

Worry burrowed deep into Owen's thoughts. He knew he'd been losing Claire. While the other kids had pulled together after Katie's death, Claire had pushed away. Owen had always figured that one day she would come back.

But now . . . was she too far gone?

A sick feeling sloshed in his stomach as he pulled into the police station parking lot and spotted the car Claire had driven off in earlier. He parked next to it and shut off the van, but he couldn't bring himself to get out of the vehicle.

"I feel like Mom would know exactly what to say right now," Catelyn said quietly.

Owen exhaled a soft laugh. "Yeah, she probably would."

"Emma would too." This time Catelyn's words were more tentative.

Owen nodded. He couldn't disagree with that.

But he also couldn't dwell on it. He had to be the one to come up with the right words. He opened his door, and Catelyn opened hers.

"Why don't you take your car home right away? I'll get Claire and meet you there."

"You're sure?" Catelyn glanced toward the police station.

Owen wasn't sure about anything anymore, but he nodded. He had a feeling it would be best if he confronted Claire alone.

"Okay." Catelyn came around the van and hugged him. "I'll see you at home."

Owen watched her go, then opened the police station door, swallowing down the bile at the back of his throat as he stepped inside.

James stood near an empty reception desk in the lobby, and he stepped forward to shake Owen's hand. But Owen's eyes were locked on Claire, curled in a corner of an uncomfortable looking chair.

She didn't look up, but he could see defiance in the set of her mouth.

It took Owen a moment to realize James was saying something. ". . . warning this time. And I trust there won't be a next time."

James glanced to Claire, who didn't twitch.

Anger flashed in Owen's chest. Didn't his daughter have any feelings at all? Remorse? Shame? Gratitude that she wasn't facing jail time or even a fine?

"It won't happen again," Owen assured James. "Thanks again for . . ." He wasn't quite sure how to finish the sentence, so he let it hang.

James nodded, had Owen sign a form, then said they were free to go.

Owen held the door open for Claire, who passed through without looking at him.

He made it into the van before he exploded. "Shoplifting, Claire? What in heaven's name did you think you were doing?"

Claire blinked at him, and he waited for her to break down in tears—to show some sign of regret. Instead, she shrugged.

His anger stoked hotter. "It's your sister's birthday. All she wanted to do was spend time with her family and have a movie night. What was I supposed to say: 'No, we can't do that because your mom died five years ago'?"

Claire's whole body jerked against the seat, and she inhaled sharply.

"I'm sorry," he said more gently. "I didn't mean it like that. But it's not fair to your siblings to expect them to give up everything we ever did with Mom. We all have to move on. I know it's hard, but it's what she would want."

Claire snorted. "Doesn't seem too hard for you."

Owen froze. "What does that mean?"

Claire slouched into her seat. "Let's just go."

Owen watched her for a moment, wondering if he should force an answer. But likely all that would happen is they would both get angrier and push each other even further away—if that was possible.

So he silently started the vehicle and headed home.

Chapter 38

"Thank you, Corazón." Emma slid the big egg into her basket, then rummaged around in the pine shavings for another. "And thank you, Trixie."

She glanced anxiously toward the house. Claire had gone straight upstairs when Owen brought her home last night, and he hadn't said much, other than that he was grateful James had only given her a warning. He'd gone to bed shortly afterward, as had everyone else.

Emma had sat at her puzzle table for a while, in case Owen couldn't sleep and wanted to talk, but he hadn't come back down. And he hadn't gotten up to sit on the porch and read their Bibles together this morning either.

She brushed aside the disappointment. He had to be exhausted.

Lord, give him the strength to handle this on top of everything else. Give him the wisdom to guide Claire. And give her the healing and peace she so desperately needs in you.

Her phone blasted from her pocket, interrupting her prayer and almost making her drop the basket of eggs.

She pulled it out, smiling when she caught Grace's name. "Good morning."

"Where are you?" Grace sounded breathless.

"In the chicken coop, why?" Emma peered around her yard as if that might explain why Grace was asking.

"Is Owen with you?" Grace's voice grew more urgent, and Emma braced herself. Surely she didn't have more bad news for him.

"Not at the moment. Why?" she asked again.

"I have good news, but I couldn't find his number."

"Oh." Relief washed over Emma. "Let me go find him. I'm not sure if he's awake yet."

"That's okay. I have to run and finish setting out breakfast. Just tell him we had a last-minute cancellation, and I was able to move some other reservations around. So we have a cabin available for him and the kids, starting tomorrow, for as long as they need it."

"Tomorrow?" A rock thudded into Emma's stomach.

"Yeah." Grace grunted as if she'd picked up something heavy. "They can move in after church. Between your truck and ours, we should be able to get everything."

"Oh." Emma couldn't find any other words.

"Emma?" Something thumped, as if Grace had set down whatever she was carrying. "Is this okay with you?"

"What?" Emma shook herself. "Oh no. Yeah. Of course it is. You're sure you guys will be okay if you don't rent it out?" In the middle of tourist season, a last-minute opening would be snatched up at a premium.

"Oh yes." It sounded like Grace was bustling around again. "I was going to refund the deposit for the family who canceled since it was a medical emergency. Their dad has to have bypass surgery. But then we got to talking about how this was actually good timing because I had a friend who just had a house fire—and they told me to keep the deposit for them."

"Wow." Emma leaned against the chicken coop, stunned.

"I know. It's totally a God thing, right?" Grace's voice bubbled. "Listen, I have to run. Tell Owen to call me if he has any questions. Otherwise we'll see y'all tomorrow."

She hung up, and Emma stared at the phone. She'd thought Owen and his family would be staying with her for a few more weeks at least. And now they wouldn't even be next door.

A God thing, Grace had said.

Well, maybe it was. God's way of keeping Emma from getting her heart set on things she couldn't have. Of helping her remain content.

She shoved her phone into her pocket, grabbed the last egg from the nesting box, and headed for the house.

The kitchen that had been silent when she went out was now full, with Owen, Kenzie, Carter, Catelyn, Cody, Mom, and William all scurrying around. Emma's chest pinched as she realized this would be the last time she walked in to this.

"Good morning, Miss Emma." Kenzie looked up from the beads she was stringing onto a bracelet. "I'm making this for you."

"Oh." Emma's heart twisted, but she made herself hold her smile. "Thank you."

Owen turned from the fridge, a jug of orange juice in his hands. His smile seemed a little duller than usual, and Emma wanted to ask how last night had gone.

But she had news to deliver. "Guess what?" She slathered enthusiasm over the words.

"What?" Kenzie was the first to ask, sounding equally excited.

"I just talked to Miss Grace, and they have a cabin available for you guys."

The orange juice landed on the table with a thunk, and Emma's eyes went to Owen's.

Before she could discern his expression, Kenzie broke into tears.

"But I like living with you," she wailed.

"Oh, sweetie, I know." Emma moved to the girl's side to hug her. "I like having you live with me too. But Grace's place is right on the lake. And it has a loft like Laura Ingalls." She and Kenzie had watched *Little House on the Prairie* together a couple of times. "Oh, and there's a hot tub."

"Oh, Kenz, you like hot tubs," Catelyn chimed in.

"I don't care about a stupid hot tub." Kenzie glared at her sister. "I want to stay here. With Miss Emma."

"Kenz." Owen finally jumped into the conversation. "This is Miss Emma's house. She was nice enough to let us stay here, but now we need to let her have her space back."

Emma wanted to protest that she didn't want to go back to having all that empty space.

"I'm sure I'll still see you all the time," she said to Kenzie. "You're going to keep riding, right?"

"Oh yes," Kenzie answered. "I'm going to ride forever."

"Well, there you go. And I'll see you at church and around town."

"But it won't be the same." Kenzie sniffled.

Emma opened her mouth, but she didn't have an answer for that.

She locked eyes with Owen, and her heart tumbled.

No, it wouldn't be the same at all.

Chapter 39

"Well, I guess that's everything." Owen stared at the back of Emma's empty truck, a strange heaviness settling over him. He was grateful to Grace and Levi for the cabin—it was spacious and airy and would give his family a place of their own.

Except, Owen had gotten used to sharing his life with Emma and Anne and William. Of crowding around the dining room table and laughing through dinner and talking over puzzles.

"Do you need any help unpacking?" Emma's voice was cheerful, but her eyes were subdued.

Owen wanted to ask if she was going to miss them as much as they were going to miss her, but that seemed like an unfair question. They had been the ones to get all the benefits from the arrangement. She would probably be glad to have her house—and her peace and quiet—back.

"That's okay." Owen toed the gravel driveway. "There's not that much stuff." Their few possessions that had survived the fire, along with the items Emma's friends had supplied and the replacement clothes they'd bought since then, fit easily inside the cabin.

"Okay, then, well . . ." Emma patted the side of her truck. "I guess I should—"

"Miss Emma!" Kenzie barreled out the front door of the cabin and hurtled across the wide porch and down the steps. "You're not leaving, are you?"

Emma's eyes came to Owen's, and the heartbreak in them almost staggered him. Maybe she *was* going to miss them too.

"I have to." Emma's voice was upbeat, but Owen heard the struggle behind it. "The ladies need their supper."

"But I'm going to miss you. I don't want you to leave me." A sudden torrent of tears spilled down Kenzie's cheeks.

Before Owen could respond, Emma was on her knees, pulling the girl into her arms. Owen could see the force of her squeeze in her taut arms.

"I'm going to miss you too."

A knot worked its way to Owen's throat. Seeing someone else love his children like that...

Emma pulled back and held Kenzie's shoulders, looking her in the eyes. "This is silly of us. I'll see you tomorrow at vacation Bible school, remember?"

Kenzie hiccupped a laugh. "Oh yeah. I'll bring your bracelet."

"I'm counting on it." Emma leaned forward and kissed Kenzie's forehead, then pushed to her feet.

She turned to Owen. "Don't be a stranger," she said quietly.

Owen shook his head. "We won't." There was so much more he wanted to say. So many things he wanted to thank her for. But the words stuck in the back of his throat. How did you thank someone for getting your family through some of the hardest days of their life?

Emma turned to open her truck door. Owen stood there, holding its edge. When she reached to close it, he caught her hand.

Shocked eyes met his.

"Thank you for everything," he said hoarsely.

Her lips dipped a little, but she nodded, blinking quickly. "You're welcome."

He let go of her hand and closed her door.

As she drove away, he couldn't help feeling like he'd left something important at her house. But when he ran through all the possibilities, he landed on only one: her.

Chapter 40

Emma eased herself into an Adirondack chair on Leah and Austin's patio, enjoying the sounds of her friends milling around her. She fingered the bracelet Kenzie had given her first thing Monday morning at VBS.

It had been such a joy to see her and Carter every day this week, even if it was only for an hour as she led the activity portion of the event. But going home to a quiet house every afternoon had left her heart aching. She missed Cody and Catelyn and even Claire.

And Owen.

She sighed and leaned her head back on the chair, closing her eyes. Yes, she could admit it, she missed Owen too.

They'd texted a couple of times during the week to finalize the design for the anniversary signs, but she hadn't seen him even once. Catelyn had brought the kids to lessons on Wednesday night. She'd said Owen was tied up at the drop zone again, but Emma couldn't help wondering whether he was trying to put some distance between them.

She didn't blame him if he was. After all, if he'd been feeling anything like she had . . .

Still, she missed his easy friendship. Once or twice, she'd thought about calling him, just to see how he was doing. But that felt awkward and too easy to misinterpret.

So she'd thrown herself into VBS and riding lessons and preparations for the upcoming county fair and the church anniversary.

"You look tired." Bethany lowered herself into an identical chair next to Emma.

"I'm fine." Emma smiled at her sister-in-law. "It's good to see you upright. How's my little niece or nephew doing?"

"The doctor says everything looks good, and I've been managing to keep some food down." Bethany laid a hand on her belly, where there was still no sign of a baby bulge.

"I got you something." James strode over, holding out a plate to Bethany. It held a stack of soda crackers and a piece of plain bread.

"My favorite," Bethany joked, taking it from him and carefully nibbling one of the crackers.

"You look tired." James's attention shifted to Emma. "I thought you'd be getting more rest now that you have your house back."

Emma shook her head, impatience rearing. Bethany's concern was one thing—she didn't always remember that Emma didn't want to be coddled. But James certainly did. "I'm fine, James."

Her fingers prickled—her neuropathy had been acting up all week—but she didn't need her brother to know that. She tucked her hands under her legs.

"Did you have your checkup today?" Worry clouded James's eyes, and Emma regretted her impatience with him.

"Yes," she said quietly. "Everything is still all clear."

James let out a heavy breath, and Emma's heart twinged. Her brother had already lost so much, and she knew the possibility of losing someone else haunted him.

Lead filled her as she realized that must be how Owen felt too.

James eventually learned to risk loving again, a little voice in her head coaxed.

But Emma shushed it. Owen didn't have only his own heart to worry about; he had to protect his kids too. There was no way he would ever risk letting them lose someone again. Especially not someone who had already been sick with the same disease that had taken their mother.

And she wouldn't want him to.

A wolf whistle pierced the air, and Emma turned, knowing already that it had come from Levi. He was the only one who could whistle loudly enough to get everyone's attention.

The chatter stopped, and Leah announced that the food was ready. Everyone bowed their heads for Dan to lead them in prayer, but before he could start, there was a commotion behind him.

"Kenzie!" Ruby's cry sent a jolt through Emma, and she lifted her head, her eyes instantly connecting with Owen's. A soft, almost uncertain smile played across his features, and Emma's lips responded without her permission.

"Hey, Owen, glad you guys could make it." Dan stepped into Emma's line of sight to shake Owen's hand, and she concentrated on getting her heart back under control. But its wild hoofbeats continued straight through Dan's prayer.

The moment everyone uttered, "Amen," Kenzie was at Emma's side.

"Hi," she said breathlessly.

"Well, hey stranger. Do you like my bracelet?" Emma held out her wrist to show it off.

Kenzie giggled. "I made it."

"Well, then you should like it extra much."

"Hi." Owen's greeting was quiet, but it nearly made Emma jump out of her skin, and all of her nerves went on high alert.

"Hi," she croaked. "How are you?"

"I'm fine." Owen's reply sounded oddly formal. "How are you?"

"Good. Good." She bit her lip, and Bethany gave her an odd look.

Emma sent her sister-in-law a silent plea for help.

"Why don't you guys take our chairs." Bethany wiggled to the edge of hers and gestured to James. "We were just getting up."

"We were?" James gave his wife a confused look.

"You want to eat, don't you?" Bethany got to her feet. "And I think I feel up to trying one of Peyton's cookies." She took James's arm and steered him toward the food, tossing Emma a "you're welcome" look over her shoulder.

Emma grimaced. This was not the kind of help she meant.

Kenzie plopped instantly into the chair James had abandoned.

Slowly, Owen moved to Bethany's chair, right next to Emma. He pulled Carter onto his lap like a shield.

"So . . ." Emma grasped for something to say. "I didn't realize you guys were going to be here." She bit her lip. Did that make it sound like she didn't want them to be here?

"Jackson told Catelyn to bring us." He gestured over his shoulder, to where Jackson and Catelyn were holding hands and laughing. He made a pained face.

Emma couldn't help but laugh. "So you're still not on board with that?"

"Is she forty-five yet?" Owen quipped.

"Daddy," Kenzie sounded exasperated. "If she had to wait until she was forty-five, she'd be older than Miss Emma."

They'd had this conversation before, and Emma knew where it was going, so she cut the girl off. "Are Cody and Claire here too?"

"Cody is by the food table. Of course." Owen laughed, but then his expression darkened. "I gave Claire a choice between house arrest and coming. She chose house arrest."

"How are things with her?"

Owen exhaled. "Okay, I guess. I think she learned her lesson, but..." He shrugged helplessly.

"I'm hungry." Carter wriggled off of Owen's lap.

"Okay, buddy, let's get some food." He stood. "Kenzie, are you ready to eat?"

"If Miss Emma is."

Owen rolled his eyes. "Kenz."

But Emma hopped out of her chair. "You'd better believe I am. Come on."

They all filled their plates, Emma concentrating hard on keeping her hands steady. Then they headed to the table where Ruby sat with James and Bethany. As they ate, their conversation seemed to return to normal, and the sense of something missing that had been hanging over Emma all week dissipated.

"The tandem chutes came in this week," Owen said after they'd all finished eating. "If you want to jump."

"She doesn't." James answered for her, giving Owen a sour look.

Emma thought about contradicting her brother just to contradict him, but then she recalled the worry in his eyes earlier.

"I'm not sure yet," she answered. "I think the next thing I want to do from my life list is climb a tree."

James snorted. "Breaking a toe wasn't enough for you? You want to break an arm too?"

Emma stuck her tongue out at him, the way she had when they were kids. "I'm not going to break my arm. Anyway, if my brother had taught me to climb a tree when we were kids, I wouldn't have to do it now."

James shook his head, but Kenzie perked up. "There's a tree at our house that Daddy says is perfect for climbing. You should come climb it."

"I'll have to do that sometime."

"How about Sunday?" Kenzie asked, her eyes hopeful.

"Oh. Uh." Emma glanced to Owen.

He nodded with a small shrug. "Sunday works. I need to check on the progress at the house anyway."

"All right then." Emma held out a hand to Kenzie. "We have a d—" The word *date* almost came out, but at the last second she managed to reshape it into "deal."

"Well," James muttered. "If you get hurt, don't expect me not to say I told you so."

But even her brother's grumping couldn't remove the smile from Emma's heart.

Chapter 41

"So I hear you're taking Emma tree climbing after church." Catelyn's eyes sparkled over the rim of her coffee cup as she swiveled on the barstool across the counter from Owen.

"Yeah," he answered, carefully casual, slicing avocado and layering it on a sandwich.

"And you're having a picnic?" Catelyn's eyebrows went up.

"Kenzie asked if we could, yes."

Catelyn and Claire both had to work after church, so it would be just him, Cody, Kenzie, Carter—and Emma. He tried to dismiss the smile from his lips.

But the truth was, he was looking forward to this. Things at the drop zone had been so crazy all week, and if it weren't for Kenzie's invitation to Emma, he might have gone in again this afternoon.

But he needed a break.

He needed to unwind and decompress and reconnect with his kids.

And with Emma.

The thought came unbidden, but he couldn't deny he was looking forward to spending time with her. It had been hard not seeing her all week. It had nearly killed him to ask Catelyn to take the kids to lessons the other night, but he and Charles had been interviewing receptionists for the drop zone, and it went later than he'd planned. He would have left the job to Charles, but he had very little confidence that his friend—who seemed to be over Emma's rejection, as well as his desire to settle down and start a family—would base his decision solely on a candidate's skills. It turned out he needn't have worried. Both he and Charles had agreed that Barb—a grandmotherly woman with impeccable organizational skills, a cheerful demeanor, and a passion for skydiving—was right for the job.

"So are you going to ask her out or what?" Catelyn cut into his thoughts, and it took Owen a moment to realize she was talking about Emma, not Barb.

"Ask her out?" His voice squeaked on the last word, and he cleared his throat. "Why would you say that?"

Catelyn rolled her eyes. "Only because you're madly in love with her."

Owen's arm jumped, and he dropped a slice of avocado to the floor. Lexi swooped in and swallowed it in a single gulp.

"I'm not madly in love with her," he said, more sharply than he intended.

Catelyn raised an eyebrow. "But you *do* like her."

"Of course I like her. We all like her. After everything she's done for our family."

"You know that's not what I meant." Catelyn set her coffee cup down and got to her feet. "We're not staying at her house anymore, so there would be no question of impropriety."

"I— It's not about—" Owen stammered. "I'm not interested in dating her. Or anyone."

Catelyn looked surprised. "Ever?"

Owen shook his head and added a slice of bread to the top of the sandwich. But his answer, which used to come so easily, got caught in his throat.

"She's great, Dad," Catelyn said quietly. "We all love her."

"Not Claire." Owen kept his voice low in case other little ears were nearby.

Catelyn sighed. "Claire is just being . . . Claire. She doesn't like anyone right now."

"She's still hurting," Owen defended her.

"I know." Catelyn's look was pointed. "Maybe she needs to see that it's okay to move on."

Huh. Owen hadn't thought of it that way. "You're pretty wise, you know."

Catelyn grinned. "I know. I got it from my mom."

Owen laughed and tossed the empty bread bag at her. "Go make sure your siblings are getting ready for church."

Catelyn lobbed the bag back and headed out of the kitchen. "You know." She turned back. "I wasn't one hundred percent sure about this move to Hope Springs. But now, I think it's the best thing that could have happened to our family. Back in Nashville, it felt like we were kind of . . . stuck in the past. But here, well, we're moving forward. Plus, you met Emma. And I met Jackson."

She pranced out of the room before Owen could respond to that.

※

Emma clung to the tree trunk, rough bark digging into her hands, her arms, and her legs. But she didn't care.

"I see my house," she called excitedly.

"Yay, you did it!" Kenzie cheered.

"I did, didn't I?" She hadn't been brave enough to look down yet, but now she did. It wasn't scary at all, not with Kenzie and Carter and Cody and Owen grinning up at her.

"We should take a picture," Kenzie said, and Owen handed her his phone.

"Smile," Kenzie called, but Emma was pretty sure she hadn't stopped smiling all day. It was so good to be spending time with them.

Kenzie snapped a few pictures, then called, "Okay, now you can come down."

Emma readjusted her grasp on the tree, lifted one foot and set it back down without moving. She tried the other foot. Then tried an arm.

"Uh," she finally called. "How do I get down?"

Owen's warm chuckle traveled up the tree. "Same way you got up. Just backwards."

"That doesn't make any sense," she grumbled.

"Start with your left foot," he instructed. "Slide it down the trunk until it reaches that branch below you. You'll need to lower the rest of your body too."

She did as he said, relieved when her foot landed on a solid branch.

Owen guided her the rest of the way down the tree like that. When she reached the lowest branch, he said, "Now sit down and jump."

She looked at him dubiously. "It's like twenty feet."

He laughed. "Okay, so we should add 'learn to judge distances' to your life list." He moved closer to the tree and stretched a hand toward her. "Come on, I've got you."

Carefully, she lowered herself to a seated position on the branch. She couldn't quite reach Owen's hand.

"It's okay," he coached. "I'm not going to let anything happen to you."

Emma nodded, took a breath, and pushed herself off the branch.

The moment she was in the air, she felt Owen's hand wrap around her forearm. Her feet hit the ground, and Owen steadied her landing.

"You did it." His hand tugged her close to him, and his other arm came around her back.

The hug lasted only a moment, but it was enough to set Emma's heart galloping.

"Good job, Miss Emma." Kenzie took her dad's place, wrapping her arms around Emma.

"Nice." Cody grinned and gave her a high five.

"I want to try," Carter declared, and Owen helped him climb the lowest branches.

As soon as Carter's feet were back on the ground, Cody asked, "Is it time for food now?"

"Ooo, you guys are having a picnic?" Emma glanced across the field toward her house. That was her cue to leave and give them some family time.

"So are you," Kenzie said, rolling her eyes like Emma should have realized that already. "Daddy made you a turkey and cheese and avocado and mustard sandwich."

"Oh." Emma turned back, her eyes snagging on Owen's. "That's my favorite."

He nodded, and her heart blipped. He knew her favorite sandwich. It was a small thing but—

"So you'll stay?" he asked, sounding uncertain.

Emma nodded. "You had me at avocado."

Kenzie giggled, and Emma suddenly remembered that she and Owen weren't alone.

Owen seemed to realize the same thing. "I'll go get the cooler."

He jogged toward the van, which was parked alongside the house. They'd toured the building before climbing the tree. The siding had already been replaced, and most of the rooms had been stripped back to the studs, but there was no longer any sign of smoke and fire damage. Soon, the contractors would put in new walls and floors and ceilings, and the house would be ready for Owen and the kids to move back in. Then they'd be neighbors again. Emma could hardly wait.

She led the kids to the picnic table, listening as Carter described the wisps of cirrus clouds in the sky.

After a few minutes, Owen returned, hefting a large cooler onto the table. "So. Now that you've conquered tree climbing, I think skydiving is the next logical step."

Emma laughed. "Yeah, because fifteen feet and fifteen thousand feet are almost the same thing." She took the sandwich he handed her.

"Skydiving is actually easier. Instead of trying *not* to fall, the whole thing is falling."

Emma snorted. "You might want to work on your marketing pitch a little bit."

Owen shrugged. "Fair enough. But I really do think you'd love it. How about Wednesday?"

His gaze landed on her, so pleading and persuasive that she almost would have said yes. But she couldn't.

"I have the county fair this week. I'm going to be there from sunup to sundown every day."

"Oh, can we go to the fair?" Kenzie turned eagerly to her father.

Owen's eyes were still on Emma, but he nodded. "Yeah. That sounds like fun. Maybe we can come say hi?"

"Of course." Emma's lips lifted at the thought of seeing them again. "If you don't mind hunting me down in the horse barns."

"We don't mind," Kenzie answered cheerfully.

Owen laughed and nodded. "No, we don't. Maybe we'll even drag you out of them to go on some rides. I seem to recall riding a roller coaster was on your list too."

Emma shook her head. "Nope. That one's not on there."

Owen frowned. "I'm sure it is. Let me see."

"All right." Emma turned on her phone, and scrolled to her list. "See?" She smirked, handing it to him.

"Yep." Owen smirked right back. "I do see." His fingers flew across the screen, and he passed the phone back to her. "It's right here."

Emma's eyes fell on the line he pointed to. Right under *climb a tree*, it said, *ride a roller coaster*.

"You just added that," she gasped with a laugh.

Owen shrugged. "All I know is it's on the list, so . . ."

Emma shook her head but grinned. "So I guess we're riding a roller coaster."

Chapter 42

"Is it time to meet Miss Emma and Ruby yet?" Kenzie danced from foot to foot, polishing off the rest of her cotton candy.

Owen checked his watch. "In a few minutes." The skip of his heart nearly matched the skip of his daughter's feet.

"Finally," Kenzie breathed.

Owen nodded. He'd poured nearly all of his energy since their picnic the other day into convincing himself that the only reason he was looking forward to the fair was for the kids.

But the moment he'd laid eyes on Emma earlier today—chatting with a student as she helped get a horse ready to show—Owen had to admit it was a lie. The reason he'd been looking forward to the fair was that he wanted to see her.

They'd only been able to talk for a few minutes before she'd had to rush off, but those few moments had been enough to make him greedy for more.

Catelyn and Jackson had taken Carter to see a magic show, Cody had gone to hang out with his baseball buddies, and Owen and Kenzie had checked out all of the animals—twice—toured the arts and crafts projects, and watched Ruby compete in and win the dressage competition.

It had all been fun, but Owen couldn't deny the pull of anticipation as he led Kenzie to the horse trailer where they'd agreed to meet Emma and Ruby.

If he was honest with himself, he wasn't sure he *wanted* to deny it anymore. Maybe Catelyn was right. Maybe his family did need to see that it was okay to move on. Maybe *he* needed to see it.

"There they are." Kenzie's voice pitched up in excitement, and Owen's heart did the same.

Ruby raced ahead of Emma, who moved more slowly than usual. And no wonder—she had to be exhausted.

Ruby careened into Kenzie, and the two girls instantly started planning which ride they should go on first.

"Hi guys." Emma reached them, her smile bright but tired around the edges. "Thanks for waiting for us." A piece of straw stuck up from her hair, and Owen's fingers slid to pluck it out.

"Oh." Her cheeks colored. "Thanks."

"Ah, yeah." He jammed his hands in his pockets so he wouldn't be tempted to do that again. It had felt so instinctive, so natural.

But judging by the way her cheeks still glowed, it hadn't been the same for her.

"So." He turned to the girls. "What's up first?"

"Roller coaster," Ruby answered definitively. "So Aunt Emma can check it off her life list."

Emma snorted. "Not that I put it on there in the first place." But she didn't protest.

They strolled toward the midway, Ruby and Kenzie in the lead. Owen walked close enough to Emma that he could have held her hand—but he kept his tucked firmly in his pockets.

The only roller coaster was a kiddie one shaped like a dragon. The track went in a circle, with slight hills and dips along the route—never getting more than six or seven feet in the air.

Emma laughed as they got in line. "I'm pretty sure even I can handle this one."

Ruby and Kenzie got into a car together, but the seats were so narrow that only one adult could fit in each, so Owen squeezed into the car behind Emma. She shrieked as the ride started, pulling a hearty chuckle from him.

"That's not funny," she called over her shoulder, but he could hear the laughter in her voice as well.

"You ride horses faster than this," he called back.

Her shoulders lifted in a shrug, and her curls bounced as she shook her head. Her blonde hair was short enough that he could just see the nape of her neck, and suddenly he found himself wondering what it would be like to press his lips there.

He tore his eyes away.

Thinking about moving on was one thing.

Thinking about kissing her was quite another.

But as they disembarked from the ride, his eyes fell on her smiling lips, and all he could think about suddenly was kisses.

"Now what?" She pulled out her phone and ceremoniously checked off "ride a roller coaster."

"I'm really not sure that counts," Owen said dubiously. "It was more like a merry-go-round than a roller coaster."

"It counts," Emma insisted.

"Can we go on the big slide next?" Ruby asked.

"Lead the way."

Owen and Emma followed the girls to the slide, then to the spinning swings, then the bumper cars and the Tilt-a-Whirl. Some of the rides they went on with the girls; others they watched, standing side by side, a little closer, it seemed, with each ride.

"Now what?" Emma asked as the girls came off the Scrambler.

"The Ferris wheel," Ruby announced.

"Yeah." Kenzie's agreement sounded tentative.

"You hate the Ferris wheel," Owen reminded his daughter. The one time he'd convinced her to ride the kiddie one at a theme park, she'd screamed and cried the entire time. The ride operator had eventually had to stop the ride and let them off early.

"Not anymore," Kenzie insisted, though she still sounded uncertain.

"I've never been on a Ferris wheel," Emma chimed in.

Owen stared at her. "How is that possible?"

She lifted a shoulder. "Kind of goes along with the whole afraid of heights thing."

"Well, now you've climbed a tree *and* ridden a roller coaster," Ruby pointed out. "I know you can do it. And you too." She turned to Kenzie.

"I'll try if Miss Emma will," Kenzie offered.

Emma laughed. "Well, I can't exactly say no now."

"Kenz, maybe you should ride with me, just in case you get scared," Owen said as they started toward the big wheel. The sun had set, and the dusky sky still held tones of silver and gold.

Kenzie shook her head. "I want to ride with Ruby. You should ride with Miss Emma, so she doesn't get scared."

"You can hold her hand if you have to," Ruby added, and both girls giggled.

"Only if it's okay with you." Owen glanced at Emma, then realized it probably sounded like he was asking if it was okay to hold her hand. "Riding together I mean, not . . ."

"That sounds fine to me." Emma's smile wavered with nerves, and Owen wondered if it was the thought of the Ferris wheel or of sitting with him that caused it. Because he was suddenly feeling pretty jittery himself—and he wasn't even afraid of heights.

They reached the line just as the lights on the Ferris wheel switched on, setting it aglow in pinks and purples and blues.

"Wow," Ruby sang out.

Kenzie turned to Owen, her eyes almost as bright as the lights. "This is going to be good."

Owen grinned. It might just be really good.

His eyes caught on Emma again, and he amended the thought. There was no might about it. It *would* be really good.

Chapter 43

Emma watched Ruby and Kenzie get on the Ferris wheel.

"Be brave," she called to Kenzie, and the girl grinned and called back, "You too."

The wheel jolted to a start, moving the girls up and backwards.

Kenzie screamed a little, and Ruby grinned and held up her hand, which was linked with Kenzie's.

If she was trying to say that was what Emma should do with Owen...

"Ready?" Owen held out a hand to her, and she stared at it. It was their turn to get in a basket.

Acutely aware that her niece and Owen's daughter were watching, Emma took Owen's hand only long enough to get into her seat. He settled in next to her, his shoulder and leg brushing hers. She tried to scoot a little farther to the inside to give him more room, but there was nowhere to go.

The Ferris wheel gave a sudden jerk, and Emma gripped the closest thing to her—which happened to be Owen's hand.

"Sorry." She laughed sheepishly, trying to pull her hand back.

But he held on, threading his fingers through hers. "It's okay. I think Ruby had the right idea."

The Ferris wheel jounced again, moving them a little higher, and Owen cinched his arm around hers, tucking it tight between them.

"Oh." Her laugh sounded breathless and silly. She had to get a grip.

But tingles were dancing up and down her arm—the kind that had nothing to do with neuropathy.

"Don't worry. It only does that the first time around," Owen reassured her. "After that it's a smooth ride."

Emma swallowed feebly. The ride might smooth out, but what about her pulse?

She knew Owen was only holding her hand to keep her from being afraid, but that didn't do anything to keep her heart from bumping all over the place.

The wheel did its jerky start-stop thing a few more times as more passengers were added. Emma searched desperately for something normal to say. But nothing about this moment felt normal.

"Get ready for it," Owen whispered as the Ferris wheel jostled toward the top.

"Ready for what?"

"This." Owen gestured his free arm toward the scene that spread out before them. His other hand tightened around hers.

"Wow." Beyond the lights of the fair, the velvety expanse of Lake Michigan stretched toward the dark line of the horizon. Lights from scattered boats dotted the surface, and white foam danced on top of the waves.

"Beautiful," Owen breathed.

Emma nodded and turned to the right, where the lights of Hope Springs poked through the trees. "It feels like we're on top of the world."

Owen's slow, warm chuckle filled her. "If you like this, you'll love skydiving."

"Mmm." Emma couldn't think of any other words because Owen's fingers were headed for her face.

He tucked a strand of hair behind her ear, his fingers grazing her cheek. He leaned closer, and Emma had a mini panic attack.

Why was he looking at her like that? Was he about to—

The Ferris wheel pitched forward, sending their basket rocking and Owen's hand tumbling from her cheek.

Neither of them said anything, and Emma wondered if she'd only been dreaming. She *was* pretty sleepy.

The wheel took them in smooth rotation after smooth rotation. The light breeze slid over Emma's cheek, gentle as Owen's hand, and her eyelids grew heavy.

Stay awake, she ordered herself.

And she thought she had obeyed, until she felt the whisper of Owen's breath over her ear. "Emma, the ride is over."

She startled, her eyes jumping open to find that her head was somehow on his shoulder.

"I'm so sorry." She jolted upright so quickly that she banged her elbow against the opposite side of the basket.

"It's okay." His smile played with her heart. "You had a long day."

He helped her out of the basket, his fingers lingering around hers for a moment before they reached Ruby and Kenzie.

"That was amazing, wasn't it, Miss Emma?" Kenzie beamed at her. "I'm glad we went on it."

"Me too." Emma tried to reorient herself. Her feet were on the ground, and she and Owen were just friends.

"So?" Owen grinned at her. "Skydiving next?"

Emma had to say no. Because if being that close to him on a Ferris wheel had done this to her, what would being strapped to him as they plummeted toward the earth do?

But she opened her mouth and the word "yes" escaped.

"Really?" Owen's eyes widened, as did Kenzie's and Ruby's.

"Yes," Emma said more firmly. She could do this without letting her feelings for Owen get in the way.

At least, she was pretty sure she could.

Chapter 44

"I can't believe you finally asked her on a date." Catelyn scanned Owen's attire as if to make sure it was appropriate. Kenzie and Cody eyed him too. Even Carter took a look before turning back to his weather book.

"It's not a date," Owen insisted, though the nerves currently crackling in his stomach said otherwise. "It's a jump. It's my job." He grabbed his car keys off the cabin's counter.

Catelyn snorted. "Maybe don't lead with that line. Try something along the lines of, 'You look nice.' Or, you know, 'smokin' hot.' Whatever mood strikes you."

Kenzie giggled and Cody made a retching sound.

"Who's smokin' hot?" Claire stumbled into the room, still in her pajamas even though it was 1 p.m. She had the day off today.

"No one," Owen said hastily at the same time as Kenzie said, "Miss Emma."

Claire stared at Owen.

"I'm just taking her for her first tandem jump," Owen explained.

"A tandem jump," Claire repeated. "Like the same way you met Mom?"

The words slammed Owen in the gut.

"Claire." It was Cody who spoke up, his voice low and warning.

"It's my job," Owen repeated.

"Right." Claire stormed out of the room, and Owen stood, torn.

"You're going to be late," Catelyn warned.

"You're right." He took a breath and headed for the door. "You all behave for your sister."

"And you have fun," Catelyn sing-songed.

Owen refused to look back over his shoulder, mostly because he didn't want to give her the satisfaction of seeing his grin. He jogged to the van, propelled by his need to see Emma.

It had been two long days since the Ferris wheel. Two long days since he'd almost lost his mind and kissed her. Two long days of wondering what her lips would have felt like on his. Two long days of waiting for another chance to find out.

You don't even know if she wants that, he reminded himself.

She'd said she didn't date, that she wasn't looking for a family of her own anymore.

But maybe . . .

Owen let out a breath. It had been a long time since he'd had to figure out a woman.

With Katie it had been—

Katie.

He stepped on the brake as he came to a crossroad.

What was he doing thinking about another woman? Katie was his *wife.*

Maybe Claire was right. Maybe he shouldn't be moving on.

He had never planned to, despite what he'd promised Katie.

But you did promise, he reminded himself. And it was what she had wanted.

He pressed his foot to the accelerator and turned his questions over to the Lord, praying for guidance. He didn't have an answer by the time he reached Emma's house, but he did have a growing desire to see where this might lead.

He jumped out of the van, but before he could reach her door, she was standing there in front of him, looking slightly nervous and entirely beautiful, and he wondered if it would be completely inappropriate to start the date—no, it wasn't a date—with a kiss.

Probably.

"Is this okay?" Emma gestured to her leggings and sleeveless yoga top that hugged her curves without being revealing.

"You look amazing," he said, and her eyes widened.

He grinned. At least he hadn't said "smokin' hot" like Catelyn had suggested.

"You said to wear something that would fit under a jumpsuit," Emma added, as if she felt the need to explain her wardrobe choice.

"And this is perfect." He had to tear his eyes off the delicate curve of her bare shoulders.

"Okay, good." She tugged at the headband that held the curls off her face, and for a moment Owen was disappointed that he wouldn't have an excuse to tuck her hair behind her ear again.

"Are you ready for this?" He led her to the van and opened the door for her, catching a snatch of her light flower and sunshine scent as she slipped past him. It was going to be difficult not to be distracted by that scent when they were strapped into a tandem rig together.

"I have no idea," she replied.

He chuckled. "Don't worry. That's how most people feel. But once you're up there, you'll wonder why you waited so long."

He closed her door and got in, locking both hands on the steering wheel so he wouldn't twine his fingers through hers the way he had on the Ferris wheel. Given that she was currently sitting on her hands, he had to assume she didn't want that.

"Nervous?" he asked, his own stomach turning about fifty somersaults a second.

She laughed faintly. "How can you tell?"

"You're bouncing your leg. You always do that when you're nervous. Or when you sit still for too long."

Her laugh turned to one of surprise. "Really? No one's ever told me that before."

He wondered if anyone had ever told her how her eyes lit up when she smiled or how she tapped her lip when she was trying to find where a puzzle piece went or how she looked serene whenever he caught her in prayer. He wondered if—

"Owen?"

"Sorry. What was that?" He pulled his thoughts back to driving.

"I was just saying that if this is too . . ." She cut off and stared out the window.

"Too?" he prompted when she didn't continue. She was usually so blunt that her hesitation sent a fresh wave of nerves through him.

Emma blew out a breath. "Weird, I guess. I mean, I know you and your wife . . . Not that this is . . . I mean, I know you're a professional, and this isn't . . ." She shook her head and pulled her headband out of her hair.

Owen resisted the urge to reach over and comb his fingers through it.

She turned to him, looking completely vulnerable, and his heart couldn't take it. He had to lighten the mood. "You usually make more sense than this."

But Emma didn't laugh. "I just mean, we don't have to do this. If you don't want to."

Owen shook his head. "Oh, no. You're not getting out of it that easily. We are jumping. Today. Together."

Emma studied him another moment, then nodded. "Okay." She pulled her hands out from under her legs and rested them in her lap.

Owen's hand stole off the steering wheel and landed on hers. He swallowed roughly as she let her fingers slide between his.

"Full disclosure?" she whispered. "I'm terrified."

"Full disclosure?" Owen repeated. "Me too."

Emma's head swiveled toward him. "You do this for a living."

He let his eyes meet hers for a second before returning them to the road. "Not with you."

Chapter 45

Emma tried to concentrate on the introductory video Owen had said she had to watch before they could jump. He was in the rigging room, getting things ready, but she could still feel his hand around hers. Could still hear the way he'd said he was nervous about this jump because it was with her.

What did that mean?

She was pretty sure he wasn't afraid they'd crash.

So was he . . .

She shook her head and forced her attention back to the TV. If she didn't figure out what she was supposed to do, maybe he *should* be afraid that they'd crash.

"Oh good. It's almost done."

She jumped at Owen's voice right behind her and looked up to find him leaning on the back of her chair, close enough that if she sat back, she could lean her head against his chest. His fresh, warm smell drifted over her, and she had to stop herself from pulling in an extra big breath.

How was she supposed to concentrate?

Fortunately, Owen hadn't been wrong about the video being almost done. A minute later, the credits rolled, and he left his spot behind her to turn off the TV.

Emma let out a long, slow pent-up breath.

"It's going to be great," Owen reassured her. "I'm going to be with you the whole way."

Emma nodded, unwilling to say that maybe that was what she was afraid of. Because ever since the Ferris wheel . . .

She'd been having hopes and wishes and dreams she knew could never come true.

She'd spent the past two days convincing herself that she'd only been imagining that he felt the same way.

But now . . .

"Let's do this!" Owen's enthusiastic words made her jump, and he laughed. "Come on." He gentled his voice and held out a hand to her. "You're going to love it."

She swallowed and took his hand. Instantly, his fingers wrapped around hers, warm and strong and secure. He led her past the big open hangar door, where Charles was inspecting the plane, to the rigging room.

"Here's your jumpsuit." He let go of her hand and passed her a shiny black suit with a red stripe down the sides.

"Flashy," she murmured, trying not to let her voice shake as her nerves kicked into high gear. She was really doing this.

Owen was already stepping into his own suit, as if it were just another day in the office. For him, she supposed it was.

The suit slipped easily over her clothing, and she reached to pull up the zipper. But her fingers had started to tremble, and she couldn't get a firm grasp on it.

"Let me help." Instead of reaching for the zipper, Owen cradled her hands in his own. "It's really going to be fine," he soothed. "It's totally normal to be nervous."

She nodded and tried to smile, although her lips felt as shaky as her hands. Owen rested his gaze on hers for a moment longer, then let go of her hands and pulled up the zipper for her.

He took a step back and grabbed something off a hook. "Now the harness." He held it out with two hands. "Come step into it."

Emma swallowed and let him help her slip her feet through the leg straps.

He moved behind her and pulled the harness up, slipping the shoulder straps over her arms. His movements were practiced and steady, and they had a calming effect on her.

"Okay, now we'll fasten you up." Owen pulled on the straps at her back and shoulders and hips until she grunted. "Good," he grinned. "Nice and tight."

He held out a pair of goggles to her. "These are for you. And you get your very own altimeter too. Give me your hand, and I'll help you put it on."

She held out her left hand, and he slipped the strap over her wrist like an oversize watch. A second, smaller strap hooked over two fingers. He squeezed her hand, then let go.

"Let me just get my rig on, and we can head out."

Emma watched as he pulled on his own harness, this one with a large backpack attached—the parachute container, she remembered—tightening and tucking the same way he had with hers. "So when we get on the plane, we're going to connect your attachment points"—he lightly touched the straps on her shoulders, then the ones by her hips—"to mine." He showed her the loops in the same spots on his harness. "And we'll be good to go."

He held out his hand, and she slipped hers into it without hesitation. Her stomach still swirled with nerves, and yet she also felt a strange sense of calm. Owen knew what he was doing. He would keep her safe.

He led her out of the hangar and across a short walkway to the plane. Charles came around from the other side of it, grinning at their interlocked hands.

"Glad he finally convinced you." Charles winked, and Emma wasn't quite sure if he meant the jump or the hand-holding, but she nodded anyway.

Charles waved them toward a small portable stairway perched in front of the plane's open door. Owen's hand slid out of hers and landed on the back of her harness, holding her firmly as she climbed.

It wasn't until she was inside the plane that she remembered she'd never flown before.

She turned to Owen. "I was so busy worrying about the jumping part that I forgot about being afraid to fly."

He chuckled. "Don't worry. I've got you for the flight too." He moved closer, steering her to a short, padded bench, which she straddled, facing the back of the plane, as the video had instructed. She felt him settle in behind her, and then his arms came around her to clip her seatbelt into place. For one crazy second, she thought about leaning back into him and letting her head rest on his chest for the ride.

Fortunately, the plane started to move, jostling her forward, and she came to her senses.

"Here we go," Owen whooped, and she could hear the exhilaration in his voice.

She grinned. This was a side of him she hadn't seen yet.

Within moments, they were in the air and Emma let herself gaze out the window. The plane tilted and turned a little, but she found she wasn't afraid at all as she admired the view of the fields and trees and lake below.

"It's even better than a Ferris wheel," she called to Owen, enjoying the sound of his chuckle over the rumble of the plane.

The video had said it would take twenty minutes to get to the jumping altitude of 13,500 feet, but the time seemed to blink by, and the next thing she knew, Owen was sliding her closer to him to fasten their connection points.

His chest was solid and warm behind her, and Emma let herself relax into him as he went over the instructions for their jump, reminding her that they would free fall for about fifty seconds before he pulled the ripcord and that if something happened to keep him from doing so, it was her job to watch her altimeter and pull the secondary ripcord before 4,000 feet.

"But nothing will happen," he reassured her. He wrapped one arm around her waist and helped her up so that they could move, crablike, toward the door of the airplane.

"We've got this," Owen said into her ear. "Cross your arms into the safety position and tip your head back." She obeyed, trying to remember exactly what the video had said, and then they were at the door and wind was rushing up at her face and blocking out all sound except Owen's countdown.

"Three," he shouted into her ear.

A rush of nerves swooped over Emma, and she had a sudden, overwhelming desire to dive back into the plane.

But Owen was a solid wall behind her, still counting down. "Two."

Emma gulped in a breath as Owen's knees bent, bending hers with them. "One."

And then they were in the air. She stuck her arms out and arched her back the way the video had instructed. Wind whipped past her face and roared in her ears, but it didn't feel like they were moving at all.

She could feel Owen above her, his hands moving to various parts of the rig, and she knew he was inspecting it just the way the video had said he would. And then his hands were in front of her giving two big thumbs up. She mimicked the gesture, exhilaration overtaking her.

This was incredible. They were floating, the world stretched out below them like an elaborate, textured mural. She wanted to call out to Owen, to tell him how amazing this was, to thank him for convincing her to jump, but the whole thing felt beyond words.

In the distance, a few feathery clouds hung over Lake Michigan at almost their exact altitude, and Emma grinned, thinking how much Carter would love to be up here with them.

Owen held up two fingers, the symbol he had said he would use to let her know when he was about to pull the ripcord. A moment later, his hand disappeared, and they were pulled into an upright position, their fall rapidly decelerating into a glide. Behind her, Owen was moving, checking the lines and the canopy.

After a moment, he held his thumbs up in front of her again. She did the same, wishing it weren't too loud to talk up here. She wanted to tell him how amazing this was. How it made her feel . . . something she couldn't exactly name. Something she couldn't ever recall feeling in her life. It was a combination of awe and joy and excitement and gratitude and . . . so many things.

They drifted in silence, still high above the earth, and Emma tried to take it all in, marveling at how something could be so thrilling and so relaxing at the same time.

She never wanted it to end, but after a few minutes, Owen gave her the hand signal to put her feet up, and she did. They were only fifteen feet above the ground now, and Owen stuck his legs out to the sides of hers. She felt the parachute slow, and then they were both seated on the ground, sliding to a stop in the grass.

Emma's breath came in short, exhilarated gasps, and for a moment all she could do was look up at the sky in wonder. She had been up there, flying.

She laughed out loud, and behind her Owen started laughing too. "Pretty cool, huh?"

Her head bobbed wildly, but she was still caught up in a strange combination of laughing and gasping, and it took a moment before she could even say, "Wow."

"It's kind of impossible to describe, isn't it?" Owen sounded like he was just as in awe as she was, even though he did this every day.

She nodded, still too breathless to say more.

"So, I was thinking." Behind her, Owen unclipped their harnesses, but he didn't move away from her. "Do you think you'd want to have dinner sometime? With me?"

Emma froze, all the air from her gasping breaths trapped in her lungs. They'd had dinner together plenty of times. But somehow she didn't think that was what he was talking about.

"I'm sorry. Was that—" Owen slid back from her and jumped to his feet. "Never mind. I know you don't—"

"I'd like that." Emma managed to wheeze the words out. She could only imagine the goofy, giddy look on her face right now, and she was very glad suddenly that her back was to him.

"Yeah?" The same giddiness brimmed in his voice. "How about tonight?"

"Sure. Let's do it tonight."

Owen whooped the way he had earlier, and Emma laughed. She felt like doing some whooping herself.

And then he was standing above her, holding out both hands.

She set hers confidently in his and let him tug her to her feet. They were only inches apart now—not as close as they had been while harnessed together, but close—and she could see the joy she felt reflected in his eyes.

He lifted a hand to her cheek, tucking in a curl that had escaped her headband.

His fingers lingered for a moment, and Emma tried to get her breathing under control.

He leaned closer, so that his forehead was almost touching hers, and Emma swallowed, realizing suddenly that he might kiss her.

Panic flooded her system.

She hadn't kissed a man in ages. She wasn't sure she'd ever been good at it. But now? She had to be really rusty.

She took a quick step backwards. "So now we pick up the chute?" she asked, her breath coming even more roughly than it had after the jump.

"Uh. Yeah." Owen looked confused and maybe a little hurt, but he started gathering the chute's lines and big nylon canopy.

"So you enjoyed it?" Owen asked, sounding like he could be talking to any old client.

Emma nodded. "Very much. Thank you." And she sounded like she could be talking to any old skydiving instructor. She pushed out a breath, resolved to do better. "Seriously, Owen, that was . . . one of the best things I've ever done."

That drew a grin from him. "Really?"

"Really." They started the trek back toward the hangar. "So about that dinner . . ." It felt bold to say it—but then again, she was feeling pretty bold after that jump.

Owen's face eased into a smile. "You still want to do that?"

"Turns out skydiving works up quite an appetite. But I wouldn't mind changing first."

"I think we can make that happen." He led her inside, where he deposited the parachute and harnesses on a table, explaining that they would be inspected and carefully repacked by himself or Charles. They both peeled off their jumpsuits and picked up the phones and keys they'd left on the table.

On the way out the door, Owen slipped his hand into hers like it was the most natural thing in the world.

And given the way her fingers curled right around his, maybe it was.

Chapter 46

Owen relaxed into Emma's comfortable couch, enjoying the familiar feel of its slightly worn fabric, as she headed to her room to change.

He'd missed being here.

Being with her.

He closed his eyes, letting himself relive their dive—her hair in his face, the exhilaration in her eyes, the joy on her lips as he'd come this close to kissing her again.

Until she'd backed away faster than if he'd turned into a snake.

Maybe he'd misinterpreted. Maybe she didn't feel the same way about him as he did about her. Maybe she was just a really nice person who had done her duty for his family and now wanted to get on with her own life.

But the way she'd wrapped her fingers around his when he took her hand. . . . That had to mean something, didn't it?

He got to his feet and paced in front of the window. She was probably confused. He'd spent so long fighting this, he'd told her he didn't intend to ever date, he'd asked her to go out with *Charles*.

He puffed out a breath.

Yeah, she had every right to be confused.

He'd been confused too.

But not anymore.

Behind him, he heard her bedroom door open, and he whirled toward her, then staggered to a halt. She had changed into a pinkish-beige dress that fell in flowing layers toward her knees, where it nearly brushed the top of her cowboy boots. Wide straps emphasized the feminine curve of her shoulders.

Her smile wavered uncertainly. "I can change if this is too . . ."

Owen's feet came unstuck and gobbled the space between them.

Her eyes widened as he planted a hand on each of her shoulders.

"This is perfect." His words whispered over the space between them. "You look stunning."

He let himself lean closer. A shaky exhale escaped her lips, but she didn't move. He leaned a little closer still, his eyes fixed on hers.

He saw the moment panic flooded them. And then she was wiggling deftly out of his arms. "So where did you want to go? There's the Hidden Cafe. Or Toiva. Or Alessandro's, if you want to get—"

"Emma." Owen's voice was slightly strangled, and he cleared his throat as her eyes met his, now looking less panicked and more . . . regretful.

He rubbed the back of his neck. "I know you said you don't date. And I said I don't."

"We did say that," she whispered.

"But I think I may need to rethink some things," he went on, daring to take a step closer to her. "Because I find myself wanting to be with you all the time. Wanting to talk to you and laugh with you. And—" He closed the remaining space between them. "Kiss you."

She didn't flee this time, but that same panic welled in her eyes.

"What is it?" He stuffed his hands in his pockets so they wouldn't go to her arms, her face, her hair. "Do you not feel the same way?"

"It's not that."

He let out a relieved breath. "Okay. Good." He slid his hand into hers. "Is this just too fast? You don't want me to kiss you yet?"

She licked her lips but looked away. "I do want you to kiss me. I'm just . . . I might be a little rusty."

Owen's laugh was equal parts surprise and relief. "Why don't you let me be the judge of that."

She looked at him, her lips lifted in a half-laugh, and it did Owen in. He brought his hands to her cheeks, raising her face toward his. Her surprised inhale as their lips met sent an explosion of joy through him, but he moved slowly, waiting for her lips to respond. When they did, he felt himself smiling.

She most definitely was *not* rusty. She was . . . perfect.

He slid his hands from her cheeks into her hair.

Her hands landed on his shoulders, and when she pulled him closer, Owen was the one to inhale in surprise. And delight.

After another moment, he pulled back gently.

Emma's eyes popped open. "Did I do something wrong?" Her voice held the same breathless exhilaration as it had after their skydive.

Owen shook his head emphatically. "That was most definitely very right."

She giggled, then clapped a hand over her mouth, and he pulled her into a hug.

Her face pressed into his chest, and he wondered if she could feel the wild racing of his heart.

"I had no idea a kiss could be so . . ." She trailed off, her arms tightening around him.

Owen pressed his lips to the top of her head. "I'd be happy to show you again sometime."

She loosened her hold on him and tilted her head up. "I just might let you do that."

He didn't need to be asked twice.

He lowered his face to hers. But just as their lips brushed, a sound from the kitchen made them jump apart.

"My mom and William just got home," Emma whisper-gasped, the panic from earlier reentering her eyes.

Owen chuckled. "Probably."

"What are we going to tell them?"

"Mmm, well." Owen stepped closer and threaded his arm around her waist. "We could tell them we just had our first kiss." He dropped his lips to her temple, then added, "Of many."

Emma's cheeks were pink, and she shoved his arm, but she was smiling widely.

"Or," she whispered back. "We could just tell them we're going to dinner."

He shrugged playfully. "If you want to be boring."

But he let his arm fall from her waist and followed her into the kitchen.

"How was it?" Anne glanced excitedly from Emma to Owen. He startled. How did she . . .

"Look at you, still glowing," Anne kept talking. "I've been thinking . . . Maybe I'll jump sometime."

Emma glanced at Owen, and he saw his own relief and amusement reflected in her eyes.

"You should, Mom." Emma really did seem to be glowing. "It was the most . . . Amazing isn't even the word for it. There isn't a word. You just have to experience it."

Anne nodded, then seemed to take stock of Emma's clothes. "You didn't jump in that, did you?"

Emma's cheeks took on more color. "No. We were, uh, just heading out for dinner."

"Oh." Anne did an admirable job of keeping any surprise out of her voice, but Owen spotted the grin she directed at her husband. "Well, don't let us keep you. You two have fun."

"We will." Owen resisted the urge to reach for Emma's hand as she started toward the door.

He fell in behind her, but as he passed them, Anne squeezed his arm, and William fist bumped his shoulder.

Owen grinned at them both and followed Emma out the door. The moment it closed behind him, he slipped his hand into hers and led her to the van.

He brushed a quick kiss onto her lips before he opened her door, then ran around to his own side before he could be tempted to kiss her again.

Chapter 47

"This is incredible." Emma kept her eyes on her nearly empty plate, but really, she meant *this*. All of this. The whole day.

Skydiving with Owen. Kissing Owen. Being here with Owen.

"It is." He reached across the table and brushed his hand over the back of hers.

The young waitress brought them their bill, giving them a sweet smile as Owen pulled out his wallet. "I love to see older couples who still hold hands," she gushed.

Emma and Owen managed to wait until she had left the table to burst into laughter.

"Older couples, huh?" Owen turned his mouth down. "How old does she think we are?"

But Emma was still caught on another word: couple.

Was that what they were now?

"Well, we don't want to disappoint the young whipper-snapper," Owen said in a reedy—and ridiculous—old-man voice. He twined his fingers with hers. "We'd better hold hands."

The waitress returned after a moment and passed Owen his card. "You two have made my night," she said. "My parents just divorced. It's good to see relationships can last."

"Thanks." Owen looked surprised, but he didn't correct the woman. "You made ours too."

The waitress smiled and hurried off.

"I guess we should go." Emma pushed reluctantly to her feet, and Owen followed suit.

"Do you want to go for a walk on the beach?" He gestured out the restaurant's wall of windows looking out over the lake.

"Yes." Emma didn't even have to think about it. "I just need to use the restroom first."

"I'll meet you at the door." He dropped a kiss onto her forehead before they separated.

She felt like a fool, grinning all the way to the bathroom, but she couldn't stop.

She used the restroom quickly, then checked her hair in the mirror. Her curls were slightly wild, and she wondered if that was from the skydive—or from the way Owen's fingers had raked through them earlier. She touched a hand to her lips, grinning to herself. Maybe their walk on the beach would lead to more kissing.

The bathroom door opened. "Oh hi, Emma."

Emma dropped her hand from her face. "Hi, Dana. I didn't realize you were back." The older woman from church had been staying with her daughter in Florida for the past six months. "How are you doing?"

"Oh, I'm great." The woman touched Emma's arm. "The question is, how are you, dear? I see your hair is coming back in beautifully. Chemo is all done?"

"Oh. Uh—" The words whammed into Emma like an ambush.

Her chemo.

Her cancer.

She still hadn't told Owen about any of it. But if they were going to be together, to be a couple, she didn't have a choice. She had to tell him right now, before things went any further.

Dana was still watching her, her forehead wrinkling more the longer Emma didn't answer.

"Yeah," Emma managed to push out. "All done. My scans are all clear."

"Praise the Lord for that." Dana pulled her into a hug.

Emma returned it briefly. "I'm so sorry. I have to get going. My, ah—" She couldn't quite bring herself to say "date," mostly because she knew that would lead to more questions. "Is waiting." She scooted past Dana and opened the door. "It was nice seeing you."

Outside the restroom, she slowed. What was she going to say to Owen? How could she possibly tell him? How would he react?

Fear turned her stomach over on itself, and she pressed a hand to her middle as she spotted Owen standing with his back to her, near the restaurant door. He had his phone to his ear, probably checking on the kids. Her stomach flipped again. She would have to tell them too, at some point.

Unless Owen didn't want to continue this relationship once he knew.

She blew a breath through pursed lips, forcing a smile to her face as Owen lowered the phone and turned toward her.

"Sorry I took so long. I ran into—" Her words died on her lips at his clenched jaw and pale face. "What's wrong?"

"That was James." His teeth didn't unlock as he spoke. "He picked Claire up again."

"Oh no. Owen." She stepped closer and grabbed his arm, her heart clenching as tight as his jaw. "What did he say?"

"She stole some things from the grocery store." Owen's voice fell heavily, and she could tell there was more he wasn't saying.

"Donuts," he continued. "A bag of chips."

It took her a moment to realize he was listing off the things Claire had stolen.

"And a bottle of vodka," he finished, voice choked.

"Oh, Owen." All Emma could do was clutch his arm. She wanted to say maybe it was a mistake, a misunderstanding, but she knew her brother better than that. He was thorough and he was fair. He wouldn't have called unless he had evidence.

"I have to go to the station," Owen rasped, unmoving.

"Of course. Let's go." Emma tugged his arm and led him to the door. "Do you want me to drive?"

He shook his head, giving her a tight smile. "I'm okay, thanks. Sorry to ruin our night."

Emma shook her head. "Your family comes first."

Owen nodded stiffly, but when they got to the vehicle, he brushed his lips quickly over hers. "Thank you."

"Always."

The ride to the station was short and silent.

When they arrived, Owen opened his door, but Emma sat, uncertain. "Do you want me to come inside or wait out here?"

He hesitated. "Would you mind coming inside? I don't know if I can . . ."

"Of course." Emma was out of the vehicle before he could finish.

She tucked her fingers between his as they crossed the parking lot but let go when they reached the door. This probably wasn't the time or the place for either her brother or his daughter to learn about their relationship.

Owen pulled the door open, and Emma entered first. It was a small station, with only three officers and a part-time receptionist, so Emma wasn't surprised to find the front desk empty.

"Come on." She gestured Owen toward the hallway that led to James's office.

The door was open, but she knocked anyway, and her brother looked up from his cluttered desk.

"Emma. What are you—" He must have spotted Owen behind her because he stood. "Ah." He strode around the desk. "Come in." If he was surprised to see them together, he didn't show it.

"Where's Claire?" Owen asked tersely.

"She's in an interrogation room to wait for you," James said, a little too matter-of-factly, in Emma's opinion.

Owen flinched but nodded. "Now what?"

"That's what I wanted to talk to you about." James directed Owen to a chair covered in rough gray fabric. "Have a seat." He raised an eyebrow toward Emma, as if asking if she was going to stay too.

"Would it be okay if I went to Claire?" she asked—not quite sure which of the men she was seeking permission from.

"Please." Owen nodded gratefully.

James scrutinized her for a moment, then nodded. "Room one. At the end of the hall."

Emma squeezed Owen's forearm on her way out the door to let him know it was going to be all right. And then she prayed that was true.

It was only a few steps to the interrogation room, but it may as well have been a mile, she walked so slowly. Going to Claire had felt like the right thing to do when she'd suggested it, but of all of Owen's children, Claire had always been the one she had the hardest time figuring out.

Give me wisdom, Lord, she prayed as she opened the interrogation room door.

Claire sat at a small table, looking younger and more vulnerable than usual.

"Hey," Emma said quietly, stepping into the room but leaving the door open.

"What are you doing here?" Claire's hard eyes traveled Emma's dress and cowboy boots.

"Your dad is talking to my brother. He should be done in a moment." She realized that didn't answer Claire's question, but it felt safest. "I just wanted to make sure you were all right."

Claire sneered. "I bet you did."

Emma had no idea how to respond to that, so she pulled out the chair across from Claire and sat. "You know—" She fiddled with the hem of her dress. "My dad died when I was a little younger than you are."

"Good for you," Claire muttered.

Emma swallowed. This was not going the way she had envisioned.

"I'm just saying," she tried again. "If you ever want to talk, I—"

"You what? Understand me?" Claire scoffed. "You know all my problems? You can fix me?"

"You don't need to be fixed Claire." Emma's voice took on a firmness she hadn't expected of herself. "You need to know Jesus' forgiveness. And you need to know there are still people in your life who care about you, even if your mom can't be here anymore."

"Like you?" Claire raised a corner of her lip in disdain.

"Like me, yes. And your father and—"

"Well, I don't want you to care about me," Claire interrupted. "You're not my mother, and you never will be."

"I'm not trying to be—"

"So you and my dad weren't on a date?" Claire waved an arm accusingly at her dress.

"I— We were at dinner."

Claire dropped her arm, looking suddenly defeated, as if the confirmation of her suspicions was too much.

"But, Claire, that doesn't mean—" Emma started to reach across the table between them but then thought better of it. "I'm not trying to—"

"Good." Claire crossed her arms protectively over her front. "Because he's going to have to choose between me and you. Which one do you think he'll pick?" Claire glared, but her lips wobbled in uncertainty.

Emma's heart went out to the girl. Did she really not know?

"He'll pick you, Claire," she said quietly. "He'll always pick you."

But Emma would never make him face that choice. She'd make it for him.

Claire blinked and looked away, swallowing hard. Emma longed to go to the girl and wrap her arms around her.

Instead, she pushed to her feet. "I'll wait in the hallway. Let me know if you need anything."

Claire's sniff was the only response.

Chapter 48

Owen mashed his temples between his thumb and forefinger, but it was impossible to make the throbbing stop. His daughter was looking at shoplifting and possession charges, but James had just finished outlining another option.

He could recommend that the prosecutor place Claire in a diversion program, where she would have to do counseling and community service. But she'd be able to stay home and not end up in a detention center.

"The diversion program here is fairly new." James's voice reached Owen as if through a thick wall. "But it's been quite successful so far. Recidivism rates are much lower than in the system."

Recidivism.

System.

Owen's stomach churned, and he gritted his teeth to keep from getting sick right here on James's floor. These were not words he should have to think about.

"Yeah." He forced his voice out past the acid burning the back of his throat. "The diversion program sounds like a good idea."

James passed Owen some paperwork that he filled out mechanically.

"Come on. I'll take you to her," James offered once Owen had completed them.

It took monumental effort to lift his feet and follow.

He'd gotten so used to doing this parenting thing alone that he'd almost forgotten Emma was here, but his heart lifted when he spotted her sitting on the floor down the hall.

"Claire wanted to be alone," she explained, scrambling to her feet.

Something was off about the way she said it, but Owen wasn't quite sure what.

James opened the door to the interrogation room, and Owen had to look away from the sight of his daughter at that table.

"You can go home with your dad," James said.

Owen heard Claire's chair scrape back, then her slow, deliberate footsteps.

She exited the room, her gaze locked on the floor. Owen should say something, but he had no words. Instead, he grabbed her arm and steered her down the hall toward the exit. Behind him, he could hear James and Emma following.

When he got to the lobby, he released Claire's arm and turned to James. "Thanks." He stuck out his hand. It sounded like a stupid thing to say to the man who had just arrested his daughter, but he knew James was doing everything he could to help turn Claire away from this path.

James shook his hand. "I'll let you know what the prosecutor says."

"Ready?" Owen's gaze shifted to Emma.

She didn't meet his eyes. "I'm going to hang out with Bethany and Ruby for a bit. They don't live far from here. James can give me a ride home when he's done with his shift."

"What?" Owen's heart stumbled. "No. Emma. I can drop you off—"

"My house is out of the way from the cabin." Her voice rang with false cheerfulness. "Besides, Ruby has been bugging me to come over to see the present she's making for the baby. Trust me, Owen, this will be for the best." Now she met his eyes, but the regret in hers didn't give him any reassurance.

"Okay," he said finally. "If you're sure that's what you want."

She nodded wordlessly.

"I'll call you later," he promised.

Again she didn't answer, though her eyes seemed to grow sadder.

He wanted to lean over and kiss her and tell her everything was going to be okay, as long as they were together. But she was standing right next to her brother, and Claire hovered next to him.

With one last look, he led his daughter out the door and to the van.

"What about the car?" Claire demanded.

They were the first words she'd spoken since he got here, and anger surged through Owen. "I'll bring Catelyn to get it tomorrow. You'll be lucky if you ever drive again. What were you thinking, Claire?"

He waited until she got in the vehicle, then went around to his side.

"I'm still waiting for an answer," he said as he started the car and backed out of the parking spot. He cast a look at the police station door, but he couldn't see Emma behind it.

"I wasn't thinking," Claire said. "Kids do dumb stuff sometimes."

Owen stopped at the end of the police department's driveway, staring at his daughter. "That's your excuse? Kids do dumb stuff?"

She shrugged.

"Claire." Owen's voice was hard enough to make his daughter flinch, but he didn't care. "You stole alcohol. Do you realize how serious that is?"

Claire shrugged again, and Owen slammed the steering wheel in frustration as he pulled onto the street. "What do you want, Claire? Do you want to go to jail? What do you think your mother would—" He stopped. He had promised himself he would never use Katie's death like that.

But Claire seemed to latch on to what he said. "What do you care how Mom would feel about it? You don't even care that she's dead."

Owen jammed his foot on the brake and pulled over to the side of the road.

"What are you doing?" Claire's eyes went wide, and she slid closer to her door.

"How could you say something like that?" All the anger had leeched from his voice, leaving it thin and empty.

Claire stared at her hands. But then she lifted her chin defiantly. "You came to the police station with Emma, for one. Are you going to tell me you two weren't on a date?"

Owen shook his head. "We've talked about this. It's been five years. We all have to move on."

"Fine. Move on," Claire spat at him. "It's not like you were even sad when Mom died anyway."

"I— What?" Owen felt his mouth open and close again, but he couldn't say anything.

"You didn't cry," Claire accused. "Not at the hospital, not at the funeral, not even at home."

"And you think that means I wasn't sad?" Owen stared at her in disbelief. "Claire, I was devastated. Your mom and you kids— You're everything to me." He took a moment to swallow roughly. "I couldn't afford to cry because I had the five of you. Carter was so little and Kenzie wouldn't talk. Cody was throwing himself into his baseball, Catelyn was trying to be a little mother. And you—" He sucked in a breath. "You were so angry all the time."

Claire snorted.

"But if you think there weren't nights that I . . ." Owen trailed off. "I was devastated," he repeated. "I didn't know how to live without her.

It's something I've had to relearn slowly. And it's something you need to relearn too."

Claire shook her head, staring out the window. "I don't want to." A single tear traced down her cheek, and Owen let out a breath.

"I know, sweetheart." He leaned across the console and pulled her into an awkward hug. "But I'll be here to help you."

Chapter 49

"Thanks for the ride." Emma climbed out of James's car, her head as heavy as her limbs.

Dark had fallen, but soft light spilled onto the driveway from the porch. At least she wouldn't have to worry about how to navigate a goodnight kiss from Owen with Mom and William home.

"Of course." James leaned across the passenger seat. "If Owen has any questions or needs anything, have him give me a call."

Emma nodded numbly, the back of her throat raw. She knew she wouldn't be seeing much of Owen anymore, but she could tell him when he brought the kids to lessons.

She dragged herself up the porch steps, the sound of James's car fading behind her.

When she reached the door, she took a deep breath and painted on as realistic a smile as she could muster. She didn't think she could handle talking about this with Mom tonight.

Fortunately, Mom and William weren't in the kitchen, and Emma let her smile dim. Maybe they had gone up to bed already.

She got a long drink of water and then made her way to the living room. She hadn't worked on her puzzle much since Owen and the kids had moved out, but tonight felt like a puzzling night.

She laughed ironically to herself at the unintentional pun. It certainly had been puzzling.

She didn't think she'd ever felt so many emotions in one day. She wanted to back up to the exhilaration of free falling with Owen. Or maybe to the headiness of kissing him.

Anything but this heaviness of knowing it was all over.

"How was your date?" Mom's voice surprised Emma, and she looked up to find both her and William on the couch, the Scrabble board spread in front of them on the coffee table. "I convinced him to play," Mom explained. "I reminded him that Cody beat me, so clearly it's not impossible."

Emma laughed thinly, the mention of Owen's son cutting at her already fragile composure.

"Is something wrong?" Mom studied Emma, concern tightening her lips.

Emma shook her head. "No." But a betraying tear sneaked its way onto her cheek.

"Oh, honey. What is it?" Mom sprang to her feet in alarm.

"It's nothing, Mom," Emma reassured her, wiping the stupid tear away. "Just a long night."

"Do you want to talk about it?" Mom gave William a look, and he got up too, crossing the room to squeeze Emma's shoulder.

"Love you, kiddo."

"Love you too." Emma's voice cracked, and more tears fell as he left the room. She loved her stepfather, even though he'd only been married to her mom for less than a year. And she loved Owen's kids, even though they weren't hers. And never would be.

"Come on. Let's sit down." Mom steered her toward the couch.

Emma wiped at her eyes. She'd always found it embarrassing to cry in front of others—even her mom.

"What happened?" Mom asked. "Something with Owen?"

Emma nodded and told her the whole story—about skydiving, about Owen saying he had to rethink his position on not dating, about dinner and the call from James and her conversation with Claire.

The only part she left out was the kisses—and her conversation with Dana, though she wasn't sure why she didn't want to tell Mom about that.

When she finished, Mom patted her knee. "I'm sure Claire will come around. It could turn out that getting caught is the best thing that could have happened to her. She'll get the counseling she needs. And in the meantime, I don't think Owen is going to give up on you."

As if to prove her point, Emma's phone dinged with a text. Since it was on the couch between them, Mom could see Owen's name as clearly as Emma could.

Emma stared at the phone a moment, then dismissed the notification.

Mom raised an eyebrow. "Are *you* giving up on *him*?"

Emma latched her fingers together, wishing it was Owen's hand she was holding. "I can't come between him and his family."

"Emma Anne Wood." Mom's voice was stern, and Emma looked up at the use of her full name. "Owen knows you'd never come between him and his family. For heaven's sake, you helped hold that family together after the fire. I have to admit that at first I was afraid his feelings for you were only as a caretaker for his kids. But I've seen the way he looks at you. His feelings for you are more than that. *Much* more."

"Well, I don't want them to be," Emma said petulantly.

Mom snort-laughed. "Tell that to my daughter who went prancing out of here with him this afternoon, completely ecstatic."

"It was just the endorphins from the jump," Emma insisted. She had landed on this explanation while she was telling Ruby and Bethany about the skydive.

"Endorphins." Mom brushed off the suggestion. "It's normal to be scared," she said, patting Emma's knee. "Falling in love can be—"

"I'm not falling in love." The words cracked off of Emma's lips, and Mom's hand lifted in surprise. "And neither is he. He can't be."

For a moment, Emma thought Mom was going to let the conversation drop.

She should have known better.

"Whyever not?" Now Mom's voice was the one that snapped. "You're beautiful, intelligent, faithful, kind—"

"Mom stop." Emma cut off Mom's list. "It doesn't matter. It's not going to work out."

"It does matter," Mom insisted. "Ask me. Ask your brother. For a long time, we both let fear—"

"I'm not afraid," Emma cut Mom off and pushed to her feet. "I'm tired. I'll see you in the morning." She leaned over and kissed Mom's head, ignoring the aching memory of Owen's kiss to her own hair.

"Emma," Mom tried again.

But Emma stepped into her room. "Goodnight, Mom." She closed the door and just stood for a moment, then made herself walk deliberately to the mirror. She ran her hands over the light fabric of her dress. When she peeled it off, the scar from her hysterectomy leered across her stomach, a reminder of what she hadn't said to Mom. It wasn't only because of Claire that she and Owen couldn't be together. It was because of her.

She pulled on a pair of shorts and a t-shirt, washed her face, and brushed her teeth. It wasn't until she was in bed and tucked under the covers that she turned on her phone and clicked to Owen's text.

I'm sorry about how it ended, but I had a great time today. Maybe we can try dinner again next week?

Everything in her wanted to say yes. But she made her fingers tap out a different answer. *I'm sorry. I guess I got a little carried away from the endorphins after the jump. But I think it's best if we stay just friends. I hope you understand.*

The reply took only three seconds to come back. *I don't.*

Emma bit her lip, staring at those two words. Maybe he deserved an explanation. But she couldn't give him one that wouldn't hurt him even more.

So she replied only, *I'm sorry.*

She lay awake a long time blinking at that screen. But no further reply came.

Chapter 50

"You both asked off of work for the grand opening tomorrow?" Owen drained the last of his coffee, looking from Catelyn to Claire, whom the caseworker had said should keep working while she was in the diversion program, in addition to the counseling and service work. She'd only been enrolled in the program for two weeks now, and Owen wasn't sure yet if he saw any drastic changes in her, but at least she wasn't in a detention center. And she hadn't gotten in trouble again—so that was something.

"Yes," both girls answered.

"Good. And Cody, you told Coach you won't be at the game?"

"Yep." Cody dug into his bowl of cereal.

"And I told Ruby to invite her family," Kenzie added. "Including Miss Emma."

"Yay." That came from Carter. "I miss her."

The other kids all stared at Owen.

"Just don't get your hopes up," he said evenly. "She's very busy."

That was the excuse he'd given them for why he and Emma hadn't gone out again. That, and the fact that skydiving hadn't been a date in the first place—like he'd told them from the beginning. He was sure none of them bought it, but at least it usually stopped them from asking more questions.

"I bet she'd come if *you* asked her," Catelyn said pointedly.

Owen sincerely doubted that. He'd seen her a grand total of four times in the past two weeks, twice at church and twice at lessons. Each time, she was polite, even friendly. But never did she indicate that their relationship had ever been more than that.

Her texts too were friendly, but nothing more, and on the few occasions he ventured to ask her out, she politely declined, insisting again that it was best if they remained just friends. She would never give him an explanation, and he could only conclude that he'd misinterpreted her feelings. Maybe it really had been the endorphins after all.

"She could be scared, you know." The offhand comment came from Cody, and they all gaped at him as he shoveled another bite into his mouth.

"What?" he asked, milk dribbling from his lip.

"Scared of what? The way you eat?" Catelyn threw him a napkin.

Cody wiped his face and shrugged. "All of us. I mean she's been single for what, like 40-some years? And then all of a sudden, it's like, 'Hey, do you want to date me and my five kids?'"

Owen snorted, but Catelyn looked thoughtful. "You know, that actually makes sense."

"Thanks." Cody grinned around another bite.

"But what can we do about it?" Catelyn tapped her lip.

"There's nothing *to* do about it." Owen grabbed his keys. "I might be late tonight." The drop zone was so close to ready for tomorrow's opening, but he fully expected a million little things to come up. "Catelyn is in charge."

"If I'm in charge, then I say you should invite her," his oldest called behind him as the door closed.

Owen shook his head and jogged to the van. It was for the best that things between him and Emma hadn't gone further than they did. If his kids were this disappointed after one date, imagine what would have happened if they'd dated a long time and then broken up.

Owen hadn't really considered that possibility when he'd asked her to dinner. He'd assumed that once they started dating, that would be it. They would remain together. That was how it had been with Katie.

Owen sighed. *I tried, Katie.* At least now no one could accuse him of not keeping his promise to his wife.

"Dad, wait." Claire's voice pulled Owen around. She ran gingerly across the gravel driveway, barefoot, wincing with each step.

"Go in the grass," Owen called, but she didn't listen.

"There's something I have to tell you." She winced as she set her foot down, and Owen cringed, his stomach immediately knotting.

"What is it?" He braced himself. Just when he'd been thinking things might be getting better.

"She's not scared." Claire's words were barely a whisper, and Owen studied her, trying to decipher them.

"Who's not scared of what?"

Claire dragged her hands through her blonde waves. "Emma. She's not scared of us. Our family."

"Oh. I'm sure she's not." He studied his daughter, trying to figure out if the comment had been her way of avoiding telling him something else. "Is that all?"

She shook her head, and the knots in his stomach pulled tighter.

"That day at the police station," Claire said.

"Yes?" Owen's fingers clenched. Please, Lord, tell him Claire hadn't done anything else illegal that day.

"She came in the interrogation room, and she said she cares about us."

Owen nodded, swallowing. He already knew how much she cared about his kids. It was one of the things that had first drawn him to her. Her big heart.

"I said I didn't want her to care about me." Claire studied her feet, twisting her big toe into a divot in the gravel. Though she wouldn't look at him, he could see the guilt on her face.

"Oh, honey. I'm sure she knew you didn't mean it. That's not why . . . Sometimes things just don't work out."

Claire shook her head violently. "I told her—" She looked up, eyes shimmering. "That I was going to make you choose between her and me. But she said—" A tear fell onto her cheek, and she swiped roughly at it. "She said you would choose me. Always."

Owen stared at his daughter a moment, processing. Then he took a step forward and pulled her into his arms. His heart squeezed as he realized what Emma had done. She'd made the choice so he didn't have to.

Claire sniffed and pulled away, wiping at her eyes. "Anyway, I just thought you should know. It's not you. It's me. And you should invite her to the grand opening."

Owen eyed her. "You really want that?"

She nodded. "Believe it or not, I really don't like seeing you so miserable."

"And you're not going to go knock over a bank or something if I do?"

Claire rolled her eyes but shook her head. "I think my days of crime are behind me. I only took that stuff because Eliza dared me. And then she ran off when I got caught." She shook her head. "Anyway, my counselor made me tour the detention center. Not really my kind of place."

A sarcastic reply about how she should have known that without a tour almost rose to Owen's lips, but he bit it back. "I'm glad."

"Well, what are you waiting for?" Claire held her hands in front of her, mimicking texting. "Invite her." She spun to go into the cabin, this time walking in the grass.

Slowly, Owen pulled out his phone. He tapped on Emma's name and then just stared at it.

He started the text five times but deleted each one before it was finished.

Finally, he had something he could live with: *I'm sorry for the short notice, but the grand opening of the drop zone is tomorrow. It would mean a lot to me if you came. It would mean a lot to the kids too. Including Claire.*

He thought about writing more, about telling her he knew what she'd done and why she'd done it and that she didn't need to do it and that he loved her for it, but all of that could wait until they were together in person.

He hit send, then got in the van.

Before he could turn it on, his phone buzzed with a reply.

I have to set up for the church anniversary tomorrow.

Disappointment whooshed from him in a hard breath.

I under— Before he finished his reply, another text came from her.

But I'll try.

He grinned, deleted what he'd been typing, and instead wrote, *Can't wait to see you*, then sent it before he could change his mind.

Chapter 51

"Let's put the collages over there," Emma directed. "And the historical items can go on those tables." She bent to pick up the box she'd carried in earlier, swaying a little as she stood.

"Are you okay?" Spencer reached out a hand to steady her.

"Yeah, fine." The truth was, her head was pounding, every single one of her muscles ached, and her vision kept going in and out, as if she were looking through a pair of binoculars that someone kept adjusting. She'd been pushing herself too hard all week. She knew that.

And it didn't help that she'd lain awake half the night, trying to decide whether or not to go to Owen's grand opening today. She missed him and the kids with an intensity that refused to relent. But she couldn't decide if that meant she should go—or she shouldn't. Would it cure the pain, or only make it worse?

In the end, she'd decided that she would wait and see what time she got done here.

"At least let me take that." Spencer wrestled the box into his own arms. "You've been running around at super-speed all morning."

"Thanks." Even though she was no longer holding the box, Emma had to gasp to take in a breath. "And then we can put these . . ." She bent forward to reach for the box that held items for the silent auction, but her vision was going in and out so fast now that she couldn't seem to figure out where to set her hand.

"Emma." The voice sounded far away, and she couldn't tell whose it was. "Emma."

"I'm just going to rest," she murmured, tipping toward the floor. She wasn't sure if the voice heard her because she was suddenly floating.

She turned her head to find Owen floating with her.

They must be skydiving again.

She smiled. "Hey, I missed you."

"I missed you too." He took her hand in his and patted it. "We're going to land soon, so I'm going to put your feet up."

"Okay." She couldn't stop smiling. Being with him was the best thing in the world. Why had she fought that?

"Ready, Emma?"

"Yes," she murmured. She was ready for whatever came next with him.

"Emma!" His voice grew louder, even though he seemed to be drifting away from her.

"Emma! Wake up."

Wake up? She wasn't . . .

She felt her eyes flutter open, but it took a moment to focus.

That wasn't Owen above her. It was Jared. And Spencer. And Sophie. And a whole crowd of people.

"Is she all right?" she heard someone ask.

"Is who all right?" She swiveled her head, trying to figure out why everyone else seemed so much taller than usual.

"You, silly." Sophie's laugh sounded shaky. "You scared us."

"What am I . . ." She realized that Sophie's legs were folded on the ground under her. Which meant that she was kneeling and Emma was . . . "Why am I lying down?" She tried to sit up, but someone had propped her feet on a box, and a hand pressed into her shoulder, keeping her on her back.

"You passed out." Jared had his fingers wrapped around her wrist.

"I did not." Emma started to argue but then snapped her mouth shut. She supposed that would explain how she and Owen had been skydiving a moment ago.

"Your vitals are good," Jared said, "but I'm going to take you to the hospital just to be safe."

"The hospital?" Emma shook her head. "That's not necessary." She tried to sit up, and this time both Sophie and Jared cradled her back to help her. "I have way too much to do here."

"We'll take care of all of this," Sophie reassured her. "You go get checked out." Her face was pinched with worry, and Emma knew all of her friends had automatically jumped to the conclusion that her cancer must be back.

"I'm fine, you guys," she insisted.

"I'm sure you are." Jared didn't sound nearly as worried as Sophie looked, and that calmed the nerves that had started to curl in Emma's stomach.

It wasn't that she couldn't handle going through cancer again—or even that she was afraid to die—but if her cancer recurred, there would be no way to keep Owen from finding out, and she didn't want to hurt him or his family. Even if they were only friends.

"But just humor us and let me take you in," Jared added.

Emma started to shake her head again, but Sophie said, "Don't make me call James," and that settled it. If her brother found out she'd passed out, he'd probably send an ambulance, a fire truck, and his own squad car.

"Fine," she sighed. "I'll go."

"Good girl." Sophie patted her back. She and Jared helped Emma to her feet.

"I'm going to carry you, okay?" Jared said.

Emma rolled her eyes but nodded. She supposed if she refused, he'd go get a stretcher.

Jared scooped her up, and Emma closed her eyes against the wave of lightheadedness that swept over her as he started walking.

"Do you want me to let Owen know?" Sophie's voice traveled alongside them. "Maybe he can meet you at the hospital."

Emma pried her eyes open, fighting back the wave of nausea. "Absolutely not."

Sophie looked surprised. "Are you sure? I'm sure he—"

"Soph," Emma interrupted her friend. "Do not tell him. Under any circumstances."

"But why—" Sophie protested, holding the door open to usher Jared through.

"Promise me," Emma demanded.

Sophie gave her a dubious look but nodded. "If that's what you want. I promise."

"Thank you." Emma closed her eyes again until she heard a car door open. Jared lowered her to the seat, causing a fresh wave of dizziness to wash over her, and she couldn't suppress a low groan.

"Sorry," he murmured. "Can you get your seatbelt?"

She nodded and reached for it.

"She's going to be okay, right?" Sophie asked Jared in a low voice—but not so low that Emma couldn't hear. She hated the sound of worry in her friend's voice. Again.

"I'm sure she will," Jared reassured her.

"Well, I'm going to send out a prayer request to everyone." Already Sophie was pulling her phone out of her pocket.

"Not to Owen," Emma called. "You promised."

"You're so stubborn." Sophie's voice was half-exasperated, half-amused. "Feel better." She closed Emma's car door, and a moment later Jared got in and started the vehicle.

"You're going to be fine," he told Emma.

Emma nodded and pulled out her own phone, her heart sick as she tapped out the short message to Owen. *I'm so sorry, but it looks like I won't be able to make it after all.*

Then she put her phone away and closed her eyes.

Chapter 52

"I can't believe this." Owen must have said it a dozen times already, but every time he looked up, more people were flooding through the doors of Above the Blue.

"Believe it." Charles clapped his shoulder, pushing back the cap he wore over his floppy curls between flights. They weren't doing jumps today, but Charles was taking groups up to see the drop zone from the air, while Owen led short presentations on skydiving basics.

"I told you Heidi is good at her job." Charles waved across the room to a petite, dark-haired woman helping Cody and Kenzie hand out goodie bags and refreshments. Owen had been skeptical when his partner had said he'd met someone who could help get the word out—especially when Charles let it slip that he was also dating this woman—but she had more than exceeded Owen's expectations. And Charles's too, if the dreamy look on his face was any indication.

"And—" Charles leaned closer. "I think she may be the one."

Owen checked his eye roll. Charles had known the woman all of three weeks. But he hoped for his friend's sake that he was right. There were few things in life more incredible than finding someone to spend it with.

He lifted his head and scanned the mingling crowds.

"She didn't come, huh?" Charles searched the crowd too.

"There's still time," Owen murmured. But he flicked his wrist to check his watch. It was after 4 p.m. If she hadn't come by now . . .

"The last group is ready to go up, Uncle Charles." Catelyn strode over, Carter trailing behind her.

"And the weather is still good," the boy announced.

Pride swelled Owen's heart. His little family had pulled together to make this day happen. If only Katie could be here to see this.

Or Emma.

"I'll gather the last group for the presentation then." He forced his mind off of wishful thinking and back to what he had to do. "Why don't you two go see if Claire needs any help at the face painting table." That had been Claire's idea—in case whole families came—and it turned out to be brilliant. Claire was a talented artist—something Owen hadn't even realized until recently—and now dozens of children walked around sporting a perfect replica of Above the Blue's logo on their cheeks.

Catelyn and Carter skipped off together, Charles saluted and headed out to the runway, and Owen went to give his last presentation. Afterward, they mingled with the guests who remained, then cleaned up the drop zone so it would be all sparkling and ready for their first jumpers Monday morning. Barb had been fielding reservations all afternoon, and they were now booked solid for the next month and a half.

It wasn't until they were about to load into the van to head home that Owen pulled out his phone.

Emma's name leapt up at him, and he quickly opened the message, the exuberance of the successful day fading as he read it. He didn't know what he'd expected. The message didn't tell him anything he didn't already know—she'd decided not to come.

He tucked the phone back into his pocket and got into the van.

"I wish Miss Emma would have been here," Kenzie chirped from the back seat.

"I know, baby. But you know she was busy with the anniversary." Owen kept his voice upbeat, as if he was certain that was the only thing that had kept Emma from attending. Not a desire to avoid him.

"Ruby and her family didn't come either," Kenzie added.

"They were probably busy with the anniversary too," Owen reassured her. "I wouldn't have scheduled the opening for the same weekend if I had known. But we'll see them tomorrow at church."

And then he would talk to Emma, tell her that his kids wanted them to be together—even Claire.

And so did he.

Chapter 53

"I still think we should stay home with you." Mom bustled around Emma's bedroom, setting a glass of water on her bedside table, tucking her blankets, and fluffing her pillows.

"Mom." Emma grabbed her mother's hand. "I'm okay."

Mom nodded. "I know." But she pressed her lips together and just looked at Emma.

Emma hated that she'd put her family and friends through all this worry. The look on James's and Bethany's and Ruby's faces yesterday when they'd shown up at the hospital . . . She wouldn't do that to them again for anything.

Fortunately, she'd only had to stay for a few hours, long enough for the doctors to determine that she was exhausted, dehydrated, and anemic, and to pump some fluids into her. Because they'd just done a PET scan a couple of weeks ago, they were confident it wasn't a recurrence of her cancer.

"Now go." Emma shooed Mom. "Or you and William will be late. Don't forget to check that they put out all the auction items. There was a box in the office that I'm not sure if anyone saw. Oh, and I told Dan that there was a stack of old church albums in the storage closet, but you might want to double-check if he—"

"Em," Mom warned. "It's all under control."

"I know." Emma threw herself back on her pillows. She hated that she couldn't be there to make sure everything ran smoothly for the anniversary, but the doctor had ordered her to at least three days of rest—and her family had decided to interpret that as bed rest.

"Here's your laptop." Mom nestled it on Emma's lap, already open to the church's page. "Stream the service. Then take a nap."

"Yes, ma'am." Emma sulked.

Mom kissed her forehead, and Emma heard her and William leave. Once the sound of their car had faded, she considered getting out of bed, but Mom had already taken care of the chickens, and Kayla had called in the staff to take care of the horses. She supposed she could work on her puzzle, but the thought of that only made her heartsick.

She pulled out her phone and scrolled to her texts, clicking on her last message to Owen. He had never responded. And she couldn't blame him. After the way she'd pushed him away for the past two weeks, not showing up at the grand opening had to be the last straw.

She blew out a breath and closed her eyes, reminding herself that it was a good thing. Yesterday's health scare was only one more confirmation that she was doing the right thing, separating herself from his family.

She drifted in and out of sleep until she heard the church service start. Groggily, she opened her eyes and pushed herself upright in bed.

The camera angle was fixed on Dan at the front of the church, so Emma couldn't see the congregation, but she could picture her friends, picture Mom and William and James and Bethany and Ruby, picture Owen with his kids, picture her whole church family filling the sanctuary.

Her heart wept not to be there with all of them, but she was grateful to at least have this connection.

When Dan started to give his sermon, Emma adjusted the computer on her lap. Her friend had never yet preached a sermon that didn't touch her, and she felt an unusual longing today as she listened, though she wasn't sure for exactly what.

"My son Matthias made this painting for me the other day," Dan started, holding up a piece of paper. Whoever was running the camera zoomed in on it, and Emma chuckled. It sort of resembled a field but was mostly blobs of color.

"It's nice, right?" The camera panned back out to show Dan smiling. "So I thanked him and went to hang it in my office. But he stopped me, and said, 'Aren't you forgetting something?' I thought about it, and then I realized, and I went and gave him a hug and thanked him again. I started to leave again, but he said, 'You forgot to pay me.'"

From the background, Emma heard the congregation chuckle.

Dan was laughing too. "So I said, 'Pay you? I thought this was a gift.' And Matthias said, 'It is. A gift you pay for.'"

Emma laughed. Dan and Jade's youngest sure was a character.

"So, being the patient father that I am—" Dan shook his head. "I explained that a gift had to be free in order to be a gift. And right there, on the spot, he decided it wasn't a gift. It was a picture he wanted to sell me. So I asked him how much he thought it was worth." Dan paused, then deadpanned, "'One thousand dollars.'"

Laughter raced through the congregation, and Emma joined in. She had a feeling she knew where Dan was going with this.

"In the end," Dan said, "we agreed that I could keep the painting for now and I would pay him back over the year by, you know, feeding him and stuff." Dan chuckled, then grew serious.

The camera followed as he paced to the right side of the church, where Emma knew her family usually sat, and she wondered if Owen and his kids were sitting with them.

"A gift isn't a gift if it's not free," Dan said slowly. "Where have I heard that before?" He opened his Bible and read, "For it is by grace you have been saved, through faith—and this is not from yourselves, it is the gift of God—not by works, so that no one can boast.'"

Emma nodded along. Ephesians 2:8-9 was one of her favorite passages.

"It is a *gift* of God," Dan continued, "given freely to us."

Emma smiled triumphantly. This was exactly where she had thought Dan was going with his sermon.

"We know that, right?" Dan said. "That's the whole reason this church was founded a hundred years ago. To worship the God who sent his Son into the world to pay the price for our sins. To live and die for us. To promise us eternal life as his free gift."

Dan strolled toward the other side of the church, the camera following. "But do we sometimes lose sight of that?" he asked. "Do we feel like maybe we need to repay God for this gift? Like maybe we need to prove to him that we're worth the sacrifice he made for us? That we deserve the life he's given us?"

Emma stilled as the questions dug their way into her heart. She didn't feel that way, did she?

"Do we ever," Dan continued, "serve him not because we want to give thanks but because we don't want to feel indebted to him? Or because we don't want him to think he made a mistake in answering our prayers? Or that he wasted his time saving our lives?"

Emma's eyes stung, and she attempted to swallow down the raw ache at the back of her throat.

She didn't know why God had spared her life. Why he'd left her on this earth when he'd taken someone like Katie to heaven so young. And, yes, maybe she did sometimes feel like she had to make that up to him. To prove to him that she wasn't wasting the extra time he'd given her.

The tears overflowed, and Emma covered her face with her hands, trying to get herself under control so she could listen to the rest of the sermon.

"You can see why we would feel that way, right?" Dan continued. "We live in a world where you can't get something for nothing, and if something sounds too good to be true, it is. But God's grace is the one thing that sounds too good to be true—but is true anyway. Everything we get from God—our life, our gifts, our salvation—it's all given to us for nothing. It's a gift. You don't have to earn it. You don't have to prove you're worth it. You can't repay it. It's yours. Because he loves you."

Emma sniffed and wiped at her still streaming eyes. She knew this—had known it for decades—so how had she let herself lose sight of it?

"Of course, just because we don't serve the Lord to earn our salvation doesn't mean we don't want to serve him at all," Dan was saying now. "It just means that our motivation is different. It isn't to repay or to earn or to prove. It's to thank. In fact, you might not know this, but the reason our church founders called this place Hope Church isn't only because it's in Hope Springs. They actually quoted 1 Timothy 4:10 in their founding documents: 'That is why we labor and strive, because we have put our hope in the living God, who is the Savior of all people, and especially of all who believe.'"

Dan scanned the congregation, his eyes sweeping over the camera as well, so that Emma almost felt like he could see her too. "There have been a lot of wonderful people who have labored and striven to keep this church going over the past one hundred years, including all of you. Out of thankfulness to God, let us continue to labor. Let us continue to strive to serve the Lord. But most of all, let us remember that his grace is a free gift. We can never earn it. We could never repay it. We can only thank him for this indescribable gift. Amen."

The service continued, but Emma bowed her head as tears fell afresh. They were cleansing tears now, tears of joy and relief.

She had been striving so hard to show the Lord all she could do for him that she'd almost lost sight of what he'd done for her. And why he'd done it.

Because he loved her.

And that love—nothing would ever change it.

Chapter 54

Owen followed the crowd filing into the fellowship hall for the anniversary festivities. He glanced down to make sure Carter was wearing his headphones—already the joyful rumble in here was plenty loud—then skimmed the heads in front of him, searching for blonde curls.

He and the kids had arrived a few minutes late for the service this morning, so he hadn't had a chance to look for Emma before church. Which didn't stop him from spending half of the service trying to spot her.

When he couldn't find her, he'd assumed she must be setting things up for the anniversary. But she didn't appear to be anywhere in here either.

"Kenzie!" Ruby appeared at their side, flinging her arms around his daughter. "I was looking for you."

"Where were you yesterday?" Kenzie's question held a note of coldness, and Owen nudged her. It wasn't Ruby's fault if her parents hadn't brought her to the grand opening.

"Sorry. Aunt Emma was sick and we had to go see her in the hospital."

Owen froze, and Cody ran into him from behind. But Owen was too focused on Ruby to apologize. "She's in the hospital? Is she all right?" His heart thundered hard in his ear, and he strained to hear Ruby over it and the crowd.

"She has dehydration, exhaustion, and anemia." Ruby ticked them off on her fingers. "But she's home now."

Owen's exhale was loud and hard. "Good." For a moment he had been afraid . . .

He shook it off. It was foolish to think that just because Katie had gotten sick, Emma would too. Besides, with Katie's illness, there had been no symptoms. Just a sudden diagnosis.

Anyway, it was no surprise that Emma was exhausted and dehydrated with how hard she pushed herself.

"So *that's* why she wasn't at the grand opening yesterday." Kenzie sounded relieved, but her comment slammed Owen's gut.

Emma had been sick, she'd been in the hospital, and he hadn't known. He hadn't been there for her.

Because she didn't want you to be, a voice whispered in his head. *She texted you that she wasn't coming. She could have told you why. But she didn't.*

True. But knowing Emma, she hadn't told him because she didn't want to worry him on his big day.

"I'm going to get some food," Cody announced. Claire and Catelyn and Kenzie and Ruby all followed, but Carter said he wasn't hungry.

Neither was Owen.

"Should we look around?" he asked the boy.

Carter shrugged, and Owen led him around the room. They admired the collages Emma had put together, as well as several historical displays with the write-ups he knew she had spent hours researching. His heart hurt that she wasn't here to see the fruits of her labor.

"What's a silent auction?" Carter asked.

Owen glanced at the table he pointed to. "It's where people donate different things and then other people bid on them and whoever bids the highest amount gets the item." He read the sign on the table. "It looks like this one is to raise money to help build a church in Thailand."

"Can we bid on something?" Carter stepped toward a sign for a trip to Europe.

"Maybe not that one," Owen murmured. His eyes fell on a logo he recognized—Hope Stables. Emma was auctioning off a trail ride.

He picked up a bidding form.

"We already get to ride at lessons," Carter pointed out.

"I know." Owen grinned at him. "This is for me."

He grabbed a pen, wrote down a bid that surprised even him, and stuck it in the locked wooden box in the center of the table.

There. He patted the table in satisfaction. If he won, he'd have her all to himself for an hour. And he could make her see that this just being friends was never going to work. They both felt too much to go back to that.

"All right, buddy," he said to Carter, chuckling at the lift in his own voice. "*Now* I think I can eat."

Carter looked longingly at the sign for the trip. "It looks like they have great clouds in Europe."

Chapter 55

Emma stepped into the barn, pulling in a deep breath. It had only been three days, but she had missed the familiar scent of hay and horse and earth. The familiar feel of work.

But this time, she was going to slow down, take it easier. She was going to remember that the work the Lord had given her to do was an expression of thankfulness, not an obligation to prove her worthiness.

"You're looking better." Kayla glanced up from the lesson she was giving as Emma walked into the arena.

"I *feel* better," Emma answered, smiling at her friend. "Thanks for taking care of everything."

"Of course. You need to learn to let us all do more of that."

Emma nodded. "I can take over here if you want."

Kayla snorted and gave her a look. "What did I just say?"

Emma held her hands up in submission. "Okay, okay. There's going to be a learning curve."

"Anyway—" Kayla's eyes sparkled. "You should get ready for your trail ride."

"Trail ride?" Emma did enjoy riding the trails around her property. But she had plenty of other things to catch up on today.

"From the silent auction at church." For some reason Kayla's mouth was twitching.

"Why do you look like that?" Emma narrowed her eyes. Her friend was up to something, for sure.

"If I look like anything," Kayla retorted, "it's happy because the bid brought in so much."

"Really?" Emma frowned. She knew the auction had surpassed its goal of raising enough to build a church in Thailand. But she'd never thought to ask how much the trail ride had brought in. She only charged seventy-five dollars for that, normally. "How much?"

"Guess." Kayla's smile grew more impish.

Emma rolled her eyes. "I don't know. Three hundred dollars." She threw out the outlandish number based on the way Kayla was acting.

"More."

"More?" she gasped.

"Five hundred." Kayla grinned.

Emma gaped at her. "Who would pay five hundred dollars for a trail ride?"

"Someone who really wants to ride with you." Kayla's impish smile transformed into an impish laugh.

"Who?"

Kayla shook her head. "I should get back to my lesson."

"Oh." Emma realized suddenly that poor little Sadie Krebs was waiting patiently for instructions. "Then tell me fast."

Kayla shook her head. "You should probably saddle up King."

"King? Are you sure?" King was good for trail rides, but only if the rider was big enough.

"Positive." Kayla turned back to Sadie.

Emma waited a moment longer, but when it was clear that her friend wasn't going to say anything else, she turned and marched toward the stable.

"Your rider will be here in half an hour," Kayla called after her.

Emma picked up her pace a bit, and by the time half an hour had passed, she had King and Scarlet saddled up and waiting in front of the stables, ready to go. She stroked the horses' noses and examined the low clouds gathering to the west. She couldn't tell if they brought rain with them, but hopefully they would hold off until the ride was done. She'd hate to disappoint her generous bidder.

She turned when she heard tires on gravel and found a red van pulling into one of the parking spots across from where she stood.

Her heart jumped. It looked so much like Owen's vehicle that for a moment she thought maybe he and the kids had forgotten that she'd moved this week's lessons to Thursday.

But only one door opened.

Only one person got out.

He spun around and strode toward her with such a large smile that she cried out, "Owen," forgetting to keep the thrill out of her voice.

"Hi." He sounded slightly breathless, and she thought for a second that he was going to pull her into a hug. But he stopped a few feet away with his arms planted at his sides.

His smile faded as his eyes roved her face. "I heard you were sick. You're feeling better now?"

She nodded, nearly saying she was feeling *much* better, now that he was here. But she couldn't say that. Not when she had told him they could only be friends.

"Because if you're not, we can wait to do this."

She tilted her head. "To do what?"

"Ride." He gestured to the horses. "Which one is for me?"

She could only stare at him.

"You always ride Scarlet, so I'm going to guess this one."

"King," Emma said numbly as Owen took the reins from her. "But. But. You're the one who bid five hundred dollars for a trail ride?"

He chuckled. "Well, I didn't know you'd find out the amount, but yeah."

"Why?" She stared at him, perplexed. She would have taken him on a ride for free anytime.

"It was for a good cause. Plus—" His discerning look traveled over her. "I figured this way it would be impossible for you to ignore me."

"Owen." Emma tried to protest, but she wasn't sure she had enough resolve right now. Instead she said, "Do you even know how to ride?"

He grinned and doffed an imaginary cowboy hat. "Don't you worry, purty lady. I can ride."

Owen jounced in his saddle. He was nowhere near as elegant a rider as Emma, but he got the job done. And just as he'd hoped it would, being out here on the horses seemed to relax Emma, so she was no longer so guarded in his presence. No longer so stiff and formal.

She'd wanted to hear all about the grand opening, and he'd told her everything—about Charles and Heidi and the incredible turnout and how all the kids had helped.

"I wish you could have been there." It was the closest he'd come to telling her he missed her, and he held his breath.

She didn't look at him, but he was watching her closely enough to see the little hint of a smile. "Me too." Then, as if afraid she'd said too much, she hastily added, "How are the kids? Other than helpful?"

"Actually." Owen tugged the reins to slow King. "I wanted to talk to you about that."

Her eyes flicked to his, and she slowed Scarlet too. "Is something wrong?" Worry creased her forehead, and he wanted to reach over and smooth it.

"Nothing's wrong." He halted King and swung his leg down. "Come here."

Emma tilted her head to the sky. "We need Carter to tell us if those are rain clouds."

Owen glanced up too, unwilling to admit he was pretty sure they were. He needed this time to tell her something—rain or not.

She dismounted Scarlet, and then she was right in front of him, and he had no idea what he'd been planning to say because that overpowering desire to kiss her that he'd been fighting since the moment he arrived roared through him.

"You wanted to tell me something about the kids?" Emma pulled off her helmet and combed her fingers through her hair, and now all he could think about was how, when he kissed her, he was going to do that too.

But first, words.

"I know what happened with Claire," he started. "At the police station."

Emma's brow furrowed tighter, and he couldn't tell if it was confusion or dismay.

"What she said to you about making me choose. Between you and her." He dared to shuffle a step closer. "I know that's why you had a change of heart. Why you decided we should just be friends. You were trying to do what was best for my family."

She shook her head, but the way she was biting her lip, Owen knew he had hit on the truth.

"I want you to know how amazing I think that is. That you would do that for us." He dared another shuffle, and now he could reach her if he wanted to. But he forced himself to keep his hands at his side. "And I want you to know that Claire is the one who told me all of this. Voluntarily. She's sorry she said it, and she doesn't feel the same way anymore. She wants you to be part of our life. So—" He let himself cup her cheek in his palm, relishing the feel of her skin against his. "No more of this just friends business."

Something wet hit his hand, and he thought at first that she was crying. But then a drop hit his neck. And another hit his nose.

"It's raining," Emma whispered.

"It is." Owen gently raised her face toward his. A rain drop glistened on her cheek, and he leaned forward to kiss it away. Then his mouth found hers. She stiffened for a moment but then relaxed into him, her lips responding eagerly.

The rain fell harder, and Owen pulled her closer, wrapping his arms tight around her back to keep her dry, letting his lips explore hers.

Her hands pressed against his wet t-shirt, every fingertip lighting a nerve in his skin. But her push became harder, and he realized she was shoving him away.

He let her go, and she stood in front of him, wet and gasping and looking remorseful.

"I'm sorry," she choked around breaths. "I shouldn't have. We can't . . ."

"Of course we can." He stepped closer, reaching for her again, but she wriggled away.

"We should get back to the barn. We're soaked."

Before Owen could react, she was swinging herself back up onto Scarlet's back.

He stared at her silently, the rain still streaming over both of them. She wouldn't look at him, and he had no choice but to get back on King.

They rode silently toward the barn, the rain lashing at them all the way.

Chapter 56

Panic streamed over Emma faster than the rain. They were almost back to the barn, and she had to figure out what she was going to tell Owen about why she had pulled away from that delicious, perfect kiss. About why they couldn't be together even if his kids were okay with it.

The heaviness in her limbs said she already knew what she had to tell him: the truth.

She led the way into the stables, leaving enough room for Owen and King, then got off Scarlet. Owen dismounted as well.

"I'm sorry our ride was cut short by the rain." Her voice had taken on that ridiculous too-polite quality she found herself using with him lately.

"Emma." Owen grabbed her hands in both of his. "What's going on?"

"Nothing." She shook her head. She had to get out of this. She couldn't do it. "I have to get this wet stuff off the horses."

"Then I'll help you," Owen said decidedly. "But I'm not leaving until we talk."

Emma let out a breath. "I just think it's best if we remain friends. Not more."

"That kiss was not a kiss between friends." Owen's growl brimmed with frustration, and he rubbed his hands through his wet hair.

Emma glanced over her shoulder to make sure they were alone. "I know. And I'm sorry. I didn't mean to— I can't— We can't—"

"Why are you so stubborn?" His voice gentled into a laugh, and he tucked a wet wisp of hair behind her ear.

Emma closed her eyes, so tempted to give in and say of course they could be together.

But she couldn't do that to him.

She slid away and turned to Scarlet, working to unfasten the bridle. But her hands had begun to tingle and burn, and she couldn't get a grip on the fasteners.

She could feel Owen's eyes on her, and she willed her hands to work.

"Let me help." He nudged her out of the way and unfastened the bridle.

Emma moved on to the saddle but she couldn't get her fingers to cooperate with that either. Silently, Owen did it. Then he untacked King.

He hung the saddles in the tack room and grabbed a brush, and Emma was too numb to even ask how he knew what to do.

She tried to pick up a brush too, but it fumbled through her fingers. She stood over it, frustrated tears welling in her eyes. She sniffed.

A pair of strong arms wrapped around her from behind, pulling her into his chest.

Oh, Emma wanted to stay there, wanted to let Owen tell her everything was fine and they could be together and she didn't have to fight it anymore.

"What's wrong?" His breath whispered across her ear, and her heart crumbled. He had been through enough. He didn't need this too.

She tried to twist away, but he held her fast.

"Not until you tell me." His chest rumbled against her back with each word.

"It's neuropathy," she whispered, painfully flexing her hands in front of her. "It's worse when I get cold. Sometimes my hands just won't work."

Owen spun her around and cradled her hands in his, pressing them to the warmth of his chest. "That's why you struggled the night of the storm too. The night you broke your toe. You should have told me."

She shook her head. "I couldn't."

She wasn't sure he heard her strangled whisper until he tilted his head. "Why not?"

"Because—"

He was looking at her so tenderly, his hands rubbing such warm circles on hers.

She focused on those hands. "Because it's chemo-induced neuropathy." The words were quieter than the horses' breaths, and yet they seemed to echo and echo around the stable.

Owen's hands stilled on hers, and she had to look up. Had to know what he was thinking.

But his pale face and hard jaw made her wish she hadn't.

"You have cancer," he whispered.

It wasn't a question, but she nodded. "I did. Last year." And then she drove the final nail into the coffin of what-could-have-been. "Ovarian cancer."

Owen made a choked sound and slowly lowered her hands to her sides, then stepped away. He strode to Big Blue's stall, and the horse poked his head over, nuzzling him. Owen didn't seem to notice.

He whirled back toward Emma so suddenly that both she and the horse jumped. "Is that why you were in the hospital the other day?"

She shook her head quickly. "I've just been pushing myself too hard. I need to slow down. Let other people help me more. Which, I realize, is ironic, given what I've been preaching to you." She cut off at his tortured look. "All of my scans have come back clean," she said quietly.

Her heart broke at the relief in his eyes as he sagged back against Big Blue's stall.

"Why didn't you tell me sooner?" Hurt and maybe anger pinged off the question.

Emma blinked at him helplessly. "How could I? The moment I found out Katie died of ovarian cancer, I knew there could never be anything between us. I never meant for any of this . . ." She trailed off. "I should have told you," she whispered. "But I didn't want to hurt you. Or the kids." Her lungs seized with the thought of them finding out.

"Yeah." Owen's voice was emotionless as he pushed himself upright.

"I don't know what else to say." She felt a desperate need to explain. "If I could change it. If I could have died and she could have lived . . ." She choked on a swell of emotion but stuffed it down.

Owen gave her a hard, disbelieving look. "Just because I wish Katie hadn't died, it doesn't follow that I wish you had died instead. For heaven's sake, Emma, don't you realize—" He slammed his mouth shut and shook his head. "We'd better get these horses brushed down." He grabbed the brush and started on King.

Emma wasn't brave enough to ask what he'd been about to say. The feeling had returned to her hands thanks to his rubbing, and she picked up the other brush and took care of Scarlet.

She wanted to tell Owen that he didn't have to help, that he could go, but her heart and her throat were both too full.

When the horses were back in their stalls, Owen stood for a moment, watching her. "I should go." The words fell heavily, and he didn't try to kiss her or hug her or touch her—or even smile.

Emma nodded silently, not quite able to bring herself to say goodbye.

Chapter 57

Owen shook two ibuprofen into his hand, then tossed the bottle into the box he'd been packing.

Their house was finally ready. They were moving back in tomorrow.

Right next door to Emma.

Owen's heart contracted as it did every time he thought of her—which was pretty much every moment of every day. If only there was a pill he could take for that.

It had been two weeks since she'd told him.

Two weeks since it felt like his world had fallen apart all over again.

He couldn't avoid seeing her at church and at lessons, but they hadn't talked—not even in the pinched, formal way they had when she'd decided they were just friends.

Now it was only a strained "hi" or a few words about how the kids were doing at lessons.

It killed him every time he saw her. It was all he could do not to gather her in his arms and tell her that he would protect her. That he wouldn't let anything bad happen to her.

But he couldn't do that. He couldn't protect her from this. Just like he hadn't been able to protect Katie.

And that was why he couldn't be with her, even though it felt like tearing a part of himself away every moment they weren't together.

"Argh." He downed the ibuprofen, then pulled the tape roll violently over the box.

"Did you say something?" Catelyn traipsed into the kitchen, a large box in her arms.

"No." Owen carried his box to the stack near the door, then took Catelyn's from her.

"That one is stuff for school."

Owen nodded and set it on a separate pile. He could hardly believe summer was over already. Catelyn would leave for school tomorrow.

"You're sure I can't drive you?"

"You're booked solid, remember?" Catelyn's smile wasn't so much patronizing as patient. "Besides, I drove all the way here, didn't I?"

"Claire was with you," Owen muttered. "And you were following me."

"Yes, and I'll be following Jackson until we get to his school. I can make it the rest of the way on my own. It's really not that far."

Owen nodded. He knew—and had given his blessing to—all of these details already. It was just hard to come to grips with the fact that his little girl didn't need him for everything anymore.

"Listen, Dad." Catelyn sounded hesitant. "I thought you should know that Emma is going to be there tonight."

Owen nodded tightly. He had figured as much when Leah had invited him to a going away party for both Jackson and Catelyn.

"I still don't understand what happened with you two . . ." Catelyn frowned expectantly. She and her siblings had been pestering him for two weeks, wanting to know why things hadn't worked out with Emma. Poor Kenzie had been in tears more than once.

"Claire still thinks it's her fault, you know," Catelyn added pointedly. "And she will until you tell us otherwise."

Owen sighed. "It's not her fault." He headed back toward the kitchen but then turned with a sudden decisiveness. "Tell everyone to meet me in the living room."

Catelyn hesitated a moment, giving him a questioning look, but when he nodded, she disappeared.

Owen stepped out onto the porch and leaned against the railing, staring out over the rolling waves of Lake Michigan.

He'd been trying to protect his children, trying to keep them from getting hurt again. But the truth was, even if he and Emma were never together, she would still be part of their lives. Kenzie was best friends with her niece. She taught them riding lessons. They went to the same church. Starting tomorrow, she would be their neighbor again. The kids deserved to know the truth, especially if there was a chance . . .

He let out a heavy breath. *Please, Lord, give me wisdom.*

He strode back into the cabin and found all the kids in the living room, the three girls crammed onto the small couch, Cody in the rocking chair, and Carter in his favorite spot by the window, studying the sky.

"What's going on, Dad?" It was Cody who asked, and he had never sounded more like an almost-grown man.

There was nowhere left to sit, so Owen remained on his feet. "I know you've all been wondering what happened with Miss Emma. Why we're not . . . together."

"It's because of me." Claire dropped her head but then perked up. "I could talk to her. Tell her—"

"It's not because of you, Claire," Owen interrupted. He swallowed, glass cutting at the sides of his throat. He couldn't do this. Not after everything they'd been through already.

"Does Miss Emma not want kids?" Kenzie asked quietly.

"Oh, honey, no. That's not it. Miss Emma loves you all very much." Owen unfisted his fingers and shoved them into his pockets.

"What then?" Catelyn flashed with unusual impatience.

"She— She's recovering from cancer." The words dragged from his lips. "From ovarian cancer."

The kids all stared at him, and for a moment Owen thought that would be their only reaction.

Then, Catelyn and Kenzie started crying. Claire leaped to her feet and strode out of the room. Cody dropped his elbows to his knees and cradled his head in his hands. Carter continued staring out the window, and Owen wondered if he understood, until he said quietly, "Like Mom."

"Yeah, buddy. Like Mom." Owen's throat ached so hard that he had to swallow several times before he could speak again. "She's okay now. The cancer is gone, but . . ."

"But it could come back." Catelyn swiped her hands across her cheeks.

Owen nodded painfully. "It could. She didn't tell us because she didn't want to hurt us. She never thought we would . . . That's why she doesn't think we should be together." He cleared his throat. "And I agree." His heart thrashed against his ribs, shouting that it did *not* agree, but he ignored it. He had to protect his children.

"Do you love her?" Claire's voice came from the living room doorway, and Owen turned to her. Her eyes were red, her cheeks blotchy.

"I'm not worried about me right now," he said. "I'm worried about how this would affect all of you. If anything ever happened to her . . ." He couldn't go on for a moment. "I couldn't put you through that again," he said finally.

"Maybe *you're* not worried about you right now, but we are." Catelyn spoke into the silence. "You need to answer Claire's question. Do you love her?"

The kids all stared him down. Owen considered his options. If he denied it, maybe they would let it go.

But he wasn't in the habit of lying to his kids. And he didn't want to start now.

"Yes," he said quietly.

"Yay!" Kenzie cheered and ran to hug him. The other kids were all smiling—even Claire—though their smiles were tempered by sadness.

"That doesn't mean," Owen cautioned, "that I think it's a good idea for us to be together. I have to consider what's best for our family. You understand that, right?"

"Yep," Kenzie answered for everyone. "As long as by 'our family' you mean Miss Emma too."

Chapter 58

"I don't think you could get any farther from Owen if you tried." Kayla laugh-frowned as she maneuvered her wheelchair next to the seat Emma had chosen at the far corner of Leah and Austin's patio. Sweet little baby Evelyn patted Kayla's cheeks, and Emma's heart ached harder than ever, but she smiled.

"You need to let it go. Nothing is going to happen. And I'm fine with it."

"Kenzie told you they're moving back into their house tomorrow?"

Emma forced her face to remain neutral as she nodded. "Do they need any help?"

"Grace and Levi are going to help. And I think Spencer and Tyler. But you could always ask . . ."

Emma shook her head. "I'm sure they'll be fine."

Kayla made an exasperated sound. "Your Aunt Emma is so stubborn, isn't she?" she cooed to Evelyn.

"It's not stubbornness." Emma heard the resignation in her own voice. "It's reality."

Kayla had been there, the night Owen had left the stables after she'd told him. She'd seen the way he could barely look at Emma, let alone speak to her, at lessons now.

Not that Emma blamed him. He had to protect himself and his children. It was what she'd been trying to do in the first place.

"Well, you must have noticed the way he keeps looking over here." Kayla's voice was low and conspiratorial as she stared pointedly across the yard to where Owen and a few other adults played bocce ball with a large group of kids.

Emma shook her head. She *had* noticed, and there was something in his look, something soft and longing, that made her think . . .

"He's probably just wishing I would leave so he could enjoy his last night with his daughter," she said.

Kayla snorted. "Trust me, that is not the look of a man who wishes you would leave."

"I should, though." Emma stood. "I have a headache anyway." It didn't matter if it was from the strain of holding back tears—it still qualified her for an early night.

"Don't go." Kayla reached for her hand, but baby Evelyn intercepted her. "I promise I'll stop talking about Owen."

Emma shook her head. It didn't matter if Kayla stopped talking about him—it didn't matter if no one ever said his name again. She'd never be able to stop thinking about him. The best she could hope for was that eventually she really would see him as just a friend.

She made her way across the patio to where Catelyn stood in the circle of Jackson's arms, chatting with Dan and Jade, who were holding hands. Emma ignored the sting of being surrounded by all of these happy couples. It had never bothered her before—and she would get used to it again.

"Hi, Emma." Something in Catelyn's expression seemed different, but Emma couldn't place it. "I'm so glad you're here." Her gaze tracked across the yard to where Owen and the others had shifted to a game of corn hole. "You should go play. Kenzie would love that."

Emma smiled sadly. It had been just as hard to distance herself from the kids as from Owen. But she had to do it.

"Actually, I think I'm going to head out. But I just wanted to say I'll be praying for you while you're at school."

"Thank you." Catelyn slid away from Jackson to hug Emma. "Take care of yourself," she whispered, squeezing tightly before she let go.

"I will." Emma hugged Jackson too, then turned to watch the corn hole game. Kenzie nailed a shot, and Owen cheered and lifted her off her feet, eliciting a squeal. Emma smiled, but as Owen set Kenzie down, his eyes came to hers. Everything stopped, and Emma was locked in that moment, in wishing she could run to him and throw her arms around him and hear him say everything was all right and he would always be there for her.

He leaned over to say something to Kenzie, then started toward Emma, and suddenly time returned with a vengeance.

Emma spun toward the house, weaving through her friends. No fewer than three people stopped her to ask if she was leaving.

She strained to retain her composure, but all she could say was "yes" as she pushed past.

She had to get out of here. If she saw Owen again, if she talked to him, she would lose the tenuous grasp she had on her emotions.

She made it out the door and broke into a full-out run for her truck, parked down the road.

She was only halfway across the yard when a voice—his voice—called her name.

She shook her head, but her feet apparently didn't get the message, because they slowed and then stopped.

She turned around as Owen's footsteps pounded the last few feet between them.

"Emma," he gasped. His face was a map of joy and hope and exhilaration.

She had to look away. She couldn't do this again.

"Emma," he said, more tenderly. He lifted a hand to her cheek, and she closed her eyes, one of the tears she'd been straining so hard to keep from falling seeping out.

"Oh, Emma," he breathed, pulling her tight to his chest. "I'm sorry." His lips pressed to her hair.

She shook her head but clutched at him. Being in his arms felt like taking a long breath after being underwater too long.

"We can't do this, Owen." Her tears soaked into the front of his shirt, and he cinched his arms tighter around her, one palm pressing into her back, the other smoothing her hair.

After a few moments, he loosened his hold and leaned her back gently so she could see his face.

"Yes, we can," he said firmly.

The desire to give in was almost unbearable, but she shook her head miserably. "I won't let you and the kids go through that again."

"I told them today," he said quietly, and Emma's heart floundered.

"You shouldn't have—" Tears started again at the thought of what they'd already been through. They didn't need more pain in their lives.

"They were sad," Owen said. "But they also wanted to know—" His Adam's apple bobbed. "If I love you."

Emma stilled, her breath trapped in her lungs.

"And I told them," he whispered, sliding his hands against her wet cheeks. "That I do."

Emma shook her head, her tears surging uncontrollably. But Owen kept his hands on her cheeks and wiped them away.

"Even then," he said. "I wasn't going to do this. I just couldn't see risking the kids' hearts like that. Risking my own."

Emma nodded. That was what she'd been trying to tell him.

"But then I saw you tonight, and I realized that being with you might mean risking loss again. But not being with you—not having your smile and your laugh and your compassion and your love in our lives at all—that would be the bigger loss."

He drew her closer and brought his lips to hers in a kiss so tender, so warm, so loving, that Emma's tears stopped and her heart stilled and peace washed over her.

When Owen pulled away, he kissed her still-wet cheeks, her nose, her forehead. "So will you stop fighting this now?"

She gave a shaky laugh. "I guess I'd better. Because I love you too."

Owen whooped the way he had when they'd gone skydiving, and Emma laughed but shushed him. "People are going to wonder what's going on."

"Well, then we'll just tell them." Owen grinned at her. "That we're in love."

Chapter 59

"I got Miss Emma's phone, Daddy." Kenzie walked past him into the living room, handing it off, as if they were spies.

"Good work. Where is Emma?" Owen dropped into the new recliner that had become his favorite, turned on the phone, and clicked over to the app Emma used for her life list.

"She's helping Catelyn with the mashed potatoes."

"Okay, good." Owen's heart couldn't have been more full. Catelyn was home for Thanksgiving, and they'd all spent the morning helping their friends prepare and serve the community Thanksgiving lunch at church.

And now they were preparing their own meal to enjoy together as a family. Or at least, that was what they would officially be if the plan he and the kids had concocted worked out.

He tapped a new line into Emma's list, then closed the app.

"I'll take the phone back in there," Cody offered. "So it's not so suspicious."

"You just want to sneak some mashed potatoes," Claire accused.

"So?" Cody grinned, and Owen passed him the phone. The boy disappeared, and Owen drummed his fingers on the armrests.

"Nervous?" Claire asked.

Owen blew out a breath. "Is it that obvious?"

"Well, you did drop about eighty brussels sprouts on the floor at church," Claire joked.

"It wasn't eighty."

"It was forty-two," Carter didn't look up from his book. "I counted when I picked them up."

"Whatever." Claire rolled her eyes, but Owen didn't mind. The change he'd seen in his daughter over the past couple of months had been nothing short of miraculous. She was doing well in school, she'd completed her diversion program but decided to continue volunteering at the animal shelter, and she'd found a new set of friends who went to their church. And maybe better than all of that, he could see her growing closer to Emma day by day. She'd even been the one to come up with the whole tweaking-Emma's-life-list plan.

"Carter, come over here a second."

Carter set his book down and traipsed over.

Owen drew him closer, speaking quietly. "You remember what you're supposed to do, right?"

Carter nodded. "I got it."

"Okay, good. We're counting on you." Owen patted the boy's shoulder.

"Time to eat." Cody popped back into the room, a beater full of mashed potatoes in his hand.

"Ew, that's so gross." Claire made a face at her brother, who took a big lick of the potatoes.

Owen followed his children into the dining room, though he had no idea how he was going to eat.

"It smells fantastic in here." Owen had helped with the turkey and stuffing, and he'd made the cranberries yesterday, but Emma and Catelyn had been putting the final touches on the dinner.

"It does, doesn't it?" Emma looked so content as she set down the bowl of squash she was carrying to the table that he caught her around the waist and brushed a kiss onto her lips.

"There are children present," Claire called.

"Oh, I'm sorry about that. Did you all want a kiss too?" Owen let Emma go and chased Kenzie down. She squealed but puckered her lips and kissed Owen before he could kiss her. He dropped a kiss onto the top of Carter's head, then moved to Claire.

"Dad," she complained, but she let him kiss her cheek, as did Catelyn.

When he reached Cody, his son held out a hand.

Owen studied him. "All right, then." He shook Cody's hand, then gripped it tighter and pulled him close enough to kiss the top of his head.

Everyone laughed at Cody's surprised splutter.

"Hey, I'm still your dad," Owen defended himself.

"I want a kiss from Miss Emma too," Kenzie cried.

"Oh." Emma stopped with the basket of rolls in her hands and glanced at Owen.

He gave her a warm smile, and she returned it, then set the basket down and moved to Kenzie, who lifted her face and puckered her lips. Emma laughed, puckered her own lips, and pecked a kiss onto Kenzie's.

"Thank you," Kenzie said happily.

"Thank *you*." Emma's eyes shone, and Owen couldn't resist sweeping a kiss across her hair as they sat down.

"Should we give thanks?" Owen asked. "Maybe we could each take a turn?"

Emma nodded. "That sounds really nice."

Owen reached for her hand under the table and bowed his head, closing his eyes as the realization of how much he had to be grateful for swept over him.

"Lord God," he started. "We are so thankful to be together for this special day. We are thankful that you never fail to provide for us and that you bring joy to us in so many ways, including through one another.

Thank you especially for the eternal joy you have promised us at your side. Amen."

Emma prayed next. "Jesus, I'm just in awe of you and what you do in our lives. Six months ago, a dog came barreling into my yard and disturbed my chickens." Owen chuckled along with the kids. "I had no idea then, Lord, how that day would change my life. Thank you for making this special family part of it. Amen."

Owen squeezed her hand, wishing he and the kids had carried out their plan before dinner instead of deciding to wait until after.

"Catelyn?" Owen asked.

"Lord, thank you for giving me the opportunity to come home to be with my family for Thanksgiving. There is no place I'd rather be. And thank you for true examples of love in my life. Amen."

"Me next," Kenzie cried. "Thank you, Jesus, for Dad and Catelyn and Claire and Cody and Carter and Miss Emma. I love them all so much. Amen."

"I'll go next," Cody said, and Owen suddenly realized that at some point in the past few months, his son's voice had lost its cracks and squeaks and had deepened into a man's voice. "Heavenly Father, thank you for all of this delicious food that I can't wait to eat," he said, and they all laughed. "And thank you for the gift of family and friends. I didn't think I was going to like Hope Springs, but I do. Amen."

"Ditto," Claire said. "And thank you also for your forgiveness. It's pretty amazing. Amen."

"Carter?" Owen managed to get out past the giant lump that had wedged its way into his throat as his children prayed. "Would you like a turn?"

"Thank you for clouds," Carter said. "And for books about clouds." They all chuckled. "And for a new mom. Amen."

Owen's head jerked up in time to see everyone else's do the same.

"Carter," the other kids all shouted at once.

Their voices overlapped one another as they turned to Emma.

"He just means—"

"He didn't mean you, he meant—"

"You know how kids are—"

"He calls everyone—"

"Guys, guys," Owen called over the ruckus. "It's okay."

Emma's eyes were darting around the table, and she looked adorably lost trying to keep up with all the noise.

"I'm sorry." Carter's eyes welled with tears. "I didn't mean to say—"

"Oh, sweetie, it's okay." Emma was instantly up and out of her seat, wrapping her arms around the boy. "I may not be your mom, but I do love you very much."

That settled it. Owen wasn't going to wait another moment to do this. Even if it meant they had to chuck out their carefully laid plan.

"Carter," he prompted. "Was there something you wanted to say to Miss Emma?"

Carter stared at him blankly.

"About putting zip lining on her life list?" Owen tried to pull his son along.

"But you didn't say—" Carter's brow wrinkled.

Owen blew out a breath. "You know what, you're right. Let's do the whole thing. Catelyn, did you do anything fun this semester?"

"Why, yes, Dad, I did." Catelyn's voice sounded intentionally rehearsed, and Owen chuckled. "I went zip lining. It was incredible."

"Have you ever been zip lining, Miss Emma?" Kenzie asked. She delivered her line perfectly—and apparently knew it, since she pulled her arms back and whispered, "Yes!"

"I— Um, no." Emma glanced around as if they'd all gone crazy.

"Oh, you should," Cody said.

"Yeah," Claire added. "It sounds like fun."

"You should put it on your life list!" Carter shouted enthusiastically.

"Okay . . ." Emma sounded more than a little concerned that they were all off their rockers. "I'll do that after dinner. Do you want some mashed potatoes?" She reached for the bowl.

"No," everyone shouted at once.

Emma yanked her hand back. "What is going on?"

"You should really put zip lining on your life list now," Claire said. "So you don't forget."

"My phone is in the kitchen. I'll get it after we eat." Emma looked to Owen as if for backup.

"The kids are right," he said. "You should add it now."

"What? Why?" Emma's forehead wrinkled until understanding dawned on her face. "Did you guys add something to my list again? I still haven't forgiven you for the last one you added." She shuddered. "Touch a snake. Come on."

"This one is better!" Kenzie sprang up out of her chair. "I'll go get your phone." She was back in three seconds, her grin wider than Owen had ever seen it.

Emma took the phone from her, still casting worried looks at everyone.

She clicked the phone on and tapped a couple of times. Her finger moved as she scrolled, her eyes narrowed as if she didn't expect to like whatever she found.

And then she froze, her eyes widening.

Owen moved toward her. His own grin felt even bigger than Kenzie's.

"I— What is this?" Emma whispered.

"Just what it says," Owen answered, joy gathering in his chest.

"But it says—" Emma licked her lips. "Get married and have a family." Her eyes met his, and he reached for her hands.

"I guess I should have been a little more specific. What it should say is, 'Get married to *me*. And have *this* family.'" He angled his head toward the table, and Kenzie giggled.

"I don't understand . . ." Emma's eyes swept over all of them.

"Then let me make it clear." Owen dropped to one knee and pulled a black velvet box out of his pocket.

Emma's gasp was loud enough that Owen was pretty sure Sophie and Spencer could hear it from down the road. She covered her mouth with her hand as tears skated down her cheeks.

Owen grabbed her free hand. "Emma Wood, when we moved to Hope Springs, my greatest hope was that my kids wouldn't hate me for uprooting them." The kids laughed, and Emma smiled a wobbly smile through her tears. "I had no idea that day Lexi led us into your yard that—" His voice cracked, and he heard one of his kids sniffle. He cleared his throat. "That it would change my life. That it would change *our* lives. I love you, Emma, and I want you to be my wife. Will you marry me?"

"I . . . Owen, are you sure?" Emma's voice shook.

"Yes!" The kids all shouted, and Owen laughed as Emma jumped.

"Yes," he said, just as firmly. "We all want you to be part of our family."

Emma's eyes roved over the kids, and Owen followed her gaze. They were all nodding earnestly.

His eyes went back to Emma, who was nodding, her now nearly shoulder-length hair bobbing.

"Yes?" he asked, hope welling through him.

"Yes." Her laugh rang across the room. "Yes, I'll marry you. I'll be part of your family."

A cheer went up from the kids, and Owen grinned and jumped to his feet, pulling Emma to him. "Close your eyes if you don't want to see kissing," he called to the kids.

And then his lips were on Emma's. It only lasted a moment before bodies pressed in on them from all sides, hugging and laughing and cheering.

"Dad," Catelyn called when the kids finally let go. "You didn't give her the ring."

"Oh yeah." Owen eased the ring from the box and slid it onto Emma's finger.

She looked at it, then at him. "I think I need to add something to my prayer of thanksgiving," she whispered.

He nodded. He did too.

Epilogue

The doorbell rang, and Emma pressed her hands to her stomach, grinning at herself in the mirror. It felt like she'd been waiting forever and only the blink of an eye for this day.

She ran her fingers through her hair. The curls had started to loosen and the roots seemed to be coming in straighter. Grace would help her put it up once they got to the church, but it really didn't matter. This day wasn't about fancy dresses or pretty hair or even the beautiful flowers that would grace the church this close to Christmas. It was about Owen and his family. About becoming part of that family.

She scooped the garment bag holding the wedding dress off her bed, grabbed the pair of white cowboy boots her friends had surprised her with at her wedding shower, and hurried to the door.

She pulled it open and was instantly tackled in a mob of arms as Kenzie and Catelyn rushed through.

"How was your semester?" she asked Catelyn as she returned the hug.

"It was great." Catelyn grinned at her. "But there will be time to talk about that later. Right now, we need to go get you married to my dad."

Emma's heart nearly burst at the words, but her eyes went to Claire, who hovered just inside the doorway, looking uncertain.

"You should see her dress," Kenzie said to Catelyn. "It's *beautiful*. Dad is going to love it." Kenzie had only come over to look at the simple long-sleeve A-line white dress about forty times in the week since Emma had picked it up from the dress shop.

"Hey, I think I forgot my lipstick," Emma said. "Could you two go grab it out of the bathroom?" She sent Catelyn a look she hoped the girl would be able to interpret.

"But you don't wear—" Kenzie started.

"It's her wedding day," Catelyn said. "Of course she's going to wear lipstick. Come on, let's go grab it."

Emma waited for them to leave the room, then laid her dress on the table and made her way to Claire, who still lingered right inside the door.

"Hey," she said. "It's okay to feel sad today. I know you miss your mom. And I just want you to know that even though I love you all very much, I would never try to replace her."

Claire nodded but bit her lip to stop the trembling.

"Oh, sweetie. I'm sorry this is so hard."

Emma took a tentative step forward, opening her arms.

Claire shook her head but stepped into Emma's embrace, letting her head fall onto Emma's shoulder. Even through her sweatshirt, Emma could feel the tears.

She rubbed Claire's back and held her close.

"We couldn't find any—" Kenzie's voice broke off. "What's wrong with Claire?"

"This is a happy day, but it's also a sad day," Emma said as Claire pulled away and wiped at her eyes. "I know how much you all miss your mom."

Kenzie nodded, her face falling. "I don't really remember her very much," she whispered. "But I think she was a lot like you."

Catelyn smiled, her own eyes tearing. "She was, Kenz. She really was."

Claire nodded, and that made Emma's eyes fill. "Could we," she started before she was interrupted with the need to sniffle. "Would it be okay if we prayed together?"

The girls nodded, and she held out a hand to Claire and one to Kenzie. Catelyn stood between the other two girls and took their hands.

"Lord of all," Emma started, "as I get ready to become part of this wonderful family, I just wanted to thank you. Thank you for Catelyn. And thank you for Kenzie." She felt Kenzie's hand swing in hers. "And thank you for Claire." She squeezed Claire's hand, and the girl squeezed back. "And thank you for Cody and Carter too." She thought of the boys, probably at the church already with Owen. "Thank you that they all had a wonderful mother who taught them so much and loved them so much and is at your side now in heaven. Thank you that they will see her again one day."

Now they were all sniffling, but she kept going. "And thank you for giving me the privilege and joy of becoming part of this family." Too choked up to continue, she gasped out an "Amen," and then held out her arms to wrap all the girls in one more hug.

"Okay, we have to get going," Catelyn finally said, wiping her eyes. "Dad will kill me if I get you there late."

Emma sniffed and wiped at her eyes too. "Let's go."

"What about your lipstick?" Kenzie asked.

Emma laughed with a shrug. "I'm not sure if your dad would recognize me in lipstick anyway."

In the car, Kenzie kept up a constant stream of chatter, with occasional interjections by Catelyn and even Claire, and it wasn't until they pulled into a parking spot at the church that the full enormity of what she was doing hit Emma.

She was about to become a *wife*. And a *mother*.

She took a deep breath, closed her eyes, and gave thanks.

She had been so certain the door to both of those things had been closed to her. *But God.*

God had made a way even when she saw none.

"Are you okay?" Catelyn asked, worry coating her voice. "You don't have cold feet, do you?"

Emma opened her eyes with a laugh. "I have incredibly warm feet. Come on, let's do this."

◊

Owen sped down the church hallway. Catelyn and the girls had left home to pick up Emma right behind him and the boys, but it had been fifteen minutes, and they weren't here yet.

Maybe they'd gotten a flat tire. Or maybe Kenzie wasn't feeling well. Or maybe Emma had changed her—

A giant breath whooshed out of him as he reached the church doors and spotted Catelyn's car. Emma and the girls poured out of it, pausing at the trunk for a moment to grab things, then hurried toward the building. Emma was wearing jeans and a sweatshirt, a long bag draped over her arm and a pair of white cowboy boots in her hand. But it was her smile that drew Owen out the door.

He jogged across the parking lot. "I was getting nervous," he called.

Emma looked up, her eyes lighting his heart on fire. "Sorry. We needed a little time for some girl talk."

"Dad, you're not supposed to see your bride before the wedding," Catelyn chided.

"My bride." Owen swept Emma into his arms and dropped a kiss onto her lips. "I like the sound of that."

"Seriously, Dad. Get inside and get ready. You're not going to get married in those old jeans." Catelyn shooed him.

"All right, all right. At least let me hold the door for my ladies."

Kenzie giggled. "That's what Miss Emma calls her chickens."

"They're *our* chickens now," Emma said.

"Really?" Kenzie sounded awestruck.

"Of course." Emma grinned at the girl. "Which means you get to help do the chores to take care of them."

"Goodie!" Kenzie cheered, and Owen laughed.

"I hope you'll still be so enthusiastic about your new chores after you've been doing them a few months. Or years. Or forever." He winked at Emma. They'd decided it would be best for Owen and the kids to move into Emma's house, since the stables were right there. The plan had been to put Owen's house on the market—but then Anne and William had offered to buy it. The best part was, now the kids would be close to their new grandparents.

Owen pulled the church door open, ushering his girls—and his almost-wife—through.

"Oh, this is beautiful." Catelyn spun to take in the decorations. With Christmas only a few days away, the church had already been adorned with Christmas trees and lights and poinsettias, leaving Emma and Owen almost no work to decorate. Which wasn't the only benefit of getting married so quickly. They'd all talked about it—Owen, Emma, and the kids—and they'd wanted to spend Christmas together as an official family.

Claire wandered to the table that stood right outside the sanctuary doors and reached for a picture on it.

"That turned out really nice," Owen murmured to Emma, kissing the top of her head. "Thank you for doing it." It had been entirely Emma's idea to include a picture of Katie on the table, along with a copy of her favorite verse, "Trust in the Lord with all your heart and lean not on your own understanding."

Emma nodded. "She's their mom, and she was your wife. She'll always be part of our lives."

Owen nodded, too overcome to say anything for a moment. How had he been so fortunate to find a love like this a second time?

"Seriously, Dad, you have to get ready, and so does Emma." Catelyn tugged Emma's arm and pulled her toward the hallway. "Claire, Kenzie, come on." She beckoned her sisters to follow.

Kenzie skipped after her, but Claire took a moment more with the picture. When she turned, she met Owen's eyes. And she smiled.

He let out a breath and smiled too, crossing the space to give her a quick hug before making his way to the dressing area. He stepped inside to find that Cody and Carter had already changed into their suits and were seated on a small couch. Cody was letting Carter read his cloud book to him. Owen had to stop for a moment. When had they grown up so much?

"Hey boys?"

They both looked up. Carter's eyes widened. "Are you done getting married already?"

Owen laughed. "Not yet, buddy. I wouldn't do that without you." He strode to the couch and crouched in front of it. "Thank you both for being my best men."

Carter nodded solemnly. "It's an important job."

"It sure is." Owen patted his knee.

"As one of your best men," Cody said, "I think it's my duty to tell you to get dressed."

Owen laughed and stood. "Yes, sir."

But it didn't take nearly long enough to put on his tux, and the wedding didn't start for another forty minutes.

He joined the boys on the couch, and they all read the cloud book until there was a knock on the door. James strode in.

"Hey." Owen scrambled to his feet. "How's Bethany?"

"So ready to have this baby." James laughed. "Just hopefully not today." He held out a hand to Owen. "Congratulations. You got yourself quite a catch in my sister."

"I know," Owen said solemnly.

"And you make her happier than I've ever seen her. You all do. So thank you."

"Oh." Owen cleared his throat. That was all he wanted. "Thank you. That means a lot to me."

"All right. Well." James clapped a hand to Owen's shoulder. "Are you ready to marry her or what?"

"I'm so ready."

Owen gestured to the boys to follow James. They marched through the lobby and into the church, and Owen's eyes roamed the rows. They'd decided to keep the wedding just to close family and friends—which was still enough people to nearly fill the church. He spotted Sophie and Spencer and Grace and Levi and Leah and Austin and all the other people he had begun to consider his own friends.

At the front of the church, he paused to hug Anne. She held him tight and whispered, "Welcome to the family."

Owen blinked back a wave of emotion. He had thought he was giving Emma a family. But she was giving him one too.

The music switched over to the processional, and Owen took his place at the front with his boys. Kenzie glided down the aisle, looking way too grown up in her emerald green dress. She cast one quick nervous look at the pews, then grinned and walked confidently down the aisle. Claire and then Catelyn followed, wearing matching dresses and matching smiles. He didn't miss the way Catelyn reached out to brush Jackson's fingers as she passed his row, but he couldn't dwell on that right now because the music swelled, pulling his eyes to the back of the church.

Emma entered the sanctuary, her simple white dress flowing elegantly to the floor, her hair pinned up in loose curls, her face radiant.

Owen took an involuntary step down the aisle, even though he was pretty sure he wasn't supposed to yet.

Emma's eyes never wavered from his as she continued down the aisle on William's arm, and when they finally reached him, it was only because William stuck his hand out that Owen was able to look away from her for a moment.

Then his gaze fastened to hers again, and he held out a hand to her and they took their place in front of Dan.

"Brothers and sisters," Dan began. "It is truly a joyous day when we get to witness the marriage of two people we care about deeply."

Emma squeezed Owen's hand, and he glanced at her tenderly. It was a joyous day indeed.

It wasn't all that long ago that he hadn't been sure he could ever find true joy again, but Emma had helped him to remember the Source of all joy, and for that he could never thank her enough.

The service continued with a song, followed by blessings and prayers, and then Dan gave a message on the verse they had chosen together, Psalm 28:7: "The Lord is my strength and my shield; my heart trusts in him, and he helps me. My heart leaps for joy, and with my song I praise him."

"My heart leaps for joy," Dan began, "every time I stand here to marry two people. And maybe even more so today than usual." He glanced out at the congregation. "Not that all of your weddings weren't meaningful to me," he said quickly, to several chuckles from the friends in the pews. "But Emma and Owen have each known their share of heartaches and hardships. They've been through a lot. There's no denying that." Dan looked at them both thoughtfully. "And yet, out of those hardships, the Lord has built a new relationship. Out of the ashes, he has fashioned a crown of beauty. Out of sorrow, he has brought joy."

Owen nodded. That couldn't be more true. Between Katie's death and Claire's behavior and the fire, his life had felt like a pile of ashes. And yet look what God had done with it.

"But it's not just a worldly joy," Dan said. "It's not just a happy ending to a love story. It's the joy you two have together—we all have together—in the greatest love story of all. It's joy in the story of God's love for us. A love so great that he saved us when we were powerless to save ourselves."

Next to him, Emma was nodding along with Dan's words, and Owen grinned. She always did that, and it was one of the things he loved about her.

"Your own love story is built on that love," Dan continued. "As you go through life's ups and downs together, know that the Lord will always be your strength and your shield. He will always be your joy and your delight. And because of him, your story will have the happiest of endings, with him in heaven one day. Until your story reaches that end, he has given you one another to have and to hold, for better or for worse, in sickness and in health—" Emma cast Owen a glance, and he shot her a confident smile. He prayed she would never have to go through cancer again. But if she did, he would be right at her side. "To encourage one another in his love, to build each other up, to serve and honor and respect one another, to pray for each other. To put the other person above yourself. And to put Christ above all."

Now Owen found himself nodding along as well.

"It's a tall order," Dan continued. "One that I don't think any of us would claim to fulfill perfectly. One that we can only attempt to fulfill with

God's help. Turn to him daily. He *will* bless your marriage, and he *will* fill you with joy in him. 'For this God is our God forever and ever; he will be our guide even to the end.' Amen."

Dan invited them to recite their vows, and Owen turned to Emma, taking both of her hands in his. "I was thinking about that puzzle we did, remember, the one with the picnic?"

Emma laughed and nodded.

"I was trying to figure out what each piece was just by looking at it on its own. And you told me that puzzles are a lot like life. We can only see one piece at a time, but God can see the whole picture. He knows how to fit them all together." He took a breath, squeezing her hands and choking back the wave of his own emotions as tears streamed down Emma's cheeks. "I'm so glad he's shown me that you're a piece of my life and that you fit right into our family. I promise to honor and cherish you, to support and encourage you, to love you always, until the end of my days."

Emma wiped her eyes and sniffled, but her voice was strong as she started her vows. "I remember doing that puzzle. And I remember thinking that there would never be room for a piece like me in a family like yours. You know I don't usually like to be wrong. But I am so glad I was in this case." She laughed around her tears, and Owen laughed with her.

"Me too," he murmured.

"I also remember the first time you told me you loved me," Emma continued. "And I cried. Because I had no idea . . ." She paused and bit her lip as tears flowed down her cheeks. Owen let go of her hands long enough to wipe them away.

"Apparently I haven't gotten over that yet," she laughed shakily. "But I had no idea that love could be so . . . amazing. And it still amazes me every day that God has brought me this kind of love. Love for you and love for your family. Our family."

Owen looked away to wipe at his own eyes, catching a glimpse of his children doing the same.

"I promise to honor and cherish you." Emma's voice was stronger now. "To support and encourage you, to love you always, until the end of my days. And I promise," she continued, catching Owen by surprise. They'd written their vows together so that they could make the same promise to each other. But she added, "To love your children always and to do all that I can to support and encourage and guide them in the Lord all my days."

Owen couldn't help it. He was crying like a baby now, and he didn't care. He stepped forward and gathered Emma into his arms, holding her tight until Dan cleared his throat.

"Uh, we should probably do the ring exchange now."

Owen held on for another second, then let Emma go as their friends laughed—though he heard plenty of sniffles too.

Owen slid the ring onto Emma's finger, then held out his hand for her to slide one onto his. And then Dan pronounced them husband and wife.

Owen pulled Emma into his arms again, and neither of them were crying now as he brought his lips to hers.

When they pulled apart, they linked hands and waited for the kids to join them. Then they all walked down the aisle together. Into their happy ending.

You're Invited...to One More Hope Springs Wedding

Thank you for reading NOT UNTIL THE END! I hope you loved Owen and Emma's story and the entire Hope Springs series. If you're wondering how all of your friends from Hope Springs are doing a couple of years down the road, you're invited to join them for one more Hope Springs wedding in the Hope Springs Series Extended Epilogue! Can you guess whose wedding it is?

Find out if you're right when you download it free!

Visit https://www.valeriembodden.com/hopespringsepilogue or use the QR code below.

And if you love the Hope Springs series, you'll find more uplifting stories of family, faith, and love in the River Falls series, featuring Grace and Levi's family in River Falls, Tennessee. Read on for an excerpt of the first River Falls book, Pieces of Forever!

A preview of Pieces of Forever (River Falls book 1)

Chapter 1

Most days, Ava could keep the demons of the past at bay.

But today, every click of the shutter reminded her of what could have been.

"Okay." She lowered the camera from her face and studied the model-perfect teenage girl standing in front of the muslin backdrop. Ava had chosen a white background to give the photos an airy, ethereal quality. "Nice job, Harper. Now, can you touch your hand to your face?"

"Like this?" Harper lifted a fisted hand to her cheek as her friend Emily, whom Ava had already done a set of shots for, giggled from behind Ava.

"You look like that statue," Emily said. "You know, the one with the guy all hunched over?"

"The Thinker?" Ava smiled as both girls dissolved into giggles. She'd been fun and silly like this once too. Some days it felt like a long time ago. Other times, like now, those days bit close at her heels. "I was thinking more like this." She lifted her own hand to her face, wincing internally as her fingertips brushed the ridges of skin that puckered her left cheek. How did she forget sometimes that this was what her skin felt like now? What it would always feel like.

She forced herself to keep her fingers there until Harper mimicked the gesture.

"Perfect." She lifted the camera and started clicking again, calling for the girl to smile, then to be serious, then to make the goofiest face she could muster. The secret to great photos, she'd found, was capturing those moments when a subject was off guard, like in the seconds after Harper pulled her goofy face and then broke into a laugh that brought out her best smile of the day.

"Great." She set her camera on the table of gear behind her. "Why don't you girls go change into your next outfits, and I'll get things set up out here."

As the girls scampered off, giggling as wildly as ever, Ava switched from the white backdrop to a black one, then reset the light levels and repositioned her flashes.

All the while, she battled those demons. If life had gone the way she'd planned, she wouldn't be in River Falls, taking photos. She'd be in New York, on the other side of the lens. She'd be the one who was giggling and rushing off to change clothes and soaking up the spotlight.

But life didn't go the way you planned.

She shook off the heaviness that tried to hang on her. She had everything she needed—her own business, her aunt, and her dog. She'd decided a long time ago that it was more than enough.

It had to be.

Ava stepped back and surveyed the studio, tapping the smooth right side of her lips.

Something was missing here.

A chair, maybe. Or no—a ladder.

She was pretty sure she still had one among her props. She stepped around her equipment and bustled toward the back room, which served as both prop storage and a makeshift changing area, with two large changing booths off to the side.

When she reached the room, she stopped in the doorway, looking around. Things were strewn helter-skelter—flowers in a pile on one table, fabrics of different hues on another, shelves crowded with wooden blocks and blankets and one of those metal washtubs everyone wanted a picture of their baby in. Scattered among it all were chairs of various shapes and colors, trunks of every size imaginable, old lighting equipment, and a variety of tripods. It was getting to the point where Ava could barely walk through the space. Aunt Lori kept offering to come and help her sort through things, but Ava always declined. She knew that to Aunt Lori, sorting meant throwing away—she'd learned that in fifth grade when Aunt Lori had "sorted" a pile of Ava's paintings right into the garbage can. Anyway, she'd get around to cleaning up back here someday.

And until then, it was always an adventure.

Her eye fell on the ladder sticking out from behind a stack of large blank canvases she had yet to find a use for. Maybe she'd grab a couple of those while she was at it. They might look artistic leaning against the ladder.

"What do you think happened to her?" The voice carried from the dressing stalls, locking Ava in place. "A fire?" She couldn't tell if the speaker was Harper or Emily.

"I think so," the other girl's voice was quieter but still reached Ava. "My mom said she was supposed to be a model or something."

"Wow. You would never be able to tell."

Ava closed her eyes, allowing herself a slow count of five. She'd heard worse. And it wasn't like the girls were trying to hurt her. They thought she was up front.

And they were only being honest.

"Wouldn't you just want to die if that happened to you?"

"Harper!" Emily's voice scolded around a half-laugh.

"Sorry. But you know what I mean. She's never going to have a boyfriend or anything."

"I heard she used to date one of the Calvano brothers. In high school."

"Ooh. Which one? They're all so hot."

"Eww." Emily made a retching sound. "They're *old*, Harper."

"Not that old. The youngest was in my sister's class, and she's only twenty."

"Well, I can't remember which one she dated. But I guess he totally ghosted her after..."

Ava's swallow sliced her throat as she backed out of the room, letting the girls' voices fade.

"Joseph," she wanted to say. He was the Calvano brother she'd dated. But she pressed her lips together and silently moved back into the studio.

There, she forced herself to pick up her camera, to double-check the ISO and the aperture, to shoot a test picture and check the white balance.

Forced herself, when Harper and Emily returned in their new outfits, to smile and nod and take pictures that would highlight their unmarred beauty.

Forced herself, when they were done, to hold her head high and say goodbye as they draped themselves over the boys who had come to pick them up.

Forced herself, as she locked the studio door, to remember that she had chosen this. That she had been the one to do the ghosting, not him.

Not that it mattered. If she hadn't pushed him away, he would have run. And she wouldn't have blamed him.

༄

Chapter 2

It was finally happening.

Joseph sat in his car, staring at the low brick building where he'd gotten his first job when he was fourteen. He'd had to beg Dr. Gallagher for weeks for that job. But finally the old vet had taken pity on him and let him help with cleaning kennels. From there, he'd worked his way up to checking in patients and then assisting the vet with minor procedures. When Joseph had graduated high school, Dr. Gallagher had promised that if Joseph studied to become a vet, he would sell him the practice one day. And now, after eight grueling years of school, River Falls Veterinary was his.

"Holy smokes," he whispered to himself. What if, after all this time, he didn't have what it took? What if he ran the practice Dr. Gallagher had spent forty years building right into the ground?

Something cold and wet pressed to his cheek, and he laughed, patting his Samoyed's soft white ears. The dog was just what he needed to keep himself grounded.

"You're right, Tasha. God's got this. What are we waiting for?"

He opened his car door, patting the roof. He'd been driving the thing for a decade, and he hadn't been sure it'd get him home from Cornell, but it had. Of course, with the loan he'd just signed to buy the practice, this old rust-bucket was going to have to get him through for a while longer.

Tasha zoomed past him, her nose instantly to the ground. Joseph wondered how many dogs had walked through the doors of this building over the years. He pulled out his keychain and grabbed the key that had been on it for less than an hour, taking a deep breath as he turned it in the lock.

This was it.

He pushed the door open and stepped over the threshold into the next chapter of his life.

Inside, everything was exactly the way Joseph remembered it, right down to the magazines in the racks and the paw-shaped treat bowl on the counter. Dr. Gallagher had even left the hideous paintings of cats in tuxedos.

"Maybe we can replace those," Joseph muttered to Tasha. And he knew exactly who he wanted to paint the replacement pictures. Assuming she would give him the time of day.

But for now, he had work to do. "All right," he said to the dog. "Where do we start?"

Four hours later, Joseph had completed an inventory, placed an order for supplies and medications, and surveyed his patient list for next week. Fortunately, Dr. Gallagher had let patients with upcoming appointments know about the transition—and the majority of them had agreed to continue using River Falls Veterinary with Joseph at the helm.

He thanked God again that he didn't have to start over from scratch.

And while he was talking to God . . . *You know how much I want things to work with Ava this time, Lord. Please make it possible. Or at least let her be willing to talk to me.*

"All right, Tasha. Should we call it a day? Go get us both some treats?" At the last word, the dog's upright ears perked.

Of course, since Joseph had just moved into his new house yesterday and hadn't had a chance to get food yet, any treats were going to have to come after a trip to the grocery store.

"Sorry, girl. I'm going to have to drop you off at home first. It's too hot to leave you in the car." After spending the past eight years in New York, it was going to take a while to readjust to the Tennessee heat.

Twenty minutes later, with Tasha safely dropped off at home, Joseph drove past the familiar storefronts that had lined Main Street since he was a boy: Daisy's Pie Shop, Henderson's Art Gallery, the Sweet Boutique, the Book Den. He crossed the bridge over the Serenity River, driving to the outskirts of town, where the grocery store was located. Sweating lightly after the short walk across the parking lot, he ducked gratefully into the air conditioned store.

He reached for a cart just as another hand landed on it.

A female hand, judging by the bright pink nail polish.

"Oh sorry." Joseph pulled his hand back and reached for another cart.

"Joseph Calvano?" The woman's voice was warm and sugary, slightly higher than most, with a taste of the South that he'd missed during his years in New York. It was a voice he would recognize anywhere.

"Madison Monroe." He turned toward her, holding out his hand, but she dove at him in a hug.

He hesitated a second, then lifted a reluctant arm to her back.

"Your daddy said you were coming home," Madison said as she pulled away, her eyes traveling to his shoes, then back up to his shoulders.

"It's nice to see you," Joseph mumbled. The last time he'd talked to Madison had been as he was running out of the prom he'd taken her to.

"You too. We should get together sometime. Catch up. You owe me a dance, you know."

"Yeah. Um—" He'd never had any desire to take Madison to the prom. He'd only asked her because he was upset that the girl he'd wanted to take—the only girl he'd ever wanted to do anything with—had pushed him away. "Sorry about that." He'd never before considered that it might have bothered Madison. She had so many guys falling at her feet, he figured she probably hadn't even noticed.

"I forgive you. On one condition." Madison pointed her perfectly manicured fingernail at his chest.

"What's that?"

"Dinner. Tomorrow night."

"Oh." Joseph's mind whirred. "I'm sorry, I can't. I'm actually, uh, actually . . ." He scratched his cheek, hoping she couldn't tell he was stalling. "I'm actually seeing someone."

Technically speaking, that wasn't one hundred percent true. But he would be seeing someone soon—as soon as he worked up the nerve to ask her. And assuming that she said yes. That counted, didn't it?

"I should have known." Madison studied his face a little too closely. "You always were too good a catch to stay single."

Joseph had no idea how to react to that. The best he could come up with was a strange sound at the back of his throat. He grabbed for an empty cart.

Madison spun her cart toward the produce section. "I'm sure I'll see you around."

Joseph blew out a long breath as she disappeared. He waited a few seconds, then entered the store, making sure to choose a different aisle than the one she'd headed for. Thankfully, he didn't run into her again as he did his shopping.

As he emerged from the store forty-five minutes later, he tried not to be disappointed that he hadn't seen the one woman he really wanted to see. The same one he'd wanted to take to the prom. It would have taken a pretty big coincidence for Ava to be at the store at the same time he was on his first day home. Not that Joseph doubted it could happen—he'd learned over the years that even the seemingly coincidental was in God's hands.

He whistled as he pushed his cart toward his car, letting his eyes rove to the deep green slopes of the Smoky Mountains that wrapped around the town, making River Falls feel cozy and protected and tucked away in its own corner of the world. He turned his head to the north, squinting, even though he knew her house was too far into the ridges to see from here.

"Watch out!"

Joseph yanked his cart to a stop at the shouted warning.

A dark-haired woman glared at him. His cart was only inches from hitting her.

"I'm so sorry." Joseph steered his cart out of the way as he apologized. "I was lost in thought. Wait. Lori?"

The woman's glare didn't ease. "Joseph."

"Hey." He cleared his throat. Wasn't this exactly the kind of coincidence he needed? "So, uh— How are things?"

"Good." The woman crossed her arms in front of her.

Okay. This was not going well. If Lori was this cold with him, what did that say about how her niece would feel to learn that Joseph was home?

"Glad to hear it." He waited for her to ask how things were with him—to give him an opening to say that he was back in town for good. But she remained silent.

Apparently, he was going to have to take things into his own hands. "I just moved back to town. Bought Dr. Gallagher's practice."

Lori gave a short nod.

"Anyway, uh—" Joseph pulled on the neck of his shirt. Had someone cranked up the thermostat on the sun? "How is Ava?"

There. He'd done it.

Lori's mouth tightened, and he resisted the urge to remind her that Ava was the one who had broken up with him.

"She's fine," Lori said finally.

"That's good." He'd been hoping for a little more information than that. But he wasn't sure he should come out and ask if Ava was seeing anyone.

"She has a photography studio."

"That's great—" He grinned at the thought. Ava had always been artistic. He bet she was a talented photographer. "I'd love to—"

"And she's getting married," Lori cut in.

"I— She's— Married?" Joseph gripped the handle of his cart. His world was tipping. "That's—" He choked on the word *great*. He wanted to be happy for Ava. He really did. "Tell her congratulations from me, would you? I, uh— Wow. I should . . ." He gestured vaguely toward his car.

He didn't wait on Lori's response before practically sprinting away from her.

He unloaded his groceries, then climbed into his car and just sat.

Ava was getting married? To someone who wasn't him? How could that be?

He'd been so sure that coming home to River Falls was more than a chance to start his veterinary practice—it was supposed to be a second chance with Ava. A chance to keep the promise he never should have broken—not even when she'd asked him to.

KEEP READING PIECES OF FOREVER

More Books by Valerie M. Bodden

Hope Springs

While the books in the Hope Springs series are linked, each is a complete romance featuring a different couple.

Not Until Forever (Sophie & Spencer)
Not Until This Moment (Jared & Peyton)
Not Until You (Nate & Violet)
Not Until Us (Dan & Jade)
Not Until Christmas Morning (Leah & Austin)
Not Until This Day (Tyler & Isabel)
Not Until Someday (Grace & Levi)
Not Until Now (Cam & Kayla)
Not Until Then (Bethany & James)
Not Until The End (Emma & Owen)

River Falls

While the books in the River Falls series are linked, each is a complete romance featuring a different couple.

Pieces of Forever (Joseph & Ava)
Songs of Home (Lydia & Liam)
Memories of the Heart (Simeon & Abigail)
Whispers of Truth (Benjamin & Summer)
Promises of Mercy (Judah & Faith)

River Falls Christmas Romances

Wondering about some of the side characters in River Falls who aren't members of the Calvano family? Join them as they get their own happily-ever-afters in the River Falls Christmas Romances.

Christmas of Joy (Madison & Luke)

Want to know when my next book releases?

You can follow me on Amazon to be the first to know when my next book releases! Just visit amazon.com/author/valeriembodden and click the follow button.

Acknowledgements

Oh goodness! What a journey this series has taken us on together. When I started writing it, all I knew was that I wanted to create a community of people who faced real-life struggles with the help of the Lord. I had no idea how many books there would be, where the characters' stories would take them, or how much I would fall in love with this place and these people. I had no idea how much I needed their stories—or how touched I would be to learn that you needed them too. But looking back, I can see how God used each one of these stories to remind me of truths from his Word that I needed to hear: truths like *perfect love drives out fear* and *God is faithful even in the storms* and *he removes our sins as far as the east is from the west* and *his grace is free*. For the chance to bring those truths to life on the page, and more than that, for those truths themselves—for the fact that they stand firm forever—I give God my highest thanks and praise.

Thank you also to my husband, Josh, for making it easy to write romantic heroes. I feel like there's a piece of you in every hero I write: an unwavering love for family, a goofy sense of humor, a light of God's love in this world. Thank you not only for being a man to model my heroes on, but also for being a model of God's love to me and to our four children.

And thank you also to those children. Each of you is as different as Owen's kids are from each other, and yet God has given you each great gifts. You are all a blessing and make this family my favorite place to be. As you grow up and go out into the world, my prayer ever remains that you will stand firm in the Lord's love, using your many gifts to his glory.

Thank you to my parents, sister, in-laws, extended family, and friends as well. One of the reasons I'm able to write characters who are surrounded by such a great support system is because *I* am surrounded by such a great support system in you. For your tireless encouragement and for reading my books and for sharing them with others, thank you.

And a huge thank you goes out to my advance reader team! Some of you have been with me from the beginning of this series, cheering on each book as it came out. And others have jumped in along the way, your enthusiasm for my books leading you to want to be part of this group. I am so grateful for each one of you, and I feel like you have become my very own Hope Springs family. A special thank you to: Anna, Sandra Golinger, Vickie, Terri Camp, Jenevieve, Karene, Lincoln Clark, Rhondia, Margaret N, Judy, Vikki, Seyi, Nancy Fudge, Michelle M, Connie Gandy, Patty Bohuslav, Darla Knutzen, Connie G, Shannon Dailey, Julie Mancil, Pam Williams, Ilona, Jan Gilmour, DS, Laura Polian, Diana A, Judith, Jenny M, Chris Little, Carol Witzenburger, Korkoi, Alison Komm, Maxine Barber, Trista Heuer, Josie Bartelt, Marlee Bedke, Jenevieve, Kellie P, Kathy Ann Meadows, Sandy H, Kelly Wickham, Ginny Durr, and Melanie Tate.

And finally, thank *you* for coming on this journey with me. I pray that the Hope Springs series has touched your heart with its stories of love, not only between the characters but between our great God and *you*. Because he loves you with an unfailing, never-ending, eternal-life-giving love—and he promises to be with you to the end.

About the Author

Valerie M. Bodden has three great loves: Jesus, her family, and books. And chocolate (okay, four great loves). She is living out her happily ever after with her high-school-sweetheart-turned-husband and their four children. Her life wouldn't make a terribly exciting book, as it has a happy beginning and middle, and someday when she goes to her heavenly home, it will have a happy end.

She was born and raised in Wisconsin but recently moved with her family to Texas, where they're all getting used to the warm weather (she doesn't miss the snow even a little bit, though the rest of the family does) and saying y'all instead of you guys.

Valerie writes emotion-filled Christian fiction that weaves real-life problems, real-life people, and real-life faith. Her characters may (okay, will) experience some heartache along the way, but she will always give them a happy ending.

Feel free to stop by www.valeriembodden.com to say hi. She loves visitors! And while you're there, you can sign up for your free story.

Printed in Great Britain
by Amazon